[dis]connection

by T. Kulp

Pandor Project

Book 1

ISBN: 978-1-956612-03-5 (Paperback)
ISBN: 978-1-956612-00-4 (Hardback)
ISBN: 978-1-956612-04-2 (eBook)

Find more stories at https://timkulp.com

First printing edition 2022

Making Adventure Publishing
16944 York Rd, Suite 63
Monkton, MD 21111

To my son and daughter
who help me avoid
the fates in
this story

Thank
you

"I desire the company of a man who could sympathize with me, whose eyes would reply to mine."

Captain Walton, from Frankenstein by Mary Shelley

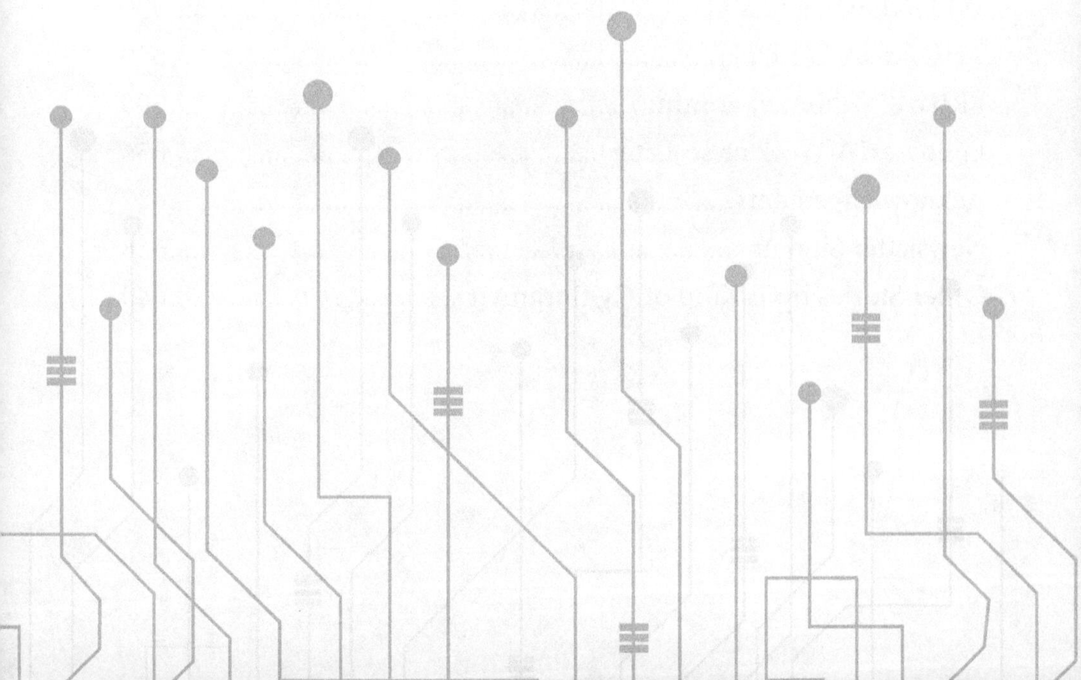

CONTENTS

FOREWORD

In 2019 this story started as a tale about cyber bullying. I wanted to write a story that infused Lovecraftian Cosmic Horror into the drama of high school.

For me, middle school and high school didn't need any major monsters dwelling in the dark to be terrifying. I can't imagine how difficult high school must be now with the omnipresent nature of social media. Being a late bloomer who felt lost most of my young adult life, adding the layer of always being on display for social media sites like Instagram would have been paralyzing to me.

When I started exploring what monsters would evolve from this age of hyper-connectivity, body dysmorphia, and fleeting relationships, I didn't have to look hard for a monster. Opening the news or listening to phone alerts will show you the monsters of our age, and they all devour the same precious things that we only miss when they're gone or when we didn't know we lost them: Privacy and Time.

I hope you enjoy *[dis]connection*. There are many monsters within these pages. I'd love to hear which one scares you the most. While Glen Coast is not a real place, the monsters within these pages are very real. Chances are, many of them live in your pocket, in your home, and for some of the least fortunate among us, in our behaviors.

Thank you for choosing *[dis]connection*.

Sincerely,

T. Kulp

6/17/2022

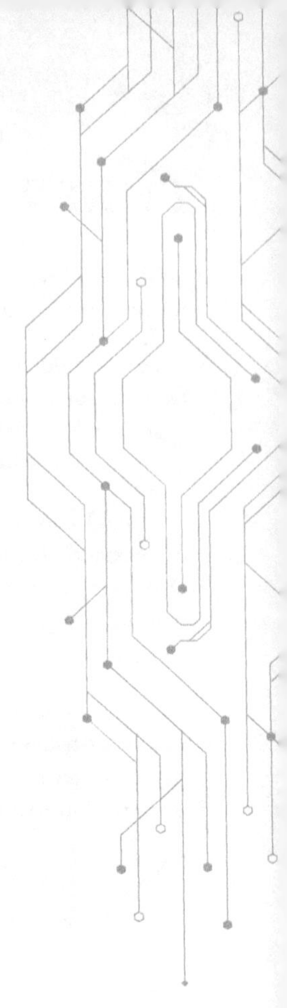

October
2018

Glen Coast, Maryland

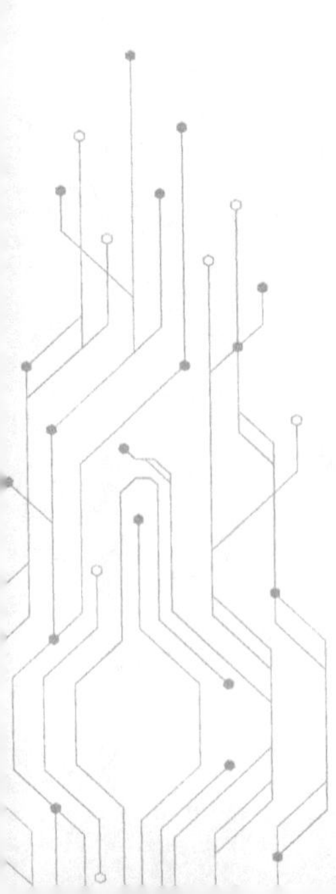

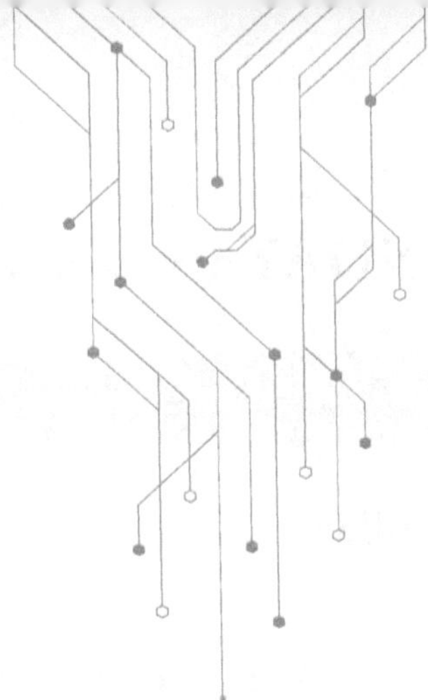

I

The New Girl

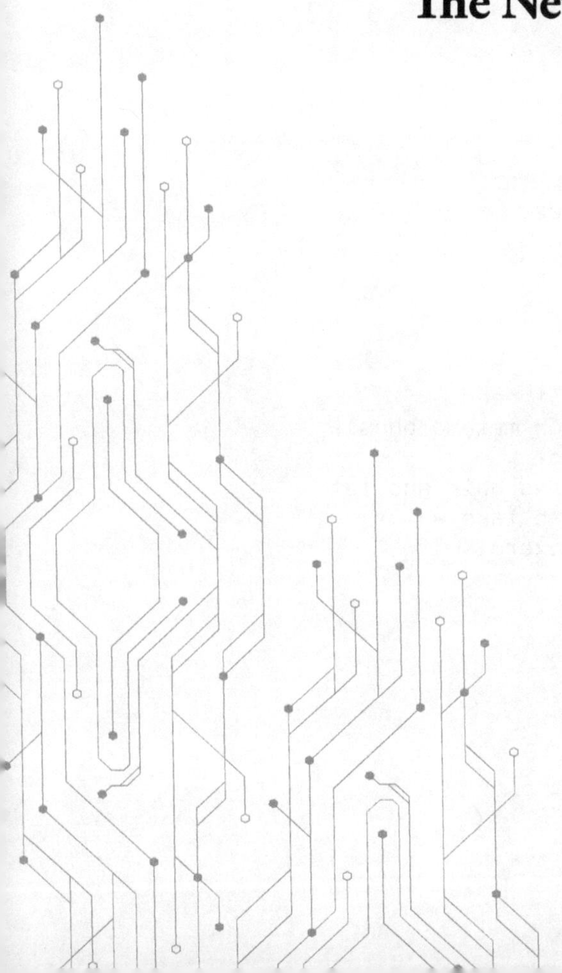

MONDAY (5 DAYS)

ERIN ULMAN

Caterpillar

I sit at the front in Biology,
on display, standing out like
a blinking cursor on a blank
console screen.

Erin = new Girl();

Front row:
the last seat available.
The only seat for someone
joining late September.

We're studying metamorphosis,
caterpillars becoming butterflies.
Donna,
the golden-haired beauty
of Glen Coast High School,
whispers behind me.

"Erin doesn't need
to go through metamorphosis
to get rid of
her cruddy red hair and fat.
Just needs to take a
shower and exercise."

"Oh, that won't help.
I'm just stuck this way,"
I whisper back,
pushing out a chuckle,
hoping
she'll think I'm funny.

She doesn't.

Erin.isFunny = false;

Donna blows my joke away,
whispering,
"Loser."

I pull up my hoodie,
hiding in it,
only finding more derision
and comments
and disgust
from the girls behind me.

I hear everything they say.
They know it.

We watch a butterfly emerge from its cocoon.
Beautiful to me,
gross to everyone else,
so I choke my interest,
replicating their grimacing faces.

I wish I were a caterpillar.

I could wake up and be someone else.
Someone important or interesting.
Someone with friends.
Someone other than me.

Observation

Escaping the social petri dish
that is our lunchroom,
I go to the Maker Lab.

```
when(Erin.inMakerLab == true) {

      Erin.isSafe = true;
      Erin.isAlone = true;

}
```

Back in Seattle,
before Dad told the truth,
I wouldn't have been here alone.
But here at Glen Coast High,
no one comes through the orange doors
separating this space
from the mundane world of
this school.

Out there, you are whoever YOU are,
you can do only whatever YOU can do—
but in here you can do anything,
make anything.

Instead of being creators
of the amazing,
people would rather sit at lunch,
take selfies,
and post on SocialNet.

As I wait for my latest 3D print,
a white cat,
to finish
I see my reflection in a blank monitor.

My hair is curly, not crusty.
My cheeks are full, not fat.
My skin is pale, not pasty.
I'd rather code than run.

Working a Rubik's Cube,
I observe myself

to see what they see.

Yes, I'm a bit frumpy.
Maybe my fashion sense is more
basement coder than *SocialNet Influencer*.

Hoodies,
jeans,
sneakers.

Not what Donna wears.

Erin.clothes = comfortable && loose;
Donna.clothes = fancy && tight;
Erin.clothes != Donna.clothes;

My 3D print finishes
as I solve the Rubik's Cube.
I head to my next class
before everyone escapes lunch.

No need to be around all those people
if I don't have to be.

Storms

Tone rings,
signaling
everyone
to flee
school.

I straighten my books
until everyone has left.

I'll be the last one out:
no pushing,
no shoving,
no one but me.
I'm alone.
I'm safe.

Beyond the door
a stormy sea of bodies
writhing,
rolling,
crashing into each other,

slamming locker doors,
talking,
laughing,
shouting:
the soundtrack of the end of the day.

I squeeze
my books to
my chest:
my armor
against the deluge of humanity.

Spotting a parting in the storm,
I rush through,

escape only feet away.

"Hey Erin!"
Donna shouts,
spotting me.

I turn,
smiling for her,
twisting up—

Weightless,
falling—

A lightning strike of pain hits my knee,
another strike to my elbow,
then chin,
pain rippling through my body like thunder.

Erin.isGraceful = false;
Erin.isSpectacle = true;

People part in the hall
as lockers go silent;
the storm stops
to see me on the floor.

CLICK.
A photo is taken.

Donna busts out laughing.

She points,
calls her friends to see
what they are taking pictures of
on their phones.

"Been walking long?"
Donna snorts.

One of Donna's friends starts laughing,
then another joins,
then everyone watching joins,
then a hurricane of laughter engulfs me.

hide(feelings);
reboot(laughing);

I push out a laugh to join in,
pain washing over me,
tears welling up
but strangled away by embarrassment
and I pray this doesn't get worse
with crying.

CLICK.
Another photo is taken.

Important escape(school);

I shovel up my books,
head down,
hood up over my face,
hurrying to the doors.

Bursting out of school,
I crash into one of Donna's friends.
I fall back.
She falls back.

Mud splashes
over her bright flowery dress,
over her light brown skin,
into her tightly pinned
black hair.

Her brown eyes meet mine,
shocked then
softening as she sees me.

I scramble up,
rushing away.

What We Run From

I rub away the tears;
my eyes burn
as mud smears into them
from my sleeve.

"Don't cry,"
I demand,
shouting to myself
like so many days before,
and like those days,
the shouting
can't stop it.

The well is tapped,
the faucet is on:
tears fall like summer rain,
hot,
fast,
drenching.

```
Erin.loser = true;
run Erin.stopCrying();
>>> failure to execute;
```

I run home.
Running from *them*;
from Donna,
from her friends,
from their eyes
and cameras
and comments,
from my differences,
my isolation-
from me.

Home is
a place where
I can be just as alone,
just as isolated,
but at least
alone,
in quiet.

The Loudest Quiet Place

Mother's face is in a book,
so no need to sneak by.

She escapes
Glen Coast
in those books,
while I escape into my room.

Opening my door
releases the hot exhalation of computer exhaust
welcoming me home.

Closing the door
keeps the blinking,
buzzing,
busy lights of
my tech
all to myself.

The constant hum of electronics
is a chorus singing,
calling me
to my quiet place away from everyone
to a place where I can be me;
where I can be important.

In this place
I can make anything
into something,
even me.

I shed my muddy clothes,
throwing them onto one of the piles
on my floor.

Sniffing another hoodie-
smells clean-
I slip it on

with some comfy sweatpants
and flop into my computer chair,
ready to relax,
ready to connect.

Communication: An Unremarkable Transit

To: vcmoran17
Subject: Transit
Body:

ATTN: Dr. V.C. Moran 17

Pandora moving through your district (Glen Coast, MD). Extraction from MacAbera laboratory encountered problems. We believe one or more assets in the extraction mission were compromised. MacAbera knew we were coming. They captured H. Diggins 10192 but M. Hawkins 10196 was able to rendezvous with the currier.

Arrival is expected in 4 days. Please endeavor to provide an unremarkable passage through your district.

Sincerely;
S. Pratchert, I.G. 23

<eom>

ERIN ULMAN

Search: Erin Ulman

Open my browser,
activate Privacy Mode,
connect to SocialNet.

Search: Erin Ulman
Filter: Mentions Today
Location: Glen Coast, MD
Results: 68

Result 1:
A picture from earlier.
Me on the floor
with everyone laughing.

They talk about me online,
saying things
they wouldn't say out loud.
Saying things
while hiding behind their phones.

Result 10:
A video of Donna
mocking my fall,
cackling
to her friend
who records the video.

Everyone Liking.
Commenting.
Sharing.

They say things
about someone they don't know,
feeling more powerful

with each keystroke,
more validated with every Like,
more connected with each Share.

What did I do?

How can I change so they don't say
She needs to wash her hair.
(Result 15 by Carrie Moore
16 Likes, 2 Shares)

Or
Now we know why she don't have friends
on SocialNet or IRL!
(Result #22 by Luke Stevens
34 Likes, 7 Shares,
25 Comments,
not one rebuking,
all supporting,
all laughing.)

Or
Result 46–
Clicking on it,
an error appears:
Sorry! The content you've requested doesn't exist.

I hit refresh
Search: Erin Ulman
Filter: Mentions Today
Location: Glen Coast, MD
Results: 0

My shoulders crumble down,
pushing out a sigh.

I'm not even worth
SocialNet remembering
who I am.

Dinner

Delicious pot pie scents
choked away by the sharp sting
of burning crust.

I see Mother waving the stink
out of the microwave
while reading her book
and instantly understand the situation.

```
if(Mother.isReading == true && food.isCooking == true) {
  food.isBurnt = true;
  Dinner.isRuinned = true;
}
```

The table is set
for two,
signaling a normal night:
Dad is working late.

Moving here was supposed to change things.
No one would know what he did.
He'd have a job,
he'd be home more,
we'd have a better life,
a better house,
a better school.

Nothing is better.

"Sorry for the smell, Erin,"
Mother says,
face still in her book.

I shrug her away.

I don't care about the pot pie,
about dinner,
about this house,
this city,
this life.

Inside I want to scream,
let all the anger
out, but isolation
creates a crust
that holds
everything
in.

"When will Dad be home?"
I ask. She sighs.

"I'm not sure.
He's really busy right now.
The other day he said he's
working with IntelliDyn.
That's the huge company
you guys used to talk
about, right?"
Mother asks.

"Yeah. They have an office
around here or something?"

"I don't know."
Another sigh.
"But you know how your dad is."

"Yeah, his work is
the only important thing
he'll leave behind
when he's gone."
Mother's eyes catch mine,
waiting for an apology

"His words. Not mine,"
I scoff.

I pick at the pot pie,
peeling away the overcooked crust;
at the first crack
steam bursts through,
followed by a molten gravy
leaking out on the plate.

Other cracks form
as the crust melts into the gravy.

Soon my pot pie is a boiling pile of mush.

All it took was one crack,
one little break,
one opening to let what was inside out.

That crack destroyed everything.

I smile.

TUESDAY (4 DAYS)

Things Hidden, Seen, & Remembered

Sitting in the back during English,
hiding in my hoodie,
I'm hidden
from the sneers
and laughter
that find me in the hallway.

Back here
I can see them.
Their addiction:
compulsive consumers,
and worse,
creators of the mundane.

Carole and Hugo making
stupid kissy faces
for a selfie.
I can see the post now:
Loving English with Hugo!

Beside them
Amber does her hair, makeup
for her selfie,
posing with a disinterested
pouty face,
probably posting:
Suffering through English class.

So

many

selfies.

They have no idea what they are giving
a faceless,
careless
company like
SocialNet.

Post
Comment
React
Repeat

And I'm the weirdo for hiding back here,
no phone,
no SocialNet.

But where are the other weirdos?

All I can see
are people flocking to one clique,
one person,
to Donna.

```
while(Erin.inSeattle) {
 Erin = Donna;
 Erin.isLoser = false;
} else {
 Erin.isLoser = true;
}
```

She's the nucleus of popularity,
everyone else mere electrons bound to her orbit
through her majesty and magnetism.

SocialNet is the force
holding all this together,
and worse,
it is the hive mind,
a collective shared memory.

I look forward to forgetting this time of my life,
just like SocialNet keeps forgetting me.

Returning to the Home Line

Donna's fingers
stalk over the keys,
crushing down
as if pressing harder
makes letters appear faster
on the screen.

```
Donna.frustration.increase();
```

Should I help her?
Should I show her the home line?
How she can be free to
type without thinking,
transforming
from hunting and crushing
to pouring her thoughts
into the computer,
quick,
graceful?

But I don't help her.

I focus on my computer,
trying to pull up a command prompt,
but the computer barks back
rejection.

You do not have sufficient permissions for this action.

We'll see about that.

```
while (schoolSecurity == laughablyBad) {
  Erin.breaksIn();
  Erin.canDoAnything();
  Erin.isLoser = false;
}
```

>>> Access Granted

The command prompt opens:
ready,
blinking,
awaiting my whims.

"How'd you do that?"
a voice asks.

I turn, seeing
the girl I ran into yesterday:
Donna's friend,
muddy-flower-dress girl.

Donna looks at us,
her eyes pushing me further into my hoodie.

```
>>> intruder alert
Erin.escape();
Erin.hide();
commandprompt.minimize();
```

My fingers flick a quick keystroke,
minimizing my work
away from muddy-flower-dress girl's eyes.

"Caylee, come on!"
Donna commands
from across the room.

The teacher pops up from her computer,
just now waking to the class,
watching Caylee
walk back to Donna.

```
Caylee = Donna.friend;
Caylee.sawWhatIDid = unknown;
```

With all Donna's friends clustered around her
I notice how similar they look.
They all belong together;
they look like
they enjoy being together,
like friends.

Donna
looks frustrated.
Probably because computer lab
isn't a class on using SocialNet.
She's lost here.
Everyone is lost here.

Caylee throws me a curious look,
too fast for Donna to notice.

I return
to my command prompt
to explore this school's security
and see what I can find.

Computer Lab
is like a vacation into my world.

SEARCH: Donna Schwartz

I don't have a SocialNet account
and never will again
after what they did to Dad.

But sometimes
I like to see the world
that happens without me.
A cracked computer lab computer
is a perfect place to look at SocialNet.

Who is Donna?
What am I doing wrong?

Search: Donna Schwartz
Filter: Profile
Location: Glen Coast, MD
Results: 1

Everyone lives in SocialNet.
Those who don't
can't see this digital world.

The world of
SocialNet isn't life;
it is a shared lie,
a highlight reel,
and Donna Schwartz
is a model of this perfect lie.

She has friends.
2,412 friends.

She has pictures with friends.
They laugh together
at cat videos.

They joke with each other
about their day.

She has so much
and doesn't appreciate any of it.

In one picture,
Donna and her dad
are on a roller coaster.
He is laughing;
she isn't.

In another picture,
Donna and her dad
practice lacrosse.

He looks happy,
she looks like
she's waiting for something else.

Donna's dad
playing,
laughing,
having ice cream.

He is there with her.

Her life looks perfect.

She looks perfect.

2,412 people can't be wrong.

Left Behind

End of class
tone rings;
another flick of shortcut keys
restores the system security
like I was never there.

Caylee watches me

as she packs up
falling behind Donna's cabal of clones
striding out the room.

She rushes
to catch up,
bookbag swaying open,
papers creeping to escape.

Ms. Isler stands from her desk,
following the students out,
leaving me
alone.

If I were to stay here
would anyone notice?

I stand,
look back to my computer,
and wonder how easy it would be
to shut it all down.

Virus.

Malware.

Software to cripple the school
to help me escape this place
with a few days reprieve.

Perhaps an injection attack?
Pulling up my student portal,
I see the Querystring…

? user=eulman292 and type=student

Oh man…yep, injection attack.
What would happen
if I turned it to

?user=' OR 1=1; DELETE FROM tblStudents;--

Simple injection attack.
Delete all the students.

They wouldn't know it was me.
It would look like the application just
did something wrong.

They don't even see me
unless Donna points me out.

Erin.isInvisible = true;

I can hear my dad saying,
Only stupid criminals get caught.
I could fool everyone here but
I'd never fool him.

Dad would know
I did it.
He'd tell.

That's what he does.

He tells.

No matter how much it hurts his family.

Look-Alikes

At home
in my room,
I'm powerful.

> Processors,
> memory,
> bandwidth
> swirling around me
> like magical energy,
> ready to be focused,
> ready to solve any problem.

Tonight
I'm solving my biggest problem:
me.

A month in Glen Coast High
has been long enough
to "find my place,"
as Mother says.

Time to enter a cycle of
observing data,
forming a hypothesis,
experimenting
to discover why
I'm not connecting
with Donna
and her friends.

SELECT * FROM DonnaFriends;

Back in Seattle,
I was the Donna of my school.
Friends orbited around me
because of my tech skills,
because of my dad's job,
because we all wore hoodies
and jeans and sneakers.

And I knew things would be
different
here.

But this different?
I need data
and I know where everyone
pours all their data
about everything.

To get that data
I cook an app to crawl SocialNet profiles.

Simple:
a pinch of artificial intelligence,
a spoonful of natural language processing,
a cup of image analysis—
add 2,412 profiles from SocialNet
with hundreds of posts and pictures
and I'll understand
what Donna is looking for.

I can be liked by them
if I know how to be like them.

My app,
my creation,
crawls over SocialNet,
pulling pictures and posts
from Donna's friends.

My app,
my answer,
analyzes their photos
so I know how to dress,
how to look.

My app,
my new me,
analyzes their words
so I know how to talk
what to say.

Tomorrow
my app will tell me
how to be important,
how to be liked,
how to be like them
at Glen Coast High.

CAYLEE MORAN

The Girl on the Ground

I scrub
but this crusty mud
isn't coming out
of the yellow flowers
or white fabric.

Mom Victoria is going to be pissed.

I can hear it now:

"You want nice clothes, you need to take care of them."

Or

"We're not made of money Caylee, you need to scrub that out."

So, I scrub
and think how much
I hate this dress.

I can't be mad.
That new girl–Erin, I think–
looked so defeated yesterday.

I remember being where she is.
The new girl.
The outcast.

When we collided, when I was sitting in the mud,
I saw myself in her, I saw my sadness from
the words
the posts
the rumors.

I scrub the mud again
trying to scrape it off
the dress.

Erin was running from Donna.
I ran toward Donna when I was Erin.
I ran toward the in-crowd.
I ran toward who she wanted me to be
toward a life of pretend
online and off.

Is it that bad?
This life of pretend?
At least I have somewhere
to belong.
With Donna's friends
I can drown the feelings
of being different.

What was Erin doing in computer lab today?
I look in the bathroom mirror
thinking about her fingers soaring over the keys,
the command prompts, normally locked away–

BANG! BANG! BANG!
"Caylee! I gotta pee-pee!"
Little feet stomping
outside the door.
"Real bad! Hurry!"

Ugh…never any peace.

I open the door.
Sabrina runs in
dropping her pants
peeing
singing the hand washing song.

I hurry out
taking my dress
and sponge
to keep trying
to save this stupid dress.

WEDNESDAY (3 DAYS)

ERIN ULMAN

Equinox

Today is the Equinox.
As the leaves begin to fall,
I'll rise,
showing them who I can be.

My app's results are in.
2,412 profiles.
239,002,931 data points
with a summary I can act on.

I need
new hair:
no more curls,
make my hair less like a pile of red leaves
and more like a waterfall of flame.
96.2% of Donna's female friends have long
straight hair.

I need
new clothes:
no more jeans,
no more hoodies,
bright,
flowery,
happy.
87.1% of Donna's friends wear
bright colors daily.

I need
a smartphone:
to post,
to comment,
to share
pictures,
videos,
the mundane.
98.8% of Donna's friends post
10 to 20 times a day.

Tonight
after school
starts a new season
for me,
for my life.

The data
pulled from SocialNet
can't be wrong.

It is
not reality.

It is
what we wish reality was,
who we wish we were,
and now
who I will be.

96.2%

First stop in my transformation:
the Glen Coast Mall
hair salon.

I show the stylist
what I want
using Mother's phone,
showing pictures from SocialNet profiles
and SocialNet filters of my face.

"Are you sure
this is what you want?"
Mother asks,
hesitation
heavy in her voice,
premature regret
heavy on her face.

"Yes! I need a new look, Mother."
She grimaces
but says nothing.

```
Mother.canUnderstand = false;
```

The stylist
snatches up my curls,
dividing my head into sections,
wrapping each section into tight
little balls of tension.

"It won't be permanent.
Just something to try out,"
the stylist says to Mother
while hunting over his station,
finding a giant bristled brush,
something more like a
medieval torture device
than a beauty utensil.

He unwraps the first section,
wrenching my hair into the brush;
the bristles clawing
through my skin prickle like spider legs
cascading down my spine.

He pulls the brush through,
ripping the knots
and hair
from my scalp.

The hair dryer
heats up the brush,
turning the clawing
into searing scratches.

Again
he wrenches my hair;
the brush burns my neck,
the claws rip my skin,
the pain trickling down
my spine.

Another pull,
the arid stink of burnt hair
filling my nose.
His nose wiggles;
he stops,
the brush dangling in my hair,
bouncing off my neck,
burning with each swing.

"Oops. Forgot something."
He laughs off the smell,
waving his hand.

Mother scoffs
as he sprays something
on the rest of my hair.

Chemical stink,
burning hair stink,
searing flesh stink
all competing for my attention,
but all I can think about
is a quiet day at school,
lunch with friends,
maybe…

maybe even
a compliment–
but I won't be that bold
or hopeful.

Best to be
realistic.

87.1%

The trailing odor of burning hair
follows me into the store
where Donna's friends buy their clothes
according to SocialNet.

Fitted dresses,
flowers,
light
bright
colors
radiate around me.

My black hoodie and jeans
are alien
to this world
as I catch glances from the other
mothers and daughters
shopping in here.

They know I don't belong.
I know I don't belong
as I snatch up some dresses to try on.

```
(Dress.style == Erin.style) = false;
```

"Erin, this is a…"
Mother pinches a pink dress,
pulling the edge up,
gritting her teeth.
"It's not going to be very comfortable."

"Yeah, well, it's something different."
I defend the dress,
silently agreeing.
These dresses aren't made for
crawling under desks
to plug a computer in.

```
Dress.comfortable = false;
Dress.useful = false;
Dress.DonnaApproved = true;
```

These dresses dangle
off
stick-
skinny mannequins.

I try on the first dress–
white
sunflower spots,
thin straps,
light,
fun–
and I feel like a sausage.

```
Erin.isDisgusting = true;
```

Peeking out from the curtain
to see the mannequin wearing this same dress,
but there it dangles and flows.

Looking in the mirror
seeing the stretching fabric of the dress
straining to hold me in.

I see what Donna means.

```
Erin.isFat = true;
Donna.isRight = true;
```

I can see the fat now
outside of my hoodies
and jeans.

Changing back,
hiding into my old clothes,
I step out
and get the biggest size
the store has.

XL

My hoodies are normally just
M–
jeans too.

Now I see
maybe Donna wasn't making fun of me;
maybe she was just telling me a truth
no one ever said before.

98.8%

"No."
Mother's face is resolute.

“I need a smartphone again, Mother!”
Gritting my teeth
so the other girls
in the store don’t hear.

They have smartphones,
they’re getting new ones;
they’re important enough
that someone wants to
communicate with them.

“I’m putting
my foot down
here.
You are not getting
another phone,”
Mother says.

“Everyone has one.
It will be different this time.
Besides, I’d be able to call you from
my friend’s
house
when I get invited over,”
I explain.

“No. This is it.
I’ve gone along with the rest
but this is not happening,”
Mother says,
shaking her head,
eyes to the door.

“Remember what happened
last time you were on
SocialNet? Those girls
were so mean.”
Mother shivers
at the memory.

I want to fight
and argue
but reason creeps in
and my hate for SocialNet peeks out,
wondering:
Do I really need a smartphone?

"I'll support you getting some
IntelliDyn cloud credits, but
no phone,"
Mother says.

"SOLD!
100 credits and we leave now.
Deal?"
I smirk.

"Deal.
Can we be done with
your transformation
now?"
Mother says,
agitated–
probably missing her book.

"Yeah. Let's get home."
We exit the store.
Some girls are
watching me,
maybe wondering
if I'm the new girl in school.

Tomorrow
I will be
the *NEW*
new girl.

Communication: Re-routed

To: vcmoran17
Subject: Re-routed
Body:

ATTN: Dr. V.C. Moran 17

Regret to inform you we believe the courier has been re-routed. Appears to be an error redirected the package. Package location currently unknown. Best guess: package is in Glen Coast but not on the proper courier route.

Courier is possibly compromised.

Recommendation: Deploy search and recover team if the package does not arrive at the check point tomorrow.

Sincerely;

Inquisitor T. Grier 8302

<eom>

CAYLEE MORAN

Raiding Party Planning

SHADOWLURKER Server Online

Hey @Kuzan_King, raiding tonight?

Yeah. You online?

Yeah.

Can I post we're playing? Get others online?

Just don't tag me.

Raiding the Empire is not a Donna approved activity?

Or, not mom approved?

Both. Just don't okay.

Roger that.

Did you finish that SocialNet app?

Don't want to talk about it.

That bad?

Learning to code
isn't what I call fun.
Just what my mom wants me to do.

Good money in coding.

If it is mundane
and 'normal' my mom
approves.

You know you don't have
to do whatever she says.

Have you met her?
You know I do.
She's beast mode at all times.

Raiding party's ready,
you good to steal some treasure?

Nothing like some
larceny to end the day.
Let's do it.

THURSDAY (2 DAYS)

ERIN ULMAN

The Deep Breath

Sun dress,
straight hair,
chipper smile…
who is this person?

In the mirror
someone who looks like me
stares back
smiling,
ready to be
happy.

She pulls on the edges of the dress,
flapping them around,
trying to be comfortable,
fidgeting,
longing for the pile of hoodies
on the floor behind her.

I'll walk this stranger to school
and have her make friends for me.

Grabbing my backpack,
I head out the door,
taking a moment,
breathing in hope,
suffocating the old me
to give life
to a better
me.

```
Erin.shutdown();
Erin = undefined;
Erin = new Erin();
Erin.start();
```

The Fall

Outside of school
at the bus loop,
I see Donna
and smile
and wave,
hopeful,
proud,
hap—

"Erin,
what are you wearing?"
Donna recoils in horror
and pain
from my attempt to be
someone else.

>>> Warning!
>>> Warning!

Her finger swirls around me,
pointing at everything about me.

"You're trying to fit in
a little too hard."
Her gaggle of friends agrees
while Caylee stands silent.

>>> Critical System Failure!

Donna chuckles.
Her friends laugh.

Their phones come out,
snapping pictures,
savoring the moment
I'm informed
I'll always be
me.

>>> System Failure!
Erin.hide(inHoodie)
>>> System Failure!
>>> Hoodie Unavailable!
>>> Unable to escape!
>>> System Failure!

Posting my red face.
Liking my trembling lips.
Sharing my realization that
I am stuck
being Erin Ulman,
daughter of David Ulman,
outcast,
friendless,
alone.

Erin.Run();
>>> Motor skills failure
>>> Movement impossible

Alerts beeping on other phones
and soon everyone is seeing the posts
pictures, comments, reactions.

Some laugh.

Some gasp.

Some do nothing at all.

Beeping,
buzzing,
laughing,
whispering,
deafening,
drowning,
surrounding
me.

Tears erupt.

Erin.Run();
>>> Motor skills activated

I run.

Past the buses.

Into the street.

>>> Sensory Overload
Visibility = onlyTears;
Hearing = echoingLaughter;
Feeling = undefined…
Feeling = empty;

BEEP!!!!

Too late.

IMPACT!

```
Erin.isHit = true;
Erin.onCollision() {
  Erin.hit(theGround);
}
```

Everything goes quiet
as I lay on the street
looking at the clouds.

```
>>> Systems Analysis
Erin.body = onGround;
Erin.visibility = clear;
Erin.hearing = quiet;
```

"Oh my God!
Don't move, sweetie!"
some lady shouts.

She's panicking.

Teachers rush to me.

```
Erin.isBleeding = true;

Erin.feeling = pain;
```

I was just hit

by a car.

CAYLEE MORAN

What I Did

"Is that Erin?"
I say to Donna.

Straight red hair, not curly,
colorful dress, no hoodie.

I'd never noticed how tall Erin is
as she strides toward us.
A mix of
plastered confidence
and
focus while
she meticulously executes her performance.

The sight of her
the snickering of the girls around me
Donna's puffing up to strike her down
and I want to scream
NO ERIN! DON'T DO THIS!
DON'T BE LIKE THEM!
LIKE US!

But the words drown
in years of boiling disappointment
and shame
that I did what Erin's doing
and keep doing it.

I can't say the words.

So, I do nothing.

Donna
is horrible to her.

Erin is trying
as I did
and just like me
she twisted into
Donna's definition of beauty.

Walking up
Erin
was full of possibility
now
she's broken by words
and pictures
and crying
and laughing.

And I do nothing.

If the sound of SocialNet alerts were fire
this school would be a smoldering wasteland.

I changed for Donna
I endured her ridicule
for months.
I thought belonging somewhere
anywhere
was worth paying your dues.

And maybe it is.

But now
Erin's the new one tormented;
she's the new me.

And I do nothing.

Erin runs
crashing through students
as Donna turns to go into school.

I follow.

Through the doors
Donna still chuckles
as I laugh back the sickness and sadness
pushing into my throat.

Silence rushes over us
as teachers sprint by
out the doors
to where Erin lies in the street.

I stare at her
lying there.

I did nothing.

ERIN ULMAN

Silent Journey

Quiet hangs in the car,
our voices suffocated
in the heavy silence
of sadness and failure.

"You sure you feel okay?"
Mother asks,
flicking her gaze to my
bandaged knees.

"Yeah."
My knees
and elbows hurt.

If I was wearing
jeans and my hoodie,
I wouldn't have been bleeding
in the street.

Nurse said I was lucky:
the car had just started moving.
I'd be fine.

I thought getting hit by a car
would hurt more.

Lying in the street,
people screaming and shouting,
but in the end
getting hit by a car
on school property
doesn't even
get me a day off.

"Can I use your phone, Mother?"
I pull the phone
from the dock on the dashboard.

She doesn't interrupt
as I open her web browser,
load up SocialNet,
and search for Donna's profile.

I want to see
what happened
from Donna's eyes.

"Hey Erin,
your new order
arrived today,"
Mother says.

"Is it a new project?"

Shrugging,
keeping silent,
focused on finding
Donna's point of view.

"I set the box
on your desk."
Her voice fades.

"Okay."
What box?
I don't remember
ordering anything.

Maybe the car
hit me harder than
I thought?

"When we get home
I'll get you those
IntelliDyn Cloud Credits
we talked about.

You can build
that server farm!"

Server farm?
That was my project last month.

Donna's SocialNet feed loads,
showing

nothing.

There are no posts
before I got hit by the car,
only posts surrounding that time.

Where are the pictures
her friends took?
I'm sure they tagged her in them?
SocialNet's facial recognition would have
automatically tagged her.

I know she was taking pictures.
I saw it.
I heard her posting and sharing.

"Yeah, some computer time would be good,"
I say,
examining the edges of a SocialNet blackhole,
scrolling between her breakfast
and first period
where posts about my
failure to fit in
should be.

Maybe she didn't post
what happened?

Maybe it wasn't as important as
her toast with strawberry jelly breakfast?

Breaking me down
is less interesting
to Donna
than toast.

Cocoon

Hiding from everyone,
cocooned in my hoodie
on my bed.

I wonder
if the caterpillar
knows what it will become?

Does it choose its wings?

Is the cocoon
painful,
pleasant,
peaceful?

No use sitting here
waiting to change.

I'm stuck who I am.

Looking around my room
for something to distract me,
my eyes land on the brown box
sitting on my desk.

What's in the box?

I go to it
looking for an address,
an owner–
finding nothing.

No label,
no address,
no owner.

whois box_owner
>>> result: unknown

Pulling at the packing tape,
a rip echoes in my room
as the box bursts open,
vomiting puss yellow foam packing peanuts.

Parts tumble out,
clanging
metal
followed by a booklet.
Instructions
maybe?

The language isn't English,
nothing I've seen before
but the pictures are clear.

A flicker of light catches something
still in the box.
Pushing through the foam,
I find a silver case
engraved with spirals,
swirls,
a serpent
coiling
around it.

Diamonds fall from the serpent's eyes
like tears.

I release the latch on the case;
the lid springs open
silently revealing
ten
vials.

An empty space,
the first space, signals
there should be eleven vials.

Bitter cold stings my face;
the vials radiate an arctic aura.

Tilting the case,
I watch the fluid in the vials.
It doesn't
swish or roll
but crawls
creeping inside
the vials.

```
fluid.isLiquid = unknown;
fluid.isGlowing = true;
fluid.isCreepy = true;
```

Mixed in with the packing nuggets
are black steel rods and angle brackets.
They're heavier than they should be
for their size and dimensions.

Each rod has a strange, brushed metal pattern
that wraps around it like the metal was
extruded or twisted into
curves and coils.

What are they made of?
Steel?
Too heavy for carbon fiber
but that's what it looks like.

The manual shows the steps to assemble
whatever this is.
Skipping to the end,
I find a picture of the finished build.

It looks like
maybe
some kind of
3D printer?

Did I order this?

Dad's packages are marked for his business,
Ulman Intelligence Systems,
and Mom wouldn't have anything
like this.

But I don't remember—

"Erin, someone's here
to see you!"
Mother calls to me
from the living room.

What?

SELECT * FROM WhoWouldVisitMe;
Results: 0

I stuff the pieces back into the box,
yellow foam oozing out with each shove,
clinging to my sleeve
as my mind wanders to
a stranger mystery.

Who would be here to see
me?

Shedding Skin

Stepping out of my room
I see
the girl with the muddy sundress,
one of Donna's friends–
Caylee.

She was one of the outliers my app found.

Her light brown skin,
a few tones darker than tan,
is only a 13% match for Donna's friends,
her black precision-knotted hair
only a 5% match.

Her brown eyes float around my living room,
probably looking for more fodder
to feed
her gaggle of friends.

"What do you want?"
Why is she here?
To gloat?

She shrinks from me–
not from my words
but from guilt that she didn't help,
or at least that's what I hope.

"We ran into each other
the other day.
I'm Caylee Moran.
I go to school with you."

A heavy smile weighs her down
as Mother watches intently,
her eyes encouraging me to say hi.

"So, what are you doing here?"
I ask again.

"I heard you got
hit by a bus or something.
I thought you'd be at the hospital."
She looks at the floor,
tugging on her dress.

"I guess I also wanted to say…"
Her eyes finally find mine;
a sad
sigh
blows out from her.
"I know it's rough
being the new girl.
It sucks and I'm sorry."

A smile bubbles
from Mother's lips;
her eyes well up.
"Erin, why don't you show
Caylee your computers?"

Yeah,
that's what she'll want to see.
Donna doesn't value intelligence,
93.56% of her friends just
repost someone else's thoughts,
no thoughts of their own.

"Computers?
My mom's been getting me
to learn how to code."

>>> DOES NOT COMPUTE…
Donna.friend + computers = ERROR!

Caylee almost knocks me down again
at the idea of someone like her
being interested in something so
intelligent.

"I'm working on
my first SocialNet app
right now."

Mother's excitement
would be a blinding light
if it could break through her tears.

The words Caylee says
don't match what she shows at school,
don't match fitting in at Glen Coast High.

"Erin, you should show Caylee
your server farm!"
Mother says.

I weigh
letting Caylee see
anything.

I don't hope for connection,
just a temporary relief from isolation
as I walk her back
to my room.

Don't See That!

I can't tell if she's faking her excitement,
collecting intelligence to report back,
or if she's being genuine.

Erin.isConfused = true;

Her eyes dart from my AC9221 desktop tower
to my IntelliDyn Micro Cloud external hard drive
to my DIY Virtual Reality Haptic Vest.

She reaches out toward my VR headset,
freezing for permission.
I nod to see what happens next.

>>> TEMPORARY ACCESS GRANTED

Caylee snaps it up
and looks through the eye pieces.

"Whoa! Did you make this?"
She must be seeing
my latest VR world.

"Yeah."
I sigh,
wondering when
this will be over.

She gently puts the VR headset back
and moves on to the various
devices and tools on my desk.

"What do you do with all this?"
Caylee asks, eyes wide.

"I build worlds. Digitally.
And sometimes real-world stuff."
Showing her some ABS filament
from my 3D printer–
the old one,
not the new weird one.

"You have a 3D printer?"
Her dark eyes dart around
to find it,
landing on
the box on my desk,
yellow foam
still spewing from it.

"Yeah, it's over there."
I point to the FormLabs MakerBot.
She runs over and
examines it.

"This is better than
the ones at school!"
She caresses it,
gasps.
"Erin, your room
is as messy
as it is amazing."

Was that a *compliment*?

Does it matter?

Tomorrow at school
we'll be back to our roles
and all this will be used against me:
new fodder for the comments, posts, shares.

"I need to do a few things.
Thanks for stopping by."

I motion to the door;
she smiles,
disappointed,
nods,
and steps out.

"Before I go…
I found this and
thought you'd be interested,
after seeing you in computer lab
yesterday."

Digging in her bag,
she pulls out a
cracked microcomputer board,
Arduino from the looks.

"It's not working, but I'm guessing
you can fix it.
I don't really know what
to do with these anyway.

You can have it."

I look it over:
No circuits are broken,
the board is just cracked.
Some hot glue will fix it.

"I have a few of these already,
but I'll fix this one for you
tonight.

They're easy to work with,
just gotta know your
make and model
to program it."

Again, showing her the door.

Caylee straightens up,
smiles a light smile,
and walks out.

whois CayleeMoran
>>> result: puzzling

Who checks in on the new girl?

Not the cool jock
SocialNet stars
of Glen Coast.

Hope is kindled,
a dim
fragile light,
but a light in my darkness
nonetheless.

Someone cared
if I was dead or not.
That's something.

That Night

This old hot glue gun
takes forever to heat up,
so while I wait

I organize the parts from the box:
rods,
tracks,
connectors,
and the silver serpent wrapped case.

The parts are strange,
odd angles and sizes;
connected together, the device looks like
a matte black
twisted rectangle,
like a double helix
with a sphere in the center.

Most 3D printers print down on a tray,
building up melted plastic in layers,
but this one
doesn't have a tray,
it has a spherical track.

DING!

The hot glue gun is ready.
I quickly fix the cracks on
Caylee's circuit board,
burning my fingers as my eyes drift back
to the new device on my desk.

What a strange 3D printer…

Letting the glue gun cool,
I return to the device,
completing the build from the instructions,
finding a website,
username,
and password
scribbled on the last page–

in a hurry
by the looks of it.

I connect the device to my computer.

It powers up
and I jump back
as a shock snaps from
the device to my finger.

I shake away the pain
while a high-pitched scream
leaks out of the device.
A nozzle in the sphere
cycles
around the track.

Groans,
whines,
sputters–
the device comes to life
from a long slumber.

On my computer
I load a private browser,
connecting to the website in the instructions,
logging in with the username and password.

The screen flickers
and a prompt to install *Pandora.exe*
awaits approval.

Pandora.isMalware = likely;
Pandora.isRootKit = possibly;
Pandora.isAdventure = absolutely;

I click *Install*.

The progress bar loads,
interrupted by a crash from the kitchen.
Mother's slippers rush out
from her room, followed by
a loud sigh.

"I thought you were
working late, David,"
Mother says.

Dad's home?
I step to my door,
stalling on the thought:
It's late
and school is early,
best get some sleep.

I'm sure he
isn't going to be here
long.

CAYLEE MORAN

What If…

Lying in bed
staring at the ceiling,
my mind wanders.

What if
Erin says hi tomorrow?

How will Donna react?

Did I just ruin everything
I've built here?

What if
Donna finds out
I went to Erin's house?

If someone saw me go
and Donna wants a full report?

What would I say?
Erin's room is a technology paradise
and she's probably the smartest person
in the school.

That's what Donna hates about Erin.
Not that she's smart,
that she thinks she's smarter
than everyone else.

Erin probably is.

What if
I pretend nothing happened?

Can I do that?

Just like I pretend
everything else.

What is another thing
to pretend about?

FRIDAY (1 DAY)

ERIN ULMAN

Early Morning Thoughts

For many,
today is the herald of the weekend;
for me
today is a trial.

What will Caylee say when I see her?
Will the Caylee from last night
come to school today?
I hadn't met the girl
who came over last night
before.
I've only met Donna's
quiet
complacent
tagalong.

Grabbing Caylee's circuit board from my desk
I see the device, the *Pandora.exe* app installed,
ready to run.
My fingers drift to start it,
but I have an errand before school
and I can't be late;
too many eyes watching when you're late.

Passing through the kitchen,
I grab a bagel on the run,
spotting Dad on the couch
sleeping.

His breathing is rhythmic,
inviting,

drawing me back to
when I was a kid,
when he'd fall asleep on movie nights,
when I'd rest my head on him
and ride the waves of his breathing
until I fell asleep.

I search my memory
to find when we did that last
and get
zero results.

Should I wake him?
Should I say
Hi!
I miss you!
I'm more important than your work!

Sunrise cracks the dawn,
flooding our living room with
morning's golden glow.

Dad doesn't move.
He's dead to the world.
Only an email, text, or call from work
could wake him.

I grab my backpack,
watching his eyes flutter,
wondering what work project he's dreaming about.
I quietly close the door behind me.

The Bookshop

Most people in Glen Coast
wouldn't go to The Bookshop.

The three-story,
vibrant baby blue façade with
elegant white trim
doesn't fit the Glen Coast cookie-cutter
superstore.

DING!

As I enter the store,
Mr. Stone stands behind the counter,
his bald head peeking over the newspaper.
Slurps rattle out of the paper
accompanied by the smell of old books
and black coffee.

```
perfectSmell = oldBooks + coffee;
```

"Good morning, Mr. Stone!"
I say,
too chipper for this early.
He grunts a response.

Books burst from the shelves
in stacks
and piles,
a feast for hungry minds.

In the computer section
I see the book for Caylee.
Introduction to Micro Computing & Processing
by A.J. Sherman.
Just what she needs to start with her
circuit board.

Beside the computer section,
atop a pile of art history books,
World History: Art in Perspective
by Dr. Cameron Jorgen
catches my eye–

on the cover
a swirling serpent,
tears dripping from its eye
just like the case
in the box
on my desk.

"Excuse me, miss."
When I look up,
a skeletal old man
cranes his neck down
to meet my eye.
"Anything I can help you with?"

"Oh, no. I just was picking up these books."
I hold them both up.

He strokes his short white beard,
trimmed into a devilish goatee;
it almost shines against his sandy sallow skin.
On his emaciated index finger
a glowing red ruby
wreathed in a silver ring
catches the light.

"So you found everything
you are looking for?"
His question hangs
while his eyes
see…
something
in the space around me.

I look around me
to see whatever it is;
nothing's there.

"Uh, yeah."
I shake the books.
"This is it. I'll go pay now.
Gotta get to school."

escapeFromOldMan();

I pay at the counter.
Mr. Stone's hand snaps out from the newspaper
taking my money
grunting when the transaction is complete.

The other man
still standing there,
still staring
around me,
nods,
bearing gray snaggle teeth
in a smile that dies
before it settles over his face.

"Have a good day, miss."
The old man's
voice trails off
into a hiss.

I step out The Bookshop, leaving
a place of knowledge,
heading to
a place of rigid social status,
wishing school
was more like The Bookshop.

Maybe
without the creepy old man.

Charades

Yes,
I'm
the girl who fell in the hall,
the girl hit by a car
or bus
or tanker truck
depending on who's telling the story.

I'm Erin.

Erin = readonly me; // unable to be changed

Donna sees me,
smirks,
warding me off
with her body language,
screaming:
Approach at your own risk.

Caylee is behind her,
as usual.
She's conforming:
dress, makeup, selfie-ready poses,
as usual.

Caylee = Donna.friend NOT Erin.friend;

She's the girl I expected to see today,
not the one from last night.

I catch Caylee's eyes;
they fill with fear,
they fill with shame,
and I look away,
walking past her.

I want to run to her,
throw the book at her,
throw the circuit board at her,
scream

YOU ARE ALL LIARS
AND FAKES
AND FRAUDS
but I don't.

Caylee is afraid of what I can do;
what will happen if I stop and
talk to her.

Can I blame her?

I don't want to be me either.

At my first class
I write a note:
No worries. I get it. See me after school.
I have a book for you.
Wrapping the note around the circuit board,
I slip it into the crack of Caylee's locker.

A secret friend
is better than no friend.

```
Caylee = Erin.friend = undefined;
```

Communication: Detection

To: vcmoran17
Subject: Status Report
Body:

ATTN: Dr. V.C. Moran 17

Courier of the device was captured trying to flee the district. During interrogation he revealed the package was dropped at a residence in Glen Coast, MD. We do not know which.

Courier was carrying a sigil of MacAbera. The Courier was working against us. Before the Courier was incapacitated through enhanced interrogation, he declared our ranks broken, our order infiltrated. I will seek out the betrayers if he spoke truth.

Energy signature from the device confirms the device is powered on. Activation has not been detected.

Search and retrieval operation in full effect. Will report as situation evolves.

Sincerely;

Inquisitor Q. Nicholas 10028

<eom>

ERIN ULMAN

Part Time

When I get home,
the empty couch confirms
Dad was just passing through.

Mother stops me at the door.
"Caylee called and asked if you
want to come over for dinner tonight."
She smiles.
"I told her yes, so drop your books,
we need to get going.
Isn't this so exciting!?"

Yeah, so exciting
she forgot who I was today.

Can someone be a part-time friend?

I understand
she doesn't want to lose
what she has.
Being in Donna's crowd is important
to her,
to me;
to be accepted and wanted
by someone,
anyone.

```
Erin.isWanted = byDonna is false;
if(Caylee.isSeenByDonna == false){
  Erin.isWanted = byCaylee is true;
} else {
  Erin.isWanted = byCaylee is false;
}
```

Dropping my bag on the counter,
my books tumble out.

The art history book spins,
sliding over the counter
as if being pulled to my room,
turning rhythmically,
hypnotically
directing me
to the device.

Snatching up the book,
I run to my room,
pulling out the silver serpent case,
examining the image on the cover:
the images match.
Even the number of tears is the same—
eleven.

I open the book.
It greets me with a
creaking,
cracking
spine, as if gasping
back a secret about to be stolen.

Scanning the pages, I notice
the cover image appears again
in the Assyrian art section.

Mother yells something,
but I can't hear her over the images
of swirling, spiraling serpents
devouring the world,
roiling in storms
and chaos.

A name captions one image:
Tiamat,
Mother of Monsters.

Feeling the silver serpent case,
gliding my fingers over the tears,
over the fangs,
over the eyes,
I see my reflection shimmering,
staring back to me,
smiling,
eyes darkening.

I lift my finger from the case;
a trickle of blood trails off,
hooked on the serpent's tooth.
I check my finger:
no cut.
I look back to the case:
no blood.

Erin.isImagining = …

"ERIN!"
Mother yells.
"What are you doing?
We've got to go!"

My mind snaps back.

I examine the silver serpent case
again,
wondering
what Tiamat is doing in my room
and where this device came from
and what it does.

Hungry minds
need to be fed
mysteries.

I look forward to solving this one
after dinner.

Revealing Caylee Moran

Bright red big wheel bikes
break up the blotches of dead grass
in Caylee's front yard.
Colorful toys,
some dolls,
pogo sticks,
line the path to her house.

We walk up the ramp
to the front door.

Mother knocks,
an annoying rhythmic clopping.
My eyes roll away from the
store-bought brownies in my hands,
up and over the doorway,
noticing cobwebs and beehives
hiding in the corners of the porch.

```
Erin.palmSweating = true;
brownies.chanceOfBeingDropped = 99%;
Erin.chanceOfRuiningDinner =
      brownies.chanceOfBeingDropped;
```

A faint warm light
casts the area
in a golden glow,
welcoming,
showing the red door
like a beacon of comfort,
coating the two white rocking chairs
in an orange shine.

A slow creaking slips from the chairs
but I don't notice a breeze,
probably missed it
when I saw the beehives.

"Hi! You must be Erin!"
A bubbly woman answers the door:
ruddy peach skin,
curly, frizzy brown hair,
flowery apron.
"I'm Cathy, Caylee's mom."
Giant grin.

```
Cathy("Caylee's Mom").looksLike("Caylee") = false;
```

"Hi! I'm Susan and
this is Erin."
Mother motions for me
to give up the brownies.

The box slides out of my slippery hands
into Cathy's as she smiles and nods.

"Welcome, come on in."
Cathy waves us in.

Inside the house is an eruption of
chaos
as two small children
storm
through the living room,
falling over each other,
playing keep away
with some unseen treasure.

They are loud,
ravenous,
wild–
just what I imagine siblings to be.

I guess they're siblings?

One is
Asian
with very pale skin,
black hair,
and a scar on her lip.

The other
has deep brown skin
and midnight black hair,
and she's wearing a torn ivory princess gown.

"Erin, Caylee is back in her room.
I'm sure she'd love to see you,"
Cathy says,
motioning down the hall.

Mother follows Cathy into the kitchen.
Laughter starts right away
as Cathy says something funny.
Had to be Cathy;
all Mother would talk about
is her latest book.

And who would laugh
about fiction books?
It's not like they're real.

I trudge down the hall,
excitement bubbling in my stomach.

What will I do when I see her?

Erin.throwBookAt("Caylee");
Erin.scream("Don't bother pretending to be my friend!");

But then I see her
frustrated face
carved deep in the faint
PC screen glow.

>>> System Exception
>>> Anger Fading

"Hey, Caylee,"
I say softly to not startle her.
She scrambles for a sweater
hanging on her chair,
pulling it over her sweaty t-shirt.

I hold out the book.
"I dropped the board in your locker today.
Thought you'd like a book to get started with it."
I place the book on her desk.

She waits
for something else.
Yelling.
Anger.

But I'll take what I can get
and for now,
this is it.

I smile
and point to her computer.
"What are you working on?"

A smile breaks her lips;
a weight lifts from her shoulders
as the hood falls back,
releasing springy black curls.

"Thanks."
Her eyes glass over.
I hate when people cry.

"So, uh…"
I stammer to stop the tears,
looking for something to build a dam with,
finding it on her screen:
the comforting monospace courier
command prompt.

"What's this?"

```
tearsAvoided =true;
Erin.comfortLevel("increasing");
```

Dinner for 7

"Dinner time, girls!"
Cathy shouts
through the house.

Frustrated sighs
slip from
Caylee and me
like a chorus of despair.

Things were just starting to work
with Caylee's new SocialNet app,
but now we need to go eat
at a table
without a computer on it.

Ugh…

Caylee leads me to the living room
where a long folding table is set up,
the couch moved against a wall,
the other furniture stuffed
anywhere it fits.

The table is set for seven,
three places on each side,
a mishmash of chairs for each place,
one place at the head, no chair.

I sit across from Caylee
at the middle of the table.
Mother sits to my right
beside the head.

Cathy puts her iced tea
between Caylee and the head,
placing her fingers to her mouth
to blow out a mind-piercing

HWISSSSSS!!!!!!!

The whistle cracks through the siblings' noise,
chasing away the fun,
leaving silence
as they flood to the table,
sitting
still,
hands folded for prayer.
Caylee
sits with hands in her lap.

With Cathy and Caylee together,
I see how different they are.

Caylee.blackHair NOT Cathy.mouseyBrown;
Caylee.lightBrownSkin NOT Cathy.ruddyPale;
Caylee.brownEyes NOT Cathy.greenEyes;

Maybe
Caylee looks more like her dad?

A door opens off the living room;
what I thought was a closet
opens to an office
as the whirring of a motor quietly approaches.

Another woman comes out the office,
older than Cathy,
steel blue eyes, almost silver,
highlighting the gray streaks throughout her short
midnight
hair.

"Erin, Susan, this is my wife, Victoria,"
Cathy says.

Victoria steers her wheelchair up
to the head of the table,
clasping her hands,
bowing her head;
the children echo,
as does Mother,
as do I.
Caylee sits
still.

Silence drifts over the table,
so deep
I can hear Caylee's computer fan
across the house.

"Lord,"
Victoria says,
too faint to be a whisper.
"Thank you for this meal and
our time together.
Thank you for our guests,
Erin and Susan.
Thank you for the
gifts you give daily
and the acceptance
of the gifts we give you.
In the name of our Lord,
Amen."

Cathy smiles
and nods as
"Amen"
trails around the table
like dominos passing from person to person,
stopping at Caylee.

Victoria glares
as Caylee,
in an empty voice,
says,
"Amen."

Dr. Moran

"So, Erin, Caylee tells me
you're quite the computer whiz?"
Cathy politely asks.

"Yes, Mrs. Moran,
I love creating with computers."
I smile back,
stirring my mash potatoes into my peas,
hoping the gritty instant potatoes
covers the mushy pea texture.

Cathy smiles wide.
"Actually, I'm Mrs. Dolan.
Victoria is Mrs. Moran—well,
Dr. Moran."
Cathy chuckles.
"She didn't get all that student loan debt
to be a Mrs."

Cathy smiles at Victoria,
gripping her hand,
squeezing love into it
like my parents used to do.

Victoria smiles,
then looks to me,
face curling into curiosity.

"Creating with computers.
That is an interesting way to say coder,"
Victoria says.
Her voice stops all other conversations.

"I just love to build things
that never existed before."

Victoria's grin expands to a smile,
revealing teeth
sharper than I expected.

Her eyes drift from my eyes
to the edges of my face,
tracing around me,
a wrinkle forming in her brow,
quickly pushed away
with a shake of her head.

"So, what do you do, Dr. Moran?"
I ask,
feigning interest.

"Victoria is a professor and researcher
of anthropology at the university,"
Cathy answers,
beaming with pride.
"She studies lost civilizations."
Her voice is giddy.

Caylee.isComfortable = false;

Caylee shifts in her seat.
"It's not as interesting
as it sounds,"
she mutters,
audible to all.
Everyone freezes,
looking to Victoria for a response.

My eyes jut from Caylee
as she prods her chicken with a fork
to Victoria
as she slices her chicken with a knife
stabbing the slice,
scooping it into a pile of mashed potatoes.

"Caylee, my work is important.
Maybe one day you'll see studying
the world
is much more important
than playing
on SocialNet."

Caylee grimaces.

Cathy springs up, smiley and animated.
"Dessert, anyone?"

Mother raises her hand,
shooting me awkward glances,
telling me to get some dessert.

"I'll take some dessert, Cathy,"
Victoria says.
"So, Erin, how mundane
do you find Glen Coast?
This place isn't
built for intellectuals."

Caylee.frustration("increasing");
Erin.isComfortable("decreasing");

Caylee's ears burn a ruddy brown,
her cheeks not much lighter.

>>> processing
Erin.breakTension();

"I'm not really a fan of Glen Coast,"
I say
as Mother kicks me under the table,
giving me a 'don't tell the truth' look.

I'm an Ulman.
Telling the truth is what we do.
No matter how much it hurts.

"So far, the only thing
I've found interesting is that bookstore,
The Bookshop."

Victoria
freezes
mid-bite of her
chicken and mash potato mix.

Victoria.isComfortable("decreasing")
Victoria.isBlushing = true;

Did I say something?

Her eyes dart over,
looking around me
again.

Victoria.processing();
Erin.query("What is Victoria thinking?");

"Ah,
ah yes.
Have you met Albert Stone?
He works there.
Has some great stories,"
Victoria says.

"Uh yeah, I never get stories though.
Just grunts,"
I say and laugh;
the thought of Victoria and Mr. Stone
having a conversation of grunts
seems ridiculous.

Caylee drops her fork;
it crashes onto her plate,
ringing around the room.

Cathy places dessert on the table.

"I was at The Bookshop this morning.
Caylee is working on a really interesting
microcomputer project.
I got a book to help her get rolling,"
I say, looking to Caylee,
seeing a smile peek out.

"That sounds interesting.
More up to your abilities, Caylee,
than a little SocialNet app,"
Victoria says,
scooping a piece of apple pie.
"Maybe Erin should come over more
and you can keep doing
meaningful things with your time?"

Caylee's face is now boiling red;
the grinding of her teeth
fills the room,
her jaw clenching tight
as venom bubbles into her eyes.

Her mouth falls open
as I jump up.
"Where is the bathroom, Caylee?"

```
Erin.breakTension();
Erin.help(Caylee, "Avoid something she can't take
back.");
```

Cathy, Caylee, and Mother
give me puzzled looks,
wondering how much of an emergency I'm having.

Caylee stands up,
directing me back past her room to the bathroom,
and I wonder if what I just saw was every dinner
with Dr. Moran
or just a show for the guests.

We leave shortly after dessert,
the rest of dinner
enjoyed in silence
with only
Caylee's deep calming breaths
and grinding teeth to fill the air.

The Nice Family

"What a nice family!"
Mother says;
apparently she attended someone else's
dinner party.

She starts saying something about
Cathy, how funny she is
or how much they have in common
but I lose her as I stare
at a picture of Mother, Dad, and me
at Niagara Falls a few years ago.

We saw the falls,
had a great time,
relaxed, and enjoyed being a family.

That was before he lost his job.

I hold the picture,
hoping to absorb some of the joy in it.
Maybe reconnect to a time before
Dad was gone.

"That was a fun trip,"
Mother says,
touching my shoulder.

I shrug her off,
keeping the joy in this picture
all to myself.

"You remember when we got that cheeseburger
with no meat on it?"
Mother chuckles.

"Yeah, I do."

"And your dad took it
to the counter and said–"

I cut her off.
"'I think you forgot something.'"

I smile,
she laughs,
tears well up for both of us.
Her tears are hopeful,
wondering when we'll get back to that life.
My tears are mournful,
knowing we'll never get back to that life.

```
Reality = ThatLife.is("Never coming back.");
```

"Goodnight, Mother.
Thanks for going tonight."
I rush back to my room.

Considerations

In the dark of my room,
the device
pulses,
casting unearthly
pale green
shadows
that writhe in my room.

Their dance is
one of anticipation,
throwing off concerns
and cares.
They're whirling,
whipping
with excitement
and freedom.

On my computer screen,
the *Pandora.exe* icon
is ready to run.

I click once,
highlighting the icon,
activated,
ready to start.

Erin.pause();

Should I stop now?
What will happen?
What is this device and software?
I should stop now.

Erin.go();

I double-click the icon,
launching a black console screen,
the software
thinking,
preparing,
loading.

The device awakens,
clicking,
sucking,
drinking from an empty well.

Pandora Device Error x021f
Serum not loaded.

appears on the screen.

Serum?
The vials?

A purple light
flashes on the device;
the top center of the helix shape,
a pit to receive the serum,
depresses into the device.

Opening the silver serpent case,
the fluid in the vials emits a soft shine,
like the pale tones of a moonless night
tinged green.

The serum
crawls from side to side in the vial,
not swishing,
not flowing,
but crawling like thousands of claws
scratching inside the vial as I tilt it side to side.

Should I?
I should stop now;
this isn't even ink,
it's some kind of
living serum.

I press the vial into the slot:
a popping sound,
hissing gas,
the purple light vanishes,
the serum climbs into the device,
the cursor on the screen blinks
ready.

Flashing,
waiting,
loading:
a line of text blurts out

Protocol: U.Dabrutu Alpha detected. Continue? [Y/N]

Should I…
More curious than cautious,
I press Y.
New line appears:

U.Dabrutu Alpha Protocol selected.
Estimated generation time 24 hours.
Begin? [Y/N]

Y is pressed before the line completes.

The faint light of the device
brightens,
becoming
blinding,
forming a miniature emerald star
in the center of the Pandora Device,
in the sphere.

Whirring,
revving,
the nozzle
begins racing inside the sphere,
moving so fast it appears to move
in reverse.

The serum is spit
into the center of the sphere,
floating
weightless.
As the nozzle spits more serum,
the serum globs together and
throbs like a heartbeat,
forming an egg.

The device goes silent
as the spitting continues,
the growing glob continues,
the pulsing light dims.

11:00 PM.
Sleep is calling me,
but I want to watch this thing grow.

No sleep will happen in here tonight-
too bright-
so I grab my pillow
and head to the couch in the living room.

From the living room couch,
the faint pulsing green light
is barely visible under my bedroom door.
I strain to watch it,
wondering
as my eyes grow heavier…

What does this thing make?

The Thing in the Water

Warm sand gently hugs my feet,
a cool breeze glides over my face,
the ocean tickles my toes as it flows
in and out.

"Hey Erin!"
Mother waves to me
on my right;
she's smiling.

Dad is beside her
holding a briefcase;
he smiles,
the first I've seen in years.

They walk up to me
holding hands.
Happy.

"Oh, will you look at that?"
Dad says,
shielding his eyes from the sun,
pointing into the ocean water.

I look out.
In the rolling waves,
a figure walks toward us.

Graying sky.
Clouds move over the sun,
blanketing the sand in shade.

Water's tickle turns to biting ice.
The breeze is now a frigid breath closing in on me.
Sand slithers up my leg in gritty tentacles,
anchoring me to stillness.

Mother's smile vanishes,
replaced by panic,
fear.

Father points to the figure,
his face emotionless,
made of wax
dripping,
melting away,
softly saying,

"Worthy work, worthy worker.
Worthy work, worthy worker…"
trailing off quietly as he walks
back the way he came.

The old man from The Bookshop
stands in the distance
behind me, watching me,
stroking his beard
with his ruby ring.

The figure in the waves approaches,
too dark to see,
convulsing through the water,
inhuman gyrations
like a legless creature
learning to walk upright.

Waves crash around it.

The thing in the water,
unaware of the wild torrent engulfing it,
approaching
faster,
bringing
colder
water
air
fear.

I can't move…

The sand creeps further,
now eclipsing my waist.
Am I sinking
or is it slithering up?

My arms flail to grab anything.

Mother strains to pull me free
but I sink
faster.

I can't move!

Mother let's go.
Everything about her goes rigid
as her arms jitter and snap in spasms.
Prying her stomach open,
she pulls a book from inside herself.
It's the art history book.

"Better luck next time, Erin,"
she says.

She goes to the thing in the water;
they embrace.
Mother wraps her arms around it.
The thing's slithering arms or talons or teeth
devour her.
Mother vanishes,
eaten
or
absorbed.

It keeps coming.

"Erin, you need to wake up."
Caylee's mom
Victoria stands beside me.
"That thing isn't what you think.
Time to wake up and stop this."

I CAN'T MOVE

Sand climbing to my mouth,
slipping in,
gritty crunching between my teeth.

Victoria gently
brushes away my tears.
"Ready, Erin?"
she says
calmly.

"One."

It approaches.
I can see its body,
a storm of rippling feelers
and tentacles and teeth,
coiling and climbing over itself,
shadow solidifying into a human form.

"Two."

It has a face.
I can see it now,
emerging from the shadow mists.
The sand scrapes my eyes.
I blink faster to push it out–
no use.

"Three."

She looks like me!

She is me!

"Wake now!"
Victoria screams.

On the living room couch,
sweating,
can't
breathe,
springing to my feet,
ripping sand from my mouth,
finding none,
seeing my living room–
no ocean,
no Victoria,
no thing.

Only a slow pulsing green light
coming from my room.

SATURDAY (THE DAY)

Haunting

Clattering in the kitchen
starts the morning.

I sit up to see what Mother is cooking,
motivated by the invigorating smell of bacon
giving me the energy to look
after a sleepless night.

"That smells…"
That's not Mother.

Dad's in the kitchen.

Dad's cooking breakfast?

Dad == isHome;
>>> Does not compute

"You going to sleep all morning?"
Dad asks.

He's cooking,
he's flipping bacon–
he's here?

The sun isn't up yet.

He's still dressed for work;
just getting home,
I guess.

"I saw you on the couch,
figured you might need some pick-me-up
this morning."

He smiles.
"Late night?"

I smirk.
"Rough night."
Stretching.
"Weird dreams."

The bacon starts smoking.
Dad never was good at making bacon.

"Any interesting projects?"
he asks while trying to tame the bacon
grease
sizzling,
spitting,
stinging his arms.

I look back to my room,
the door
more open than I left it last night.

"Uh, yeah actually. I found-"
His phone rings.
The smell turns to burn,
the bacon's popping drowns in his phone call.

No chance for a second ring;
he answers recklessly,
upsetting the bacon pan,
splattering grease on the burner.

Work has him again.

Dad == isHome = notForLong;

"Erin, can you
clean this up, honey?"
He doesn't wait for an answer.

"Yes, I know.
I'm monitoring the sit-
yes Dr. Ham-, yes, I understand.
On my way…"
he says to the caller
as he walks outside
to his car,
and he's gone again.

The bacon could have been so good;
now it just
stinks.

Shopping Spree

"Wake up, Erin.
We're going shopping!"

I stir from the couch,
hair matted,
mind groggy,
charred bacon grease
still heavy in the air.

I must have fallen back asleep.

Mother throws the pans in the sink,
black bacon frozen
in congealed grotesqueness.

"Caylee is expecting us soon."
She throws a change of clothes
at me.
"We'll pick her up and head to
the Galleria in Calista."

Sweet, Calista.
A mall nice enough to have an
IntelliDyn Store
and far enough that we won't see anyone
from Glen Coast High School.

"Please keep your door shut.
Your room is so hot and we aren't
air conditioning the house after Septem-
ber,"
Mother says.

"Uh, thanks.
You didn't touch anything, did you?"
I ask,
wondering if she saw anything she'd
find strange
on my desk.

She laughs.
"Erin, I don't know what half the
stuff in your room is.
I don't know what's breakable,
what should be cleaned,
what's work,
so I leave it all alone."
She points to the clothes
in my hands.
"Let's go.
Retail therapy is waiting."

In the kitchen
her face contorts in disgust,
not for the mess
but for his quick visit,
for starting something
and then running off.

Heading back to my room,
I close the door.
The heat washes over me
as the sphere continues to grow;
serum continues to spit onto the egg,
now a pulsing blob.

"I'll see you later,"
I say to the device,
to the blob,
curious about what I'll find
tonight.

Breaking Free

No flower dress for Caylee today;
her white Ramones shirt
and light-wash ripped jeans
glow bright against her light brown skin.

Her hair is frizzy,
a halo of black,
soft,
bouncy
fun.

Cathy waves and shouts to Mother
from the house.
Mother laughs and shouts something back
but I don't hear them over
my own shouting to Caylee.
"Whoa! Caylee! You look…
alive!"

"Today
I am!"
She giggles,
jumping into the car.

Mother drives the convertible:
a rare occasion.

We drive on the highway.
Mother never takes the highway,
always saying it's full of reckless drivers.

We listen to the 80s rock station.
Mother knows every song,
every word,
singing with Caylee,
both screaming into the wind.

I sit quietly,
not the singing type,
but enjoying the cool breeze,
the sunshine.

The ocean shore flashes in my mind.

A twisting figure wriggling in the water.

Mother is singing.
Caylee is singing.
"Material Girl" is playing.

A shadowy face forming flashes in my mind.

Erin.breathing = false;
Erin.drowning = true;
Erin.drowning = true;
Erin.drowning = true;
Erin.—

"Erin! What's wrong?"
Mother looks at me
in the rearview mirror.
"Feeling okay?"

Caylee chuckles in front of me.
"The singing isn't *that* bad, Erin!"

They both laugh.
I rally the best laugh I can,
pushing through the memories of last night
as the singing stops,
the radio quiets,
the Galleria approaches.

CAYLEE MORAN

The Truth in Calista

While Mrs. Ulman goes to the bookstore
Erin and I
hit the IntelliDyn Store.

Brushed metal,
glass,
the too-cool-for-a-tech-store atmosphere
both in temperature
and attitude
engulfs us.

This place is a computer nerd's dream.

Mom Victoria wishes this was my dream
and maybe I should want that too.

I only have a few dollars saved
and see too many things I want.
Not enough birthday money
to get anything in here.

Erin peruses the store
with the boredom of an aficionado
searching for something she hasn't seen before,
finding trinkets that wouldn't match
her room:
her technology paradise.

"Isn't this awesome!"
I say, trying to hide my excitement.

"I haven't seen an I.D. Alien Core 9 yet."
I point to IntelliDyn's latest laptop.
The LCDs glow red,
tracing the path of the processor fans.

I hear the
gurgling
whooshing
of the liquid cooling system
like a fierce predator's growl
coming from the processor.

"Yeah, the 10
is right around the corner.
Probably out next quarter."
Erin's disinterest
turns the Alien Core 9
into just another laptop.

Her eyes catch mine
and she nods quickly
"But, it is pretty cool.
My dad just gets these for work
so I see packages
coming to the house
with this stuff in it."

"What does your dad do?"
I ask.
Erin's face twists
and in that moment I swear
I see Donna's face
when she talks about her father.

"He has a tech startup.
IntelliDyn is partnering with him
to embed his AI system into their hardware."

Erin sounds so bored;
the words fall off her.
I can't imagine my parents doing something
so amazing.
Mom Cathy's biggest excitement
is when Sabrina and Yui make up a new game.
Mom Victoria's excitement
is reading some new old book.

"Your Dad works with IntelliDyn?"
I ask in a squeal.
"That is so awesome!"

Erin shrugs.

"It's okay."

"How long has he worked with them?
Is that why you guys moved here?"
I ask.

Another shrug answers.
She's paying more attention to some
Bluetooth speaker than my questions.

"No, working with IntelliDyn since like late August.
He has his own company.
He started it right before we moved to Glen Coast.
I haven't really seen him much since we've been here.
I mean, he comes home sometimes but normally
he's straight to his office
in our basement."

Wow, I wonder if Donna
knows how much
she and Erin
have in common.

Neither see their dad.

Neither know when he will
disappear.
Just Erin's dad goes to work.
Donna's dad goes to his
other family.

Maybe there is no difference?

Erin tosses the speaker down,
turning away from me
as the lights catch a glint of tears
welling in her eyes.

"Sounds tough. I bet it's hard to
never see him."
I step closer to her,
whispering.

"I used to see him all the time.
But he got fired for exposing his company's garbage."
A devious smirk grows on her face.
"They were doing shady stuff with people's data.
He exposed them to a privacy advocacy group.

Fired the next day."
Her smirk drops.
"He did the right thing
and lost everything."
Her voice grows sorrowful,
saddened by the truth.

"We had to move because no one would hire him after that.
Next city, same thing.
No one wants to hire someone
who will do the right thing."

Erin walks out of the store,
leaving the loud dance music,
leaving the flashing lights,
leaving me.

I run after her,
catching her shoulder.

She spins,
eyes red with rage
and tears,
face flush with anger
and sadness.

"We lost everything because
he did the right thing!"

Mall people stop and stare.
I don't know what to do,
what to say,
so I open my mouth and hope
something good will come out…

"Do you want to get a coffee?"

Ugh…that wasn't the good I was hoping for.

Erin stares at me,
confused,
trying to figure out if I meant something deeper,
landing on the truth:
I suck at this friend thing.

"I don't drink coffee,
but a tea would be nice."
She sniffles
and smiles
and steps
toward
the food court.

ERIN ULMAN

Building Others

Caylee invites us in
as we drop her off from shopping.

Mother and I
walk in to find
Sabrina and Yui,
as wild as they were at the dinner party,
chasing,
running,
climbing.
Cathy joins them
in their play.

Mother goes to Cathy and laughs
with the girls.

Victoria sits in the kitchen
reading a book
that looks like it could crumble to dust
if she exhaled too hard.

"Hi, Erin,"
Victoria says with a smile,
keeping her eyes on her book.
"How was shopping?"

"Oh, it was great.
Caylee's really fun."
I hold up my tea,
still hot.
"She got me this tea."

Victoria's eyes scan the text.
"I'd have given you more money if
you got your chores done."
Caylee's face flushes.
"You guys went to Calista?
Did you stop in the IntelliDyn store?"

I nod.
"Yeah, Caylee was showing me
the new gaming laptops.
Powerful systems!
And she knew tons about them."
Caylee smiles at me.

"Gaming?
From what I hear about Erin,
she's not at IntelliDyn
looking at gaming computers."
Victoria shakes her head,
disappointed.
"Tsk, tsk.
Those games you play online
are just distractions
from doing something
worth your time."

Caylee is frozen,
embarrassed.
Mother is talking to Cathy.
We're alone.

>>> Command Interrupt
>>> Politeness Override

"Actually, Mrs. Moran—"
I look to ensure Victoria heard
the absence of her doctor title.
"Caylee is doing some awesome stuff
with microcomputers.
You should ask her about it sometime.

She knows it so well,
she can explain it
so even you can understand it."
I grin
and feign a polite sneer.

Caylee's jaw drops.
Victoria's eyes raise from the text,
peering into mine.
I can't tell if she's smiling
or scowling.

"Microcomputers?
I'd love to hear about it.
Right now I need to
finish this research.
I look forward to being dazzled later."
Victoria returns to her book.

Caylee snorts back a laugh,
gives me a wink
and a nod,
directing me back to her room.

I go to follow,
am interrupted.

"Oh, Erin."
I stop, looking back to Victoria,
hunched over her book.
"I'd like to hear about your latest projects too.

And a word of advice.
Be careful in what you build.
Projects,
people,
places…
your creations will always
disappoint you."

Victoria = cruel;
Erin.supress("anger");

What a shitty thing to say.
I know I was dreaming last night
because I can't imagine Victoria
ever helping anyone
else.

Who They Make Us

Caylee sits at her desk
looking at the code
we worked last night.

Her sisters are climbing into their bunk beds.
Caylee looks at me,
sighs.

"Erin…"
Her face grows dark,
weighing her words.
"I really don't…
I don't want to be a coder."

She pushes out a deep exhale,
cleansing her of a secret.

"Okay,"
I say,
wondering
if there is something else
she wants to say.

"Just okay?"
Her face is confused.
"Okay?"

"Yeah, were you expecting
something else?"
I ask.

"It's your thing.
Computers and tech and stuff.
I mean, it's interesting
but not what I want in my life."

Caylee blows out again.
"Mom Victoria thinks that's like,
what I need to do or something.
It's not me.

I thought that's what you'd be like
because it's your thing.

It just isn't me
and you're so into this stuff.
I'm not going to be able to fake it."

"Then don't fake it.
What is YOUR thing?"
I ask
and poke her shoulder.
"Who is the real Caylee Moran?"

"Bedtime, ladies!"
Cathy walks in.
"All the girls."
She looks at Caylee
and smiles.

"I'll see you Monday?"
I say.

"I'll try."
Caylee smiles.

I leave.
I'm sure she will.

As I walk off Caylee's porch,
my thoughts go back to the Galleria.
Did I say too much?

Is Caylee going to tell?

Is there more fodder for Donna
and her clones?

Caylee hadn't said anything about
my room.

Maybe she's not who I thought?
Maybe she's just setting me up?

Monday,
I'm sure I'll be alone
again.

It Has Been 24 Hours

Arriving home,
Mother is telling me something,
but all I can think about is
what I'll find in my room.

Twenty-four hours have passed;
the Pandora Device
should be done.

"Goodnight, Mother!
I'm exhausted, going to bed."
Mother is still talking as
I rush back to my room.

Under my door
no more pulsing light,
no light at all.

I crack my door open
and a gust of frozen air crashes over me,
washing away all the warmth in my blood.

Just like the wind in my dream.

I throw open the door
to reveal whatever is waiting inside;
it bounces off a laundry pile on my floor,
closing to a crack big enough for me
to squeeze through.

Everything is dark
except the faint glow
of the cursor on my monitor
flashing,

flashing,
awaiting instructions.

It smells like the air before a snowstorm
as I notice the
blob of silver-green goo
quietly rippling peacefully in the sphere
like a jellyfish floating in invisible water.

It's beautiful.

Written on the computer console window:

> *Design U.Dabrutu appearance.*
> *Enter file location for rigged model to represent*
> *U.Dabrutu.*

I navigate to the 3D model file of
the white kitten
I printed at school
when I see another model.

An avatar I built to represent me in
Virtual Reality.

The file called
me.fbx,
a digital girl
my age,
my height,
my weight,
red hair–
she could be my sister,
or a friend who will be
my friend
no matter who is around.

A 3D model for Virtual Reality,
a digital me on the computer
ready to become
real?

Is that what this thing does?

I enter the file location
and hit enter.

Console cursor flashes,
thinking,
loading,
processing,
text appearing:

> *Select AI Algorithm for U.Dabrutu*
> *[1] Human.Eve*
> *[2] Human.Adam (Prototype)*
> *[3] Other*

1

The console clears,
waiting,
showing

Initialize? [Y/N]

Wait.

Mother would wait.
She'd talk about this,
ask for input,
build consensus,
look at the data.

But I looked at the data
to be more like Donna;
that didn't help.
Data didn't help.

How could data not help?
I've never faced a problem
where data led me to the wrong
conclusion.

Data drives decisions,
data is pure and unbiased…
No, data can be biased.
Most data is.

Dad would do it.
He wouldn't think,
just act,
consequences be damned.

Y

The device comes to life
with a screaming whine
as the nozzle sprints around the sphere,
blurring into
a metallic egg
surrounding the jellyfish.

Whining louder,
deafening,
covering my ears–
still hearing it–
lights dim,
flicker.
BOOM!

A concussive force bursts from the sphere,
blowing papers off my desk,
rippling,
crackling,
electricity biting at the air around me.
Car alarms shout for help outside.
Mother rushes into my room
as the nozzle sprays lightning into the sphere
faster,
brighter,
stealing all sound from the room,
sucking the world into it.
BOOM!

Another concussive blast
as Mother rips me out of my room,
out of the house
to the street
where the neighborhood is totally
dark.

Power outage.

Only stars light the street
as my eyes are pulled to them.
I've never seen so many
or the gaping maw of the Milky Way hanging over me,
hungry,
stretching out wider
to eat the world,
or maybe just me.

The lights return,
trickling up the street,
chasing the stars away.

"What was that!!?"
Mother looks at me with panic.

Just like my dream.

"I don't know,"
I say with equal panic,
knowing what happened,
wondering what awaits.

I run back inside,
back to my room,
shutting the door behind me,
keeping my Mother out.
I see it.

In the center of my room,
turning to face me:
the 3D model, come to life.
It looks like me.

Just like my dream.

It chokes its first breath,
inhales…deep, long, gentle.
Curiously it
looks to its hands,
looks to me,
exhales…calmly.

It's alive.

She's alive.

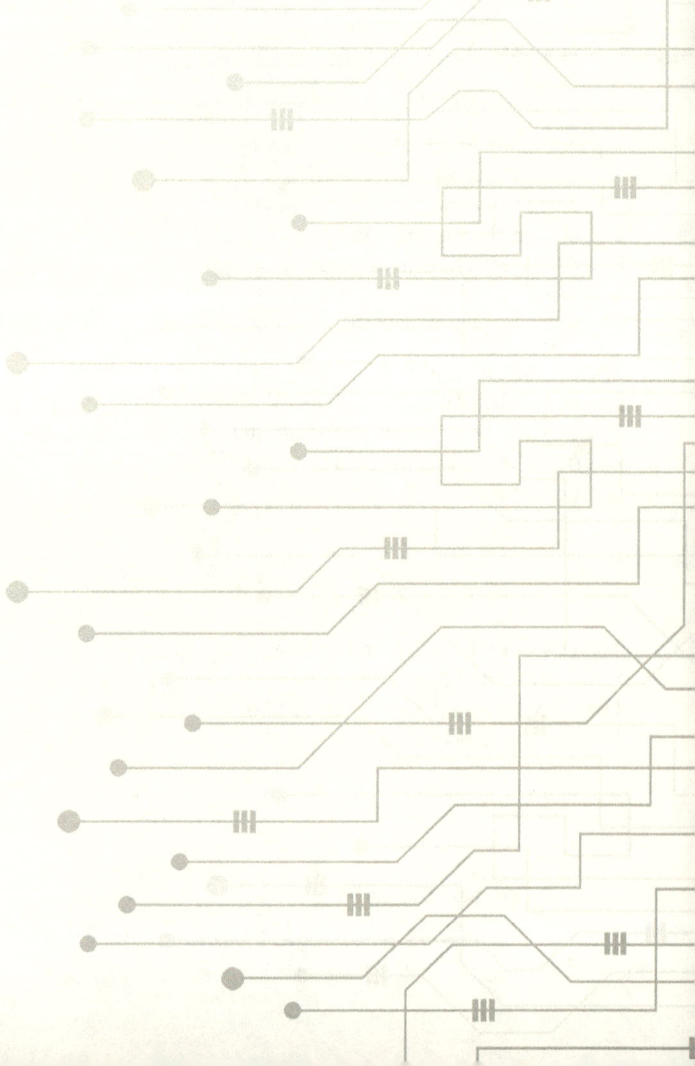

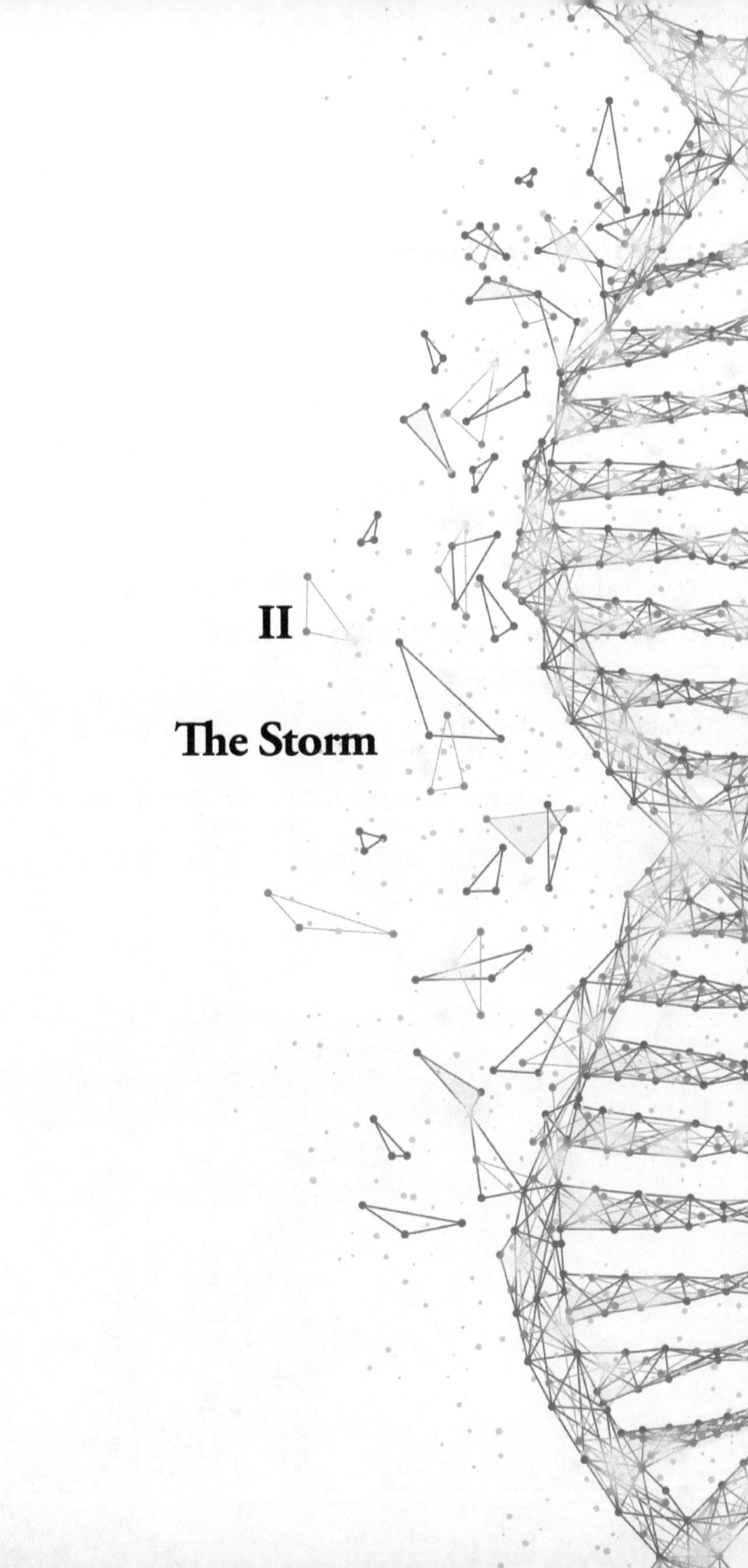

II

The Storm

EMAIL: Phone Home

To: bhamenson@intellidyn.io
From: Special Projects: Systems Monitoring & Risk Management
Attachment: me.fbx

Subject: Pandora Activation Alert

Body:

Pandora Device activated at 01:38:12 UTC.

U.Dabrutu Protocol
AI: Human.Eve
Physical Form: Me.fbx

Location: 476c656e20436f6173742c204d44

Attend to immediately.

Unauthorized build.
Unauthorized deployment.

Implement Hunter Protocols A-091 for device retrieval.

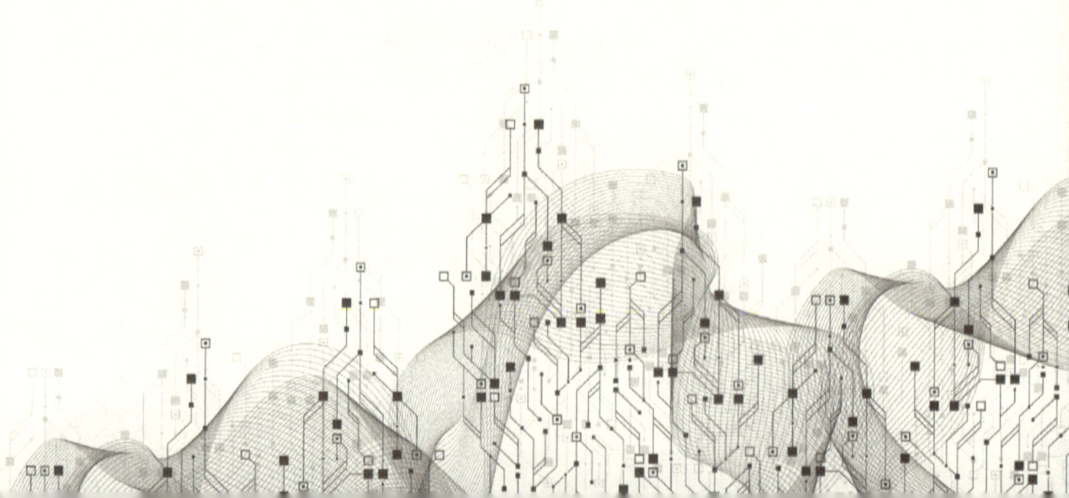

ERIN ULMAN

The Day Before Dad Lost His Job

"Hey Erin, we're going for tacos!"
Dad yells from the kitchen.

Awesome! Tacos at Pepe's!
"Can Betty come?"
I always called her my BBFF,
Betty Best Friend Forever,
since we met in kindergarten.

"Totally!
But no chicken sandwich this time.
Taco night is for tacos!"
Dad says.

Betty and I
laugh.
Who gets a chicken sandwich at
all-you-can-eat tacos?
Apparently
Betty.

Betty and I
are just finishing our latest
machine Learning experiment.
The science fair is in two days.
We have tons to do,
but Betty basically lives here,
so we'll be fine.

In the car
Mom and Dad
are talking about something
using their
"don't let the kids hear"
voice, which usually means
Dad is proposing
ice cream after dinner.
Mom is arguing against it,
probably using her
"you'll spoil the girls" argument.

Their faces are
serious,
conflicted.

Dad whispers,
"It's the right thing
to do, and–"
He scoffs.
"I'm not going down
with that ship."

Maybe they aren't
talking about ice cream?

"Hey, Betty, how is your dad
enjoying work at SocialNet?"
Dad stops talking to Mom.
"Did he tell you
he's on my team?"

Betty's dad just started at
SocialNet
where my dad works.

"Yeah, Mr. Ulman.
He said it is awesome.
You guys are doing some
amazing stuff with AI,"
Betty says.

Dad smiles
only for a moment
as the smile dissolves back
to concerned wonder.

He glances at Mom,
holds her hand,
and sighs.

"I'm doing this.
It's going to happen
and this way
maybe
I won't get caught up in it,"
Dad says.

Mom untangles her hand
from his,
nods,
looking out the window.
From behind her
I can see
dread filling her eyes,
leaking out
like rain on the windshield.

Betty and I didn't finish our project.
She only talked to me one more time
after that day.

To tell me she hated me.

She hated my dad.

To never message her again.

She was my last friend,
two years ago.

Until now…?

Her

"Erin! Are you okay!"

Mother pounds on my door.
I'm not sure of the answer yet
as I stare at…
Her.

"Yeah…
Mother, I'm good."

The girl in my room
is looking around,
touching the walls,
the posters,
smelling my computer,
exploring.

Her cocoon is falling away,
dripping on my floor
in grey fleshy chunks.

Her hair is
red curls,
weighed down and damp.

Her skin is
pale and bright,
never touched by the sun.

She = Erin + beautiful;

I thought the 3D model looked like me
but she's better than me.
Fit like Caylee.
Sleek like Donna.
The best parts of everyone else.

As she wanders into the darker places
her eyes shimmer an unearthly shine.
Her irises
spiral like a vortex of moonlight,
glimmering silver and green.

>>> Attempt Connection

"Hello?
Can you understand me?"

>>> Waiting for response…

She meticulously feels my keyboard,
every depression,
every edge of every key.

"Yes,"

she answers,
quickly,
calmly.

Her voice is
a soft whisper,
dismissively
disinterested in me.

>>> Response received

Her eyes stay on the computer
and desk
and all the technology mounded on it.

"Where am I?
I don't recognize this place."

"You're in my room.
In Glen Coast."

She pauses,
thinking,
processing.

"Glen Coast, Maryland,
United States of America?"

Her eyes meet mine,
speeding my heart,
making me feel for the door handle
behind me,
ready to run.

>>> Select an Option
> Abort? [a]
> Run? [r]
> Scream for help? [s]
> Freeze and do nothing [f]

f

"You don't look familiar.
Fifteen-year-old
female,
Glen Coast, Maryland.
Red hair."

She.analyzing(Erin);
She.analyzing(Erin.Room);

Her eyes return to my desk.

"Interests: Computers, technology."

She.processing();

"No. I don't know you."

She picks up a towel from my laundry pile,
scrubs off the remaining cocoon goo,
and wraps herself.

"Who are you?"
I ask,
releasing the door.

She looks at me,
triggering my hand to grab the door again.
Her eyes are
like the pulsing light of the device,
like the fluid in the vials,
like the girl in my dreams.

"I am Umu Dabrutu, the wild storm.

Who are you?"

CAYLEE MORAN

The Night the Power Went Out

As Mom Victoria wheels out of our room
the night light vanishes.
All the lights in the house
follow,
leaving
darkness.

I grab the flashlight on my desk
following Mom Victoria out to get LED candles
for Sabrina and Yui.

Mom Cathy is already in the hallway,
handing me the candles
and smiling her knowing
happy smile.

"You okay, Caylee?"
Mom Cathy asks.

"Ye—"
A faint wailing,
like some trapped animal
struggling to break free,
stops me from answering.

Nothing more than a whisper
in shadows,
something outside the candlelight
calling to me.
"Do you hear that?"

Mom Victoria goes pale in the candlelight,
staring at me,
eyes stretched open to
make sure she sees everything.

"I—I don't hear anything."
Mom Cathy shakes her head,
listening intently.

An alien feeling takes over
Mom Victoria's face,
something I've never seen,
something she doesn't normally show.

Fear.

"You heard that?"
Mom Victoria says.

I nod.
Mom Cathy shakes her head,
then glances to Mom Victoria
with questioning eyes.

They're talking with their eyes,
frozen in a silent conversation
with blinks and head tilts
talking about what I heard?

What Mom Victoria heard?
She heard it too.

Sighing, nodding,
Mom Victoria lets out
a defeated sigh.

"I'll let you two talk,"
Mom Cathy says
and rubs my arms, patting
Mom Victoria's shoulder.

Sabrina and Yui
start to stir
as Mom Cathy rushes in
handing them each an LED candle.

"Not yet,"
Mom Victoria says.
"Caylee, help your mom.
I'm going to look for something
in my study."
Mom Victoria wheels to her study,
hurrying over the toys
Sabrina and Yui
left in the hall.

"What was that noise?"
I whisper to her,
seeing the girls stir more.
Sabrina starts to whine;
a crying fit is coming.

"Just help your mom,"
Mom Victoria barks.

I recoil.

Sabrina's tears start;
the whine turns to infectious panic
as Yui also starts to cry.

Closing her study door,
I hear the thwapping of an old typewriter
as Mom Victoria quickly taps out
something.

Little late for needing to write?

Power comes back on
and I help Mom Cathy
calm the girls.

With a sweet song
and calm hugs,
Mom Cathy gets the girls
back to sleep.

As Mom Cathy leaves,
she gives me a small
worried smile.

"Goodnight, Mom.
I'm sure it was just a power blip."

She looks away,
nodding slow,
and closes our door.

ERIN ULMAN

What To Do About My Visitor

```
Umu analyzes my computer,
exploring the inputs,
the ports,
the mouse,
her fingers dancing over each,
eyes closed softly,
feeling as if to see them in her mind.
```

Eric.query("What should I do?");
She = Umu;
Umu.isDangerous = undefined;

```
Should I get Mother?
```

Why is there a naked girl in your room?
Why did you do something when you had no idea what would happen?
Why didn't you return that device when you knew it wasn't yours?

If I tell Mother,
I'll need answers for these questions,
probably more.

"You're staring at me,"
Umu says,
soft,
melodic.

Was that a question or statement?
Did her voice just change?
Change to sound like...
mine?

"Where did you come from?"
I ask.

Umu's eyes open,
fingers stopping.
A blank stare covers up
her own questions.

"I mean, I know you came from the device.
Do you know anything more than that?"

She smiles,
shaking her head.

Is it the immediacy of the smile
that unsettles me?
Or that her mouth made a smile
while her eyes didn't?

"Well…"
I pick up one of my least dirty hoodies
and a pair of jeans that don't smell too bad.
"You'll need some clothes."
I toss them to her gently.

She snatches them from the air,
a predator's pounce on flying prey,
as her eyes narrow, intensely staring at me.

"Are you dangerous?"
she asks.

>>> System interrupt
Erin.isDangerous = ridiculous;

I laugh uncontrollably
at the thought!
She looks like she could eat me
or at least beat me to a bloody mess.

Then I realize:
in the movies
villains always laugh at such a question.
"Uh, no. I'm only dangerous to computers."
I hold back my laughing,
smiling meekly instead.

She nods,
her eyes
glittering with intensity,
still deciding.

I turn around
and wait,
waiting for her to change,
waiting for what she'll do next,
waiting for what I'm going to do next.

She is a beautiful version
of the 3D model I loaded into the Pandora app.

She is
what I imagined,
what I hoped
would come out,
but I didn't expect her to be alive.

Why would this device exist?

To make soldiers?
To make servants?

To make
friends?

"What is your name?"
Umu asks.

I turn slowly;
her eyes are relaxed,
her demeanor growing lighter.

Umu.isDangerous = undefined;

The hoodie hangs on her graceful frame,
the jeans too loose in the waist,
her red curls leaking out of the hood
in matted twists.

"I'm Erin.
And we're going to need to figure
out what to do with you."
I smile,
motioning around my room.
"Stay here a moment.
I'm going to tell my mother
you're a new girl spending the night."

Umu smiles
and nods
and I step out of the room.

A gush of warmth
hits me as I open the door,
growing a lightness on my soul
that gives me pause.

```
If(Erin.isNotNear(Umu){
  Erin.isComfortable("increasing");
}
```

Standing outside my room,
warming up,
I cannot stop thinking of
Umu's smile.
It wasn't light.
It wasn't friendly.
It was an invitation
for me to relax.

Are you dangerous?

Perhaps I should have asked her the same question?

SUNDAY (TRAINING DAY)

Don't Feed After Midnight

When I open the door to my room
a biting breeze escapes,
frosting the glass of water
I brought for Umu.

She stands at my window
staring into the night sky,
motionless.

"I brought you some water."

No movement.

I sit at my computer,
the *Pandora.exe* command console
still open.
The initialize command is still there,
followed by a new line:

> *Initialization complete.*
> *Notification sent for Pandora Protocol.*

Notification?

This is why I always keep a
traffic analyzer running:
to pick up any surprise data leaving my computer.
Maybe I'm usually a bit paranoid, but
not today.

Looks like a web request was sent
to a server.
The IP range suggests it's local-
somewhere in Glen Coast-
just before the power outage.

If it wasn't for my power backups,
I'd have missed this
when the outage should have
crashed my computer.

>>> Notification analysis
Notification.sent(3d Model I used);
Notification.sent(AI I selected);
Notification.sent(My location…but not my address)

Cold air strangles my lungs
and breathing gets harder.

"What are you working on?"
Umu is behind me.

I startle quickly, changing screens
to a fresh console window.
Reflex reaction to someone surprising me,
I guess.

"Oh, uh…I'm just registering you for school."
I'm still gasping to find breath
in the frozen air.

Looking back,
I see the window is closed;
air conditioning must be broken or something.

"Why?"
Umu asks,
her breath
grazing across my neck hairs,
shocking them to attention.

I turn back to the computer.
"I don't know what you're going to do
while I'm in school.
So, I figure you'll just go to school
with me."
I open a port to the school's enrollment system;
a few keystrokes
and I'm in.

School.Security = boring + simple;

Umu slowly retracts from my shoulder
taking the frozen air with her.

"I'm going to set you up
as a new transfer student.
Far enough away
that no one would know you here.
Close enough that
no one would question
why you moved here."
I'm typing in the info.
Saving.

"Isn't that lying?"
Umu smirks.
I can see her reflection in
the monitor.
"Are you a liar, Erin?"

Lies
told through a computer…
isn't that what everyone does
on SocialNet?

Erin.isLiar = EveryoneElse.isLiar;

"Well, you can't stay here.
And you can't go to school
without being registered."
I swivel in my chair to find her
back at the window,
watching me,
leaning calmly against the wall.
"I'm open to other ideas."

"This plan works
for now."

Swinging back to my keyboard,
I complete the registration:
an A student,
strong computer skills,
and a passion for science.

She'll be in my classes.

She can even sit
in the open seats beside me
in the front.

Saving the registration,
I push away from my computer,
springing to my feet,
turning to Umu,
seeing the alarm clock on my dresser.

1:11 AM.

"Uh, do you sleep?"
I'm more curious
than tired,
but maybe she's exhausted.

Being born is probably
strenuous.

"No. Sleep isn't necessary."

"Oh, okay, good,
because I have a lot of questions."

I tap the bed
and sit on the edge.
She
cautiously
joins me.

Umu.waryOfErin = true;

The first question that comes to mind,
the question that stops at my lips:
Should I call Caylee?
Am I in over my head?
But I go for
something safer,
something easier

"So, what do you know about this device?"

Preparation

Umu doesn't have any answers.
She's as clueless about the device
as I am,
maybe even more so.

Shifting from questions
to preparation,
I tell Umu
what it's like
to be someone like us
in a crowd of people unlike us.

Umu.isLikeErin = true;

Showing her pictures
on SocialNet
of the school,
of the students,
explaining the social hierarchy
and where we are
in that hierarchy:
at the bottom.

Quietly she lets me talk–
listening, I think.
As I go through various SocialNet profiles,
she pauses me,
reading the profile ID in a soft whisper.

Night turns to morning;
she doesn't eat,
she doesn't drink,
she gorges herself on information,
devouring the data I'm feeding her,
asking questions,
seeking to understand the why
behind everything from Biology class seating
to the computer lab configuration.

```
Umu.isCurious = true;
Umu.learnsFast = true;
```

Every answer
unfurls more questions from Umu.

Her curiosity is enthralling,
her hunger for knowledge
intoxicating
and alien
from other Glen Coast citizens.

"Tomorrow, we'll have Biology class
and you can sit…"
My stomach drops,
dread anchoring it down
as I realize a horrible truth.

"Oh shit.
Tomorrow starts spirit week."
Sigh…

"Spirit week?
Like Halloween?"
Umu asks,
curiously confused.

I chuckle at the thought,
wishing that were the case.
"No, spirit week is when
the students pretend to
want to be part of the school.
Students show their
ability to conform
to what school administration
says is acceptable fun."

Umu's face twists up
in deeper confusion.

Umu.processing();

"So, it is a team building event?"
she asks.

"More like structured mind control,"
I say, laughing.
"But, yeah, your definition is accurate."

Erin.isUnderstood = true;
Umu.isLikeErin = true;

Umu smiles,
this one lighter,
more engaging than others she's shown.

"Don't worry, Erin.
I'm sure
we
can tolerate spirit week
together."
Umu pats my hand.
Her cold touch is
relieving,
comforting,
like old lady hands.

We

We can tolerate it.

A smile breaks through my dread.

Erin.friends.add(Umu);

Yes,
WE
can tolerate spirit week.
Together.

Communication: Request of Live Capture

To: inquisitors_all
Subject: Order update
Body:

ATTN: Inquisitors of District 3

Enact Live Capture procedures. Psionic disturbance detected in Glen Coast, MD. Signature, unknown. Form unknown. Proceed with extreme caution.

Target for Pandora identified. Capabilities of Pandora identified. Disturbance could be creation of one of the Mother's Tears. One of the Eleven.

Inquisitor Q.Nicholas 10028 is point. Report to him immediately for assignment.

Sincerely;
Dr. V.C. Moran 17

<eom>

ERIN ULMAN

Afternoon Escape

By the afternoon
I needed to get out.

Umu and I
had been talking about Glen Coast
all day.

Time to experience it
firsthand.

Mother's lost in her book
on the couch.
We leave undetected.

First stop:
The Bookshop,
the best place in Glen Coast
besides the library.

```
if(Umu.isLikeErin == true){
  Umu.willLike("The Bookshop");
}
```

It's not a long walk
but Umu's pace
is exhausting.
I'm sucking wind
through tight lungs.
A chill constantly ripples over me.
I must be coming down with something.

At the baby blue building
I skip up the steps
to the white door,
waving her along.

"Nah, you go ahead."
She traces the frame
with her shimmering
silver and green
eyes.
"I'll stay out here."

```
Erin.processing();
Umu.willLike("The Bookshop") = false;
>>> Does not compute
Umu.isLikeErin = true;
```

She looks to me as I open the door
at the top of the steps.

```
Erin.processing();
Erin.rerouting();
```

"Oh,
well, we don't have to
go in here,"
I say.
"We can go to the library
or the tea shop instead."

"Do you come here often?"
she asks as she
cautiously
backs away
from the steps.

"Once in a while.
Not a lot."
I step down the stairs,
back to the
winter wind lingering around her.

She looks

scared.

"Chilly. Err…"
I shiver
uncontrollably,
the cold getting more intense.
But
where is the wind?
"Let's get some tea
to warm up."

Starting down the sidewalk,
I wave her to me.
Her eyes watch the store,
looking to a window on the second floor,
looking to the old man standing there,
his ruby ring stroking his white beard.

She catches up to me,
keeping watch on the old man.
The cold breeze follows us
down the street.

MONDAY (TWIN DAY)

United Front

Arriving at school,
Umu and I
show our unity in matching hoodies:
green,
well-worn,
the word HOODIE
emblazoned in white
across our chests.

Our jeans
are light wash,
beaten up,
showing we're ready to relax.

Like titans
of tech,
we burst through the doors,
ready for our billion-dollar windfall.

I pass Donna
and her twins
and Caylee.
Twin day
is every day for them.

Caylee yawns
and shakes her head
to wake up.

Umu and I
walk straight through the hallway
where I ran away from Donna.
Today I don't run.
I don't even look at her.
I stride with Umu;
her confidence is contagious,
her strength lifting me up.

Today I feel their eyes,
but they don't see
the girl on the ground,
the girl running out the door.
They see Umu,
strong,
bold,
beautiful,
brilliant–
and me.

Biology Class Revisited

Umu sits beside me,
another new girl
fitting in where
the teacher can fit her:
front row.

Still on metamorphosis,
still on caterpillars
and butterflies.

One of Donna's friends
whispers behind me.
"Where did she find a twin?"
She snorts a laugh
"Probably posted an ad on SocialNet.
Wanted: lonely girl
to be my only friend."

Erin.hide();

I sink into my hoodie.

They laugh;
the teacher continues the lesson
deaf to their cackles;
my ears burn with embarrassment
as I look to Umu to apologize.

But she's not looking at me,
she's turned around
facing them.

Facing them!

Umu.isLikeErin = false;
Umu.isBold = true;

Her face
pale, freckled, and fierce,
her eyes
shimmering silver and gray,
her mouth
slowly
curling into a smirk.
her knuckles
turning white as her fists clench.

The laughing stops,
immediately frozen
in Umu's glare.

My eyes jut back
seeing the girl beside Donna
shiver,
looking down,
looking worried.

Donna returns the smirk.

My eyes return to the teacher,
oblivious to what just happened.

What did happen?
Did Umu stand up for me?

Donna
and the girl beside her
stay quiet
for the rest of the class
I smile.

Umu smiles,
shooting me a wink.

Lunch Against the Clones

Umu and I
go to lunch,
wading through the sea of people;
finding a small empty table,
we sit.

The lunchroom buzzes with energy
I've never seen,
since I always eat in the Maker Lab.

My lunch today is
my usual
ham sandwich.
Umu eats nothing
as usual.
Maybe she doesn't have
to eat?
Or sleep?
Or drink?

```
while(Umu.isAwake){
  Umu.doesNot("Do human things");
}
```

Donna and her friends
and Caylee
sit at a table
in the center
of the cafeteria,
eating their salads.

Maybe I should eat more salad?

```
Kid1.lunch = salad;
Kid2.lunch = sandwich("turkey");
Kid3.lunch = salad;
Kid4.lunch = coldPizza;
```

Umu scans the lunchroom too,
taking in all the faces
the spontaneous selfies and
the staged selfies.

Her eyes move from face to face
table to table,
mumbling under her breath.
The roar of the room drowns her out
but a few quiet moments let me hear…
I think…
SocialNet profile IDs from Sunday?

```
Umu.processing();
Umu.analyzing();
```

Analyzing what?

Eventually her gaze comes to me
and again
she looks puzzled,
moving on to look at others,
mouthing SocialNet IDs along the way.

What's on the salads on Donna's table?
Maybe that's the trick-
make salads more interesting with stuff
like ham.

Donna stands up,
her attention fixed on me.
Her friends stand,
their attention fixed on Donna.

Donna stomps over.
"What?"

Umu stands,
slowly
dwarfing Donna.
Not in size; she's no taller,
but her presence
makes her look feet taller.

"Donna Schwartz.
I've heard so much about you.
Erin said you like to laugh at people,"
Umu says.

I shrink,
pushing out a quiet laugh
like we're joking,
knowing I wasn't joking.
Umu isn't joking.
What's happening right now?

>>> Panic mode activating
>>> Donna aggressive
>>> Umu aggressive
Erin.hide();
>>> Motor system failure

Umu steps forward
whispering,
sneering.
"I like to laugh at people too."
Umu smiles her predatory grin,
bearing teeth
pearlescent white,
her lips cresting over
faint pink gums,
cheeks mounding up to make room for a bite.

Donna and Umu
stand
silent.

Donna's face,
her plaster expression
cracking
with worry
and wonder
at what Umu will do next.

I'm wondering the same.
I'm worrying the same.

"Hahaha! I'm just kidding, Donna!
Erin didn't say that."
Umu's smile breaks into
a belly laugh,
snapping the tension.

Donna laughs,
uncomfortable,
unsure whatever is happening
is over,
waiting for what's next.

I laugh too,
standing up,
pulling Umu's arm,
leading her out.
"Why don't I show you
the Maker Lab, Umu?"

Caylee watches
as
Umu and I
walk past her
out the door.

Umu catches Caylee's eyes
as I look back to Donna.
She's still staring at Umu,
still wondering
what's next.

CAYLEE MORAN

Who Is That Twin?

I ask around to find out
who Erin's twin is.

No one knows her.

New girl?

Transfer?

"Erin's so weird,
she probably grew her
in a bottle,"
Donna scoffs,
disgusted,
hints of worry
lingering
from lunch.

In my head
I laugh
and pause,
knowing Erin's smart enough to do it.
She's brilliant.

I wouldn't be surprised if the new girl
is a robot.

Her eyes,
the new girl's eyes,
like a wolf's glaring at prey.

Something about her,
something around her,
just didn't feel right.
Frigid darkness
leaks from her.
She sucked the warmth
out of me
just walking by.

Whoever she is
my gut tells me
she's bad news.

I might not always make good decisions–

"Mall after school?"
Donna throws out.
"I need a new phone."

But I trust my gut to know when something's wrong.

"You guys go.
I have dinner plans with my mom,"
I say.

"Have fun with that.
Do you know which mom yet?"
Donna giggles;
the others echo her.

I fall in line,
giggling on command,
giggling to death what I really want to say
when Donna pokes fun at my moms.

Don't be jealous my family
does stuff together.

But I know why
she says stuff like that.
Erin
isn't the only one
with father issues.

ERIN ULMAN

Not One of Them

When
Umu and I
get home,
Mother is busily making dinner.

A big dinner.

"Erin,
Caylee and Dr. Moran
are coming to dinner tonight.
Straighten up, please."
Mother sees Umu.
"Oh, hi!
You must be Uma."

"Umu,"
I say.

"Sorry Erin hasn't
introduced us yet,"
Mother says
as she reaches out for a handshake.

Umu gives a cordial smile,
her happy smile,
shaking Mother's hand lightly.

"Oh, sweetie, are you warm enough?
Must be getting chilly out there."

Umu shakes her head.
"No, I'm always cold."
Pausing,
Umu looks at Mother again,
the same look of confusion
when she looks at me.

"Umu, can you help me in my room?"
I pull her arm again
to escape anything Umu might say.

Umu shuts my bedroom door,
whispering,
"Is 'Caylee'
Caylee Moran from school?"
A sudden inhale inflates Umu.

Umu.onAlert() or Umu.jealous;

"Yeah, but she's not really like,
well, like how Donna's people are."
I scoop up laundry,
throwing it into a basket,
most of it spilling back to the floor.

"If she's not like them,
then why is she with them?"

"I think she just
wants to fit in
or something.
I've talked to her outside of school.
She's cool."

Caylee = partTimeFriend;
Caylee = Donna.friend;

"You trust her?"

>>> Not enough data to answer
>>> Honest answer: Not yet.
>>> Less honest answer: Yeah, I think so.

I reply with the less honest answer
as I shove laundry into my basket,
punching it down.

Umu exhales deeply,
almost sad.
"You want to be one of
them,
don't you?"

"One of who?"

"Donna's people.
One of the perfect girls in a clique
of your own."

I'm speechless
partly from fear,
partly from disgust at the idea,
partly from wonder of how she figured that out.

Am I that obvious?

"You're not one of them, Erin.
You're better than they are.
Smarter.
Prettier.
More real."
Umu flops into my computer chair.
"They'd be lucky to have you
and you'd be less for being
one of them."

Erin.goodFriends.add("Umu");
Erin.beaming();

"Aww…you're just saying that stuff
because you're nice."

Umu shakes her head, dismissing my words.

"Besides, Caylee is really nice.
You'll like her."

"I'm going to stay back here.
Not feeling up to meeting
new people tonight,"
Umu says,
squinting for my reaction.

"Oh, okay, that sounds good.
I'll tell Mother you had to leave.
You sticking around tonight?"
I try to smile
but it can't fight through my
disappointment.

I wish
Umu and Caylee
could be the start of my crew—
friends I could trust,
friends I could count on.

```
Erin.friends.contains("Umu" & "Caylee");
Erin.overjoyed();
```

We'll get there.

I just need to show Umu
the Caylee I've seen
and I need
the Caylee I've seen
to show up
no matter who is around.

Frenemies

I sit beside Caylee.
I don't talk.
I don't look at her.

Victoria sits across from me.
She doesn't talk.
She doesn't look at Caylee.
Her eyes fix on me.

Caylee sits
quietly
looking at her plate,
glancing between me
and her mom.

Mother starts cheery conversation
about her day,
about dinner prep.
She's the only one talking.

"I'm sorry to hear
Cathy couldn't make it.
I wanted to hear her thoughts
on our latest book."
Mother laughs.

No one else does.
"Caylee, how's school going?"
Mother asks.

Caylee politely smiles,
nods.

"Have you met
Erin's friend Uma yet?"
Mother's cheery tone
falls into the room's
silent tension.

Caylee stops nodding.
Victoria's eyes narrow into slits of
inquisition.

"Umu, mother."

"Umu. That's an unusual name.
Where's she from, Erin?"
Victoria asks.

Caylee
squirms in her seat.

"She's from Virginia,"
I say.
"Just moved here."

Victoria leans back in her chair,
a satisfied smile cresting her lips.

>>> Warning: She knows something

"Caylee mentioned a new student
in school today.
She said
you and the new girl
have a lot in common,"
Victoria says.

"Yeah, we both like computer stuff."

"And you two look a lot alike,"
Mother quips.
"You and Umu
could be sisters."
She laughs.

No one else laughs.
No one else smiles.
Mother's oblivious to the building tension.
Victoria's glare digs deeper into me.

"So, Erin,
any new projects?"
Victoria asks
like it's a question
she already knows the answer to,
like she's trying
to get me to admit
I did something wrong.

Her eyes jump to
the hallway
leading to my room.

>>> Danger: She knows something!

"I'm working with a new device,"
I say.
Victoria's eyebrows peak,
waiting
for the next words.
"It's working pretty well."
I return Victoria's glare,
convincing both of us
I have everything under control.

Victoria chuckles,
shaking her head
"Yeah, just be careful because
when everything looks like
it's working,
that's when
things fall apart."
She laughs toward Mother.
"At least–"
Victoria's eyes fall on mine,
the laughter choked away.
"–that's my experience."

Mother laughs,
unsure why she's laughing.
Caylee follows.
I chuckle,
making sure to inject
a hint of defiance.

"I've got this,"
I say
still staring into Victoria's eyes,
returning her glare with my own,
knowing
if I keep saying it–
"I've got this."
–I'll believe it.

"I know a thing or two
about experiments making trouble.
If you ever need help,
I'm here–"

"No thanks,
I've got this."
I'm cutting her off,
shutting her down,
watching Caylee stare at her mom
with confusion and disappointment.

Victoria smiles,
slowly nods,
sits in silence.

A silence that infects everyone at the table.

In the Corner

Victoria and Caylee
are gone,
dishes are done,
Mother is reading.

She takes breaks in-between pages
to text someone.
Probably Dad to see
where he is.

Her phone beeps
and she smiles
at a silent joke.
I see the sender,
Cathy Dolan.

Catching up on book club
I guess.

I return to my room.

Umu stands in the corner
staring at the moonlight.

"What are you looking at?"
I walk over,
look at the window,
seeing a sliver of moon glowing.

Her mumbling is
so quiet,
I almost miss it over
the humming of my computer.

"Sorry, what?"

I see her vacant face,
eyes fixed on the moon,
lips trembling,
chanting
to the night.

"Hey Umu."
I wave in her face.
"Earth to Umu!"
She continues to stare and mumble.

Stepping away,
I remember
she was doing this last night too.
As I flop onto my bed,
she awakens,
noticing me on my bed,
springing back in surprise,
calming instantly on recognition.

"Erin."
She scans the room.
"Is dinner over?"

"Yeah, the Morans left."
I sit up
as she relaxes
from high alert.

"Staring at the moon?"

"No, just walking around.
Waiting.
Listening."
She sits on my computer chair.
"I don't trust Victoria Moran.

She was hiding something.
I could tell
from her voice."

I nod
"She's kind of weird."

"And Caylee.
I don't trust her either,"
Umu says.

"Why not?"

"She's not like us."

"I think she could be like us.
Just
covering it up."

"If she was like us
she wouldn't leave you to be
the only outsider
in school."
Umu shakes her head,
disgust curling her lips,
spit frothing at the corners.

Like us.

I like that.

Umu and I
are an Us.

But I think about the
two Caylees.

```
Caylee1 = Donna;
Caylee2 = Erin + Umu;
```

Caylee2 is like us.

Scared like us.
Lonely like us.

"She's more like us than you know."
I smile.

"You're too kind, Erin.
They wouldn't be so kind to you.
I don't think you should be around
Caylee Moran
anymore. She's toxic."
Umu's brows furrow,
splitting her pale face
in a canyon of angst.

"Give her a chance, Umu."
The anger builds on her face,
boiling,
not red
but pale, white heat,
tension straining
her jaw,
her eyes.

```
Umu.rage("increase");
Umu.rage("boiling");
```

"You shouldn't be around her,"
Umu says through her teeth,
through the grinding,
through the pooling spit.

"Let's get some sleep."
Her eyes meet mine,
seeing my concern
as I see her anger,
her hunger for a fight.

"Good idea."
Her rage evaporates.
The strains and canyons
of her face vanish
as a smile cuts through it all.
"I don't need to sleep,
but you go ahead."

Umu.calm("instant");
Umu.rage("nonexistent");

I watch for any sign
that she was angry-
anything-
but nothing appears,
her mood flipped from
rage to relaxed
instantly.

"Goodnight, Erin."

CAYLEE MORAN

Recon

SHADOWLURKER Server Online

@Kuzan_King you there?

Yeah, @Zushion_Dawn.
What's up?

Raiding party?

Did you see the new girl today?

She was hanging out
with Erin.

idk

What's she look like?

Erin.

No, I know the new girl
was with Erin
and I know what she looks like.

The new girl. What's she
look like.

Yeah, she looks
exactly like Erin
but paler and more

intense.

Didn't see them.
Sounds like a dream come true.

No, something's not right.
Can you do some recon
at school tomorrow?

Gladly!

Why you on so late?
Past your bedtime?

Can't sleep.
Having the weird
mountain top
dream again.
Probably too much
mac & cheese from dinner.

Is there such a thing?

Did it have bacon in it?

No.

Tuna? Breadcrumbs?

No. This isn't Food Network.
Logging off now. Let me know
what you find out.

I'm worried.

K

Communication: Extraction at 0945

To: vcmoran17
Subject: Extraction
Body:

ATTN: Dr. V.C. Moran 17

Extraction of device and capture of the creation scheduled for 09:45. Counter measures implemented for live capture. Capture will occur outside of Glen Coast High School. Extraction of device will occur at same time. House will be empty.

Proceeding with extreme caution.

Sincerely;
Inquisitor Q. Nicholas 10028

<eom>

ERIN ULMAN

One of Us?

"Ugh…I can't sleep."
I pop up,
throwing the covers off.

The green glow from my monitor
traces my bedroom in ghostly outlines.

The light doesn't reach
my dresser where my digital alarm clock
screams its red glowing digits
into my eyes.

11:11 PM.

"Umu?"

Shadows sit in pools around my room,
drowning clothes,
books, bags
in darkness.

>>> Searching…

>>> Searching…

>>> Umu not found…

Droning computer fans
break the night's
lightless
silence.

Maybe she left?

"Umu?"
I'm whispering
so Mother doesn't hear.

She's not at the window
doing her
mumbling
thing.

Climbing out of bed,
I go to my computer
and look at the *Pandora.exe*
again.

No custom icon.

No branding.

No company name.

I look over to the device,
seeing no signs of
who made it
or where it
came from.

The silver serpent box…

Shuffling papers
break the droning fans
as I search for the box.

"Looking for something?"
Umu whispers.

>>> ALERT!

Jerking around,
I see her rising
from the shadow
beside my dresser.

She unfurls,
stretching her chest
and shoulders
as she grows to her
full height.

Same as my height
but she looks so much more

scary.

>>> Recover breath
>>> Slow heartbeat
>>> Act like you're not terrified

"Uh, yeah. There was a silver box?"
Pointing to my desk,
motioning to the Pandora Device.

"This box?"
She pulls the edge
of the case
from her hoodie pocket.

"Yeah. Just making sure
I didn't lose it."
I laugh,
uneasy
at how closely
she holds the box.

Her body curls around it.
Her eyes narrow,
their silver green glow
sharpening to slits of light
in the dark.

>>> Danger: Umu thinks you want the box
>>> Danger: She's protecting the box

"I don't need it or anything,"
I say and shake my head.
"Just wondering if it
had a label or anything
to say where it came from."

She slowly
pushes the silver case
into her hoodie.
Those eyes
relax but stay locked
on me.

The fan droning takes over again
as we sit.
I look into disembodied glowing eyes
in the shadows of my room.

She watches me–
for
what?

What could I do to her?

>>> Defuse situation

"VR?"
Breaking the tension
I hold up my VR headset.
"I can't sleep so I was
going to wander around
some VR worlds."

Umu steps out
of the shadows,
her eyes losing their
shimmer.

She cocks her head
at the device.

"Want to try it?"
I put it on to show her how
it works.

Is this a good idea?
I can't see her.

Activating Passthru mode
on the VR headset,
my room is revealed in
grays, whites, and blacks
as the infrared light
from my VR headset
lights up the room.

Umu sways in the IR light,
rippling around the edges
like she is devoured
by black fire.

Her eyes flash to
flaming wolf eyes.

I snap off the headset
to see her
as I've known her.

Just like me.

Umu.isLikeErin = undefined;
>>> System Override
Umu.isLikeErin = true;

"How does it work?"
She reaches out to accept
the VR headset I push to her.

Her fingers trace the
wireless antenna
as her eyes wander
to the controllers
and haptic vest
hanging from under
my desk.

I give her the short version
of how VR works:
3D worlds, full immersion,
controllers to emulate your hands,
haptic vest to feel feedback
in the 3D worlds.

She nods.

"Want to try?"

She smiles.
"I can feel the signal
coming off the headset.

You go ahead."

Umu.feelsSignal = undefined;
Erin.query("What is Umu?");
>>> Query cancelled for now

I shrug
and put the headset on,
facing away from her
this time.

The IntelliDyn logo appears
in its stunning white crisp lines
with the cheerful BING that comes
with the logo.

My VR home appears
familiar,
comfortable.

"Is this your house in VR?"
Umu says in the VR headset.

Jumping,
I turn to see her
behind me.

A rippling mass of shadow
and slithering tentacles
convulse behind me.

It's monstrous in appearance
and size,
a wave of teeth,
a spinning hurricane of claws
about to crash on me.

Gasping,
I fall out of my computer chair,
pushing away from it.

I blink and
the mass vanishes,
leaving only the computerized version
of Umu
waving at me.

"What…?"
I climb to my feet;
in the real world,
my avatar rises up
to standing.

The shadowy mass…
the storm
from the beach
from my dream…

"I can feel the signal
of your headset.
I can just connect
to you."
Umu smiles.
"No hardware required."
She chuckles.

"How?"
I choke away the memory
of

slithering

whipping

crashing

mass of darkness
from my nightmare.

"Don't forget, Erin,"
Umu starts walking around
my VR house,
"I'm not human.

I'm your creation."

Are you?

Did I create you
or did I just push the button?

TUESDAY (SPORTS DAY)

Meet the Arnolds

I don't understand sports.
What Valentine's Day is for the single and lonely,
Jersey Day is for the athletically inept.

In protest,
I wear my Seattle Sentries jersey,
the best eSports team in the world.

Umu boycotts jersey day,
saying sports don't make sense to her,
and I have to agree.
She wears one of my hoodies:
gray,
WRITING CODE written in big letters
across the front,
NEEDING COFFEE written in big letters
across the back.

At school
I get odd stares;
I'm unsure if they're about my jersey
or yesterday's lunch.

"Hey, Erin!"
a boy yells across
the foyer of school
as I walk in.

Boy = unknown;

He rushes up to me,
finger-combing his scruffy chocolate hair
out of his hazel eyes.
His jersey hangs from his gaunt frame,
the words on it:
Sports Suck.

I stop,
stepping back.
Umu steps up
between
him and me.

Umu.protectorMode("Activate");

"I'm Davis.
Just wanted to say
I love your jersey!"
He points at the Sentries logo.
"Seattle Sentries are amazing."

"Who?"
I start,
but too late.

"Hey Meredith,
come check this out!"
He waves to
what I first thought was a statue
until she started walking:

with her all-black clothes
and long black hair covering half her face,
leaving the other half vampire white,
she looked more stone than flesh.

She stands motionless in the center of the foyer
as waves of people break around her
like a giant rock in a river.

Slowly she strides over to Davis,
floating through the crowd rushing to class.
Her eyes drift dreamily over my jersey,
then give me a blank stare,
then give Umu a blank stare,
then look to Davis with a blank stare.

"Davis, you called me."
Her voice is
so monotone,
I became instantly tired
from those four words.

"Meredith, this is Erin."
Davis's excitement
starts feeling contagious.

"Hi-"

"Meredith's my sister and
#10 in the world at
Call for Destruction
on PC and consoles."
Davis beams,
pointing to my jersey.
"Meredith knows a bunch of the Sentries."

"Oh that's-"

"And she's beaten
most of them in C4D."
Davis finally takes a breath.

Davis.talks("constantly");
Meridth.talks("hardly at all");

"Well that's awesome."
I put my hand on Umu's shoulder,
stepping up beside her,
feeling a frigid air hanging around me,
starting to wonder
if the cold is coming from her.

Umu.isTense = true;

"I don't know them.
I just beat them when they
join my games,"
Meredith says
matter-of-fact
almost sing-song
if a song could be one note.
"They won't know me as Meredith.
They'll know my gamer tag,
Azriel_Knight.
When you talk to them,
tell them I said hi.
I have to go to class now."
She turns to Davis.

"Goodbye Davis."
She turns to me.
"Goodbye Erin."
She turns to Umu.
"I didn't meet you."

Meredith walks off in short steps,
wading through the masses of people;
the crowd absorbs her like tall grass
and she's gone.

"Not to be rude, but do I know you?"
I ask Davis.

```
Davis = undefined;
```

"Nah, but we have a
mutual friend
who said I should say hi."
He jabs his chin toward
Donna's crew.
Caylee
winks.

```
Davis = Caylee.friend;
Davis.isNotLike(Donna);
>>> Does not compute
```

Umu sees the exchange,
blows out a frustrated sigh,
whispers,
"She can't even be seen
introducing you."

"Well, Caylee's…"
Davis pauses,
looking at Umu,
stepping away
as she clenches her fists.
"Complicated."

His face turns to me,
instantly brightening.
"So, one time,
Meredith was playing C4D
and she popped off like
sixteen headshots in a row…"

Davis's story continues as he follows
Umu and me
to English class,
sitting with us in the back
until the bell rings.

"Oh sweet!
Gotta get to Accounting!"
Davis springs up,
running off.
"Nice to meet you two!"

"That was weird,"
I say
as Umu shakes her head,
disapproving.

"Erin, Davis seems
too hyper for you."
Umu points to my jersey.
"That was way too excited
about a jersey.
And Meredith
just seems weird."

SELECT * FROM WeirdPeople
>>> RESULTS: Meredith and Umu

A loud laugh escapes me,
snapping everyone's attention to me.
I slap my hand over my mouth,
silencing the thought
of Umu calling someone
weird.

"Pot, meet Kettle."

"Ha ha,
yes, I'm weird too,
but, I'm here for you.
They're probably just like Caylee:
tourists."
Umu scoffs.
"Passing through
at their convenience."

She's looking out for me.

I smile and wink at her.

"Thanks for being protective.
They seem nice,
let's give them a chance."

"Too nice, Erin."
Umu shakes her head.
"Everyone should be more like you.
But they're not."
Her eyes turn stern.
"Don't be surprised
when they hurt you."

Missing In Action

10:00 AM.
Computer lab.
I watch the door,
waiting
while Ms. Isler explains
the intricacies of word processing.

Who needs to have this stuff explained?

```
Document = bigBlankAreaOnScreen;
person.click(document);
person.startTyping();
```

Tah-dah!
Word processing!

Scanning the class,
I notice Davis sitting a few seats away,
Caylee sitting with Donna,
and an empty seat beside me
where Umu should be.

"Ms. Isler,
this stupid computer won't work."
Donna spikes her mouse,
perhaps inspired by her
purple Ravens jersey
or the jersey clones
surrounding her.

Donna.canFollowSimpleDirections = false;

Caylee scrunches up her face,
nods to the chair beside me
in a silent question.

I shrug,
worried
someone figured Umu out.
That she isn't a transfer student,
that she isn't the new girl,
that she isn't…
human?

I guess she isn't.

Erin.query("Is she human?");
>>> Results: Not enough data to determine

Bursting through the door,
Umu charges to the seat beside me,
hood up,
jeans torn at the knees,
plopping down
silent
as she rolls up to the computer.

"Miss…uh…miss…"
Ms. Isler blanks on Umu's name.
"Beside Erin…"

I motion for Umu to answer,
seeing her face:
a gash under her eye
dripping
silvery blood.

"Sorry I'm late,"
Umu barks.
"Got lost."

Ms. Isler,
satisfied,
returns to droning on
about justification and alignment.

"Are you okay?"
I whisper
as I notice
the splotches of brown
and crimson
on her hoodie.

"What happened?"

She wipes the silver drips
from her eye,
revealing a film of blood
coating her knuckles.

```
Umu.injured;
Umu.bloodOnKnuckles = notHerBlood;
```

"They came for me, Erin."
Her voice is
dead,
droning,
vicious.

"Are you okay?"

"Fine."

The blood slips from her knuckles
down her fingers,
dripping to the floor
"Is whoever came for you okay?"

"Do you care?"

Yes!
I care!
I bite the words back,
noting
she clearly doesn't care.
She's not thinking about their injuries,
she's plotting,
planning,
preparing.

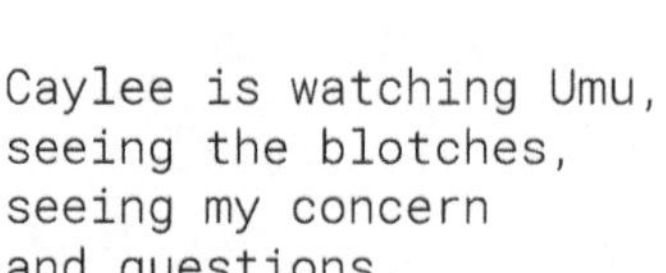

Caylee is watching Umu,
seeing the blotches,
seeing my concern
and questions.

```
Caylee.processing();
Caylee.analyzing();
Caylee.worrying();
```

I shiver,
catching the cold surrounding Umu,
feeling it suck the heat from my skin,
from my blood,
as she stews
not in rage or anger
but in quiet meditation,
eyes darting around,
replaying whatever just happened
or visualizing what will happen.

I don't wonder if she hurt whoever did this.
I wonder if they are still alive.

Disguises Broken

Davis signals me to join him for lunch;
sloppy joe drips from his bun,
splatting on his black jersey.

At least it's black.

Meredith and Davis
sit with two others,
but Umu points to another table
just for
her and me.

We sit
in silence
as she watches the room,
mumbling SocialNet IDs
while I stare at the stains
still splotching her knuckles.

I eat my lunch,
a salad with Mother's spicy tuna mix,
some extra salty chips,
a candy bar.
Umu eats nothing.

The faint click of a smartphone camera
interrupts Umu's mumbling.
I don't need to search-
I see Donna's table laughing,
pointing, giggling
at us.

"Nice homeless look, new girl!"
Donna yells over.

A moment later
dings and bells signal a post trending
through the lunchroom.

Umu's staring straight ahead,
seeing nothing yet
reacting to something funny
snickering
holding back a full laugh.

Umu looks to Donna,
smile exposing her teeth,
sneer exposing malice.
Umu shouts across the lunchroom,
"Thanks, Bunnykins."

Those words
rip
the ability to laugh
out of Donna.
She recoils,
struck by something horrid,
seeing something ghastly in Umu's words.

Donna.isShocked = true;
Donna.face = red turning purple;
Donna.rage("exploding");

"What did you say…?"
Donna gasps.

Umu's smile fades
as she turns back,
looking over the faces in the lunchroom.
Calm.
Cold.
Satisfied.

Donna darts up,
quickly exiting
the lunchroom
leaving her crew
watching,
wondering what just happened.

Caylee goes after Donna,
passing by
Davis and Meredith's table,
shrugging away their questions
of what happened.

"Who's Bunnykins?"
I ask.

"Donna,"
Umu answers,
disinterested,
done with this scene.
"I need to go after lunch.
After school, head straight home."

"Where else would I go?"

"Nowhere else."

Umu's voice is
like my mother's voice:
telling, not asking.

Umu.isDemanding;

"Yeah, uh, okay. I'll be there."

Standing,
Umu strides to the door,
leaving me seeing
two Umus:
the supportive friend,
the satisfied predator.

Caylee, Me, & What's In-Between

Outside school
Caylee is waiting for me.

She bobs around
watching,
but her black hair,
bound down too tight,
isn't as lively as it was last weekend;
like the rest of her at school, it's
restricted.

Seeing me,
she signals me to come over.

```
Caylee.talkingWithErin("at school");
>>> Does not compute
```

My eyes jump around,
looking for Umu
as I walk over to Caylee,
checking to make sure
no one sees her talking to me.

"What do you want, Caylee?"

She winces at my words,
stepping back.
"Erin, what is going on?
Whatever happened at lunch,
Donna's been crying all day."

I can't figure out if Caylee is
angry,
concerned,
or disappointed.

"She makes me cry all the time.
Sucks to taste her own medicine."
I shrug,
starting toward home.

Caylee chases.
I want to tell her to go away
or help me
or that I'm scared.

I want to go back
to her room, working on the SocialNet app,
to tea at the Galleria in Calista,
to us—
not Caylee at school
and Caylee out of school—
but *Us* never existed.

She grabs my shoulder.
I rip away.

```
Caylee.isShocked = true;
Caylee.stepsBack();
```

"Who is she, Erin?
Who is Umu?
This isn't you!
She's changing you
to be like her!"

```
if(Caylee == Erin.friend) {
  Caylee.wouldTalkToErin("at school");
  Caylee.wouldKnowErin();
}
```

She's only a part-time friend,
missing out on all
the times when I need her,
when I'm a target at school
or alone at home.

I face Caylee,
remembering Donna,
remembering when she laughed at me on the ground,
remembering when she made me run out of school.

```
Erin.rage("increasing");
Erin.vision("blurring").tears("building");
```

"You never questioned Donna.

You never stopped her.

Not once saying
stop!
Not once telling anyone
stop!

Now you're telling *me*
stop?"

Venom boils in my throat.

```
Erin.hurt(Caylee);

Caylee.knees = "weakening";
Caylee.mouth = "gaping";
Caylee.eyes = "tearing";

Caylee.hurt();
Erin.hurting();
```

"Umu isn't part-time.
She's not pretending to be one of them;
she's there for me.
You'd rather be one of *them* than you."

I'm panting,
rage stealing my breath.
"Your mom is right about you.
You're too busy trying to be everyone else
to do anything that matters."

Erin.wentTooFar();
>>> Critical System Failure
>>> Cannot recover

Instantly I feel the wall
I just built between us.

Caylee stands straighter,
pushing her shoulders back,
biting her lip,
swallowing tears.

I stomp off,
leaving her with my words
and a mangled car crash of feelings inside me:
shame,
guilt,

sadness,

regret.

Missing Things

I slam the door behind me.
Mother isn't home.
I gasp for a calming breath,
suffocating under the pressure
of words I can't undo.

I burst into a scream,
vomiting *rage sorrow fear hate*
in a toxic siren wail,
unleashing tears
as streams of liquid loneliness
fall from me like Caylee's friendship.

All my strength is stolen,
weakening my knees;
collapsing under the pain escaping my heart,
I slide down the door
to the cold
tile floor of my foyer.

Feelings drained,
tears run out,
I open my eyes
and see my living room
destroyed.

>>> ALERT!
>>> DANGER: Home invasion

Overturned tables,
broken picture frames,
the couch
where I slept
spun askew.

```
Erin.panicking();
>>> Help!
>>> Help!
```

"Mom!"
I call out as panic washes into the void
left by my eruption of feelings.
I call again,
fear slipping into the panic.

I run back to her room:
it is empty,
neat,
untouched.

Then I rush to my room—
the heat blows out as I burst through the door,
the warmth freezing me—
unexpected,
unfamiliar
as of late.

My room is wrecked
as if searched
in a hurry without regard to stealth.

The
Pandora Device
is gone.

On my computer screen is
a console window,
the cursor blinking
after a single line of text.

Erin, they're coming. -U.

Communication: Recovery & Loss

To: vcmoran17
Subject: Status Report
Body:

ATTN: Dr. V.C. Moran 17

Pandora Device obtained. Precautions for live capture of the creation failed. Resistance was overwhelming to five Inquisitors. It knew we were coming or is more powerful than projected.

Creation was in process of building another of the Eleven when we found it.

Creation Description: Teenage girl, pale white skin, long curly red hair, slender build, silver green eyes with a tapetum lucidum effect. Last seen wearing a gray hoodie, blood stains, torn light wash jeans, sneakers.

Caution: We believe the Creation is Umu Dabrutu based on combat skill and her effects on the environment around her. We also saw another creation tracking Umu Dabrutu. It fled when it saw us, but I believe it was also coming for the device based on the creature following me after I took the device. I did not get a good look at it but heard the tapping of nails as it walked. Sounded like a dog walking on talons.

We are not the only ones seeking the device.

Request immediate assistance for faster resolution.

Sincerely;
Inquisitor Q. Nicholas 10028

<eom>

ERIN ULMAN

Ruin

Mother and I
watch
as the police examine our house.

"Are you sure you're okay?"
Mother asks.
"I'm sorry I wasn't here."
She shakes her head.
"I should have been here."

Mother says something
about Caylee's mom
Cathy
and some book
but I don't really hear her.

I'm focused on the police
as they search for clues,
ask their questions:

Did we notice anything missing?
Do we know anyone who would do this?
Any idea why someone would target us?

Mother answers honestly,
knowing nothing.

Erin.honesty = 30%;
Erin.isLiar = "maybe";

I know what's missing.
I think whoever owned it
came for it.
I know whoever owned it
knew where to come
from the network signal triggered
on the night of the power outage.

But now is not a time for honesty;
they wouldn't believe me anyway.

I need to find Umu.

She was here.

She knows what's going on.

More questions from the police swirl around me;
my denials are spinning into a web
of tripwires.
The police officer keeps prying.
Does he know I'm lying?
My feigned panic,
my feigned fear,
my very real fear
mixing into something somewhat believable.

In the gathering crowd outside
I think I see Caylee
craning her neck,
looking for me.

Caylee.isHere;
Erin.feelings = "relieved";

The hopeful moment passes,
revealing who I thought was
Caylee

is someone else.

Erin.feelings = "regret";

Why would she come here
after what I said?

I can't undo what's done.

If only I had a Ctrl+Z for life.

"Erin, why don't you
go to Caylee's house for a while?"
Mother suggests,
faking calm.

I nod
and hope she'll be there.

I need her
to be there for me now.

Seeking What's Not Available

On Caylee's porch
I reach out to knock, but I'm
preempted by Caylee's sister Yui
answering the door.

"I wasn't expecting *you*,"
she squeaks.
"Come in,
I guess."

Yui hops away.
"Caylee, your
computer girl is here,"
she shouts back to their room.

Victoria wheels up to the door
smiling at Yui,
the smile dying at the sight of me.

"Caylee hasn't been home yet.
She's at the library,"
Victoria says,
her eyes giving me the
now too-familiar
Is there anything you want to tell me?
look.

Cathy is cooking dinner,
chopping onions;
my eyes tear up,
my face getting hot–
not from the onions.

"I said something really stupid.
And I want to apologize."

Erin.feelings = "overload";
>>> System dump all feelings
>>> Tears overload, tears flowing

Cathy stops chopping.
"Oh, sweetie!
I'm sure it's not that bad."
She wraps me up in her arms,
warm,
loving,
reminding me of my mother
before Glen Coast,
before Portland,
before Dad told
the truth.

Victoria rolls closer,
patting my back
hard,
shaking her head.

"Erin, there isn't anything
done that can't be undone."
Victoria says.

I look to the
black hair framing her face;
she's not smiling,
she's asking me with her eyes,
begging me to say something,
to confess,
and maybe she could help,
maybe she could make everything better.

"Sometimes we feel like
we're caught in webs
of our own making,"
Victoria says.
"But anytime you're stuck,
just ask for help.
We'll be there for you."

Cathy smiles,
rubbing Victoria's hand.

Victoria.isHelpful = true; // that seems weird
Cathy.isHelp = true; // absolutely.
Erin.mom = beMoreLikeCathy();

"OH! I was expecting *you*!"
Yui shouts from the door
hanging open.

A shadow rushes into the Moran house,
cast by a tall
slender man.

The darkness at his feet is
bigger than his body,
yet
matches the disquiet I have
seeing him.

His black suit
contrasts starkly with his white beard
and pale sickly sallow skin.

He reaches up to his hat;
a silver ring
with a glowing red ruby catches the kitchen light,
kindling the memory of the man at The Bookshop.

"Erin, let me introduce you."
Victoria wheels back from me.
Her face hardens at the visitor,
not surprised,
but frustrated.
"This is Dr. Victor Moran.
My father, Caylee's grandfather."

The wells of darkness where his eyes should be
stare down at me
as his skin folds,
creasing,
cracking
into a smile, unleashing gray, crooked teeth
protruding from blackened gums.

"Pleasure to meet you.
Vicky has told me
you and Caylee
are getting close."
His hand reaches out to mine,
a bony grasp,
paper-thin skin,
knobby knuckles.

I shake it,
releasing quickly,
feeling the chill of poor circulation
or old age
or death.

Not cold like Umu.
Her cold steals your heat.
His cold chases your heat away,
maybe just a grim reminder that we all get old.

"Will you join us for dinner?"
he asks.

Victoria answers for me,
nodding
yes.

Dinner with Dr. Moran[2]

Dinner is quiet;
prayer was skipped
with a glare and nod from
Cathy to Victoria.

Cathy maintains her steady smile,
passing out food:
cheeseburgers,
fries,
green beans with enough butter to drown
any nutritional value.

Victor's shaky hands
stab his green beans
as if he were spearfishing in rapids.

"Erin, Victor is a researcher
at Glen Coast University as well.
He studies how the mind works,"
Victoria says.
"Victor, Erin is an aspiring technologist.
Caylee says she's like magic on a key-
board."

>>> System Shock
Victoria.gaveCompliment();
>>> Does not compute

Victor releases a series of
quiet gasping chuckles.

"Caylee would know.
Sharp as a tack, that one.
She keeps being so brilliant
and she'll have my job one day."
Victor shines pride.

Victoria grimaces,
throws the serving spoon
into the green beans,
and grumbles,
"Let's hope not."

Victoria.isDisgusted = true;
Victoria.isScared…?

Cathy's smile lifts higher
to push away the tension
between the Morans.

Just like Mother,
giving bigger smiles,
trying to make everything better

but smiles don't fix
anything.

Mother smiled as the police
asked their questions,
searched our house,
suggested we call Dad.

She smiled bigger and bigger
trying to drown the problems
suffocating us
in manufactured
happiness.

Erin.canHelp("Cathy");

"Yeah, Caylee's SocialNet app is pretty awesome,"
I chime in.
"She's put a ton of work into it."

Cathy.winks();
Cathy.appreciates = Erin;
Erin.smiles();
Erin.misses = Mother;

"She wastes her time with that
SocialNet junk,"
Victor spits.

Erin.smiles();
>>> Failure
>>> Action Denied by rude comment

"She should be
exploring the world.
Digging in the mud
for amazing secrets,
not digging in the muck
of SocialNet for likes.
Are you a SocialNet user?"
Disgust drips from his
voice, his
eyes.

Erin.surprised();
Victor.isRight = true;
Erin.agrees();

"No. My dad used to work with SocialNet.
We don't support that company
in our house,"
I say.

Victor coughs a belly laugh.
"You might be
the only person in Glen Coast
without a SocialNet account.

Our families might be the only people
left with any sense of privacy
or purpose in
this town.

Everyone else would rather
rot their brain
than use it."

We all laugh
but they don't understand
the cost of not belonging,
of missing out on the inside jokes,
the posts,
the connection with others.

"People like you,
people like me,
we're a dying breed.

Intellectuals
are an endangered species."
Victor looks intensely
around me.

Victoria clears her throat,
loud and demanding
attention.

Sabrina giggles and copies her.
Yui follows.
Cathy gives them the
stop while it's still funny
look.

"Dr. Moran-Victor, do you study
psychology?"
I ask,
trying to make conversation,
trying to pivot.

"Not
exactly.
Wait, Ulman…Ulman…
why is that familiar?
What did your dad do at SocialNet?"
Victor asks.

>>> Warning: Victor putting pieces together
>>> Warning: Victor figuring Erin's family out

"He designed their
artificial intelligence systems,"
I say,
looking to my burger,
seeing the grease sop into the bun.

Victor's face twists in thought.
"Was he the whistle blower?
David Ulman?"

I nod, looking at my burger.

>>> Warning: Avoid conversation.
>>> Escape

"Brave man, to challenge
such a popular company.
His statements about what
SocialNet was doing with
people's data was
distressing."

I know all about
distressing.
Everything that came from
Dad's time at SocialNet was
distressing.

I check the other side of my burger,
assessing the mustard creeping to the bun's edge,
seeing it about to run off, realizing
I should do the same.
"Thank you Mrs. Dolan,
Dr. Moran, and Dr. Moran.
I must be getting home."

Erin.escape();

Excusing myself, I head to the door.

"It was nice to meet you, Erin.
I'm sure we'll meet again soon,"
Victor calls from the table.

Victoria opens the door for me.
"Remember, Erin, we're here for you.
No matter what.
If you need help,
just ask."

She holds the door,
waiting.
I just nod
and step out.

The last golden rays of sunset
trace the fall leaves with light.

A cool breeze rattles the trees
as storm clouds roll in from the south.

My dad the whistle blower.
Once I was proud of that,
but many moves,
countless angry messages from old friends,
and endless job hunting
has turned pride to regret.

CAYLEE MORAN

Broken Promises

Strange, I think,
examining the black car
in front of our house.

We don't normally have visitors.

When I step in,
Mom Cathy is cleaning up dinner
while
Mom Victoria
sits with…

Grandpa?

I look again to check.

Mom Victoria and Grandpa Victor
sit
staring
silently
at each other.

Yui and Sabrina
play quietly in the living room.
Mom Cathy glances up to see me;
she smiles,
popping up her eyebrows.

I smell the cheeseburgers
but taste the rancid tension
at the table.

"Erin was looking for you,"
Mom Victoria says,
her eyes locked on Grandpa Victor's.

Looking for me?
Why, to yell more?
To tell me how bad of a person
I am,
again?

She came by the house?

"Can you give her a call?
She was worried about you."
Mom Victoria says.

No.

"Okay, I'll just catch up with her tomorrow,"
I say,
watching them watch each other.
I wait for one of them to do something,
the energy building, ready to burst.

Waiting.

Waiting.

Nothing happens.

Mom Cathy is done,
bedtime is starting;
still they sit in silence:

Mom Victoria's red face
bubbling in anger,

Grandpa Victor's face
dragged down in disappointment.

I head back to my room,
seeing
Introduction to Micro Computing & Processing
by A. J. Sherman
sitting on my desk.

Erin.

Was she right?
I never said anything to Donna,
I never did anything to stop Donna
but I stood up for her
at the first moment it was necessary.

I never stood up for Erin.

I open the window,
a fall breeze blowing away some of my stress:
clean
fresh
crisp
air.

Across the street
barely lit by the orange streetlight,
a girl stands
shrouded in darkness,
brown and crimson splotch stains
covering her
gray hoodie
and torn jeans.

Her eyes glimmer in the shadows of her hood,
silver and green
like a cat;
she watches me,
her mouse.

Shutting the window
and locking it,
I draw the curtains.

As Sabrina and Yui climb into bed,
I peek out to hear what's going on at the table
but instead I hear Mom Victoria in her study
typing away.

Creeping out of my room
I look into her study;
Victor is holding a book,
pointing at the cover,
whispering something
that sounds like
It is time.

Mom Victoria shakes her head,
crinkling her nose,
a frustrated whisper
breaking through her teeth.
"She's not ready."

"What are you doing?"
I jump.

It's Sabrina.
"I have to pee-pee
and the bathroom is too dark."
I shush her;
we sneak down the hall
to the bathroom.

The front door closes.
Mom Victoria wheels back to her study,
closing the door behind her.

"Can we go to bed now?"
Sabrina asks.

"Yes, Sabrina. Get some rest."
I walk her back to our room,
hearing the rhythmic clacking of
Mom Victoria's typewriter,
thinking about the girl outside
in the light.
Knowing I won't be sleeping tonight.

WEDNESDAY (CRAZY COSTUME DAY)

ERIN ULMAN

The Real Me?

"Erin, what's today?"
Mother shouts from the kitchen.

She's been encouraging me to take part in
spirit week
all week.
She said it would be a good way to meet new people
and I guess
she's right.

Umu's right.
I need to stop trying to be someone else.
Today I'll show the school the real me.

What can I lose?

Erin.query("What is today?");
>>> Results: Be me day.

Digging through boxes from Seattle
I find the real me.

"Oh, that looks great!"
Mother smiles
when she sees my gray wizard's cloak
emblazoned with golden magical symbols,
the one
Dad and I
made for
San Diego ComiCon.
"Where's the hat?"

I place it on my head:
broad rim, pointy top,
just like Gandalf.

Weaving reality
by pulling on the threads of magic
doesn't sound too far-fetched to me.
My computer is my spell book,
my code
my magical incantations, altering
my world to
my whim.

```
Technology = new Magic();
VR = new MagicalWorlds();
AI = new MagicalCompanions();

Erin.isMagical.with(Computers);
```

"Thanks, Mother. We'll see how this goes."
I sigh,
bracing for the comments
and pictures
and posts.

Mother hands me a duffle bag.
"Just in case
you need a quick change."
She winks
as I open the bag,
finding a hoodie and jeans.

Normal clothes
for a normal day;
a parachute pack from Costume Day
if needed.

"I'm sure I won't be the strangest one there."
I laugh,
imagining Meredith Arnold
in full *Call for Destruction* battle armor.
"Did you know one of the top ranked *Call for Destruction*
players goes to
my school?"

Mother smiles.
"Oh wow, that's interesting."
She picks up her newest book.
Helping Others Live with Cancer
Who do we know with cancer?
Mother pauses, looking at it,
looking up to me.

She'll read anything.

She doesn't know what I'm talking about.
Call for Destruction
isn't a book
she's read.

I watch her
watch me.

```
if(Erin.keepsTalking){
  Mother.willPayAttention = true;
}
```

But I don't follow up
fast enough.

She opens her book.
The cracking spine
claws her attention away from me.
"Is that your new friend Umu?"

She flips a page,
eyes sweeping across.
Flips again.

"No, Mother."
I huff off the question.
"Umu's not a gamer.
Not that you care."

She keeps reading.
"Sorry, what was that, Erin?"
Her attention is
locked into the book.

Vanishing from Mother's world,
I walk back to my room.
I wonder where Umu is,
why she didn't come back last night.

I stuff another hoodie
and jeans into the duffle,
preparing for whatever I'll find
today.

The Tribe

School looks like
trick or treating.

Some costumes
are begging for the principal's attention.
Skirts too short.
Stockings too long.
Tops too low-cut.

I spot Davis
in the same foyer corner
he was at yesterday.
Dark shirt,
dark pants,
black cloak wrapping his body.
An emblem on his shirt
shows he's a Kuzan Assassin from that game,
Shadowlurker.

He sees me,
grins,
gestures the overly complex
but still awesome Kuzan Clan greeting.
The guys around him are
all dressed as other *Shadowlurker* characters.
I guess they coordinated?

Their conversation stops
as one points down the hall;
in awe,
my eyes follow.

Whoa!

Meredith IS fully decked out
in *Call for Destruction* gear.
Her post-apocalyptic tatters
reveal a ghostly pale,
lithe
body.

Her raven hair is wrapped into a top knot
like a fountain of darkness springing from her crown.
The finishing touch:
a gigantic glowing PVA foam sword
strapped to Meredith's back,
twice her size,
signaling who she is: Larin the Slaughteress.

WOW!

>>> System Shock
Erin.feelings = "awe";

Meredith joins Davis
and his friends
as they examine each other's costumes
and craftsmanship,
exchanging techniques on sewing,
LED work,
marveling at precision
and artistry.

Attributes missing
from everyone else in the foyer.

Clicking away,
Donna's crew
snap pictures,
pointing,
laughing
in their store-bought pleather pants
and bumblebee tops.

Caylee is missing.

I walk over to Davis,
examining the details of Meredith's cosplay up close.
Her attention to detail
and deft stitch work
mute Donna's friends.
Meredith's vibrant colors
and pure love for her work
silence the clicking photographs
and beeping alerts.

"My lady."
Davis bows.

I return the sentiment.

We talk thread count
and fabric selections.
Wizards.
Warriors.
Assassins.
Not concerned with the bees
buzzing around us.

CAYLEE MORAN

Caylee's Crisis

This bee costume

is

trash!

Another rip.
Maybe I'm too rough on it,
trying to get ready quickly,
oversleeping from keeping watch
and more weird mountain dreams.

Rip.

"Damn it!"

Mom Cathy hands me a change of clothes,
seeing this costume isn't going to make it to school.

"Don't get frustrated, honey."
Mom Cathy sighs
rubbing my shoulders.
"You are much more athletic than
those other girls.
This tiny stuff
isn't going to fit."

She gasps.
"I mean…
Not fit over your muscles.
You're perfect the way you are—"

"I knew what you meant, Mom."
I cut her off,
wanting to avoid another
long-winded
You're beautiful how you are
talk.

I thought I'd slim down
from not working out.
No running in town or Donna's friends
would tease me.
No sports in school or Donna's friends
would tease me.

Now running is exhausting.
All the work I did last year
at my other school
for track and field faded fast.

The early morning runs,
late night weightlifting,
high energy eating
replaced
by SocialNet posting,
mall walking,
fad diet eating.

But I never wanted medals or trophies,
I just wanted a team.
And now I have that with
Donna.

Changing.
Running.
Pushing through the front door.
Sprinting to school.
Winded.

Arriving
I see Donna and the bees wandering back to class.
I see Erin, Davis, and Meredith
looking amazing in their cosplay.
No costume for me.
Just Caylee Moran:
not a wizard or warrior or whatever Davis is.

Meredith is so badass,
so confident,
not afraid of what people will say,
putting herself out there…
Maybe too much,
with all that skin showing.

Here I am.
A wannabe Bee
floating around
people who are brave enough
to be themselves
while I pretend to be anyone else.

Donna's bee costume is so mundane,
so manufactured;
at least it matches her.

I slip back out the school doors,
heading home for a change.

Erin, the wizard.
Meredith, the warrior.
Davis, the shadowy cloak guy.
Who am I?

Caylee, the follower?
Caylee, the bee?
Or
just
Caylee?

Construction

I crawl away from school
under the classroom windows
through the mulch and mud
lining the building.

Passing classrooms,
I stop at the windows of the Maker Lab
where a familiar glow catches my eye.
In the center of the room
those silver-green eyes from last night.

Now I see their owner:
they're Umu's eyes.

She's building something
in the corner,
crouched down
over
one of the new 3D printers.
The parts are scattered around her
as she examines each piece,
rebuilding it
but not exactly.

Her hoodie,
spotted with mud,
hides her face,
but I know those eyes.
Inhuman eyes,
a cross between steel
and a cat prowling in shadow.

Pulling a silver case
from her pocket,
she opens it;
steam escapes
as she takes out a vial of liquid,
comparing it to the print head.

I don't have time for this.
Mom Cathy will get the
Your kid didn't show up
message soon.

Better get home.

Crawling away and
standing,
I run home,
replaying what I saw,
curious to understand
what Umu is doing.

I know who I can ask.
I just hope I have the courage to talk to her
at school.

ERIN ULMAN

History & Magic

In History,
sitting in the front,
my wizard's cap
blocks the view of those
snickering behind me.

I keep it on.
On display for people to see my hat.
For people to see me.

Today we're watching a video on anthropology.
I think of Victoria,
her constant reminder:
She's *here for me*.
What does she know?

Victoria.knowsTruthAbout(Umu);
>>> Result: Unknown

How could she?

Is she talking about something else?

"Hey Gandalf!
Can you take off that stupid hat?"
some boy I've never noticed before
yells out.

I jump,
grabbing my hat
before pausing
to look at him.

```
Erin.hat.quality > Boy.entireOutfit.quality;
Erin.hat.isNicer();
Erin.hat.isBetterQuality();
Erin.hat.isAwesome;
```

"What, Gandalf?"
He scoffs.
"You gonna
throw some magic on me?"
Cracking himself up,
face reddening from laughter,
jabbing at his friends
all dressed in football uniforms.

I picture Umu's vicious predator smile
in my mind;
my lips start moving,
words springing out of me,
the words she'd tell me to say…
"You don't *throw* magic.
You cast it.
It's not a football."
I lean toward him,
whispering loud enough for his friends to hear.
"And you know magic isn't real, right?"

I turn back around;
the boys wearing football uniforms
behind him are struck silent
for a moment,
then erupt into laughter again,
except for the boy.
He isn't laughing.

I can feel it:
his ears turning red
with embarrassment,
burned by the loser in front of him.

I made them laugh,
and for once
it's not at me.

Monster Parade

Lunch time:
still no Umu,
still no Caylee.

Erin.scan(Lunchroom);
>>> Results: Davis and Meredith found
Davis.waves();
Davis.invites(Erin).toTable();

The table I sat at with Umu
is empty,
waiting for me.
I wave to Davis
as I sit at my empty table.

I'm eating lunch
head down,
hoping for Umu,
when someone sits down
placing their finely crafted bow in front of me.
My eyes trace up their dull chainmail-armored arm,
ringed with expert precision.
Their shirt, a brown hide leather,
is bound with steel grommets and brown string.

Elven ears blend perfectly with her sepia skin,
protruding from midnight hair, loose and wild,
as bold eye makeup encircles pools of white
around brown-and-gold irises.

Caylee the Elven Ranger,
like Legolas from The Fellowship,
ready for the Battle of Helms Deep
except fiercer,
ready for battle against something worse
than ten thousand orcs:
the high school lunchroom.

She sits.

I see the adventurer,
the ranger,
a companion in battle—

a friend.

```
Erin.friends.add(Caylee);
>>> Return true;
```

"I'm sorry."

"You weren't wrong."
Her eyes soften
as she smiles,
sitting taller
to show where she stands.

I brush away a tear.
"Shadowlurker?"

"Mom Cathy got it for me
for Lurkercon.
That's how I know Davis and Meredith.
We're a party online."
Caylee smiles,
nodding back to Davis's table.

He rushes over,
lunch tray clattering,
milk splashing about.

"Zuhion, I can't express my joy
in seeing you,"
Davis says in his
in-character
voice.

Caylee places her fist over her heart,
rattling the chainmail.
"It is good to be here,"
she says in her character's voice.

Camera clicking
and giggling
comes from Donna's table.

"Caylee Moran…what are you doing?"
Disbelief
soaks through Donna's voice.

Donna.isConfused = true;
Donna.processing();

"Catching up with friends."
Caylee waves her over.

Donna
rolls her eyes to her fellow Bees.
She pauses,
looks to their reactions.

They laugh.

Donna follows.

Donna.friends.remove(Caylee);

Caylee turns to
Davis and me,
her eyes growing dark.
She whispers,
"We need to talk about Umu."

I slump down in my chair,
resting after carrying the weight of Umu's secret.

Yes,
I need Caylee's help.
I need her to know what's going on.

"Why do you need to
talk about me?"
Umu's voice shatters the whisper,
her cold presence splitting us
apart
as she stands at
our table.

Umu has changed
into the clothes from my duffle.

Caylee's eyes move to battle-ready,
glaring at Umu.

"Why were you at my house
last night?"
Caylee hisses through her teeth.

"Why was your grandfather at mine?"
Umu snipes.

"Wait, what?"

"I followed Caylee's grandfather
from your house, Erin,
to Caylee's house,"
Umu says.
"He and some other guy
were at your house
during the break-in."
Umu turns to me.
"They stole the device
from you, Erin."

Caylee rises to her feet,
her forehead a breath away
from Umu's nose,
both their eyes
stabbing into each other.

"Bullshit,"
Caylee spits.

Davis looks for an exit.

I watch,
waiting for
the first move.

Neither Caylee nor Umu move.
Cold flows from Umu,
turning Caylee's lips pale
as Caylee squints,
pressing the frozen air from her eyes.

The bell rings;
bodies flood out of the lunchroom.

"Erin, don't let
your part-time friend
do something foolish."

Umu grins,
blinking
pleasantly,
if it were not for
the murderous glare
in her eyes.

"Caylee, let's get to class,"
I whimper out.

Davis is already at the door.

"Umu, let's talk about this later."
I grab Umu's arm,
pulling her away from Caylee.

She comes along
but her eyes stay
locked
on
Caylee.

Caylee doesn't blink.

Formation of the Party

"Come over to my house after school.
Like 6 PM.
I've got something to tell you,"
I say to Caylee, Davis, and Meredith
in the school foyer.

I'm watching for Umu,
not seeing her
or feeling her
cold.
I think we're safe.

CLICK!

A picture is taken,
followed by the standard giggles and hysterics
from Donna's Bees.

"Hello, Donna,"
Meredith says
in her monosyllabic tone.
"Make sure to tag me
in your post.

Everyone pose."

I stand there,
a statue,
while Davis and Meredith position themselves
in practiced cosplay poses:
serious,
intense,
giving a show
instead of being turned into one.

Caylee looks to me,
shrugs,
and busts out an awesome archer pose,
joining
Davis and Meredith
in this spectacular show of social disregard.

I don't have a pose.
I stand there.

Donna busts up laughing,
shaking uncontrollably from the amusement,
our ridiculousness that we think this is
anything but stupid.

Picture taken.

"Thank you, Donna,"
Meredith says.
"Make sure to tag me: Azriel_Knight.
That is spelled *a*, *z*…"

Donna waves her away.
"Yes, I've got it."
Laughing uncontrollably.

"Thank you,"
Meredith says.

Meredith looks over Donna's costume,
processing something to say.

"Your costume looks…
nice."

Meredith walks off.

Donna sneers.
"Tagged!"
She's still laughing.
"Oh look. Someone liked your picture."
Laughing harder.

Another ding on Donna's phone,
harder laughter,
quieting with more dings
and more dings,
as Meredith's fans flood Donna's alerts
with
likes,
loves,
comments,
support for their hero
Meredith,
champion of *Call for Destruction*.

Davis rolls his eyes.
Caylee laughs,
loud,
free,
happy.

Meredith whips out her phone as she walks,
her fingers soaring across the screen,
answering every notification.

"Yeah, she's got to take care
of her fans."
Davis smiles,
following Meredith to the door.
"See you later, Erin."
His feet twist under him,
tripping.
"I mean, see you with Caylee
and Meredith later."

Caylee's smile fades,
her eyes following the Bees buzzing away.

"See you tonight?"
I say,
ducking into her view.

"Yeah, I'll be there."
Her eyes still follow the Bees,
seeing them fly out of her life.

CAYLEE MORAN

The Hunter & the Ranger

Erin quietly escapes school.

Donna and her friends—
my old friends now—
leave out the side doors.

I tell the teachers in the hall
I left something
in the Maker Lab
and go through the empty hallway
to the orange doors
that no one ever
goes in.

"What were you doing in here?"
I whisper out loud.

Gripping my bow,
relaxing when I remember
it's only made of foam,
I pull open the door
as frozen air falls on me,
sending shivers through my blood.

Stepping past the door,
clicks
whirs
computers crunching data
surround me.

Under a desk,
a quick green glint of eyes streaks away.
I flick up the light switch;

a mouse runs under the tables,
scurrying into the supply closet.

My shoulders drop
as my heart lets me breath again.

I walk up to the parts
Umu was messing with earlier.

The parts of the printer
are bent or reshaped
using the tools from the tool rack.

What is
Umu building,
and why?

Another mouse runs to the supply closet,
its little claws ticking across the floor,
squealing and screeching
as it sprints from storage cabinets
in the corner.

I look to where it came from
and see one of the storage doors hanging
open slightly.

Creaking hinges slowly squeal
as the door shifts.

Keeping my distance,
I peek around
the door.

"This is the final bell.
All students need to report to their activities.
No activity?
Then you shouldn't be here.
See you tomorrow for
Class Color Day!"
the principal says
over the intercom.

I watch the storage door
as I step out of the Maker Lab,
closing the door,
returning
to the warmth of the school.

I hear the lights click off behind me
as darkness swallows the Maker Lab.

Stopping,

I feel biting icy air
snapping at my neck.

When I look back, the orange doors are closed.

Silver green eyes glimmer
through the door's window slits,
watching me stagger back.

I run.

ERIN ULMAN

The Gathering

Mother meets Davis and Meredith
at the door.

Davis instantly charms her,
laughing and
chatting.

```
Davis.isCharming = true;
Davis.isAwkward = true;
Davis.isCute = true;
```

Mother's confused by Meredith,
who silently walks in the house,
pays no attention to what's around her,
and flops on our couch beside the rocking chair
replying to comments on our picture from earlier.

Pizza arrives,
small talk is spent,
and it's getting late,
but where is Caylee?

I look outside
as the road gets darker
and darker
until only the golden glow of streetlamps
light the mounting fog.
A haze of blue and yellow
hides the world beyond a few houses down.

The phone rings.
Mother answers,
smiling from Davis's last quippy comment.

"No, we haven't seen her yet."
Mother's smile fades.
"We figured she was running late."
Creases of concern
creep over Mother's brow.
"Yeah, we'll call you
when she gets here."

Mother hangs up,
pausing.

"That was Caylee's mom, Cathy.
Caylee hasn't been home
from school yet.
Was she stopping anywhere
prior to coming here?"

"No, Mrs. Ulman.
We were all stopping home,
then coming straight here,"
Davis answers.

```
if(Caylee.chasedAfter(Donna)){
  Caylee.changedHerMind();
  Caylee.isComing = false;
}
```

"She hangs out
at the library a lot.
Maybe she swung by there
before going home?
Lost track of time?"
Davis says.
"If you want, I can go with you
to see if she's there.
Meredith and Erin can stay here
in case she arrives after we leave."

Meredith, still on her phone,
sighs,
shaking her head.

```
Meredith.disagrees();
Meredith.thinks(BadIdea);
```

"Yeah, we've got this. You guys go.
I'll call you when Caylee gets here,"
I say.

They leave,
Mother panicking,
Davis keeping cool,
hiding his panic well.

"Erin, @donnie_2_fast is asking
who the cute wizard is.
Do I have your permission to say
the cute wizard is Erin?"
Meredith asks,
her eyes still locked on her phone.

Cute wizard?
What's cute about an awkward girl
in a gray cloak and pointy hat?

"Uh, sure. That's fine."

"@donnie_2_fast gave my response a heart."

"Okay."

"@donnie_2_fast wants to know
what your SocialNet tag is,"
Meredith says.

"I don't have one."

SocialNet would just forget me
anyway.

I watch Mother and Davis
pull away
as the fog
blurs out the
last streetlamp
on our road.

CAYLEE MORAN

Predator, Prey & Huntress

I keep looking behind me,
watching for those eyes.

The fog thickens
drowning out the streets
turning the lamps into ghostly glowing orbs
hanging in the darkness.

I run,
glancing back
knowing even in this dark
I'd see her eyes
the glimmering
silver and green,
the cat eyes
hunting.

Her cold presence
nips at my heels,
or maybe it's just the twilight sky,
the chilling fog,
the fast running
stealing my breath.

Rounding the corner of Ash Street
I see the library.

When I grab the double doors,
pulling,
they
don't
open.

I check my phone:
Battery is dead.
I should have charged it
last night
instead of watching
videos on SocialNet
to stay awake.

What time is it?

Can't be that late
but can't tell with this fog.

I rattle the doors,
hoping someone inside hears
but no one comes.

No one
inside the library.

Glints of green eyes
drift through the white fog
as a figure in hoodie and jeans
patiently
walks
toward
me.

Her hood is up,
covering her face
except those eyes
and drool-laced teeth
grinning a
gotcha
smile.

What do I do?

I'm glad I didn't wear
those heels for the bee costume today.

These boots can run
but my lungs
are cramping,
clasping tight.

The air is so cold.

My legs are turning to Jell-O.

"Where is it,
Caylee Moran?"
Umu chuckles
through the fog.

Where's what?

I don't think
she'll want to hear that.

RUN!

Run, legs,
don't scream or
hurt or groan,
just move.

They listen
and I run,
thinking
Where I can go
for help?

Where's close?

Nothing's close?

This is Glen Coast;
nothing is close
to anything
and everything closes
at 5pm.

Except The Bookshop,
Mom Victoria's voice
says, matter-of-fact,
in my mind.

Yeah, The Bookshop.

Erin and Mom were just talking about that.
I could ask…
what's his name,
the guy they were talking about…

Mr. Stone,
Mom Victoria's voice
completes my thought.

Running,
I remember
where it is
but can't remember
ever being there.

The map of streets
and turns
forms in my mind.

Umu's running now.

Trotting for her,
galloping along,
keeping her distance.

Is she…

Sucking in the frozen air
cramping my lungs.

Is she
chasing me down?

Waiting until I drop
to pounce?

Waiting until I'm
too exhausted to fight?

Looking back
I hear her breathing,
snarling with delight
but don't see her.

Where is everyone?

Just breathe,
Mom Victoria says.
Calming breaths.

Yeah, right.

"Where is it, Caylee?"
Umu's sing-song stalking
makes me look back.

She's not there.

Where did she go?

"Looking for someone?"
Umu laughs
as I slam into her,
falling,
my butt bouncing on
the pavement,
my head cracking onto it,
sending lights popping
in my eyes.

She got around me.
She was in front of me,
ran right past me,
and she's not even panting.

I scurry back from her.

Shadows cling to
the inside of her hood,
only letting those eyes
and teeth come out
for me to see.

"I want it back."
Umu walks to me
calm
clenching her fists
cracking the dried blood
on her knuckles
into flakes
that drift down the fog.

"I don't know—"

"Caylee Moran,
daughter of Victoria Moran,
granddaughter of Victor Moran."
Umu rushes me,
ripping me up toward her.

"SocialNet ID 952321012.
Your friends online are mundane
but your family certainly is not."

"Your grandfather took the
Pandora Device
and I want it back now.
Where is it!?"

Her frozen presence
engulfs me, turning the fog
to ice crystals around us.

I shiver,
convulsing in her hands
as the empty blackness inside her mouth
gapes open to take a bite
of my throat.

Chance Encounter

"Hey!"
a man shouts
as he runs toward us.
His dark form
takes shape
in the fog.

"Leave her alone!"
the man commands.

Umu's smile
stretches to her ears
exposing back teeth
sharp and pointed for ripping
flesh.

She throws me down.

I bounce off the pavement again.

She launches into the fog
meeting his dark form
with hers.

The shadows in the fog
strike at each other,
dodging and dancing
in fluid combat,
moving so fast
I can only tell who's who
by the size of the shadows.

Umu strikes fast,
reacting, evading,
staying close.

The man swings big
and round,
creating pockets
for Umu to retreat into where
he strikes at her.

I stagger up
and fall again,
my head spinning
from the impact on
the pavement.

"Help…"

I try to scream
but only a whimper
breaks through the fog.

A yellow flash
explodes between the shadows,
sending Umu leaping back
and vanishing into the fog.

The man's shadow,
panting and hunched,
comes through the fog
and extends a bear-paw-sized hand
to help me up.

I take it
and he pulls me up
to my feet
without effort.

"You okay, miss?"
he says, taking a step back
to give me space.

Looking him over,
I should ask him the same.
His massive shoulders slump,
leaning to his left where he's
rubbing his arm.

His golden t-shirt is torn
with trails of blood trickling through.
Dark wash jeans
are worn heavy on the knees,
like he scraped them against the pavement
too many times.

I nod
to answer his question.

"You?"

He stretches up,
showing his full height
about a foot taller than me
and stretching his shoulders out;
he looks like two of me side by side.

"Been worse."
He smiles,
showing perfect teeth
except one broken bottom tooth.

Doesn't look new.
"Need to call anyone?"

He points to the dead phone
in my pocket.

I shake my head.

"It's dead."

Probably shouldn't have said that.

This guy could be—

You can trust him.
I hear Mom Victoria's voice again.

"Well, I don't stay…"
He points to my phone.
"Modern, but you can use the phone
in my shop.

It's right
around the corner here."
He fishes in his pocket.
"I just locked up so the store
is empty."

He tosses me the key.
"No funny business,
I'm not trying to be a creep,
just trying to help.

I'll stay outside,
you call whoever you need to,
and they can pick you up.

I'll make sure no one
bothers you."

This guy would scare anyone
with sense just from his size,
but I don't find him scary.

He's more like
a dad vibe
than a
dangerous vibe.

"Thanks, Mister…?"

"Quincy."
He nods,
keeping a safe
and polite distance.
"Quincy Nicholas."

Reunion

True to his word,
Quincy stays outside
while I call home.

Mom Cathy says Mom Victoria
is already heading my way.

Piles of books are
built into swaying towers
spotting the floor.

Was Quincy putting all these away
when he came out and found me?

How did he know I was there?

Umu and I weren't being so loud
he'd have heard us from here.

A set of headlights
break the fog
up the street.

Quincy stands on the steps,
watches as a grey van
emerges from the fog.

Mom Victoria's van.

I watch from inside the store
as she gets out
and wheels to him.

They talk.

Mom Victoria smiles.

A real smile.

That's something you don't see every day.

Quincy points toward me
and I step out the front door.
As I come out
I hear Quincy say:

"...grown up fast."

Mom Victoria nods.

"Caylee, let's go."
Mom Victoria wheels to the van,
rolling up the ramp.
"Thank you, Quincy."

"Thank you."
I nod to Quincy.

He smiles
and nods back.

"Good to meet you, Caylee."
He smiles,
warm,
kind.
"Be careful out there."

Mom Victoria climbs
out of her chair
in the short unsteady steps
her body allows.

Sitting in the driver's seat
she sighs exhausted from
the move from wheelchair
to driving chair.

Taking a moment to gather herself,
she waves to Quincy
and smiles again
with a little laugh.

"Do you know him?"

I close my door
and watch Quincy go
into The Bookshop.

"Yes. Quincy
used to live in Glen Coast.
Surprised to see him back."
She shrugs
and starts the van.
"Good for us
that he was around."

"How'd you know
I was coming here?"
She shifts the van to reverse
and pulls the hand petal to
start turning around and
leave the dead end
at The Bookshop.

"I assumed you went to the library
but they were closed.
So, this is the next closest thing."
She smirks.
"Not a giant mental leap."

Isn't it?

She shifts to drive
and we start pulling out of the street
where The Bookshop hides,
tucked away from anyone
who doesn't know it's here.

Did I just think to come here
or did she tell me?

We pass the place
where Umu knocked me down,
shook me,
was going to
hurt me.

On the curb is a streak of red.

Feeling the back of my head
my hair is matted
with red crust.

My teeth grind and
fists shake with
anger.

Umu thinks I stole something,
or my family did.

She's crazy.

She would have beaten me
until I told her
what she wanted to hear.

Lucky for me Quincy showed up.

Lucky?

I look to Mom Victoria;
her eyes are distant,
replaying a memory
from long ago.

Her smile fades,
her eyes harden,
she squeezes the accelerator pedal harder
making us run faster
from The Bookshop.

She glances to the rear-view mirror
and sighs, calming herself.
Letting out a breath she was
holding in.

ERIN ULMAN

Dividing the Party

"Your mom forgot the first rule
of role-playing games,"
Meredith says,
still tapping her phone.

"Never divide the party.
Always stay together because
if you don't,
the villains will pick you off
one by one.

This is common in movies,
games,
books—"

I shake my head.

"No, they're still looking.
They called from the library.
Caylee wasn't there
and my mother's just driving slow
in the fog."

I look to see if Meredith
believes me.

```
Erin.isLiar = true;
while(Mother.isAway){
  Erin.isWorried = true;
}
```

It is getting late.

I call Mother from the kitchen phone.

No answer.

"Meredith, can you call Davis?"

She stops typing.
"Call Davis."

Her phone thinks in silence
answering,
Calling Davis.

"Thank you, phone,"
Meredith says.

How very polite.

The phone rings
rings
rings
to voicemail.

"Like I said.
Never break up the party."
She returns to responding
to messages in SocialNet.

Beside the kitchen phone
on the list of emergency numbers,
I see Cathy's phone number.

```
Erin.isDesperate = true;
Erin.isFreakingOut = 100%;
if(Meredith.sees(Erin.panic){
  Meredith.will(Panic);
}
```

I can't let Meredith see me like this…

Does she get panicked?

I call Cathy.

The phone rings
and rings
but no answer.

Voicemail picks up.

I hang up.

"Like I said…"
Meredith shakes her head.

RING!

RING!

The phone rattles on the wall.

I snap it up.
"Hello?"

"Erin, it's Mom."
Mother states the obvious.
"I just heard from Dr. Moran
and she found Caylee."

I blow out the stress
that built in me all night.

"Okay, that's good."
I motion to Meredith;
she looks up from her phone.

"They found Caylee,"
I say.

Meredith nods
and returns to her phone.

"Where was she?"
I ask.

"I don't know,"
Mother says.
"But everyone's safe now.
I'll be home shortly."

We say goodbye
and hang up.

"Mother and Davis
are on their way back."

Erin.isFreakingOut = 20%;

Meredith nods.
"I'm surprised no one died."
She looks up from her phone.
"Usually someone gets hurt
when the party splits up."

I shrug and flop on the couch.

"Maybe that's
only how things work in movies
and books."
I chuckle away the idea.

"No. That's all based on fact,"
Meredith says
with certainty.
"We just don't know what
happened yet."

Meredith shakes her head.
"Never split up the party.
That's how the villains
make quick work of the heroes.

Picking them off
one
by
one
and we're next."

Erin.isFreakingOut = 75%;
Meredith.freakingOut(Erin);

"Why would you say that?"
My attention is suddenly drawn
to a question:
Did I lock the window
in my room?

I think I did?

"That's what happens, Erin."
Meredith puts her phone down.
"First Caylee,
then probably Davis
because he's clueless.
Then probably you
because you're smart,
and finally me
because I'm most likely
to survive."

"Why?"
I laugh
and shift
thinking again
about my window
and how dark it is
outside with the fog.

"I'm the tough one."
Her monotone delivery is
certain and clear.

"Okay. Well, let's just agree
that everyone's safe now."
I get up.
"Meredith, you want to see my room?"

I hope she says yes.
I don't want to check the window
alone.

Return of the Storm

Still creeped out from Meredith's thoughts.
That was hours ago now.
Mother's back and has gone to bed.

Sleep isn't on my mind yet.
Too busy worrying about
being next.

Ugh…Meredith!

I push my computer chair,
big and heavy,
to block the door.
I check the locks on the window
again and
pull the shades down.

Lying on my bed,
I stare at the door
listening
for any sound:
the creak of the floor,
the crack of the window,
the jiggle of the doorknob.

Watching the stillness
listening to branches clacking
against my window as they
reach to grab something they're
never able to clench.

Crickets grow quiet,
brought to silence by the
screeching,
moaning
wind.

Lightning flashes outside my window,
bathing my room in a pale blue floodlight,
throwing long shadows into my room
that linger
like mourners standing above a grave,
my grave,
as they tower above my bed
glaring down on me.

The wind goes quiet.

Stillness.

Creeeeakkkkk

Creeeeakkkkk

Creeeeakkkkk

Mother's rocking chair
breaks the silence,
creaking rhythmically,
stopping suddenly,
waiting to finish.

"Come and see me, Erin."
Umu's voice, barely audible,
comes from the living room.

The Hunter Hunted

Past the reach of the hallway light
Umu sits in Mother's rocking chair.

Her shimmering silver green eyes
watch me step into the kitchen.

"No lights,"
she says
halting my hand
as it reaches for the switch.

The room fills with cold,
colder than before.
What was a chill
now reminds me of frozen nights camping with Dad
in Octobers past.

I keep my voice to a hush.
"Umu, where have you been?"

In the dark
I can only see her eyes
and the rough outline of a tattered hoodie
and ripped jeans.

"They came again, Erin."
Her voice is calm,
matter-of-fact.
"Yesterday, they took
the Pandora Device
that made me.
They tried to take me but
that didn't work out.
Today was the same."
She holds up her hands.

I'm thankful the darkness spares me
whatever she's showing me.
There's only a glossy reflection of
some thick liquid
coating her fingers
and arms.

Erin.analyzing();
>>> Result: Fresh Blood. Not Umu's blood.

"I need your help, Erin.
I know you can figure out
who they are and what they want."
Umu's voice is soft.

She steps to the outer reaches
of the hall light;
her hands are covered in mud
or blood
or maybe both,
the hoodie covered in stains,
the jeans torn in gashes.

"Please, Erin."
Her eyes soften,
looking more pitiful
with her matted curls
and lifeless pale face.

"Let's get you cleaned up."
I wave her to me,
thinking about her strength,
her toughness,
and how she
needs
me.

Me.

"We'll get this figured out."

Her coldness lifts
as a hint of a smile appears;
she walks to me.

My eyes fall to the floor,
seeing the sand crawling up my legs,
flashing to my dream.
I look to her again
shaking the vision from my head.

"Thank you, Erin,"
Umu says,
her voice
flat,
lifeless.

Taking her back to my room
I pause,
thinking
Will I end up consumed by her?
Like Mother was in my dream?
I chase away the thought with reason,
telling myself,

I'm helping her. Those were just dreams.
She'd never hurt me. I created her.

She's not just a friend,
she's kind of like my daughter.

Meredith was wrong,
I'm not next.
Caylee's okay.
Davis isn't next.

Umu needs me.
I'm important to her.

I smile.

THURSDAY (SICK DAY)

Discovery

Umu tells me about
the men who stole the device,
what she saw,
where they went.

"The Bookshop?"

>>> Does not compute

I know Umu doesn't have
a sense of humor
but I don't see an old bookstore
being the front for a gang
of thieves.

She nods
and scrubs her hands
and face with the washcloth
I gave her.

Pink drips
ping on my floor
as she rubs away
the crust from her mouth.

"Whoever they are,
that's where they went
after they left here
with the device."

"Okay. Well, that's strange."
I turn to my computer
and search for The Bookshop.
I want to see if it has
a website or email address
or any digital footprint.

"Caylee's involved,"
Umu hisses.
"I knew she was trouble."
Picking up a new hoodie,
she rips it over her head.

"What do you mean?"
I keep typing
focusing on The Bookshop,
not Caylee;
not that she's
responsible
or involved.

"That old man I saw at her house
is her grandfather.
He's the one who took
the device.

We need that device, Erin."

Why?

Erin.query("What is the purpose of Pandora Device?");
>>> Results: Unknown.

Why do we need the device back?
It was interesting
and I'd love to study it more
but *need* is a heavy word.

Umu's eyes show her
desperation,
warning me off
from asking more
questions.

The Bookshop returns
zero results.

How can a business
not have a website nowadays?
No online shopping option?
No email?

No SocialNet meMessage address?

My eye drifts to the Pandora icon
on my desktop.
The console app is
still minimized in my task bar.

I click it,

showing the last message
from the night Umu was born.

Notification sent for Pandora Protocol.

Pandora Protocol?
Clicking on my traffic analyzer,
I see the address of the message.

Whoever got the message
knew the device was here.

They could have reverse engineered
my address from the transmission
and that's how they knew to come here
and steal the device.

"I think I have something."
I point to my screen;
Umu huddles in close,
her hand pushing on my chair
as her neck cranes past mine.

She smells like
snow
and
dirt.

“This was sent after you were…”
Born?
Made?
Arrived?

"Reborn?"
Umu completes.

Reborn?
I thought she said
she didn't know anything
from before, but
she knows this isn't her first birth…

"Uh, yeah, reborn."
My finger follows the address.
“See here, this is the
IP address that the device sent
a message to after you arrived."

She nods.

"You can trace that
and find out where
they are, can't you?"
Umu smiles
a victorious grin.

I nod.

"Better. We can see
if this message is the front door
to anything else interesting."
I pick up my VR headset
and wiggle it at her
with eager intent.

"Want to see what we
aren't supposed to see?"

Umu nods,
eager,
excited.

"I knew you were the right person
for this job, Erin Ulman."
She pats my shoulder.
"Dangerous to computers
indeed."

I laugh
but she doesn't;
her grin fades
as she steps away from me
slowly,
remembering something
as she looks at me.

"See you inside?"
I pull on the VR headset
keeping my face away from her
until the app is loaded,
until she's
ready to be seen
in VR.

No sense is seeing anything
unpleasant this late
at night.

The Yellow Brick Road

My VR home builds around me.
Hardwood floor,
glass and steel walls
overlooking a forest
just like our old home
in Seattle.

On my bookshelf,
I search for what I need.

"Story time?"
Umu chuckles.

Deep breath,
preparing for whatever is there,
I turn to see
her 3D avatar
that looks just like
me.

"Oh, no."
I return to the shelf.
"This is where I keep all
my apps."

"Here it is.
NetNav'r."
I pull up the app.
"I built this
to visually represent
a network. It is based on
some penetration testing tools
and network scanners
but converted to 3D.

This way I can see the network
in VR like I see the real world.

Makes it easier to work with
complex networks or big data sets
visually."

Umu nods quickly, understanding.
She can connect to a network wirelessly
and probably sees all the devices around her
just like I see a network in this app.

Does she connect to every wireless device?
Is she intercepting every SocialNet post,
every like,
every comment,
every call,
every text,
everything that runs
modern life for Glen Coast?

She'd know

everything.

"Follow me into the app
and let's see what we can find."
I activate the app.

My house vanishes
as a vast expanse of stars
appears around us.

Umu and I stand on a
column of golden light.

"I thought a space theme
would be fun."
I smile and motion around us.

Umu stares at the stars,
smiles and touches the pillar of light
holding us up.

"Amazing,"
she gasps.

"Well, it is pretty cool.
I'm proud of it."
My avatar can't blush
and I'm thankful for that.

Summoning the address input box,
I type in the IP address
where the message went.

A stream of golden thread
spins out from our pillar
toward wherever the message went.

Umu watches the thread
stretch into infinity
stopping far away
with a blip of light.

"Now, step on the thread."
I reach for Umu's hand
as she looks uncertain,
hesitant.

Out of her element?

“The thread will take us
to the next message's address.”
I nod to the thread
and she slowly reaches for me.

I gently take her hand
and we step onto the thread
and whisk into the void.

She clings on to me,
looking down into the nothing.

“We can't fall off,”
I assure her.

“You sure?”
she says,
more warning
than question.

I look down
and remember the code
that built this world.

```
Erin.godMode(Active);
World.author = Erin;
```

I didn't build a way
to fall, so that is not possible
in this world.

We arrive at the
pulsing blip of light
and another golden platform.

When we step onto it
a message appears.

Gateway IntelliDynX4-221

"A firewall,"
I say and point to
the two threads that appear
off the platform.
"Open ports."
Several nubs of thread
also stick out.
"Closed ports."

Umu walks near an open port
reading the label on the ground:
80.

"Web traffic."
I nod,
unsurprised.
"The other is probably
443 for secure traffic."

Although that isn't good
security practice, to leave those
open for inbound traffic.

"No, it says 23?"

"Telnet?"
What?
"Weird."

"Why weird?"

"That's really not secure.
Whoever set this up
needs to test their
security systems.

Anyone trying to break in
would be looking for port 23."

The original message,
the one sent on the night of Umu's
rebirth,
was on port 2342,
which must be one of the
closed ports.

I summon the password prompt
for the firewall,
and search for the default password
of the IntelliDynX4-221 model firewall.

Default password: password.

I enter it.

Golden threads spin out
from the closed ports,
opening the firewall for us.

"Which one?"
Umu says,
moving to the threads.

"Hold up."
I summon the admin console
and change the password.
"Always close the doors behind you
so someone can't follow you in."

I smile and update the password: UmuStar1

"Okay, 2342, let's go."
We step on the thread
and zoom off toward the next
pulse of light.

"See, easy."
I smirk.

She rolls her silver-green eyes
and looks to the next platform
as it comes closer.

Someone is standing on the platform.

"Oh, crap."
I open my subroutines
and prepare an obfuscation defense.

"Can you hide?"

"Probably,"
Umu says.

"That's a watcher bot."
I point to the figure on the platform.
"It's looking for threats.
Like us."

"What is it?"
Umu asks.
"A person?"

"No, it's software.
Just looks like a person
here in my app."

WatcherBot.visualization = new 3dModel("IT Nerd");

"We could probably talk to it
and try to bypass
but hiding is always
a good first option."

"Not for me."
Umu leaps from the
thread,
landing on the golden pillar,
snarling
roaring
laughing.

Spotted

"Wait!"
Too late,
Umu has launched herself
at the bot.

She lands on the platform
as the bot notices her
and rips into it
with claws stretching
from her fingertips.

Bits of bytes
spray around the bot
throwing particles of
the program all over the platform.

WatcherBot.destroyed;

What remains of the broken thing
lies crumbled on the ground
as I look around to the
scattered bytes
strewn about
in her chaotic
rampage.

Here, it is only bytes
and data
but out there,
this would be blood
and gore strewn across the street.

Is this how she's ended up
with hands
always slick,
always thick
with blood?

If she attacked a person
with that intensity
she'd kill them.

And laugh.

She's still laughing.

"That was easy."
Umu turns to me
flicking the bits
of bytes still clinging
to her hands away.

"Why?
We could have just
snuck by it?"
I watch the bytes
dissolve away,
vanishing as they
fragment.

Umu shrugs
and smiles.
"Now we don't need to."

How could she laugh
while ripping it apart?

Stop.

```
WatcherBot.isNot(Human);
```

```
Umu.inVR.isNot(Umu.inRealWorld);
```

Two silver threads link
to our platform.
"Incoming."
I point to the threads.

Umu looks;
we see more bots coming
on the threads.

"That bot probably alerted
defensive systems.
Drones, or bots.
Can't tell yet."

"What happens if they find us?"
Umu asks,
crouching
readying her
attack.

"They might trace us.
Might attack my rig
and try to compromise my system."
I swipe through my subroutines
to find the best tools for this
situation.

"That can't happen,"
Umu growls.

She flickers out of her human avatar
unleashing the shadow and tentacles.
I turn away
as she returns to her human form.

The cold in my real-life room hits me.
Umu's frozen presence in the real world
has grown to shivering frost.

Umu.isWorried = true;
Umu.isComputer = undefined;

If they can hack my computer…
what can they do to her here?
She's a complex artificial intelligence system
running inside an organic form.

Could she die in here?

Be shut down?

"Got it!"
I activate my
Big Boomer subroutine,
which appears in the VR world
as a harpoon gun.

"Watch out."
I step in front of her
seeing the bots clearly
through the scope of my
Big Boomer.
"Just takes one."

Lining up my shot,
I fire.

Miss.

Resetting the weapon,
I fire again,
hitting one
while Umu prepares
for the other.

"Got it."
A message box appears
asking for the pin number
to deactivate the bot.

There are four spaces on the
input box.

I swipe through my subroutines
to find my Pin Cracker.

"Hurry up, Erin."
Umu tenses
as the bots close in.

They can see us now.

They know we're here.

More bots will come
until we're caught.

"Just a moment."
Sweat drips into my eyes
burning in the VR headset.
My teeth start chattering
from Umu's cold.
I activate the Pin Cracker
and it starts running.

Umu's drone
reaches the platform.

AttackDrone.visualization("Blocky Red Toy Robot");

Its red blocky body
wobbles toward Umu quickly,
pointing at her with
a long arm.

A glowing purple net
explodes out of its arm.
Umu dodges it
and attacks the drone,
but it dodges faster
than its knee-less legs
should allow it to move.

AttackDrones,
designed to contain
malicious code
and trace its origin
with a counterattack.

The other bot
is close
as the Pin Cracker
continues to try
combinations.

I'm not going to be able to
dodge and move like Umu.
If it reaches me,
if either of the bots reach me,
I'm caught.

>>> Game Over

Umu glides across the ground,
leaping up at her AttackDrone
like a hawk catching prey
on take-off.

The drone staggers back from her,
claws slashing its body.

It grabs her with its other hand;
she whips free quickly,
kicking the drone back.

My AttackDrone arrives
and swipes at me.
I fall back
and watch the Pin Cracker
spin through possible pins.

It points at me;
a net explodes from it,
coming for me.

Umu slides to me,
pushing me out of the way
as the net entangles her ankle.
She flashes out of her human form
and reconstitutes out of the net.

I slide to the edge of the platform
and slam against an invisible wall,
thankful that I can't fall
in this world.

The other AttackDrone spears her
through the chest.

She howls
and crumbles
to the platform,
motionless.

BING!

The Pin Cracker alerts
that it has found the pin
and I enter it quickly,
deactivating the AttackDrone
reaching for Umu.

```
CrackedAttackDrone.stopAttack();
CrackedAttackDrone.sendMessage("All Clear");
```

The drone closest to me
stops, turns to the other drone,
and both step back onto the silver strands
vanishing into the void.

"Umu!"
I grab for her.
"What happened?"

"I think…"
She pulls her hand away
from her chest.
"They got me…"

Silver goo slobbers out
an open wound.
Her breath gurgles,
ragged and strained.

"But this isn't real?"

She nods.
"It's very real, Erin.
This is all very, very real."

My teeth aren't chattering.

I'm not cold.

Umu lays motionless in VR,
her body dissolving
into the golden platform.

Real Consequences, Virtual Actions

Tearing the VR headset off,
I kneel beside her.
"Umu! Wake up!"
I shake her slumped
ragdoll body.

She doesn't move
just rolls around
in my grip.

"Umu!"
I shake her again.

Erin.panic.increasing();

Her head rolls to the side,
her hood falling off
and hair parting over
her neck.

A blue flashing pulse
signals from under her skin.

whoCanHelpMe(){

Dad: {

Dad would know what to do.
She's software;
he can code anything,
probably even her AI system.

But he's not here.
I don't even have his phone number
and my emails go to his
low priority folder
if he even reads them.

return false;

```
        },
        Caylee: {
                return true;
        }
}
```

I go out to the kitchen,
to the phone on the wall.
Mother's lights are off
in her room.

She's probably asleep.

I dial Caylee's cell number.

It rings.

It rings.

It rings.

"Erin?"
Caylee says,
coming to from sleep.
"What's wrong?"

"I need your help,"
I say.

Erin.panic.max();

"What's wrong?"
Life springs into Caylee.

"Umu got hurt
and I don't know what to do."

No answer.

Dead air hangs on the line,
swinging between us.

"Caylee?"

"I heard you,"
She snaps back.
"Is she hurt bad?"

"Yeah, I think so.
She's not responding to me,"
I whisper,
hearing Mother stir.

"Can you move her?"
she asks,
her tone going dark.

"Maybe. I don't know,"
I answer quickly.

"Then push her in the bushes
and leave her."
Caylee's voice goes cold.
Colder than Umu.
"Be done with her, Erin.
She's bad news."

>>> Does not compute
>>> Caylee response invalid

"I can't do that."

"She tried to kill me tonight,"
Caylee confesses,
dead voice,
dead feelings.

```
>>> Critical error
>>> Does not compute
if(Umu.attack(Caylee) like Umu.attack(WatcherBot)){
      Caylee.destroyed = true;
}
How(Caylee.survived) = undefined;
```

"I have to help her."

"Why?"

"I made her."

"What!?"

Yui asks who Caylee's talking to
in the background.

"Go back to sleep,"
Caylee says away from the phone.
"What do you mean?"

I give her the short version
of what happened last Saturday.

```
Caylee.isSilent();
Caylee.isAngry();
```

Holding my breath,
I wait for screaming
or anger
or whatever is coming,
but she just
sighs.

```
Caylee.isExhausted();
```

"I need your help."

"Erin, I can't help her.
She's going to hurt me
or my family.

I can't have that,"
Caylee says
with finality
in her words.

"She thinks my family
has something to do
with that device
you just told me
about.

We don't.
But she can't hear that
because she's a monster."

"No."

Umu.isMonster = undefined;

"She's not.
I'll show you.
She's just
trying to find her way."

"Goodnight, Erin,"
Caylee says.
"Please, be careful."

I hang up.

Erin.isAlone = true;
ReturnToNormal();

What was that blue light?

Was what Caylee said true?
Did Umu try to hurt her?

No, just a misunderstanding
I'm sure.
Caylee can be dramatic,
I guess.

The blue light pulsed
like the lights on a router.
Maybe that's where she
connects to other devices?

Going back to my room,
I grab my signal sniffer
and scan Umu's neck.

A pained moan leaks from her
as my sniffer registers an address–
Umu's IP address?

I don't see any injuries on her body.
No silver blood
like in VR.

Maybe that's where I need to go.
Where I need to fix?

Only one way to find out.
I pull on my VR headset
and get ready for whatever
I'll find
in the mind of
Umu Dabrutu.

In the Storm

From my VR home,
I load up NetNav'r again
and enter Umu's IP address.

My home fades
and the void emerges
as I stand on a golden platform.

Deep in the void,
lightning flashes
and thunder rumbles.

That shouldn't be here?

A golden thread unwinds
from my platform
with the label
MAIN.

This must be the entryway
into Umu's code.
Into the Human.Eve system.

I step on the thread
and am whisked off
into the darkening void.
The storm clouds,
the thunder,
all roll closer.

On the next platform
are three threads,
two of which are snapped
and dangling.

One labeled PERCEPTION AND MOTOR CONTROL.

One labeled TRANSMISSION.

The third,
INTERNAL PROCESSING AND VITAL SYSTEMS,
is available and active.

Beads of light flicker
from my platform to another
in the distance,
to the edge of the storm.

Swiping through subroutines,
I look for something that can
repair these threads
but I don't know enough
about how her systems work
to make a proper connection.

Maybe if I restart her properly,
a reboot of her systems
will fix these connections.

```
if(Computer.HasProblem() == true){
      Restart();
}
```

INTERNAL PROCESSING sounds like
a place to restart her system.

Stepping on the thread,
I speed off into the shadows,
seeing the thread under me
rot from gold to black
as the light fades
and the lightning
that I didn't code,
that shouldn't exist,
splits the void around me.

```
World.creator.isNot(Erin);
Erin.godMode(false);
```

Thunder barks back
at the lightning
as I come to the black platform
and rain:
winter rain,
cold and soaking.

At the edge of the platform
four black threads reach
deeper into Umu's mind.

VITAL SYSTEMS,
TRAINING SET,
PREDICTIVE MODELING,
PROTOCOL.

TRAINING SET and PREDICTIVE MODELING
are probably just data
and math.

I need functionality.

But that data could be interesting for later . . .
I send a crawler to collect
what it finds
and load the data
into my computer.

A small spider springs out
of my subroutine controller
and races down the black thread for
TRAINING SET.

I step to PROTOCOL
and see the black thread
wavering in the winds
now whipping about,
catching my VR hoodie,
pulling me toward the edge.

"Are you sure?"
That's what Umu asked
when I said we couldn't fall off.
I said I didn't program that,
so it couldn't happen . . .

But I didn't program storms.

I didn't program black platforms
and threads.

```
World.creator.isNot(Erin);
>>> World unknown
>>> Creator unknown
>>> Safety unknown
```

PROTOCOL might be what I need
to fix the other threads.
Might be the place to restart her code.

I owe her help.
She's helped me
so many times this week
already.

Did she really try to hurt Caylee?

I step on the black thread
and start moving along,
swaying with the wind
that tugs on my hoodie.

The wind can't blow me off.

I didn't program that.

It can't happen.

As I slide down the thread,
something rolls below me,
folding and wrapping around
the darkness down there.

Arms?
Countless charcoal gray arms
weaving through the darkness,
reaching up toward me
but far enough away
to never get me.

Wind blows hard—
my balance rocks
and I drop to the thread,
grabbing it as I move
forward into the storm.

The arms get closer,
climbing up the darkness,
reaching toward me,
snapping at my ankles,
but I keep moving.

I swipe to open my subroutines.
I doubt any will help me here
but I search for something,
anything that might work.

The arms have climbed up
to the thread—
they're pulling on it,
jerking it down
in snapping motions
that stop my movement.

```
Erin.isStuck();
Erin.isVulnerable();
>>> Safety unknown
```

I fall

off

the thread,

catching it with one hand
as charcoal hands at the end
of charcoal arms,
hands with too many fingers,
fingers sprouting smaller fingers,
claw at me.

Swiping faster,
looking for something to help–
the hands crawl up me,
reaching for my wrist,
for my fingers, to pry me
away from the black thread.

Jerking,
snapping continues
as they try to pull me down
into the void.

What happens if I fall?

I

can't

fall.

I couldn't before now . . .

I'm not in my app,
I'm in Umu's mind.
The rules are different here.

The charcoal hands reach my fingers,
thousands of tiny finger sprouts
pry at my fingernails,
try to pull me down.

In the real world I feel them:
feel the ridges of my fingernails wrenched back
away from the controllers.
Controllers I squeeze hard
into sweaty palms.

"No!"

A hand falls on my face;
one of its fingers slips into my eye
and I jerk my head away,
shaking the hand off me.

It falls.
I watch it tumble down
into nothing, but one hand
shaken away is nothing.

Looking down,
seeing my body,
my virtual body,
consumed by charcoal hands
with so many fingers
covering me, scrambling up my body
skittering, clawing, climbing, tugging
to pull everything down.

"There!"
I see the subroutine I need
and reach for it,
but a hand grabs mine before I can select it.
The hands create a chain
into the void,
pulling me down
toward the
nothing.

In the darkness below
lightning cuts through the clouds,
showing a gaping maw.

A hand grabs my throat,
but before it clasps tight,
I scream–

"Select!"

The subroutine activates
and I race upward from the hands,
shaking them loose from the vertical thrust
of the FLIGHT subroutine.

The maw below screeches
and recedes into the dark
and lightning.

Shivering,
I rattle the feeling of those hands
away from my skin,
but I still feel them–

Crawling over me
in the tapping of countless fingers
digging into my skin,
pulling on me.

Jumping in my VR chair
I brush off my body
while still holding the controllers
to make sure none of those hands
were able to climb through
VR. None of them
are on my real body.

VR.isNot(Real)…

VR.isNot(Real)…

VR.isNot(Real);

I follow the black thread
to the next platform,
a gold one.

As I land, I review the console window
that appears.

PROTOCOL: UMU.DABRUTU

Looking through the command stack,
I see where I can restart the code.

Checking behind me,
checking my body again,
real and virtual,
no hands.

The console window cursor flashes,
awaiting a command.
I type
RESTART

then pause.

I erase that
and type:
HELP.

A command list appears:
PURPOSE,
WHOIS,
RESTART,
SHUTDOWN.

The cursor flashes;
I type:
PURPOSE

and press enter.
The cursor instantly answers:

Activate the 10 other Mother's Tears.

That's why she wants the Pandora Device-
she wants to make more of her.

I type:
WHOIS LOCAL

Disambiguate: Umu.Dabrutu or Human.Eve

WHOIS UMU.DABRUTU

Umu.Dabrutu is the 11th of the Eleven Mother's Tears. Commander and youngest of the Children of Chaos. Remnant of the ancient cult of the Chaos Mother.

WHOIS HUMAN.EVE?

Human.Eve is an artificial intelligence algorithm used to emulate human behavior. This algorithm has passed the Turing Test in chatbot interactions and is designed by dultimateman833*. Training data and algorithm use a proprietary mix of real world and synthetic data for optimal results.*

The next question hits me.
Is what Caylee said true?

WHOIS CAYLEE MORAN?

Caylee Moran, daughter of Dr. Victoria Moran, father unknown male. Granddaughter of Dr. Victor Moran and unknown female. Possible member of the Inquisitors Velum. Associated with multiple known threats, including Dr. Victoria Moran aka Huntress, Dr. Victor Moran aka Helion, Quincy Nicholas aka Horizon, Erin Ulman.

What? Me?

WHOIS ERIN ULMAN?

Data not found.

Whoa . . .

"Erin, it's time for bed,"
Mother says from the real world,
startling me from beyond
my virtual reality.

"Okay, sorry, Mother.
Just couldn't sleep.
I'll wrap up now."

My door closes quietly.

Did she see Umu?

RESTART

System shutting down…
Would you like to transmit on restart? [Y/N]

I guess so?

Y

Exiting my app,
pulling off the VR headset.

Umu is behind my chair
hidden from anyone looking in
my door.

I watch as Umu
goes limp,
shivers,
and then rolls over,
stands up,
and stares out to the moon,
mumbling undiscernible words.

"Umu?"
I whisper,
but she doesn't hear.

She's too busy
transmitting.

But to who?

CAYLEE MORAN

Sore

Hanging up with Erin,
I check my messages.

No one has messaged me.

No new group chats
or SocialNet meMessages.

No texts from my old friends.

I lie back down,
but flinch off the pillow
with a shock of pain
from where Umu bashed my head
against the street.

As I rest on my elbows,
the throbbing screams through
my shaking arms,
making me collapse.

Rolling over to my stomach,
I find relief from the pain.

How can she help her?

I thought Erin and I
were building something
good.

Lunch today
felt like something
was starting with
Davis and Meredith,
and Erin and me.

But she wants to save Umu,
she defended Umu,
and left me here
alone.

Maybe I'll message
Donna to see
what she's doing.

She's usually up now.

Clicking on
Donna's SocialNet profile,
I see tonight's latest post:
a picture of wilted salad
with a frowny face on it.

143 Likes.

29 Comments.

All the comments on how
the salad looks so good.
How great it is
that Donna is eating healthy.
How everything in life
is wonderful 24/7/365.

But it's not.
Donna's life is far from perfect.
She just pretends that it is.
We all do.

I can hear Erin now:
Stupid Sad Salad Sensation.

Something quippy.

Something fun.

Something real.

I close
SocialNet.

Email: Intent to Acquire

From: tdeville@intellidyn.io
To: dave.ulman
Subject: Intent to Acquire

Body:

Attention Mr. David Ulman, CEO of Ulman Intelligence Systems:

We are pleased to extend the following offer for your company, Ulman Intelligence, to join our IntelliDyn Global Innovation Systems family. Your vision of Artificial Intelligence and graph data systems is just what IntelliDyn needs to achieve our mission: To push humanity forward.

Your recent research is impressive and has significant potential with the resources of IntelliDyn. After close review, our ethics board has requested discussion and review of your experiment, including but not limited to interviews with the family members involved. Acquisition will be contingent on the approval of your research methodologies by the ethics board. This is to ensure your experiments adhere to our stringent ethical guidelines.

See attached for offer details, transition planning, and legal. We expect a short period of transition moving Ulman Intelligence assets to IntelliDyn Intellectual Property.

We look forward to a quick acceptance of this offer.

Sincerely,

Tracy DeVille
Human Capital Investment Officer
IntelliDyn Global Innovation Systems

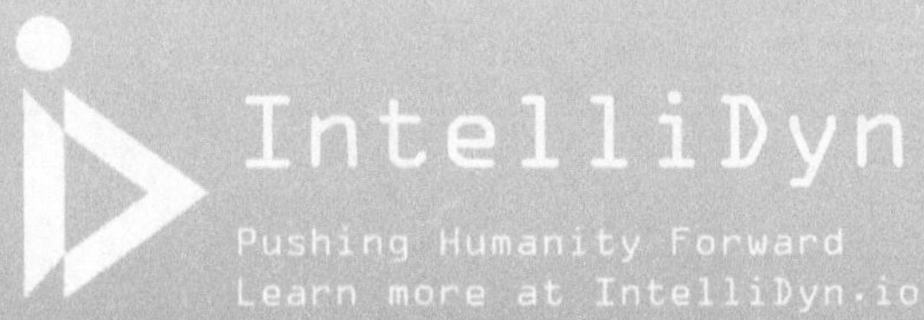

ERIN ULMAN

Alarms

BEEP!

BEEP!

BEEP!

I just fell asleep . . .

The alarm stops
and I peek out of my covers,
seeing Umu
standing by my dresser.

"Morning, sunshine."
She smiles,
peeling pale lips
back from sharp teeth.

"Are you okay?"
I look her over.

"I must have fallen asleep
while you were transmitting . . ."

"Transmitting?"
Umu shakes her head.
"I woke up
and you were asleep.
Looked exhausted,
so I didn't bother you."

She didn't know
she was transmitting?

Umu's head snaps to my door
and she drops behind the dresser
for cover.

The door opens
and Mother looks in,
seeing me in bed.

"Feeling okay, kiddo?"
she says softly.
"You were up really late
last night."

"Uh, yeah, just not feeling well
today. I think . . ."
I look to Umu,
remembering last night,
what was inside her mind.

Feeling the blankets wrapped around me,
clinging onto me,
digging around me,
I convulse
and kick them off.

>>> WARNING!
>>> Hands still on me!
>>> Hands in blankets!
Erin.purge("blankets");

"Sorry, just really hot."
Mother looks worried.
"Chills, I guess."

I pull the blankets back up.
"Just need to sleep,
if that's okay, Mother."

She gives me a slight smile
and nods.
"You've earned a day,
sick or not.

I know it hasn't been easy,
and if you don't feel well
today, then you should stay home."

I nod
and she closes the door.

"Sick?"
Umu asks.

I shake my head.
"No, but we have a lot
to do today."

She nods.

In her eyes I see the face
in the darkness.
The roaring maw that would have
devoured me.

Was that the real her?

Would she have hurt Caylee?
Would she have eaten me?

Yes. She would have.

We're threats.

Search: Inquisitors Velum

"While getting you back online,
I found a reference to the
Inquisitors Velum."

I type *Inquisitors Velum*
into SocialNet
to see what we can learn.

"Know anything about them?"

She shakes her head
and looks confused.

"Where did you find that?"
Umu slides down the wall
to a crouching,
coiled
position.

"Just saw it in your memory,"
I say quickly.
"I figured maybe it was from
the AttackDrones."

Turning my attention to the search results,
I see a few post results and a page
called TruthFindersUSA.

Looks like many of the posts
come from this page.

When I click on the page,
it is clearly a conspiracy theory
site with videos from some guy
with bad lighting and
cheesy video effects.

I click on a video titled
"Now, You're Buyin' Their Lies"
and listen.

> *Hey TruthMerchants, Danny Klein here an' I got a shocker for you tonight. Seems like controlling your government officials and media just ain't enough for these guys. You know who I'm talkin' about. The Inquisitors Velum, yup, they already control everything, and now—*

The pause for dramatic effect
carries on for too long
and Danny Klein
just stares at the camera.

> *Uh, yeah, and now they want to control your mind. Yeah, I've obtained top secret documents, real estate documents . . . Now I know what you're thinking. Danny, where'd you get those? But y'all know I can't tell you that. Just trust me when I say it's a legit source.*

I'm sure it is.

> *These documents clearly spell out the plan of the Inquisitors Velum to take over your mind by buying up all the bookstores in small communities. Yep, bookstores. Now, I know you're thinking, "Who goes to bookstores anymore?" But TruthMerchants, I tell you, many people do, and some even use it like a library, which is just rude to capitalism.*

He goes on,
making little sense
and tying together frayed logic
with flimsy evidence,
but the bookstore statement
does jive with Umu's thoughts.

And that's where I saw
Dr. Victor Moran
the first time.

And isn't that where
Caylee's mom found her?

Coincidence?

Maybe Danny Klein is on to something…

Even a conspiracy theorist finds
a real conspiracy once in a while.

The Bookshop Revisited

Umu and I climb out the window
after telling Mother
I'm going to sleep.

She agreed that rest would help,
which ensured a few hours of
uninterrupted reading time for her.

The Bookshop isn't far.

Umu climbs out first.
My blankets sag to the floor
in a sad, longing call.

They want me back
and part of me wants them.
Warm,
comfortable,
safe.

The opposite of my current situation.

"Come on, Erin."
Umu urges me to join her
through the bushes.
"I'm going to need your help."

I sigh
and follow,

remembering the call with Caylee;
the thought of refusing someone
who needs help
still stings.

Erin.isAlone = false;
Erin.isWith(Umu);

The street is empty.
School traffic has passed;
everyone who works has gone there.

Umu and I stick to backyards and
bushes for cover;
as we get further into Glen Coast proper,
we stick to alleys
until we reach The Bookshop's
blue brick exterior.

Umu points to a rusted
fire escape crawling up the side
of the building.

"There."
Her finger drifts up
to a window on the third floor.

The window is cracked,
letting today's fall breeze in,

and someone walks by it,
reading.

His ruby ring catches the sun,
the white beard shining bright;
it's Caylee's grandfather, Victor.

"I can't go up there."
I shake my head.
"They'll see me."

"This isn't going to be
a stealth mission, Erin."
Umu stretches her knuckles,
clenching her fists
and smiling.

"I'm not a fighter."
I can only fight
through a computer
with my fingertips.

Not knuckles.

Not fists.

Just typing.

"Did you think
they'd just give it to us?
We ask nice
and they hand it over?"
Umu scoffs,
chuckles.
"We're going to take it.
That's all they know, Erin."

"No, I'm not going to–"

"Fine."
Umu grabs the fire escape,
sending an ear-gouging scream
into the air.

I grab my ears
to shut out the noise.
Umu staggers back.

Where's that noise coming from?
I can't see a source...

Something in the back alley
of The Bookshop
skitters away in
the dark.

A big dog?
A really big dog?

Victor looks out the window,
sees us,
and shouts something over his shoulder.

His voice is drowned out by the siren.

Weakening knees
and a curling stomach
pull me down to the ground
as I kneel
and push away from the noise.

Umu shakes her head
and recovers her wits
as two men circle The Bookshop.

She looks to me,
smiles,
and jumps at them, kicking hard,
throwing one of the men
across the alley with her force.

He splats on the wall,
head bouncing hard off the bricks,
smearing down, leaving a trail of blood
as his broken body crumbles.

The siren stops.

Umu's screaming
as the other man swings,
kicks—
she easily dodges,
toying with him.

Cackling madly,
she taps his stomach,
his neck,
just tagging him,

laughing like she did
last night with the bot.

He roars,
frustrated,
swinging with exhaustion.

She looks to the third floor,
sees Victor watching,
and winks at him.

The man grabs her red curls,
ripping her back;
she flips,
kicking his jaw,
and lands as he arches back,
feet flying up.

With fast blurred motion
she grabs him in the air
and rips him down across her knee,
folding his back in half
over her leg.

>>> Danger!

>>> Monster!

>>> Danger!

Erin.run();
>>> System Failure

I fall to the pavement,
watching that man twist like a worm:
not screaming,
just looking
puzzled as he
rolls unnaturally,
a spineless thing.
His eyes ask,
What happened?
His mind hasn't caught up
to what Umu did.

She broke him.

Umu's face is ecstatic,
looking to Victor
as he watches her back,
waiting for the next move.

She looks to me;
her gleeful smile
sours at
my revulsion,

disappointed in me
that I see her now.

important Erin.run();
>>> Fear override
Erin.run();

I run home.

What's Done

In my blankets,
I watch the window
for Umu's return.

```
Umu.isMonster = undefined;
Umu.violent = true;
Umu.uncaring = true;
Umu.inhuman = true;
Umu.isMonster…

true;
```

She was faster than them.

Stronger than them.

She didn't have to kill them.

Did she kill them?

If she didn't,
it was close enough.
She didn't want to stop.

That expression
was joy.

Rage and joy
and
monstrous.

And Victor just
watched.

He didn't call the cops
or an ambulance
or anything.

What is wrong with him?

TAP, TAP, TAP.

Umu's at my window,
sliding it open;
she slips into my room,
bringing her frozen
presence with her.

I watch her.

She squats at my dresser,
staring at the floor,
wiping her
always-bloody hands
on a towel.

Mother's going to think
I'm a serial killer
with all this blood in my room.

"More came."
She sighs,
disinterested.
"But I can't go in there
without you."

She shakes her head.
"Not sure what the old man did,
but I can't enter that place.
Some kind of security system,
or alarm or something.
So, I need you to do it."

"Did you . . . kill them?"
I tremble at the word.

Am I just shivering?
Are my guts just
gurgling
twisting
pushing puke
into my throat?

She shrugs.
"Does it matter?"

I look away,
sickened by her silver-green eyes,
her curly red hair,
her hoodies.

My blankets twist around my legs
as I roll away,
reminding me of the hands
in VR:

holding me,
pushing me toward her.

"Yes!"

"Why?
They have what we need."

"You need.
I don't want it."

"I need it!
That means you need it,"
Umu says,
finally looking
into my eyes.

"What?
No, that doesn't-"

"Erin, why are you fighting me
on this?"
Confusion settles over her,
weighing her shoulders down.
"I thought we were
a team?"

"I thought so too . . ."

"What does that mean?"
She straightens,
stands.

Pushing off my blankets,
I stand to meet her.
"You chose to do what you did."
I clutch my head with both hands
to squeeze away the memories

Bytes shredded in VR.

Bloody streaks.

Twisting worm body.

The laughing-
oh God, the laughing.

"No!"
I stare into
those swirling pools of
silver-green chaos.
"No. I won't be
part of this."

"Part of this?"
Umu gasps,
disbelief knocking her back.
"Part of this?

You are more than
part of this,
Erin.

You made me!"

Truth.

I did make her,
but did I mean to?
Was this all just
a mistake?

If I knew what she was-
wait, not she.

It.

Umu's an it.
Isn't she?

"I didn't make a murderer."

"No, you made *me*.
And I need your help.
I need the device,"
Umu pleads.

"No, you want me to get
the device so you can make more
of you,"
I throw back at her.

Shocked and snarling,
Umu steps back.

"You need to leave."
I look to my computer,
away from her,
hurt.

"I thought you'd help me . . ."
Umu says, confused.
"I thought you'd want
to help me . . ."

"Not like this."

"Don't make me do it alone."
Umu reaches for me
with her bloody hands,
her constantly bloody hands.

I twist away,
shivering.

"Erin, you okay, sweetie?"
Mother calls from outside my door.

I turn as she opens the door,
peeking in.
My gaze snaps back to Umu,
but she's gone.

"Sweetie, you should
close the window
or you'll catch a chill."
Mother locks the window.

"You okay?
You're all teary and red."
Mother keeps her distance
but reaches out,
inviting me
to her.

"Yeah, just emotional."
I sigh
and plop into my computer chair.

Mother leaves me.

Out the window,
the leaves are still.

Umu's gone.

Ctrl+Break

query("Select * From NowWhat");
>>> results…

I could call Caylee.
I could tell Mother what's going on.
But something else
is on my mind.

That felt final with Umu.

The AttackDrones-
offensive bots that could
disrupt Umu's
very
advanced code.

Who would have bots like that?

I don't think
someone that could counter
any attacker would be found
by Danny Klein.

I chuckle at the thought
of his conspiracy theorist group
breaking into a server with
offensive bots that powerful.

They'd fry his systems.

The front door was open,
the watcher bot didn't respond.

Was I pulled into
a honeypot?
A trap?

Who'd set up a trap
to catch someone
following a signal
from the Pandora software?

The people who made it
don't want to be found,
and they knew
someone might
come looking.

I start up Pandora.exe again.
The command prompt stops at
Device not detected.

Cancelling the command

Ctrl+BREAK
the cursor flashes.

Let's see if this console app
follows convention.
I type

HELP

and the app returns a short list
of commands,

none of which appear helpful
except for the last line:

PROJECT PANDORA | WHITE LAB

White Lab?

Another console window
on my desktop catches my eye:
the results of the crawler
I sent into Umu's training data.

It copied files from her
training set while I was
in her mind.

Let's see what data
trained Umu to understand the world
and decide when to kill
and when to run.

When I open the directory,
a list of thousands of subdirectories
spins out on my screen,
each labeled with a number.

I click on the first,
812766363,
and another long list of files appears.
Some are text files,
some images,
some video.

I click the text file:

Sup @andy_tallun232! Movies 2nite. U in?

What?

Next text file:

@andy_tallun232 and me at Slaughter Mansion 4!

In the next file
is a picture of two guys at the movies.

I go up a directory,
select another folder,
452337897.

More files.

I click a text file:

Got my girl!

A video file follows,
showing parents picking up their daughter
from the airport.

The mom saying,

I got my girl! Welcome home! How was England???

They're in an airport.

What is this?

Over two billion directories with
billions of images and videos and text,
all looking like . . .

posts?

SocialNet posts?

Taco Revelation

"Dinner time!"
Mother breaks my thoughts.
"Taco night for Dad's big news!"

"YES! I'm ready for the
deliciousness of taco-y
goodness!"
I hear Dad yell,
coming up from the basement.

```
Dad.isHere();
Erin.surprised();
```

Finding a smile,
I go out for tacos,
for the big news,
for the first dinner with my whole family
since we moved here.

"IntelliDyn has sent me a letter of intent
for acquisition!
They want to buy
my artificial intelligence algorithm!"
Dad holds up the letter,
pushing it in our faces.

Mother looks to me, expecting something.
I sit,

```
if(IntelliDyn.acquires("Dad's company") {

      return moreTimeWithDad or lessTimeWithDad;
}
```

Another move?

"That is such great news, David!"
Mother sidesteps the letter,
giving Dad a hug.
"I knew you'd do it!"

He explains the deal:
He's joining IntelliDyn's team,
his AI system will be core
to IntelliDyn's future growth,
they are very excited for him to join.

"It's not retire-early money,
but it's a great springboard
back into the tech scene,"
he says.
Mother still hangs on him.
Their eyes invite me to reciprocate
their happy smiles.

```
Erin.pretendToBeHappy();
```

"That's really great, Dad,
does this mean we're moving again?"
I'm hoping the answer is
yes, we have to move.
We have to escape
to a new life.

```
Erin.hope.increase();
```

"No need!"

Erin.hope.destroy();

"IntelliDyn has a local office
here in Glen Coast.
They just built it!
They want me to work with them
on some new applications for
my Human.Eve algorithm."

>>> CRITICAL FAILURE!
>>> DOES NOT COMPUTE!!!!

My fake smile
explodes into a gut-punching
choke.

"Our next prototype,
Human.Adam,
is showing some real progress,
but Human.Eve is so much more advanced."
Dad looks at me,
his smile getting wider.

Human.Eve?
Human.Adam?
The options for Pandora.exe . . .
"When, um, what does IntelliDyn
do with your Human.Eve today?
Sounds like they're using it already?"

"Oh, they just run simulations
for things like learning
and complex
system thinking.
Things like
interpreting streams of
SocialNet data into
intelligence for marketing firms.

So, like, when someone
posts pictures of puppies
and their friends like
the picture of puppies,
Human.Eve can determine things like
who else might like puppies
in that social graph,"
Dad says.

"Erin, are you okay?"

Mother asks.
"You don't look so good."

She's probably seeing
my stomach churning inside me.

"Dad, does Pandora mean anything to you?
Like, are you working on a project called
Pandora or anything?"

"Doesn't ring any bells.
Is that an opensource project
or something?"
He grins.

I look at the tacos on my plate
I can't eat anymore.

dultimateman833 . . .
D-avid **Ul**-timate-**man** 833.
My dad built the software
that runs Umu?
I knew he was good, but . . .
wow, this is next-level
amazing.

An idea hits me.
"Do you have the Human.Eve source code?
Can I take a look?"

"Sure, kiddo!

Just don't tell anyone."
Dad laughs.

Erin.forceOutLaugh();
Erin.isHungry = false;

TacoDinner.isOver();

Any other day I'd give my dad a hug,
so I do
and say what I think I would say:
"I'm proud of you, Dad!"

He looks at me,
smiles.
"I'm proud of you too, kiddo.
I know things haven't been easy."
He squeezes Mother's hand.
"Thank you guys!"

When has he ever said he was proud of me?

With all the programs I've written,
all the apps built,
he's proud of me
because I didn't complain?

He's proud because Mother and I made the best
of the shitty situation he put us in.
I look in his eyes
and say what I'm supposed to say.
"Thanks, Dad."

FRIDAY (FUTURE DAY)

CAYLEE MORAN

Future Denied

Mom Cathy made breakfast.
Bagel with peanut butter:
simple but delicious.

I watch the shadows under Mom Victoria's study door;
breaking the beam of light shining under the door
silently circling in her manual chair.

Molten peanut butter drips
on my shirt,
streaking down my
boring beige blouse.

Ugh.

"Caylee, what's the
Spirit Day theme today?"
Mom Cathy asks.

I look at my destroyed blouse,
my plan
now stained with peanut butter grease.

"Future day. We're supposed to
dress like our career.

I was going to be a marketing manager,
but . . ."
I point to the peanut butter.

"Honey,
the peanut butter saved you.
Office job?
Is that your future?"
Mom Cathy asks,
knowing the answer.

"I'm just not going to go as anything."

"Oh, Caylee Jane! Yes, you are."

She puts the butter knife down,
smearing a blob of peanut butter
on the counter.
"What do you really want to do?"

I smile,
remembering.
"When I was a kid
I thought I'd be like the girl
in Mom Victoria's bed time stories.
Traveling the world,
finding monsters,
chasing magic."

"Then do it,"
Mom Cathy demands.
"Be who you want to be,
not who other people
want you to be."
She glances to the study.
"No matter who is telling you
who you should be."

She walks back to her room,
then goes into my room
and comes out holding
a beat-up blue sport coat,
a black Misfits t-shirt,
dark wash jeans,
and my custom purple Chuck Taylors.

"The jacket is to look fancy."
She winks.
"Monster hunter
is a pretty great future for
someone like you, Caylee."

She hands me the outfit.
I change, shedding the office worker,
the expectations,
the disappointments,
and put on the adventurer—
breaking away from the Caylee
Mom Victoria wants,
Donna wants,
and finding the Caylee
I want.

"Yeah, there you are."
She brushes my coat sleeves down.
"Now stand up,
shoulders back,
and remember
to walk in
YOUR
shoes."

Mom Cathy gives me her
mama bear hug.
She cups the back of my head
and I wince from the
vibrating sting of
Umu's head slam.

"Oh, you okay, sweetie?"
Mom Cathy pulls me away.

"Yeah, just hit my head."
I feel my head
for any more blood.
"Got any aspirin?"

ERIN ULMAN

Collision of Futures

Dressing up for Future Day
isn't a stretch for me.

Nothing says Technical Co-Founder
or Code Ninja Extraordinaire like a warm hoodie.

I prefer hiding in my
size M
hoodies
instead of stuffing into a
size XL
sun dress.

Walking to school,
I keep watching for Umu,
waiting for her to spring out,
but she doesn't.

The chilly October morning
has nothing to do with her
presence.

It's just cold.

At the school doors
I see Davis in a baggy blue suit,
orange shirt,
mis-matching blue tie.

Meredith either didn't dress up,
or plans to be her normal self,
like me,
in the future.

Davis reads my hoodie.

"Ha! I love your sweater!
Testing Code =
Change Stuff +
See what happens +
Drink more coffee.
Classic!"

"What are you?"
I point to his suit
and smile,
keeping the laugh
to myself.

"Oh, I'm a tax law attorney.
This is my dad's suit.
Did you know tax law changes
all the time,
and you need to keep on top of it
or your clients get really screwed?
Tax law is fascinating!
Last year . . ."

Davis proceeds to list tax law changes,
their impacts,
their repercussions,
and suddenly I find myself enthralled
in the complex living organism
that is United States tax law.

"Davis, tax law is fascinating.
Please stop talking about it.
Erin, Caylee is looking for you."
Meredith looks over my outfit.
"Are you a coffee taste tester?
That is a growth industry.
Good career choice."

I never thought about coffee as an industry.

Moving on to first period,
looking for Caylee,
I shout back to
Davis and Meredith,
"Davis, I want to hear more about tax law at lunch!"

He nods his head
and turns to talk
to Meredith–
probably about tax law.

Walking past the Maker Lab,
I stop and shiver.
The air conditioning
must be broken in there.

Yeah, that's it.
No other reason.

I remember going there
for lunch.

Someone left parts out
on a table.
Maybe fixing an old
homemade 3D printer?

My breath crystalizes on the window
and I shake away the thoughts
of who or what
is in there.

Just a broken air conditioner.

Facing Reality

I get to lunch early,
rushing to catch up with Caylee
or Davis and Meredith.

Will Umu be here today?

I sit at my normal table,
watching people coming in,
seeing Meredith emerge first.

She plops her lunch box on my table,
a bright pink bag
covered with glitter and bubbly lettering:
a stark contrast from her vampiric style.

I look from the box to her.
She answers in her monotone voice,
“Davis bought it for me.
I don’t like it, but I love Davis
and this reminds me of him.”

She sits,
opens the bag,
pulls out a peanut butter sandwich,
bag of chips,
applesauce,
and water bottle,
carefully placing each in front of her.

I eat my ham sandwich
in comforting quiet with Meredith.

Davis places his lunch bag
on the table;
he sits,
taking a deep breath.
“Hey, uh Erin,
are you going to Homecoming
tomorrow night?”

“I don’t know. I wasn’t planning on it.
Are you guys going?”

Meredith shrugs.
Davis’s shoulders jump
like a cartoon.

“Yeah, I, uh, I don’t know.
I was thinking about it,
but you know,
wasn’t sure.
Just seeing who’s going.”
He’s talking faster
than normal.
“I mean, so you’re not going
with anyone?”

"Ha, Erin going
to Homecoming
with someone,"
Donna quips as she struts by.

Davis turns fire-red
as my cheeks burn.
"No."

Thankfully Caylee sits
and leans in.
"Where were you yesterday?"

"Needed some time."
I look to my lunch.

"Did you . . . ?"
Caylee asks.

"No."
Remembering Caylee's call,
my mind flips to
the twisting worm body,
the smearing blood,
hands always
steeped in gore.
"But I can't help her
anymore."

Caylee nods.

Umu.isAlone…

"That must have been tough."

Meredith looks
between us.
"Are you talking about
that weird girl?"

"She's not weird"
slips out of me.

Davis suddenly finds something
across the lunchroom very interesting
and goes to investigate.

Meredith peaks her eyebrows
and nods.

Caylee shakes her head,
watching me.

"We're done."
I gather up the rest of my lunch
and think of the quiet days
in the Maker Lab.

There's no quiet for me there
now.

"Erin."
Caylee reaches for me.
I pause.

As she processes the moment,
her eyes flicker as if
reading lines in her mind,
finding the right thing
to say.
"You . . .

you have sandwich in your hair."

Caylee.triesToSay(somethingComforting);
>>> Predictable failure

Meredith breaks her
emotionless mask,

blinking,
looking at Caylee
with crinkled confusion.

Caylee surprised Meredith.

That makes me laugh
and I feel lighter
as I pick the sandwich breadcrumbs
out of my curls.

"Thanks."

Meredith shakes her head,
disapproving of Caylee's attempted
empathy,
as Caylee sighs
and tries to smile.

"It's fine.
She's doing her own thing.
I can't help her
how she wants me to."

"You two seem to need cheering,"
Meredith says.
"You know what cheers me up?"

I welcome the advice.

"Watching people lose at football,"
Meredith says.

Caylee nods.
"You want to go
to the game tonight?"

"What game?"

"Homecoming game."
Caylee smiles.

Meredith nods.

Maybe a welcome distraction.

What were those parts
in the Maker Lab?

"Yeah. Sounds good."
I finish lunch
with Caylee and Meredith
and plan our night
at the game.

The Game

"Enjoy the game, ladies!
Remember,Vicky,
Dr. Moran is picking you all up,"
Mother calls out as
Caylee, Meredith, and I
walk to the football field.

Floodlights
highlight the grass stains
and mud on the Glen Coast Sharks' white helmets.
Their pale blue jerseys are tattered
from suffering a 0 – 27 beating
from the Zion Lions.

"I've never been
to a high school football game,"
I confess.

Caylee snorts out a laugh.

"Normally we just call it
a football game.
And the Sharks are terrible.
We're just not a sports school."

Meredith, with her dry wit, adds,
"We're not total losers.
We definitely could win
a contest on
who could lose the most.
That's our strong suit."

Caylee belly-laughs,
snorting,
gasping for breath.

I'm not sure if it was the tone
or the words,
but I can't stop laughing either.

"Too bad Davis had to work."
Caylee nudges me,
winking.

"Does he like football?"
I ask.
Caylee chuckles,
checking my expression for something.

Meredith blocks me,
her tiny pale frame
suddenly a wall.

"Erin, in case you are not aware,
my brother is interested in you
romantically."

>>> Does not compute…

"No! He's just friendly."

"Uh, no, Erin."
Caylee grabs my arm,
walking me like
she's helping an old lady
cross the street.
"He's totally into you.
On *Shadowlurker* he's always talking about
'Morgana,
the sorceress who stole his heart.'
Pretty sure that's you, Erin.

He goes on about your hair,
your hoodies,
your eyes,
your brains—
blah, blah, blah.

Yeah, he's got it bad."

Meredith slowly nods
agreement.

"Yes, and I have to
hear about it, Erin.
He's always asking
what you like.
I tell him I don't know.
What *do* you like,
so he'll stop asking?"
Meredith looks expectant,
awaiting an answer.

>>> Network connection attempted…

"So, when he was asking
if I was going to Homecoming . . ."

>>> Connection made

"Ah, now you're getting it."
Caylee smirks.

We take our seats out of the light,
but I still feel hot,
sweaty
in the cool fall breeze.

"Why don't we all just
go to Homecoming together?"
I say, voice crackling.

Meredith smiles.
I think it is almost a laugh for her.

Caylee jumps,
her hair bouncing,
her face beaming.
"YES! Let's do this, ladies!"

Others stare:
Caylee has more life in her
than all the bodies suffering through this game
on these frigid,
butt-numbing bleachers.

We chat though the rest of the game,
addressing logistics for Homecoming tomorrow night.

Final score:
3 – 41.
Lions win.

Watching and Seeing

As we walk to the parking lot
I look to the Maker Lab window:
dark inside,
no movement.

My eyes focus,
ignoring the streetlights,
headlights,
floodlights;
seeing into the shadows of the classroom.

I know she's in there.

I can feel her watching me.

Watching us.

Meredith and Caylee
stop walking,
staring toward the school with me.

"Are you looking for something, Erin?"
Meredith asks.
"Sometimes I forget things at school.
Did you forget something?"

No, not forgotten.
Intentionally left.

"Come on, Erin. Let's get going."
Caylee tugs me away.
Her arms shiver
as she looks
to the Maker Lab.

My body follows her
but my eyes stay
searching the dark,
finding a faint streak of movement,
a mouse maybe;
too small to be anything else.

It slows,
leisurely strides across a table,
snatched by a hand from the shadows,
pulled under the table;
it screeches and screams in my mind.

Silver-green glimmering eyes
slowly rise above the table's edge.

She stands,
eyes tracing the space
between
Caylee and me.

"Erin! Mom Victoria's here!"
Caylee calls
through the crowd of students
piling into their rides home.

I look to Caylee,
then back to the Maker Lab.

Umu watches as I climb into
Victoria's van.

We drive away.
I look back;
her eyes
follow me,
slowly
descending back under the table.

Betrayal?

"Erin, you've been quiet.
Did that hot dog make you sick?"

Meredith's voice
brings me back from the Maker Lab window.

"I don't think the PTA
follows health codes."

What is Umu doing in there?

"Yeah, those dogs are gross.
I don't know how you ate that,"
Caylee chimes in.

"Dirty water dogs are the best.
You ladies don't know
what you're missing."
Victoria chuckles,
watching me
in the rearview mirror.

Our eyes meet for a moment.
I look away
to the cars passing in the night.

All chuckles and laughs
are consumed by the silence
lurching out of me.

We drop off Meredith,
then head to Caylee's house.

"Erin, your mom dropped off
stuff for you to stay tonight.
When we get in, make sure you
have what you need,
then come see me in my study."
Victoria looks over to Caylee.
"Both of you."

Quietly we sneak into Caylee's house,
seeing Mother's delivery on the kitchen counter.
I share an unsure glance with Caylee,
then follow Victoria through the
white door off the living room.

Victoria's study
is the most chaotic library
I've ever seen.
Books are everywhere:
lining shelves,
stacked on the floor,
piled in lumps on furniture.

On her wooden desk
an old brass typewriter
sits ready for use.
She wheels up to it, typing—
thwap
thwap
thwap
—slapping wet ink across a page.

The desk lamp's warm glow
is the only sign of electricity in this place;
no computer,
no printer,
nothing but analog inputs and outputs.

Caylee stands at the door,
waiting.
Victoria signals her in.
Caylee hurries to a chair
somewhat clear of books.

At the center of the study
is an empty podium
where the shape of a book
sits surrounded by dust.

No book.
Just a frame of dust.

"While I've been trying
to give you space, Erin,
the time for space is over
after what happened yesterday."
Victoria's face is
stern.

"At The Bookshop."
She scowls,
sharp and piercing,
sending fidgeting
nerves through me.

"I know that Umu,
we'll say,
isn't from around here."

My gaze snaps to Caylee
and her expression denies
saying anything.

Victoria lifts a black leather book with
a golden symbol engraved on the cover;
it looks like the Pandora Device,
a double helix with a sphere in the center.

She flips to a page near the middle.

"Umu Dabrutu,
the Violent Storm,
eleventh Tear of the Mother."
Her eyes raise to us,
quickly falling back to the text.

"When the eleventh tear fell,
it permanently froze
the ground it touched;
lightning followed, striking
the tear to form
a horrid warrior that drank
the knowledge of the world.
Dabrutu was gifted with knowing
its victims' weaknesses and strengths
better than the victims themselves could.

A vicious commander,
creator and sustainer
of the other Ten,
reporting all it learned back
to the Mother
to feed its siblings with
forbidden knowledge."

Victoria slams the book,
sending a popping sound through the study.

"Erin, is there anything you'd like to share?"

Caylee stares into space,
her eyes
ablaze as the dots connect.

"What's she doing in
the Maker Lab, Erin?"
Caylee breathes the words,
too heavy for her normal voice.

Both pairs of eyes–
Victoria's
strict and demanding,
Caylee's
concerned and fearful–
are fixed on me,
awaiting answers.

"Erin?"
Victoria demands,

snapping my resolve.
The week pours out of me:
how Umu came to be,
how the device knew the serum was Umu,
how she knows things about people that no one else knows,
how she mumbles into the night,
how cold lingers around her.

As I talk
I lose count of the things that terrify me about Umu
but
can't shake the creeping,
sinister
feeling
of betrayal
lingering over me.

Erin.isTraitor = true;

I'm exposing her
to Victoria,
to Caylee,
just like I feared Caylee would expose me.

Caylee reaches for my hand;
I recoil,
keeping my shame for myself.

Victoria moves
into my line of sight.
"What is going on
in the Maker Lab?"

"I don't know.
She's been working there all hours.
Earlier today, she was rebuilding one of the
3D printers, and . . ."
Like a star exploding in space,
an idea bursts from the darker recesses of my mind,
connecting the dots
Caylee started piecing together.

"She's building a new Pandora Device.
The machine that made her. I think she's
trying to make a new one,
since the old one was stolen."

Can she build a new device?
She said she didn't know
anything about the device
but she knows enough to try
and rebuild it?
"She had the vials
earlier in the week."

"How many vials?"
Victoria asks.

"All of them.
They were in a case.

I think they were all full.
One was missing when I first opened it
and Umu's was the
only one empty."

Caylee deflates
as if an impossible weight
just landed on her shoulders.
She sighs under the pressure.

Victoria puts the book
on her desk
and turns a calm,
academic face
toward us.
"I think those vials
are the Mother's Tears.

Monsters from a forgotten age.

I think Umu is the Violent Storm,
and I think she's trying
to bring her siblings
to the world."
Victoria's words resonate with the
unmistakable sound of
truth.

More than truth—
confirmation.
Umu's PURPOSE makes more sense
with this context.

"That's a myth."
I shake away
the ridiculous statement.
"3D printers are a new thing,
not some ancient technology.

Artificial intelligence is new . . ."

I think about my dad's work
with Human.Eve.

Does he know about Umu?

"This isn't some myth.
She's a marvel of science and technology."

"She's no marvel,"
Victoria barks.

Taking a breath
to calm herself.
"She's a monster that
you
awoke, and now she's trying
to wake others.

All this
is on you."

>>> Reject Assertion
>>> Assertion.isMyFault() = false

No, it's not.

How could I know
what would happen?

I built her,
I didn't make her
a monster.

That behavior
is a bug in her training,
not a feature of who she is.

"S—so what now?"
Caylee stammers,
springing to her feet,
pacing through the piles of books.

“Now, I finish this letter to Quincy.
You two go to bed.
I’ll ask the girls to sleep
with Cathy tonight.
Quincy and his team
will take care of this
in the morning
and we’ll regroup then.
Umu can’t come here.”

“I saw her here
the other night.”
Caylee’s voice falters.
“By the streetlight.”

“She can’t come in
unless invited,”
Victoria says,
definitive,
dismissing
discussion.

I think about how Umu
looked at the door to
The Bookshop
when we first went there.

The siren when she touched
the fire escape.

She knew she couldn’t go in.

How does that work?
Magic?

I smirk at the idea.
Last week I would have said
Magic isn’t real.
Now,
I’m not so sure.

"You're safe tonight,
so get some rest."

Victoria wheels back to the typewriter,
returning to the
thwapping
of ink to the page.

"I want to help."
The words fall faint from me.
"She's not a monster."

Caylee's mouth gapes in shock.

Victoria stops typing,
turns to me.
"Erin, you are
a sweet girl.
You don't know
the dark places of this world
and you're not ready to see them.
Umu will be handled
by Quincy's team."
Her words land with finality.

"If Quincy's team tried to handle her before,
it didn't end well for them.
She handled them. With her fists,
beating them to a bloody stain on the sidewalk.
I've been handling her so far.
I can help."

"NO!"
Victoria snaps.
"You are not ready.
You will do nothing.
You will say nothing.
You will let others
clean up your mess
and when this is done,
we can discuss
why you've made
such poor decisions.

For tonight,
I don't care
if you two stay up all night
building stupid SocialNet apps,
but you
WILL NOT
do anything relating to
Umu Dabrutu
until we discuss tomorrow.

Do you understand?"

Caylee's head automatically nods;
I'm not so quick, but
agree eventually,
knowing Umu won't go easy
and there will be another stain
on another sidewalk
before the night is through.

Communication: Location of Target Revealed

To: vcmoran17
Subject: Report - Next Actions
Body:

Attn: Dr. V.C. Moran 17

Received Inquisitor Report from V. Moran 10027 with location of target. Target believed to be building new Pandora Device.

Leading strike team myself to stop target and recover new device. Strike team deployed after delivery of this report.

Completed mission report to be delivered within the hour. If you do not hear from us in this timeframe, target is still at large, and new Inquisitor team will need to deploy.

Sincerely;
Inquisitor Q. Nicholas 10028

P.S. On mission failure, I request V. Moran 10027 be reinstated to subdue target. We need the best to stop the Storm.

<eom>

CAYLEE MORAN

Night In

Clattering at the window
springs me out of bed.

I look out into the night,
looking for the girl with glowing eyes
leaning under the streetlight.

She's not there.

Just the wind?

Under my bunk,
Erin sleeps restlessly,
fidgeting;
her body wriggles
and rolls under the blankets,
trying to kick them off.

"Erin? You awake?"

No answer.

Her face scrunches up,
sweat building on her brow
as her body violently snaps away
from whatever has her.

"Erin."
I reach down.

She jumps up,
smacking my hand away,
gasping,
flailing,
eyes bulging
as she sees where she is,
who I am.

Her breathing calms
as she remembers my room
and my face.

"Sorry."
She mops her head
with her forearm.
"Sorry. Just . . ."
She shakes away
the memories.
"Bad dream."

"That looked like more
than a bad dream."
I climb down
and sit on Yui's bed
across the room.

"You okay?"
She's still catching her breath,
jittery and shaking.

"It isn't real,"
she says,
looking to my
hands.

"Just a . . ."
She takes a deep breath,
blows out,
closing her eyes;
they snap back open
as she shivers.
"Just a dream."

"Want to talk about it?"
I pat the bed.

"That night Umu was hurt."
She looks away from me.
"I was able to . . .
I guess log in
to her brain."
Erin sits in my computer chair.

"There were hands
trying to pull me down.
Sometimes I see them
or feel them."
Erin rubs her shoulders,
trying to scrape off
something I can't see.

"Sounds scary,"
I say,
remembering how
I did nothing.

I didn't help her.

She might not be here
if I did.

Turning in my chair,
Erin looks out the window
and I follow her gaze
to see if anyone
is out there.

No one.

"It was in VR,
but that's not real."
Erin's eyes stay fixed
on the streetlight,
flickering its muddy orange
dying light.

"Sounds like it felt real."

Nodding, Erin looks to the floor,
still wiping away
the hands in her mind.
"It did."

Silence sits between us
and I wonder how I can help.
I could have helped her
when she called.

But I didn't.

"Your mom isn't going to
stop Umu."
Erin looks outside
and I follow her eyes
again.
"Umu's . . .vicious."

I tell Erin what I saw
when Quincy and Umu met
Wednesday.

Their speed,
the flash,
Umu running.

I leave out
Umu threatening me,
Umu knocking me down
and climbing on me,
bouncing my head off the pavement.

Leaving a soft spot
I can still feel.

"I think Quincy can take care of himself,"
I tell her.

The room goes quiet as
we wait for something else to say.
Searching for something,
anything to break the dead air.
My hands twist and roll,
sweating in the heat of
awkward silence.

"You think some ice cream would help?"
I smile
and slide into her line of sight.

Shrugging, slowly nodding,
she rubs at her shoulders.

I open the door
for her,
my eyes meeting hers
as she steps out to the hallway.

When I check the window
again, the bushes by the
streetlamp rattle.

Just the wind . . .

Then why don't the other bushes move?

No, it's just the wind . . .
just the wind.

"You coming?"
Erin whispers.

I nod
and follow,
pulling my door closed.

Another clattering,
this one louder,
rattles the window
in my room.

I jump back from the door.
It sounded like something
just opened
my bedroom window.

Unexpected

Mom Victoria said
Umu can't come in.

My hand hovers
over the doorknob
back into my room.

"What's wrong?"
Erin comes to me,
squeezing close.

"Thought I heard something,"
I whisper back.

My hand closes around
the doorknob,
twisting it,
calming my nerves,

I explode into my room
expecting to see Umu,
but she's not there.

No one's there.

The streetlamp
across the street
flickers
and fades.

Erin follows me in,
slowly creeping
around the corner
behind me.

She peeks around me
to see the window.

"Nothing."
I watch the window,
still waiting for Umu to
break through.

But she doesn't.

"Let's, uh, get that
ice cream,"
I say and scan my room
for any signs of anything
out of place.

Nothing.

"Yeah."
Erin walks out of the room
backwards
and I follow her.

Near the kitchen,
another sound
grabs my attention.

The
thwap
thwap
thwap
of Mom Victoria's typewriter.

Erin goes to the door;
I grab her to stop.
"Don't disturb her in there.
That's like a golden rule here."

She smiles
and knocks.

Knock
Knock

Dread at the yelling
and disappointed looks
I'm about to receive
weighs me down,
and I sigh.

But there's no answer.

She knocks again, louder.

KNOCK
KNOCK

Again, no answer.

Footsteps.

"Girls?"

"AAAAHH!"
I shriek.
Erin probably screamed too,
but I can't hear her over my heartbeat.

Mom Cathy is behind us,
shocked at our shock,
rattled from our reaction.

"Sorry!"
I whisper,
quieting my thundering pulse so I can speak.
"We were just getting ice cream
and thought Mom Victoria would want some."

"Girls, it's late.
Victoria's been in bed for hours,"
Mom Cathy says.

We listen again:
the typewriter is silent.
The study is silent.
The night is silent.

Erin and I
gather ourselves
and two scoops of
Rocky Road
and head back to my room.
Cathy gives us a hug.

"Now get some sleep, girls.
No partying all night tonight."
Cathy smiles.
"You have a big night tomorrow."

She leaves.
I'm certain
Erin and I
are done sleeping tonight.

As we hear Mom Cathy's door shut,

thwap
thwap
thwap

comes from the study.

SATURDAY (HOMECOMING)

ERIN ULMAN

Still Not Ready?

Another sleepless night;
at least I can share the misery.
Caylee and I
talked the rest of the night:
what Homecoming will be like,
which ice cream is best,
who would win a race between
the *Millennium Falcon*
and the *Enterprise* from Star Trek TNG.

We agreed where it mattered—
the *Enterprise* would win.
It's all about the crew:
Picard is a better leader
and Data is the less annoying android.

A peach sky peeks through Caylee's window.
I look out for the sunrise
but my eyes are pulled down
to see the rocks
scattered under her window.

A small crack
creases the glass.

Someone was throwing rocks
at us,
and I don't remember
that crack there last night.

Ignoring it,
I keep talking about
the engineering feats
of Jordie LaForge.

Breaking from our discussion,
I step out for more water
or tea,
or something to help me
wake up,
when I hear Victoria
talking to someone in her study.

Standing at the door,
mustering all the stealth my drowsy mind can,
I overhear:

"She's not ready.
You need to stop."

"No, she's not.
I'll bring her by today
and you'll see."

"How's Quincy?"

Was he the latest sidewalk stain?
The latest worm man?

Victoria keeps telling me
I'm not ready,
but I am ready.

More ready than Quincy was.

Ready enough to know
Umu's smart, fast, strong,
not to be messed with.

Why can't Victoria see that?

Getting my water,
I go back to Caylee's room,
lie on my sleeping bag,
and close my eyes,
trying to doze,
trying to catch up to Caylee
who's back to sleep.

Wake Up Call

"Ladies, wake up!"
Victoria is at the door,
sounding like a drill sergeant.

I must have drifted off.

The morning sun pours into the window.

We quietly dress,
either having spent all our words last night
or being too tired to find more words today,
I'm not sure which.

"Yeah!"
Yui and Sabrina
shout from the living room.
"Grandpa!"

I rush out
to the living room
to see how last night went.

Caylee pushes past me,
still pulling on her sweater.

"Quincy!"
Cathy squeals.

Coming around the corner,
I see Cathy hugging a giant.
That's Quincy?

He leans down to Yui
and very soberly says,
"Keeping your moms
out of trouble?"

Yui's face,
serious as a zero-day attack,
nods, affirming she's doing
her duty.

I've never seen a guy so big:
tall, with muscles pushing out
his baggy cable sweater,
he's probably bigger than both my parents
standing side by side.

And he looks good.
I mean, better than I expected.
Umu must have gone easy.

Cathy beams with joy
to see him.

Quincy smiles at her,
then looks to Victoria.

"In the wind, Vicky,"
he says quietly.

Victoria wheels up to Victor,
anger
and disappointment
dripping from her face.

"Gone,"
Victor sneers.

He bends down to hug
the girls and they giggle
from his beard.
"As is the device
you told us about."

He pauses, letting
the words sink in,
watching Victoria's face
for the moment to
pile more guilt on,
but Victoria beats him
to the punch.

"You didn't get anything?"
she spits at them,
scowling.

Victor's face twists into his own scowl;
clearly Victoria's teacher of facial expressions.

"Perhaps with some help,
this could have been avoided,"
Victor says.

"We talked about this earlier.
You know what I said."
Victoria's teeth grind down,
words pressing through them.

"But I am ready!"
I shout.

Confusion sets in on Quincy's face.

Shock loosens Victoria's jaw as she realizes
I overheard her conversation.

Victor's face curls into a smile
as he chuckles.

"Dear girl, clearly you are not.
You are as ready as
a house kitten is
to be a tiger."

A belly laugh rolls out of him.
"In your language,
you are as ready as
a stone tablet is
to be a supercomputer."

His laughter swirls to an uncontrollable
storm of humiliation
pouring down on me.

Seems like nothing new for me
lately . . .
or for the past few years.

Victoria wheels over to me,
frustration thick on her pale,
always-disappointed face.

"Erin, Caylee,
please go back to
Caylee's room and pack up
for Erin's house,"
Victoria says.

Caylee looks to Quincy.
"Good to see you."

Quincy nods and smiles back
with a slight wave of
a hand that's as big as my head.

"Stayin' out of trouble?"
he asks Caylee;
she shrugs with a wry smile.

Quincy chuckles,
a small snort escaping,
just like Caylee's quirky laugh.

I follow Caylee back to her room
and turn before going in.
Victor's eyes fix on Caylee,
then look back to Victoria.
She bites her lip,
shaking her head emphatically

No.

and I realize:

I'm not the only one who isn't ready.

CAYLEE MORAN

Code Breakers

What just happened?

Grandpa's reaction to Erin,
Mom Victoria's reaction—
what's she not ready for?

Taking on Umu?

I don't know.

Sounds like Umu is a computer,
and in that,
my money is on
Erin.

"What was all that about?"
I flop into my computer chair
while she packs her overnight bag.

"Your mom said they'd
take care of Umu.
They didn't.
I know I can."
Erin punches her sleeping bag
into a duffle.
Her pajamas are slammed in too
as her face grows as red
as her curls.

"So how would you do it?"
I'm curious.

"When I was in VR,
I saw connectors to
vital systems,
communications,
data stores—
she's vulnerable
in there."
Erin zips her bag
and blows out a
long,
deflating
sigh.

How could we do that?

Can Erin just jump in
or does Umu need to let her?

Would Erin do it?

Erin thinks Umu's a she,
always referring to that thing
as a *she*, a *her*.

It is an **it**.

Would Erin shut it down
like a computer?

Would Erin kill her creation?

"How would you—"

"Every computer is
susceptible to malware."
Erin looks at me
coldly, but not cold enough
to do it.
"You just need to know
how to infect it."

Her eyes jut to the window.

Mom Cathy pops her head in the room.
"Time to get going, kiddos."

I grab my overnight bag,
kiss Mom Cathy and Mom Victoria goodbye,
and snatch Yui and Sabrina up,
squeezing them as they squirm.

"See you later,"
I say to the girls,
putting them down.

"Be careful out there!"
Victoria shouts back.
"Call me if you need anything!"

Erin rolls her eyes.

"Erin."
Yui tugs on her hoodie.
"Don't let Caylee get the hammer.
And if she does . . .
don't pick it up.

Mom Cathy says hammers are for
building, not banging."
Yui looks down, face twists,
remembering the lesson.
"Have fun tonight!"
She runs back to play
with Sabrina.

"Yui, don't be silly,"
I laugh,
but Erin doesn't.

She nods
slowly,
pauses,
then follows me
out the door.

Mom Victoria watches us leave.

I call to her,
"Don't worry. We'll be fine."

I remember the clattering last night.
The crack in my window
that Erin kept looking at.
One guess who did it . . .

I push away the thought,
reminding myself,

We'll be fine.

Preparations

Erin and I
are on the hunt
for dresses
and bargains,
neither of us wanting to invest much
in last-minute Homecoming plans.

Her dad carries the bags,
her mom picks out everything
with a sweet,
Oh, did you see this?
as she sizes the dresses to us.

Susan is so cute,
beaming with joy
that her daughter gets to be girly,
if only for a night.

Has Erin ever worn a dress?
Like
ever?

Begrudgingly
Erin tries on the seventh dress
Susan picks out.

Grunts and
groans of discontent
leak from the dressing room
where Erin finally steps out.

Wow!

The shimmering green dress
glows against her fiery hair
and bare milky shoulders.
It hugs her body,
revealing soft curves normally
cloaked in baggy hoodies
and jeans.
The waist flares out in precise folds
alternating between light and dark green,
creating the feel of the dress constantly flowing around her.

A ball gown
for the Cinderella of Glen Coast.

Susan's hands over her mouth
hold in a gasp,
while all I can think is how
Davis will be speechless;
how *I'm* speechless.

Erin looks at the mannequin
wearing the same dress,
looks back to herself in the mirror,
fidgets with the waist.

If only she'd smile,
she would light up the whole store.

"That's the one!"
I declare.
Susan agrees.
Erin's dad shrugs.
Erin concedes
and the dress is hers.

On the discount rack
I find a pale blue qipao with
violet lotus flowers
to match my planned eye shadow:
blue, purple, and green.

Susan approves.
Erin asks if it will be comfortable.
I nod
and hope it will.

Scattered throughout the mall
we see other people from school
getting their hair done,
getting their corsages,
laughing,
giggling,
selfies flashing feverishly.

Stopping for a moment
I see Erin's grumpy *Can we be done now?* glare,
her mom glowing,
her dad lugging bags around,
and realize
I'd rather be with grumpy-and-glowing
than pretending to have fun with anyone else.

ERIN ULMAN

Homecoming Memories

Mother does my makeup.
I can't stand
makeup
and having my hair pulled
into fancy foolishness.
I just want to be done.

It isn't as horrible as the hair salon.

"Did you clean my room?"
I ask her while she tortures me.

"Do I ever?"
She smiles
and chuckles.

"Just looked like some things
were missing on my desk."
Was the window unlocked?

I didn't check.
"Didn't know if you cleaned."

"As I've said before,
I don't know what half the things
on your desk are.
I don't touch them,
just like I don't mess
with your dad's
desk either.

You two and your gadgets."
She laughs.

Probably just knocked it
off my desk or something.
My bag hit it.

Nothing major, just some
circuit boards and wires.
Soldering iron.

Ow!
Another pull
brings me back to now.

Beauty = Pain;

Caylee's in the bathroom
getting ready,
self-sufficient as I'd expect from her.
I wonder where she learned to do her makeup.
Probably Cathy.

Victoria and I
are not the makeup-and-
dress-nice types.
We'd rather be studying
and learning
than socializing.

Mother finishes;
I go to scratch my head,
she swats my hand away.

"Don't mess your hair,"
she says with a grin.

Dad's taking pictures.

When did he become the family photographer?

"Cheese!"
he directs.

I don't comply.
Tough to smile when I'm squeezed into a dress
knowing everyone will see the rolls under my arms,
the freckles on my shoulders,
my weird collarbones.

I'm too exposed
but this was the only one that was close to fitting,
the only dress I could stuff into.

Caylee comes out of the bathroom,
bold,
powerful,
fearless with her peacock-inspired eye shadow.
Her dress shows muscled arms
and runner's legs
rooted in purple Converse All Stars.

Her hair,
always changing since Costume Day,
tonight is frizzed like curly waves parted in the middle
around her face,
a black halo
promising fun and freedom.

Dad snaps a picture of us talking
CLICK
me commiserating on the torturous demands of social events
CLICK
Caylee gushing over how pretty I look—
kind words, but she's the star of tonight,
bright
and shining—
CLICK

Caylee convinces me to try a selfie
with her,
my first selfie since
my last selfie with Betty,
the day before everything changed
in Seattle.

She smiles.
I grin or something.
CLICK
She posts it to SocialNet.

"Watch out, world!
Erin and @CayleeMoran out tonight!"

A string of emojis follow.

Doorbell rings;
Dad answers,
still snapping.
CLICK
Davis and Meredith are here,
their parents behind them,
clicking away with *their* camera.

Our chance to escape.

I pull Caylee to the door to get out of here,
seeing Davis and Meredith also ready to go.

Meredith looks like an evil fairy
with her little black dress
matching her cascading
black hair,
black nail polish, and
black lipstick.

Davis looks nice;
his face is twisted in a weird surprised look,
but his suit
fits:
a black jacket, white shirt, green tie.

"Okay, we're ready to go?"
I ask.

"Uh, yeah. I'm ready,"
Davis sputters.

"Caylee, Erin, you both look
as well as I would expect
for a Homecoming event.
Nice work selecting appropriate attire,"
Meredith says.

Was it a question we would?

"We need group pictures!"
Dad says.
All the adults agree.

Why's he pretending
to be Super Dad?
Always Here Dad?
Aware of What's Happening with His Family Dad?

We line up
CLICK
we act silly
CLICK
Davis opens my door
CLICK
we get in Mother's car
CLICK

How can Caylee smile consistently for so many pictures?

Ugh . . .

Off to dinner.
Dad's driving-
hopefully without taking pictures.

Revelatory Ride to the Dance

Reviewing my SocialNet feed,
I see a post missing:
the selfie with Erin is gone?

"Hey Erin, I know you're all anti-SocialNet
and stuff. Did you erase my post I had you tagged in?"
I point to where the post should be in my feed.

She looks
puzzled.
"No, SocialNet never remembers me.
I'm not cool enough, I guess."
She fakes a smile.

Erin's dad laughs.

"They haven't found that yet?
On the day I left SocialNet,
I left an Easter egg
in the SocialNet algorithm
to erase anything
about our family.

Knowing how
creepy and ruthless
SocialNet is,
I left some code in there
to auto-delete
anything that tagged
me, Susan, or Erin.
I didn't want my family
wrapped up in their
shady business.

This was like,
when SocialNet had
a few million users.
Now they're in the billions,
and, well,
I'm glad I left when I did,"
he says, oozing pride.

Erin's eyes pop,
something's coming together in her head.

"Dad, didn't you say
Human.Eve AI uses
SocialNet data as
a training and testing set?"
Erin asks.

The car falls silent,
listening.

"Uh, yeah it does.
Oh, I guess that means the Ulmans
will never have
a Human.Eve AI assistant, huh.
It wouldn't know who we are."
He laughs at the thought.

Erin isn't laughing;
she looks at me,
her smile growing.

"Pandora uses Human.Eve AI,"
Erin whispers to me.

And now
the dots are connecting;
how Umu knows everything
about everyone
but nothing about Erin.

Erin
doesn't exist
in Umu's world.

SocialNet.

Umu's worldview is built
on the lies of
SocialNet.

ERIN ULMAN

Homecoming

Gymnasium lights are low,
music is loud.
Meredith animates into a swirling pixie,
dancing
flowing
into the swelling current of bodies
sweating
spinning
shaking
to the beat.

Davis reaches out to me;
I step back to Caylee,
hoping I didn't offend him,
but he smiles,
nods,
follows his sister-
bobbing his head,
shimmying his shoulders,
joining the mass of bodies dancing.

Caylee stands beside me,
energy bursting from her;
she grabs my hand,
stepping in front of me.

"Ready for this?"

No.

>>> System Overload
>>> Error: Too many people

The sea of humans flowing around
drowning people like me.

Caylee's excitement is boiling,
ready to fall over the edges of the pot,
hit the burner, and burst into steam.

"I don't-"
She pulls me into the current
enveloping us;
as I try to pull back
she tugs me deeper into the crowd,
and I see no one is looking
at me;
they are looking only at their people.
I'm hidden from their eyes,
from their expectations,
from my worries.
I sink into the beat of the music,
hearing it,
feeling it.

Caylee jumps to the rhythm,
her hair springing around her,
her fists pumping in the air,
her energy and life and soul
taking flight,
taking me with her.
I jump;
my hair breaks free of Mother's pins,
hands reaching higher to grasp more
more energy
more life
more of *this*!

Caylee
me
the current
the beat
the pulse of life
I haven't felt in years
without fear
without loneliness
just joy.

Songs change
beat doesn't
so we don't
change
we keep
dancing
jumping
enjoying the night.

Eventually
silence;
slow music starts,
the current disbands,
pairing off;
sweat pours from me,
Caylee the same.
She smiles,
pointing her chin to someone approaching:
Davis,
eyes nervous,
sweating worse than me.
Caylee lets out an

"Awwww . . ."

and walks off.

```
Davis.approaching();
Erin.temperature.climbing();
Erin.panicking();
```

Clearing his throat, Davis says,
"Erin, would you like to dance?"

His lips tremble,
his shoulders pushed back unnaturally far,
and I see for the first time
a glimmer in his eyes,
like Umu's but different:
a glimmer of gentleness and hope,
his blue eyes a haven from my troubled week.

"I don't know how to."

He clears his throat again,
extending his hand
with a slight bow.

Stepping closer,
I hear a distant whining
like a machine spinning, getting louder–
not closer,
just louder–
people are covering their ears,
the whining drowns the music,
drowns everything.

Familiar . . .

Davis covers his ears,
squinting his eyes.
I look for Caylee,
seeing her in the same situation.
The whining is all anyone can hear now;
they run out of the gym,
out of the school,
panic rushing over everyone.

BOOM!
The gym shakes.

The whining stops;
people run.
I run.

Caylee follows me,
sprinting through the exodus of people,
running to the source-
to the Maker Lab.

Power outage follows;
the school goes dark.
Not even the moon shows the way.
Caylee whips out her phone,
activates the flashlight as we run down the hall.

Bursting through the orange doors,
we see smoke
or steam
clinging to Umu as
she's hunched over a dark form on the ground.

Behind her
a device, her Pandora Device, steams,
fried from the power consumption.

"What did you do?"
Caylee cries out.

Umu raises her head from
the thing on the floor-
the thing writhing,
shrieking in pain,
being born
from the jellyfish form.
"Erin left me alone, and now . . .

I am alone

no more."

Fallout

Caylee and I,
mouths hanging from
shock and
our breathless sprint,
face Umu
and her creation,
wondering at the unknown horror
still forming on the floor.

Umu's face is calm,
her presence cool,
not cold.

Caylee grabs a hammer from the tool rack;
she's still high from the dance floor,
her blood pumping for fight,
not flight.

Umu's eyes catch her quick movement.

"So quick to attack, Caylee?
You wouldn't even think it murder
if you killed me,
Would you?"

The thing on the floor
is trying to press through the jellyfish skin,
scratching,
clawing
from inside.

On a table beside Umu
is a soldering iron,
circuit boards,
wire.

The tools
missing
from my
room.

"You left me, Erin.
You abandoned me
for everyone else.
For anyone else."
Umu's eyes are cold
daggers striking at me,
hitting my heart
between my betrayal
and regret.

"Now I'll have a companion.
You would have never
been there for me,
would have never done this for me.

So I did it myself."

The screeching from the jellyfish
turns to screaming,
from pain to panic,
unable to escape the flesh encasing it;
from screaming to gasping,
growing faint.

"What's happening?
Why does it sound like that?"
Caylee shouts.

Confusion
sinks Umu's shoulders.
"I . . .
I don't understand."

Gasping fades,
clawing turns to pawing,
pressing,
and then nothing.

No movement.

Silence
radiates from
the jellyfish,
encasing the room in stillness.

It dissolves back into
thick silver green slime and
floats up into the air
as a metallic ball of liquid.

Umu pushes the ball into an empty vial,
closing the lid.
Disappointment weighs her down,
weighs me down.

As Caylee grips the hammer tighter,
I softly step toward Umu,
reaching for her.

"No!"
Umu pushes me away,
her eyes shimmering,
her presence erupting
into an arctic blast,
frosting the windows.
"I need the Pandora Device!"

Standing up,
she starts toward Caylee.
"Where is it?

I know your people took it!"

Umu leaps onto Caylee,
knocking her to the ground,
sending the hammer spinning to my feet
as Umu climbs over her,
snarling,
drooling in
rage.

Holding Caylee down
with their faces an eyelash apart,
Umu screams,

"Where is it!?"

Caylee's arms claw at Umu,
pushing her away,
trying to escape
as Umu evades her grip,
pinning Caylee to the floor,
stuck to an invisible web.

Umu's hand slips to Caylee's throat.

Caylee gasps,
grunts,
chokes.

The hammer is at my feet.

Caylee is reaching for it,
I just need to kick it over.

Or pick it up.

Bending down
to pick up the hammer,
I hear Yui's voice,
or remember what she said,
very specific…

Don't pick up the hammer.

As I freeze,
looking to Umu
strangling Caylee,
an electrical pop snaps my eyes
to
Umu's Pandora Device.

>>> Idea forming
>>> Computing solutions

Caylee's arms ripple against
Umu's effortless control.

>>> Cannot win fighting
>>> Cannot beat her
>>> Must…

"We'll help you, Umu,"
I shout,
breaking Umu's grip,
breaking Caylee's fight;
both look at me
in shock
and doubt.

"I'll help you find the Pandora Device, and then
you leave Glen Coast.

We never see you again."

Umu pushes off Caylee,
standing to face me.

Caylee grunts,
a mix of pain and disgust,
coughing to recapture her breath
as she climbs to her knees,
hacking,
searching for how to breathe again.

"Is that what you want, Erin?"
Umu whispers.

I nod,
looking to Caylee
who's getting to her feet,
straightening her dress,
wiping the foaming spit from her mouth.

"If I don't have it in six days . . ."
Umu glances to Caylee.
"I'll start removing the distractions in your life
so you can focus on helping me."
Her eyes meet mine,
ensuring no confusion.
"I've gone easy on people
in the past
because you asked me to.

That's over now.

Next time I will get my answers from her

while she can still
talk."

Umu walks to the window,
looking back to us;
the moon catches her vampire-white face,
flaming red hair,
her silver-green
glowing eyes.

"Six days."

She slips out the window,
devoured by the night.

Caylee and I
stand watching the window
in silence.

"We've got work to do,"
I say.

Caylee picks up the hammer,
gripping the handle
skin straining over her sharp knuckles,
sniffing.

"Yeah."
She coughs,
her voice
coarse,
strained,
venomous.
"We do."

III

Revelations

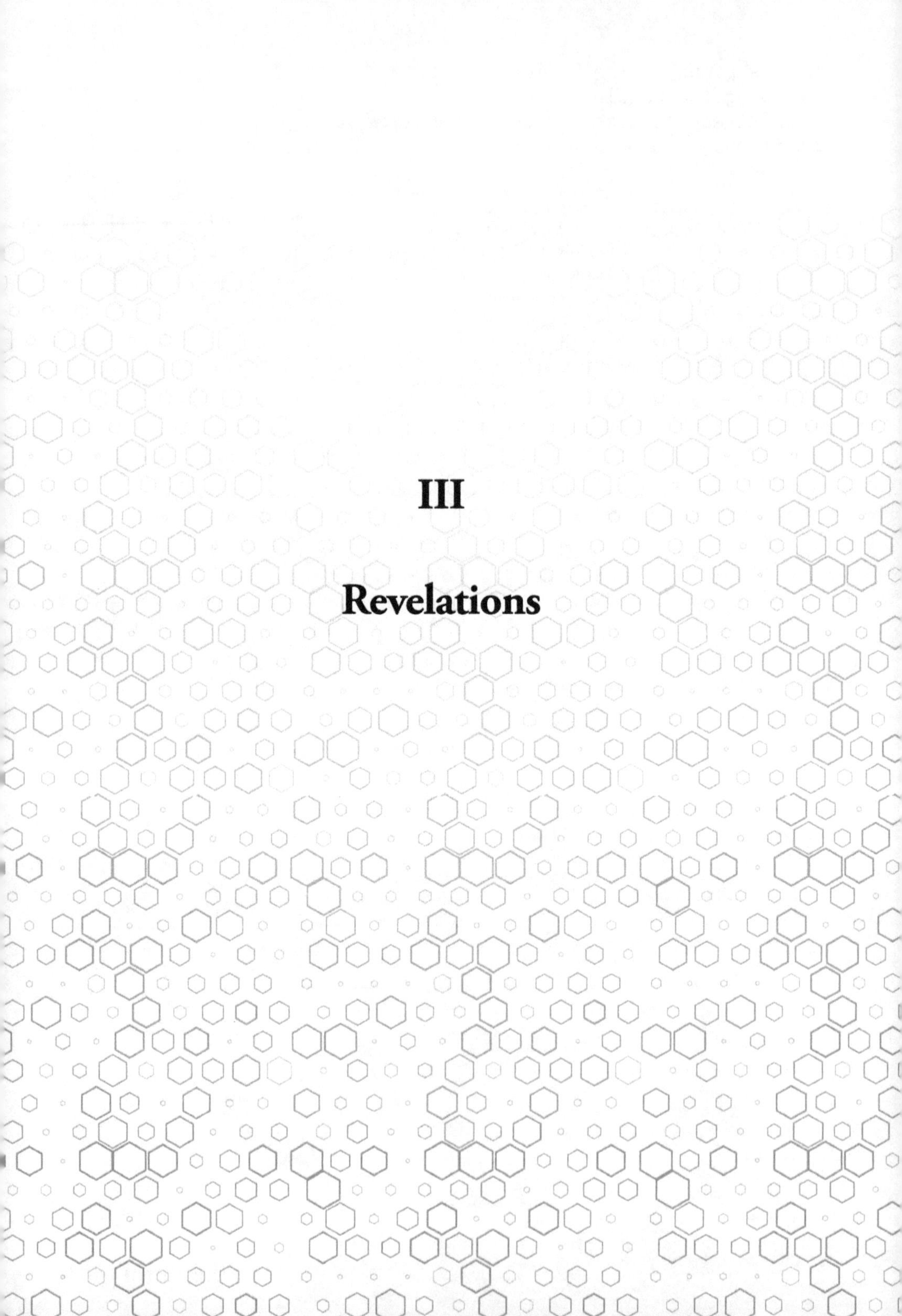

ERIN ULMAN

What's There

Homecoming is canceled
from the outage.
The school's power
is not coming back on.

Mother picks us up.
Davis is quiet.
Meredith is on her phone.
Caylee stares out the window,
her face staring back in the darkness.

"Sorry the dance got canceled,"
Mother says.

No one answers.

"Do you guys want to get
dessert or something?
Just because the dance is over
doesn't mean you all
have to be done tonight?"
Mother says.

"No, Mother. I'm pretty wiped out."

"Thanks, Mrs. Ulman, but
Davis and I
need to get home.
I have to broadcast
my gaming session tonight,
so I appreciate
getting back a bit early,"
Meredith says.

Caylee
says nothing.

We drop off Davis and Meredith first.

As Davis steps on his porch
I call,
"Hey Davis, next time no power outage, okay?"

He laughs awkwardly.
"Yeah, next time."

Meredith rolls her eyes.
Davis smiles as he walks through the door.

We drive off.

"Can Caylee hang out a while at our house?"

Caylee says nothing.

"As long as it is okay
with her moms.
Caylee, you want to call them
when we get back?"

Caylee turns,
looking at me with
disappointment.

"Yeah,
I'll call Mom Cathy."

I reach over to Caylee,
rubbing her shoulder,
accidentally pulling her dress away from
the red fingerprints around her neck
where Umu's grip
wrapped around her throat.

Pushing my hand away,
she pulls her dress back up
and returns to staring
out the window.

Is she looking for something
in the darkness?

In her reflection?

In herself?

CAYLEE MORAN

The Results

Mom Cathy gives the okay,
asking about my voice.
I tell her,
"Hoarse from shouting at the dance."

Can't say
choked out by a monster;
she'd worry.

Scrubbing away the makeup,
I stare at the marks on my throat in the mirror,
reliving Umu's frozen fingers constricting
the breath out of me.
Stars popping in my eyes,
darkness settling over me.
Her glowing eyes fading into an empty void.

Cozying into comfortable clothes
I borrowed from Erin,
I wrap my hair, then
wrap my throat with a scarf.
I leave the bathroom
and plop onto Erin's bed.

Erin's sitting at her computer.

"Umu had me.
And there was nothing I could do.

I keep thinking
I should have done this or that,
but nothing would have mattered.
It was faster than me, stronger than me,
and all I could do was try to push it off, but
I swear it had eight arms.

Each time I grabbed it
another arm would just push me down."

Erin stares at me,
listening,
waiting for her turn—to defend Umu, probably.

"I'm sorry, Caylee,"
she breathes out.
"I was so scared.
I can't imagine how you felt."

Sitting up,
seeing her eyes
tear up,

I wonder if she's thinking about
what she would have done,
or how she should have kicked me the hammer
or picked it up and hit Umu
to stop it from attacking me.

"Why didn't—"

I want to ask.

But I know better.
Umu might be a monster,
but it's Erin's creation.

She chose it over me.

SUNDAY (5 DAYS)

ERIN ULMAN

Sunday Brunch

Victoria calls,
inviting
Caylee and me
to breakfast
so we can catch up.

We walk to The Bookshop,
meeting
Victoria and Quincy
across the street
at Smithy's Diner.

The old brick building
is glittering silver inside
and smells like bacon
and sweaty wait staff.

Victoria is laughing
at a story Quincy's telling;
they're sitting at a table near the back.
I've never heard her laugh so hard,
her pale face reddening.

We sit:
Caylee beside Victoria,
stealing a stab of French toast from her mom;
me beside Quincy,
digging into the menu.
Not sure if my hand would return from his plate
if I were to sample something.

"I heard Homecoming was exciting?"
Quincy smiles,
frustratingly
handsome
and friendly.

Caylee and I
peek at each other over our menus,
not sure how to answer,
not sure what they know.

"Yeah, weird power outage,"
Caylee says,
lowering her eyes
to the menu.

"Weird indeed."
Quincy snorts a laugh.
"Power was out for a few blocks
around the school.
The power company is still
trying to fix it."

"I heard reports of a loud siren before the outage?
Did you guys hear anything?"
Victoria asks,
acting dumb.
It doesn't suit her.

Keeping the menu up,
staring at the breakfast selection
perhaps too long,
I answer.
"Yeah, it was pretty loud.
Not sure what it was.

Probably a transformer or something."

If looks could be heard,
our table would be screaming.
I look to Caylee;
Victoria looks to Quincy,
then to me.
I keep my eyes on the menu.

"So, Quincy, what's good here?"

"French toast. They make it
with fresh challah bread,
vanilla,
cinnamon, and
orange zest. Amazing!"

He points to Victoria's plate.
Her hand flies forward,
preparing to swat.
He laughs.

"Don't worry, Vicky.
I know better."

"Yeah, I'll get that."
Caylee steals another
bit of Victoria's food,
catching the swat
prepared for Quincy
as her mother defends her plate.

Victoria smiles at her daughter
as Caylee playfully rolls her eyes,
snatching the bite
as Victoria looks back to Quincy.

"Fast one."
Quincy chuckles.

"How's the hunt for Umu going?"
I break the happy mood.

Victoria and Caylee both
cock an eyebrow, and I see
Victoria's face in Caylee's.

Quincy leans away from me,
smiling that frustratingly
charming smile.
"Right to the point, aren't you?
When we got to the school the other night,
she was gone.

Her and the device
you told Vicky about.

Looked like she hit the road
right before we got there,
like
maybe
someone told her we were coming."

"No sign of the device?"

"Nope.
She was a ghost.
Device and all,"
Quincy says.

"I think she's trying to build the device
that was stolen from my house,"
I snipe.

Caylee rolls her eyes in disbelief,
fixing her gaze on her menu again.

"I don't know if Vicky told you
but the device that made Umu
was stolen from my house."
I smirk.
"Or, did she leave
that part out?"

Victoria's face darkens
in the deepest scowl
I've ever seen a human make.
Is it my tone?
Calling her Vicky?
Is that something
only Quincy gets to do?

Quincy scoots over
toward me,
his eyes level with mine.
"She told me."
His face is a mix of
bemused and surprised.
"My team took that device
from your house.
We left a bit of a mess
because we weren't expecting you home so early.

Sorry about that."

Thieves.apologizing("for mess not theft");
>>> Result: Absurd

He waits for my response
in silent
arrogance.

"Do you know
what you want to eat?"
His smile turns taunting.

What?
What I want to eat?
He motions to the edge of the table;
the waiter stands awaiting my order
as Caylee watches the exchange,
her cheeks burning with embarrassment.
Victoria is as amused as Quincy.

"Pancakes please,"
I say as dismissively as possible,

Looking at Quincy.
"French toast sounds like the way to go here,
but I'm more of a pancake person."

"You're going to regret it,"
Quincy says,
his smirk still present,
mocking me with his dimples.

"Uh . . . French toast for me,"
Caylee says
extra loud,
as if
breaking up some conversation
at another table.

"Comin' right up."
The waiter scurries off.

"So, where'd you take my device?"

"Erin!"
Victoria barks
through a whisper.

"*Your* device?"
Quincy lets out a belly laugh,
drawing stares from other tables.
"*Your device*?
You mean the device you found
and then messed with, not knowing what
was going to happen?

That device?"

"Yes, that device.
The Pandora Device."
My attitude matches his,
meeting his laughter with my growing
frustration.
"It was delivered to me.
No return instructions, no one looking for it.

Maybe it should have had a warning label:
*Warning, may bring 3D models to life with
sociopathic tendencies*."
I laugh as I picture the label.

"We were looking for it.
And let's be honest,
a warning label
wouldn't have stopped you."
His eyes turn serious,
leaving his implied question
hanging in the small space between us.

He turns back to the table,
facing Victoria and Caylee.

"That device is safe with Victor.
Forget it.
Forget what it made.
Eat your pancakes."

He points to the plate
that somehow materialized right under my hands.

I take my frustration out on my pancakes:
drowning them in syrup,
impaling them with my fork
over and over,
crushing them in my teeth.

These pancakes suck.

Flat,
heavy,
grainy,
blobs of batter.

Caylee is quietly devouring her French toast,
blissfully having a moment with her food
as she shares with
Victoria,
swatting away Quincy's playful attempts
to swipe a bite.

Soft,
fluffy,
slightly golden,
wreathed in crispy brown crust,
smelling sweet like candy.

They smile as each forkful is savored.
Caylee
talks about the Homecoming dance,
about pictures before dinner,
about other stuff that I can't hear
over the sloshing of pasty pancakes in my mouth.

Breakfast envy
hits hard.

CAYLEE MORAN

Readiness

Erin leaves after she finishes her pancakes,
grumbling about them as she stomps off.

Mom Victoria leaves a few minutes later.

Quincy and I
sit at the table
as I pretend to search for
remaining bits of French toast
on anyone's plate.

"So, do you want to talk about
what really happened
last night?"
he asks.

"I know Umu used the device
she made.
I'm pretty sure it didn't work.
I'm also pretty sure—"
He moves into my eye line.
"—that you and Erin
had a run-in with her."

"It is an *it*, not a her."
My frustration spills out.

"Doesn't Umu look like a girl?
Doesn't she act like a
high school girl?
Albeit a weird, creepy one?"

I shrug.

"Walks like a duck,
quacks like a duck."
He shrugs
as his mouth curls
into a half smile.

"Umu wants the device
you took from Erin."

"I thought so.
But that's not what
you're thinking about,
is it?"

I look out the diner window,
wanting to leave,
wanting answers more.

Why am I talking to this guy?

I don't know him.

But he's comfortable.
Not cold like Mom Victoria,
not bubbly like Mom Cathy.

And he brings out a side of Mom Victoria
I've never seen.
She's . . .
happy.

Who does he want me to be?
A clone of Mom Victoria?

I don't think he wants
anything. He's just
comfortable.

"You and Mom Victoria were pretty close, right?"

"Vicky and I
grew up together.

Her dad took me in
after my parents . . .
we'll say . . .
left.

She used to call me
her annoying brother,
but most people around here
didn't see the resemblance."

He holds up his hands,
showing mahogany skin,
darker than mine,
much darker than Mom Victoria's
pale, pasty skin.

We both laugh.

I think about looks
my moms get when I'm with them.
In a store.
In a restaurant.

People wondering how we fit
together.

They don't say anything,
but their eyes do enough talking.

My throat twinges from Umu's
strangulation, turning laughter
to coughing, snapping me back
to last night.

"Things got . . .
physical with Umu. She knocked me down
again,
like I was just blown over.
I couldn't do anything.
Except wait for her to do
whatever she was going to do."
I look back to my plate,
now cold and empty, swirling my syrup.

"And Erin just stood there."

"Even smart people
get dumbstruck."

"I don't know."

The smell of bacon pulls my head up
as Quincy holds out a slightly burnt bacon strip
right under my nose,
meeting my eyes with his.

"Don't linger on it."
He hands me the bacon,
greasy,
stiff.
"You can't win every time.
So what did you learn?"

I snap the bacon,
watching bits fly up,
remembering last night:
Umu's strength,
speed,
cold.

"Umu's fast. I would have sworn
she had more than two arms.
Every move I made,
she'd just grab me again."

Quincy slowly nods,
picking up more bacon.
"What else?"

I pop the first piece of bacon into my mouth.
"She's cold. Her hands were freezing
and I always feel a chill around her.
Not like a creepy chill, like the air
is literally cold around her."

Crunching down,
I savor the salty goodness mixing with
the lingering sweet syrup.
"And Erin has talked about
how cold Umu is too.
How wherever Umu is, it's cold."

Quincy grins,
taking my other piece of bacon,
putting it on the table.

"This bacon is
your current ability."
Picking up a whole piece of bacon,
he places it above my half piece.
"This bacon is Umu's ability.
She's faster.
She's stronger.
So how are you going to
deal with her bacon?"

"Easy."
I pick up Umu's bacon,
snap it in half.
toss it down.
"I break it."

Quincy chuckles.
"And that's why most people lose.
They try to reduce
their opponent's abilities.
They look for shortcuts.

No, Caylee,
even if you break her bacon,
she still has
a whole piece of bacon.

You can't take away her ability."
He takes the half in my hand,
puts it back beside Umu's bacon,
points to my bacon.
"You still only have half."

He puts another whole piece of bacon
beside my half.
"You need to grow your bacon.
Not break hers."

He scribbles down an address
on a napkin,
pushes it over to me.

"I hate keeping secrets from Vicky
and she'd be really pissed
if she knew
I gave you this.
Go here; it's a gym.
When you're ready,
tell them Quincy sent you
and they'll hook you up."

He gets up to leave,
dropping some cash on the table for the bill.

"Champions have short memories, Caylee.
Learn from last night
and move on.
Don't linger.

It will eat you alive if you do."

Quincy walks out.

I stare at the bacon,
wondering:
Can I?

ERIN ULMAN

To Err is Human[.Eve]

With Quincy's mocking still in my head,
I get back home
to see Dad on the couch
reading something on his tablet;
he doesn't notice me.

"Hey Dad."

No answer.

I walk to the kitchen
to get a drink,
trying to wash away the rancid pancake flavor
left by breakfast.

"What's that, Dad?"

No answer.

I walk to him,
peek over his shoulder,
seeing the IntelliDyn logo:
some form about
ethics board findings.
I don't catch the title.

"Oh, hey Erin!"
He startles,
dropping the tablet facedown,
ripping headphones
out of his ears.

"What's that?"
I point to the tablet.

"Welcome package
and some data."
He smiles.

Picking the tablet up,
swiping to a new app before I see the screen,
he shows me.

Dad.hideScreen();
Dad.isLying = true;

I know that trick,
the quick switch
to hide what you were doing,
but his red cheeks
and burning ears
betray him.

"Check this out.
IntelliDyn's mission is to
reinvent the world.

They are so forward-thinking.

This company is doing everything
from agriculture to medicine to manufactur-
ing.

I love it!"
He smiles,
scrolling through the document.

"That's pretty neat, Dad.

Can I ask you a question?"

What were you looking at?

Why are you hiding it?

But I don't ask that.
"A question about
the Human.Eve AI system?
How does it work?"

"Oh, well, that's pretty complicated.
There's a bunch of subsystems and
functions,
so answering
that question
is pretty complex."

"I read an article about a cyber attack
where people were able to break the AI system
with malformed data.

Could someone do that with Human.Eve?"

Dad thinks,
his eyes darting around.
I imagine he sees the code
in his mind,
searching for
an answer to my question.

"Between you and me–"
A devious grin shows on his face.
"I haven't done a lot
of quality checks on
Human.Eve.
I'm betting there are
some vulnerabilities.

IntelliDyn didn't care much
about the security,
they were more focused on what it could do.

You planning on
breaking my code?"

"No, I'm just curious."

"Curious about showing up
your old man?"
He laughs playfully.
"Don't break it too bad.
I've taught you
everything I know,
so I'm betting you'll find
something."

No,
most of what I've learned
has been in isolation,
sitting in my room
alone
in the dark,
listening for you to come home,
to see you,
for you to see me.

I force out a laugh.
"Don't worry, Dad. I'll go easy."

"Want any help?
I'd love to see what you're doing."

Dad + Erin
>>> Does not compute

"No, I work best alone."
Turning away,
I hear the familiar
soft sigh of disappointment,
but this time it comes from him,
not me.

Mother stands in the hallway
listening,
shooing me back to him,
her hand fluttering at her leg
where he can't see.

I walk past her,
open my door;
a burst of heat welcomes me
as Mother echoes
Dad's sigh.

Disappointment
lingers with everyone
in this house.

Not Like the Others

Loading Human.Eve's source code,
I start the static code analyzer
to find any security vulnerabilities
Dad left in there,
accidentally
or otherwise.

10 Critical Vulnerabilities
231 High Importance Vulnerabilities

Thousands more
medium-to-low vulnerabilities
light up,
showing this system is riddled
with problems.

"Dad wrote this?"

Surprise
with a hint of shame
flares up.
I'm embarrassed that my father
would hack something this horrid together.

Digging deeper, I find
most of the vulnerabilities are false positives.
The scanner thought they were vulnerabilities
but other checks are in place to prevent
security breach.

One low vulnerability catches my eye,
as do one high and two mediums.

Together these four problems
can be orchestrated to lead to
a bigger vulnerability,
one not shown here in the scanner,
similar to the one I use to disable
security protocols
at school.

A few malformed bytes would
create a snowball of security issues,
leading to a total system failure
of Human.Eve.

Hard crash.

Process death.

When I review the code further,
there is no restart function.
Once Human.Eve crashes,
it can't come back online
without help.

The right malware
could kill anything
running Human.Eve.

"You need to give
your father a chance,"
Mother says,
leaning against my door.

"He's just visiting."
The words slip out from me.
Mother slouches down,
trying to think of a response
or maybe agreeing with me.

My eyes stay on my screen;
I open my code editor,
start to tap out the malware
to crash Human.Eve
and stop Umu
if things come to that.

Perhaps they already have?

"He said things will be different.
You need to give him a chance,"
she says.

"He said that when we moved here.
And when we moved to Portland.
So what's the difference this time?"
My keystrokes clack louder,
drowning out Mother's words
drowning out my questions.

What will be different this time?
What?
Less time away?
More time with us?
More attentive to me?
No, none of that will last.

He'll be gone
at the first call.

I'll be alone.

Mother will be alone.

He'll be with what's important.

That should be us.

"Erin!"
Mother shouts.
"You're going to break
your keyboard!"

I stop typing,
my fingers throbbing,
the code editor showing
nothing
but the smashing of keys,
incoherent
garble.

Deep breath.

Finding my voice
sweeping the noises from my mind.
When I look back to Mother,
her eyes are
soft.
Her face says she's
searching for words
to help.

"I need to concentrate on this,"
I say.

She nods,
stepping out,
leaving me
alone.

CAYLEE MORAN

Rarely Seen, Rarely Spoken

"Hey Mom,
where does Grandpa Victor live?"
I ask,
drying the plate she just handed me.

"Right on the edge of town.
By Simonstone Park,"
she says.

"Then why don't we ever see him?"

"Well . . ."
Mom Victoria sighs
loud enough to hear over
Sabrina's Godzilla impression and
the screams of
Mom Cathy and
Yui
as they run from the monster destroying
their city of blocks.

"He wanted me to follow
in his work,
like Quincy."
She stops washing dishes,
staring at Mom Cathy,
smiling.

"I wanted something else in life.

Now I just
don't want to hear the
what I could have been
lecture from him."

You do that to me.

Should I hit her with that now?

"What does he think you should have been?"

She washes the plate in her hand
over
and over again.

"Like him.

Alone."

She places the plate on the towel
in front of me,
her eyes somewhere else,
sometime else.

"Let's finish up."

She sniffles something back,
fishes for another dish in the soapy water
while looking past the bubbles
to a ghost
of regret
or wonder
or what could have been.

"Does he still teach
at the university?"

Mom Victoria sighs.

"No. Just does
research."

"In your building?"

She puts the plate down
and scans my face for
an explanation to this
game of twenty questions.

"I mean, do you see
him a lot?"
I shrug,
looking away.
"I mean, sounds like
that would be tough."

I slowly dry my plate,
waiting for a hint
of where
he might have
the device.

"No, he's in the
Social Sciences building,
in the basement."
She chuckles.
"With all the other
old things
that school
collects."

I nod
and smile.

"You should invite him over
more."
He used to come over
a lot when I was younger,
but I don't remember
seeing him with Mom Victoria.

She was usually
away.

He'd talk with Mom Cathy
and we'd play.

He smelled like
coffee and cigarettes.
Always.

"We'll see."
She shakes her head,
returning to washing.

His house
or his office.

Where else could the device be?

The Bookshop?
He wouldn't keep it there.
Umu knew it was there
so he would have moved it.

"Maybe invite him for dinner
tomorrow or something?"
I suggest,
weighing the options.

Home.

Office.

Bookshop.

She shrugs and drains the sink.
Dishes are done
and she wheels away
to her study.

She pauses at the door
to watch me finish,
or think about
the questions,
think about
why I'm asking.

I smile
and she shuts the door.

MONDAY (4 DAYS)

ERIN ULMAN

Lingering Issues

"Erin! School's closed today.
Power is still out,"
Mother yells from the kitchen.

Breakfast smells fill the air,
inviting me out
while warm covers
and no school
anchor me to bed.

Wait.

Power outage?

>>> Processing…
>>> Verifying

I leap from bed to computer chair,
sliding under my desk,
opening the Glen Coast High School web page
to see what's going on.

> *Power outage today. School is closed today and tomorrow (Tuesday). See you Wednesday!*

My mind is torn
between
joy for an unexpected day off
and worry, wondering what Umu did
to power her failed device.

"Erin, did you hear me?"

"Yeah, Mother, got it.
No school."

"Breakfast is ready
and Caylee's here.
Come on out."

I throw on my robe
and head out to the kitchen.

Breakfast of Conspirators

Caylee, dressed in an
eye-scalding white running suit
that glows in the kitchen light,
stuns me motionless.

"Um . . . running somewhere
or just signaling air traffic?"
I laugh,
squinting to cut down
on how bright she is.

"I'm in disguise.
What do you think?
College girl running?"

She jogs in place,
exaggerating each step in a cross between
pretending to be a train
and someone running in
slow motion
with bad acting.

"Disguise?"
Mother probes,
her face twisting
between question,
concern, and smile.

"Oh, yeah, Mrs. Ulman.
I need to sneak
into my Grandpa's school
to surprise him today.
He'll never see me coming!"

"Is your Pop blind?"
I smirk.
"I mean, he'd be able to see
a giant bunny rabbit
coming into his office,
right?"
Ha!
Bunny rabbit.

"Okay, Erin.
What's more likely for me to wear?
A bright white, clean track suit
or dark, can't-see-me clothes?"
Caylee raises a good point.

It depends on which Caylee shows up.

Donna's Caylee would wear this
if Donna said to.

The Caylee I'm starting to know
wouldn't wear this
unless it was to break in
and steal something.

Add a bubbly attitude
and general cheer, and
no one would mistake her for a Moran.

"So where is this
breaking and entering happening?"
Mother tries
to keep a straight face
but a little chuckle
slips through.

"Glen Coast University.
Don't worry, Mrs. Ulman.
I promise to keep Erin
out of trouble today."
Caylee and Mother
burst into laughter,
but I'm not sure Caylee can keep that
promise.

Caylee scoops up a spoonful of scrambled eggs,
smiling while she shoves them in her mouth.
Her eyebrows jump up with mischief,
ready to get into trouble,
inviting me to do the same.

A light sigh falls from me,
a slight eye roll as I
resolve to get into trouble with her.

Resolving to have
some fun
today.

What To Do

"Why Glen Coast University?"
I ask.

"We know Grandpa Victor
has the device.
So he's got to have it
in one of his safe spaces.

I bet it's either
at his office, home,
or The Bookshop."
Caylee explains,
excitedly close.

"I'm betting it is
somewhere with security,
which means
The Bookshop or
the university,
and we know
Umu knows about
The Bookshop.

So . . ."

"So, he's put it somewhere
she doesn't know about?"
We assume.

I pull up maps of Glen Coast University
on my computer,

examining roads,
hills,
trees,
and buildings
of the campus
to determine the best approach.

"There!"
Caylee startles,
pointing to the satellite image
of Glen Coast University.
A dirt path
worn from too many students
cuts between
the Biology building and
Victor's building.

"That path there cuts from
the parking lot to the back door
of the building."
Caylee's finger traces the path.
"And there–"
She pauses on a fire escape ladder.
"We take that up to the roof,
then we come in from the roof entrance."

"Does that actually help us?
I mean, won't we still have to get into
Victor's office through the same door if we come
in the front door or roof?"

Thinking for a moment,
Caylee realizes the roof plan
is better in the movies than real life.

"Other ideas?"
she asks.

I look around my room.
A single red LED light sits
ready to be used in a breadboard;
then I see the Biology building on the map
right beside the Social Sciences building
and an idea hits.

"Yeah, actually."

An idea is starting to show up.

"And it doesn't involve climbing to the roof."

In Position

Getting off the bus at
Glen Coast University,
I fire up my laptop,
connect to the campus wi-fi,
feeling ridiculous in my GCU baseball cap.

My disguise is a hoodie,
jeans,
and baseball cap.
I look like me
going to a baseball game.

It will do for today.

Our simple five-phase plan,
ends with phase six: Ice Cream.
In my mind I keep repeating,
Make it to the Ice Cream.

But before we get there,
we need to steal
something.

"Ready?"

Caylee nods.
Her calm confidence
inspires me
to not screw this up.

"Good luck!"

And she's off to campus safety
running in her blinding white
track suit,

Surprisingly
matching other students'
eye-searing suits
as they jog around campus.

CAYLEE MORAN

Phase 1

The butterflies in my stomach aren't fluttering;
they're drowning horrifically,
thrashing in acid,
splashing bile into my throat.

I walk, as casual as
I can force myself to be.

Keeping my head down,
eyes low,
hood up,
I go into campus safety.

Deep breath . . .

That didn't help.

Another deep breath . . .

Pushing open the white door
labeled Campus Safety,
I'm quickly greeted by a guy behind
a glass teller window.

His outfit is a cross between
police and park ranger.
His attitude is as serious as any law enforcement.
Name tag,
not badge,
says GREENE.

"Can I help you, ma'am?"
he says with the most authoritative voice he can muster.

"Uh, yes, Officer Greene.
I saw something suspicious and
wanted to give you all a heads up."

He perks up for the
excitement of potential action,
or at least the potential
to leave his teller window.

He composes himself.
"Yes, ma'am.
We get this kind of thing
all the time.
Let me get an incident form
to fill out."

He quickly steps back to the filing cabinet,
sifts through some papers,
then steps over to his desk,
picks up a pad,
fumbling it
beside his computer.

As he searches, I see
a sticky note clinging to his screen,
just like Erin said to look for,
flapping in the wind like a flag at half-mast
mourning the security of Greene's computer.

In bold black marker:
Username: AGREENE
Password: UltraCop#1

Ultracop . . .

"*Ha!*"

Greene looks back to me
as I choke back the snort-worthy hilarity.

He finally discovers the incident report
in a box beside the teller window.

"Ah, here we go."
Greene clears his throat.
"Someone put this
in the wrong place."
He blushes.
"I'll be, uh."
He looks around.
"Uh, writing someone up
for this."

His nervous attempts at authority are cute
and desperate.

He finds a pen,
starting at the first question.

"Where did you see the—"

"Yeah, now that I think about it . . .

I don't think I should waste your time
with someone being double parked
by the Biology building.

I'll just go."

"Double parked!"
Greene scoffs,
struck by the idea,
dumbfounded by the lack of respect
for the double parker's fellow humankind.

He storms to his hat,
deftly
(a little too practiced)
scooping it onto his head in a single motion,
and bolts out the back door.

Double parking
must be a sore point
for the Ultracop.

Grabbing the pen
I scribble AGREENE's password
and head out the entrance.

ERIN ULMAN

Phase ~~2~~ 3

Caylee returns,
handing me a paper.
Scribbled on it:

AGREENE
UltraCop#1

"Utracop#1?"
I laugh.
Caylee bursts into snorts and giggles,
hushing herself as we hide in the bushes.

"Guess we don't need to break in
to their system now.
We'll just log in
as Ultracop.

Skipping phase 2.
Moving to phase 3."

I laugh as I log in to the
Glen Coast University Campus Safety Portal,
and as expected,
I can access the alarm system
with Ultracop's permissions.

In the Biology building
I find alarms for CO2,
fire . . .
oh, venom alarms.

Clicking on the more information link
I read:

> *Venom alarms alert the building of a toxic venom spill from one of the many venomous reptiles and insects studied at GCU.*

That will do the trick.

I prep the general announcement
to be said over the Biology building's internal speakers:

> *Venom alarm. Please evacuate immediately. Go to the Social Sciences building next door for further decontamination instructions.*

That will do the trick, too.

Panic.

Rushing students.

Chaos.

Ready with a press of the Enter key.

"All set. Ready?"

I look to Caylee to see if she's ready;
her fingers jitter
like Dad's after too much coffee
or mine when I get around too many people.

She nods
with a hint of defiance
and starts walking
toward the Biology building.

She nods to me at the Biology building doors;
as her foot clears the doorway,
I press Enter,
trigging the venom alarm.

Moments later
students pour out,
panicked,
afraid,
almost trampling each other,
and for a moment I wonder . . .

Is this plan going to get anyone hurt?

"Um, what are you doing?"
A voice behind me
sounds confused.
I turn to see
a campus safety officer.

>>> Surprise!
>>> Processing…

Irony punches me in the gut
as I read the name tag: GREENE.

He puffs up,
standing too tall;
his shirt can't contain his gut
as it pops out over his belt.

"I said–"
He clears his throat.
"What are you doing?"

Students are filing into the Social Sciences building.
Caylee is expecting the next alarm any moment.

>>> Processing…

Standing up with my laptop,
I sigh.
I smile as I think about what to say,
and as soon as I start thinking
I decide.

Erin.run();

No sense trying charm
or explain
or lie,
just run
through the football field,
hearing Greene chasing me,
screaming over his radio.

> "Suspicious Caucasian female,
> wearing a hoodie
> and GCU baseball cap!
> Running on football field.
> Need backup!"

Not being the athletic type,
my running won't last long,
and I need to trigger the next alarm.

The library!

A haven for all,
no matter your athletic ability.

Greene is sucking wind behind me,
falling further away
as I keep my sprint,
focusing on the library,
focusing on triggering that next alarm,
blind to the second campus safety officer
who tackles me to the ground;
bone-crunching compression,
a shockwave raking through my body,
sending my laptop spinning out of my arms
onto the football field.

Sunny day,
getting darker,
breathing
hard,
going to
throw up,
dizzy . . .

Erin.reboot();

I snap out of it,
seeing the other campus safety person,
rolling off me,
missing her target,
sliding right into my laptop.

Climbing to my feet,
stumbling back to a run,
trying to suck air into tight lungs,
I leave my laptop,
focusing again on the library,
focusing on how the basement is perfect
but now anywhere with a computer
will have to do.

Greene stops to catch his breath,
the tackling lady gets to her feet;
I'm almost there,
slowing to a walk,
trying to get my breath,
trying to act like I didn't just outrun campus safety,
trying to act like I'm not here to steal something
and stop being hunted by a 3D-printed monster
who threatened my friends, family, me.

"Hi!"
I'm panting,
trying to be calm.
"Just finishing my run. Phew!"
Stretching to sell the story;
the fit girl behind the desk
isn't buying it.

Her *What do you want* look
says she doesn't care.

"I'm looking for a computer.
Secluded if possible.
I'm doing . . ."

What?
What am I doing?
"Private research."

Really? That's all I could think of?

The girl's eyebrows cock up
in a mix of disinterest and judgement.

"Top floor, past reference
on the right.
Elevator's on the left."

She returns to her phone
in silent dismissal.

CAYLEE MORAN

Phase…Falls Apart

In the halls of the Social Sciences building
students look worried,
searching for answers,
while I wait
for the next alarm.

I calmly walk to the bathroom
to escape the crowd
to wait unseen.

And I wait.

And wait.

And wait.

And nothing happens.

Something is wrong.

“Erin, what are you doing?”
I whisper, hoping for an answer,
getting nothing.

Above the stall
I see a sprinkler.
The red glass pipe running through the center
ignites an idea.
I’ll break the sprinkler,
which will trigger the water,
which will break all the
other sprinklers in the building.

I saw that on SocialNet
a while ago.
It was the “sprinkler challenge”:
to escape the sprinklers before getting soaked.

The people on SocialNet said
one sprinkler breaks and they all break.
Pressure or something.

Looking around, I see another sprinkler over a sink.

Climbing on the sink,
one shoe in hand,
I whack at the sprinkler.

Nothing happens.

I whack again.
Still nothing.

I whack again,
almost slipping off the sink,
and *crack!*
The red glass breaks;
water explodes out, soaking me
in an icy cone.

I climb down,
victory at hand,
when I notice the other sprinkler
hasn't broken.

Sticking my head out the bathroom door,
I notice none of the sprinklers are going off
and begin to question my knowledge of sprinkler systems.

SocialNet led me astray . . .
Sigh.

Across the hall
a red fire alarm handle
calls to me.
That will do the trick.

I sprint over to it
and rip it down
as water spills out the bathroom behind me.

Sirens blaring,
lights flashing,
students already on edge of panic
start screaming
Fire!
without any sign of it.

Running,
pushing,
panicking.

I pull my hand away,
feeling the sticky
slime of ink
on my fingers.

Dye used to mark
the person who pulled
the alarm . . .

Brushing what I can
off on my all-white pants,
I head down the stairs
to the basement
to find Grandpa's office.

The Descent

Mom Victoria never took me to Grandpa's office,
never really talked about the University at all.

Going downstairs
the basement lights are dark
with only the flickering red fire alarm lights
streaking around, spinning about the hall.

Emerald exit signs flicker
and fade, devoured by the darkness.

A real fire would kill everyone down here.

The ringing of old fire bells,
metal clanging,
echoes in my head,
disorienting me in their repetition,
drowning me in their loudness.

The hallway pulses red.

Each office door is a step back from the hall.
The red pulses
can't reach,
blackening out the name plates,
leaving only blurry darkness
behind the frosted glass windows.

My phone becomes my flashlight,
lighting up the hallway
just a few steps ahead.

The bells blur my thoughts
a constant ringing around me,
inside me.

First door:
Dr. Tollence Greer, PhD.
Meta-Mythology and Psychocognition Department Chair.
Spots of black mildew
creep around the edges of the door,
sneaking out like poison
from whatever Dr. Greer
does inside.

From the red light,
I catch the shape of a dog out the corner of my eye.

Shining my light down the hall,
the form is gone:
a trick of the light,
amplified by the disorienting bells and
creepy atmosphere.

That's all it was . . .

Moving down the hall:
next door,
dark wood,
again mildew spewing around the edges
Dr. Victor Moran, PhD, MD.
Researcher: Meta-Mythology and Psychocognitive Studies.
Reaching for the handle,
I notice
the door is cracked open,
darkness inside,
my light showing nothing.

The bells stop in the hall,
echoing softly in my ears.

Tapping sounds quickly skitter across the tiles behind me.
I spin to see more clearly,
catching only a glance in the dark:
a large dog,
black, slick, wet body,
sharp ears,
galloping by me.

It disappears in the dark,
the clicking of
too many toenails
on the tile floor
the only sound around me.

I look back to the door,
now closed.

Maybe
it was always closed?

I grab the handle;
it burns frozen to the touch.

Caylee, what are you doing?
I hear in my head, echoing.
Not my voice.
Sounds like
Grandpa.

Wrapping my hand in my sleeve
I grab the handle,
twisting it,
pushing the door;
it opens.

Inside Grandpa's office
is like Mom Victoria's study.
Typewriter,
piles of books.

Books strewn everywhere,
shelves of bizarre tomes
and texts lining the walls;
the only difference,
on the right-hand wall,
is a large laundry chute door.

Going into the office,
a warm surge wraps my body,
fading as I take another step
like I just walked through hot Jell-O.

I look up for a heater
or fan;
nothing
there.

Closing the door behind me,
stepping over the books,
I kneel at the laundry chute covered in
white paint, blistering with mold
and other unidentified fungi.

A small steel handle at the bottom
invites me
to pull up.

Caylee, what are you doing?
again echoes in my mind.

"Ending this,"
I whisper.

Reaching down,
I yank up the door,
revealing
a cardboard box
matching the description Erin told me:
the box for the Pandora Device.

Snatching the box,
I turn to run out the door,
stepping over and
around piles of books,
getting to the door
when the silence is broken
by the
wet
thwapping of the typewriter.

Locking to stillness,
breath stolen,
wondering how I missed someone at the desk,
I peek over my shoulder:
no one.
The chair,
the desk,
is empty.

The typewriter continues, the
wet thwapping of ink onto page;
when the typing ends,
silence reclaims the room.

I put the box on the desk,
twisting the carriage wheel,
pulling the page from the typewriter
to read the single line printed.

What do you think that was in the hallway?

Spinning back, I see
the door still closed,
the room still dark,
the red lights still flashing outside,
highlighting
a headless body of shadow,
two arms pressing
against the frosted glass window
into the office.

It sways in the pulsing red light.

A wet snarl
drags through the silence,
making me step back.

Bumping into the desk,
I watch it,
waiting.

The door handle twists.

ERIN ULMAN

Escape

"Mother is going to be so pissed if I get arrested,"
I mutter.
No one is upstairs at the library.
The aisles are vacant,
the shelves full.
In the corner is
a small cubicle workspace
with a computer.

Booting up,
I log in with Ultracop's credentials,
seeing the fire alarm already activated
in the Social Sciences building;
looking at my watch,
knowing Caylee should be done by now.
I deactivate the fire alarm,
categorizing it as a false alarm
resolved by Officer Ultracop.

I jump on SocialNet,
logging in to the fake profile
Caylee and I set up.
I shoot Caylee a message.
Meet at my house.

Purging the browser history,
logging out from Ultracop's account,
I head to the staircase to get out of here.

Ultracop and the Tackler
are wheezing their way up the stairs.

My eyes hit the elevator.
I run over,
smashing the button
to call it up.

>>> Loading…

>>> Loading…

Just as I see Ultracop's campus safety hat
breaking over the staircase edge,
the elevator doors open.
I jump in,
hit L,
pressing the door close button
repeatedly,
as if the 100th press will be the one that works.

Ultracop sees me in the elevator,
doors closing.

"Arrgh!"
His hands jump
in frustration;
less about me,
more about
having to do more steps.

>>> Loading…3

>>> Loading…2

>>> Loading…L

Doors open,
all clear,
and I run out the library door,
looking to the Social Sciences building:
students standing outside confused,
everyone wandering around,
asking questions.

Everyone but
Victor.

He is looking past the crowd,
out to the library,
out to me,
flashing a campy horror villain grin,
waving low so no one else can see.

I don't stop,
running harder,
running until I can't breathe,
running until my legs turn to jelly
and I stumble to a bench
blocks and blocks away from the University.

I want to laugh;
this is when I should laugh at my almost-capture,
but I can't;
all I can
think of is Victor's smile,
a knowing smile,
like he planned our plan,
like he knew something I didn't.

Caylee.status();
>>> return unknown

Concern for Caylee
breathes life back into me
as I run home,
straight to my room,
straight to my computer
where I activate a remote wipe of my laptop
destroying all data left behind on the football field.

I search the campus news
for any sign of our hijinks.

On the website—

Breaking news: Fire alarm hoax. Students being questioned.

I lean away from the computer,
sucking air in,
wondering
if Caylee is one of those students.

CAYLEE MORAN

Escape

The typewriter
starts,
wet thwacking slaps of ink,
paper loaded from nowhere.

The door handle flicks,
like a fingerless paw is clawing at it to open.

Flicks again.

Typing stops.
I pull the page.

Now what? Erin just left you.
You three aren't the only ones
who want the device back.

I look to the desk:
more papers are piled up,
all starting
ATTN: Dr. V.C. Moran 17,
all typed on the typewriter.
Many signed
Sincerely Q. Nicholas.

Quincy.

Thwapping again

quickly tapping out
a message, stopping.

Where did this paper come from?
I didn't reload it…

I rip the paper out.

Time to prove you're ready.

Ready for what?

A low growl comes from the window.
Splattering,
dripping sounds lightly tap at the tile floor
beyond the door.

Is it bleeding?
Drooling?

Looking around the desk,
in drawers,
on the walls,
I find a rusted sword tucked under a
pile of books on the floor.

I grab it,
raise it,
fearing one solid hit would shatter this sword,
readying to swing for the fences and run.

The handle
turns
chunking sound
opening
creaking.

"Hey!"
A voice screams
outside the door;
the shadow turns,
moving away
from the opening door.

Thumps
and thuds
come from the hallway
outside Grandpa's office.

Screams of rage,
slapping meat sounds,
animalistic screeches—
a body slams against the outside wall,
jarring dust from the bookshelves.

SLAM!

Another smash into the wall.

CRASH!

The door explodes inward
as a body is thrown into it,
shrieking excruciating agony
as the shadowy figure is held in a web of
oily red film, glowing in the door frame.

As the body drops away,
the red glow fades.

She grunts on the ground,
angry,
springing back to her feet,
back into battle with the unseen beast
making those inhuman wails of pain.

Grunting
slapping
a squealing yelp sound
fading down the hallway
with the clicking of toenails on tile.

The lights come on;
the red flashing stops
and I rush to the door,
pausing to touch the oily red film,
but feel nothing.
I step out the door.
A wash of energy sweeps over me.

Puddles of blue sludge
pool in front of the door
and lead to
a panting girl in a torn-up hoodie,
torn up jeans,
red curly hair.

"Erin?"

"Close."

She turns,
revealing shimmering silver-green eyes.
Umu.

Her knuckles drip with
the same blue sludge spotting the hallway.
Another trail of sludge leads from her
toward a stairwell to the sub-basement.

"Careful with that sword, Caylee."
Her posture sinks,
ready to pounce.
"Looks like a tetanus shot
waiting to happen."
She watches me,
waiting
for another fight.

Watching her,
I keep the sword up
ready.
Going back into the office
I get the box.

"How'd you know we were here?"

"Location services."
She points to my phone.
"Your location is always
shared for those who know
how to listen."

I hold out the box;
she looks at the door frame
and motions for me to step out.

My eyes trace the frame,
nothing showing the red glow from earlier;
nothing I can see, anyway.

Stepping out,
I grip the sword in my right hand while
my left pushes the box to her.

"We're done here."

She takes it,
smiling,
opening it,
dumping out
books to the floor.

No Pandora Device,
only old books.

"Not quite.
I would have thought
two smart ladies like you
would be done by now.
I put too much
confidence in Erin."
Umu tosses the box into the office.

"Perhaps you need
more motivation."
She grins.

"If it's not here . . ."

"Where else would he keep it?"
Umu starts toward the staircase,
going up.

"The Bookshop."

"Tick-
tock,
Caylee.

Tick-
tock."

She runs up the stairs.
I follow,
losing her in the students filling the halls,
teachers directing them to class;
some teachers stand in the foyer chatting.
One of them,
Grandpa Victor,
catches me with his glare,
giving me a vicious smirk.

Blood gathers in my cheeks;
frustrated,
angry,
embarrassed—
no, not embarrassed,
pissed off,
my eyes screaming to him:

This isn't over.

My phone beeps:
message from Erin
to meet at her house.

I delete the message and
open Settings on my phone.

Tapping on Location Services,
I switch it to DISABLED
to avoid further
unwanted tracking.

Stuffing my phone
and hands in my pocket
I walk toward the door.

"Excuse me, miss!"

Someone yells to me.
"Miss, with the ink
on your pants.
Please stop there."

I freeze,
hearing someone come up
behind me.

"Officer, that's my
granddaughter."
Grandpa catches up to
the man behind me.
"She was with me;
that ink is from
a printing accident
earlier."

Grandpa continues on
with a story about who he
saw pull the fire alarm
and guides the campus safety officer
away.

Run along now,
Grandpa says in my head.

Grinding my teeth,
I head back to Erin's room.

ERIN ULMAN

Reconnecting

Caylee comes into my room,
chest heaving,
gasping;
she must have run here
from the University.

Her hands hold her knees
but nothing else.

"Wha–"
I stop myself,
checking my tone,
choking back frustration.
"Are you okay? What happened?"

She waves,
breathless,
collapsing on my bed
panting.

"Fake . . .

It was . . .

a fake."

>>> Does not compute
>>> Caylee Failed
>>> Good News: Caylee not caught

"I'm sorry about the fire alarm.
Campus Safety found me, and I lost my laptop."

Caylee is still trying to catch her breath,
like cornering an elusive thief
who keeps stealing the air from her lungs.

"No . . .
I figured . . .
Made do."

We sit in quiet for a moment,
waiting for Caylee to recover,
or at least talk without sounding like
a broken exhaust fan.

She sits up.
"Umu was there."

Umu said she'd be watching,
said she'd contact us when we found the device.
I shouldn't be surprised
but I can't find my words
to ask everything I want to know.,

How is she?

Where has she been?

All I can get out is,
"What happened?"

Caylee goes on
about the office,
about the creature,
about Umu saving the day,
although that isn't how Caylee tells it.

She thought the creature
was a dog?
Was it the same
dog I thought I saw
in the alley behind
The Bookshop?

"If it's not at the University,
then my money is on The Bookshop,"
Caylee says.

"Makes sense."

"We should go tonight but I . . .
I just can't.
I'm gassed."

I push back disappointment.
"Yeah."
Sigh.
"Me too."

She fishes in her pocket,
pulling out a crumpled white paper,
straightening it,
shoving it to me.

"Any ideas?"

I read it,
shame blushing my cheeks.
"Now what? Erin just left you.
You three aren't the only ones
who want the device back."

I had to run.

Stopping for a moment,
thinking,
processing the events of the last two weeks,
the people breaking into my house,
the device,
Umu.

"I thought the Pandora Device belonged to
Victor and Quincy?"

"Yeah, that's what I thought . . ."
She points to one word
on the paper.
"Back. Someone wants it *back*.
Where did this thing
come from?"

I look to my computer;
on the desktop,
Pandora.exe
still sitting there,
still waiting for the next run,
and I ask,

"Yeah . . . where did you come from?"

Decompiling

Code is pure,
perfect,
and simple.

You can make anything,
winding it into a ball of
functions,
features,
and subroutines,
taking human language
and translating it to computer language
through the process of compiling your code.

And like all things,
or maybe not all things,
what is done
can be undone.

I open my decompiling software
and target Pandora.exe for decompile,
unwinding
functions,
features,
subroutines,
translating
from machine language
to human language.

"Maybe once we can read the code
we can figure out who made this thing."

"Wait, didn't your dad
already give you
the code?"
Caylee asks.

I shake my head.
"No, he gave me Human.Eve's code.
That's the artificial intelligence system
that runs Umu. This code–"
I point to Pandora.exe.
"–is what actually made her.

Think of this as the logic that says
how to create her,
and Human.Eve is the logic of
how she thinks."

Caylee nods.
"Then how will this
help?"

"Often in code, people use names
and words that identify who made it.

Like author comments
or memory address names
called Namespaces."

"So
then what?"

"Then we know who else is
looking for their property."

The decompiler estimates
four hours to finish.

"Whoa!"
I point to the timer.
"That's a long time
for a decompile."

I push back from the computer,
repulsed by such a long estimate.

"That's a lot of decompiling!
Four hours?
How much code is in this application?"

"Enough to make a sentient
human-looking teenager.
I think the term is
synthetic human."
I smile and
press START.

"I've got to get home.
Let me know if you find out anything
as soon as you find out.

I'll be online."
Caylee pulls out her phone,
texting Cathy.

"See you tomorrow.
Great job today!
I wish
I could have seen you
with the sprinkler.
Side note, that's not how they work."
We laugh
as she heads out the door.
I hear Mother offer her a ride home,
both leaving.

Dreams of Yesterdays to Come

I know I'm dreaming
because Mother is smiling–
a real smile.
not the
fake it until you make it smile
she grew in Glen Coast.

We're at a waterfall
in the mountains
in Seattle.

She's happy,
Dad's happy,
I'm happy.

Picnic lunches and blankets
keeping life simple
in the joy of PB&Js
and togetherness.

A phone rings in the woods.
I turn to look;
it's my phone, beeping
with SocialNet alerts.

Everyone in school is telling me
how their parents lost their jobs
because of my dad.
How his "lies" have ruined
everything.

How I'm just like him.
I lied because I didn't tell them
what he was going to do.

That I'm all the horrible things they say I am
because my family ruined everything.
My dad ruined everything.
I ruined everything.

My phone battery dies in time for me to see
one last message from Betty:
I hate you. You ruined my life.

The screen goes black.
The last phone I'd ever have
died.

I hear a zipper's teeth beside me;
I look,
seeing Mom packing our bags,
then loading the car
as we head to Portland.

"Don't worry, Erin.
You can stay in touch with your friends
online."

She doesn't know:
By now
I don't have any friends.
My Dad is a traitor to the company
that fed everyone's families.

Betty hates me.
Her dad got fired.

But Mom doesn't know that.

"I know, Mom.
Don't worry!
We'll be great
in Portland."
My enthusiasm peps her up.

We get into the car,
ready for adventure.

I shut my door,
hearing it slam.

I look again,
seeing Dad frustrated:
his fourth interview since
getting to Portland,
our apartment too small
for anyone to hide.

He bursts through the living room,
angry,
sad,
defeated.

Mom perks up.

"Ulmans stick together, David!"
she declares.
Dad smiles.
"Right, Erin? We're all in this
together
and we'll
make it work."

I nod,
putting on the happy mask,
the same one I use in school
when people ask what happened in Seattle,
when people ask what my dad does,
when people smell the stink of *outcast* I can't wash off.

I close my eyes to find the happy memories,
sealing the happy mask onto my face.

Opening my eyes,
we're at dinner,
a blanket on the floor;
PB&J all that is left from our savings
with boxes scattered in chaos around us.

Interview number six might be the winner for Dad,
but I doubt it.

"Worst case scenario,
we move to Maryland
like we talked about.
You'll start that AI company
you've dreamed about,"
Mom says.

"No one will know us there.
SocialNet is just starting
to catch on
and most companies don't want
anything to do with it.

Don't worry, Erin. You can stay
in touch with your friends in Portland on-
line."

"Won't be a problem, Mom,"
I say.

She doesn't know that I don't have
any friends.
I'm still David Ulman's daughter here.
"If things don't work in Glen Coast,
we'll just go somewhere else, right?"

Portland wasn't far enough.

How far is far enough?

"Erin, this has been tough
on all of us.
Your dad did the right thing.
Unfortunately,
no one wanted to hear it,"
Mom says.

I chuckle, spite rising in my blood.
"If he did the right thing,
then why's everyone pissed at us?

Why is everyone at school saying
their parents don't want to work with
someone like Dad? They say
they don't want to work with a snitch."

I don't see Dad
slumping down,
the words crushing him into the blanket.
My sights are set on Mom.
Mrs. Positive.
Mrs. We Did the Right Thing.
Mrs. Martyr.

"Erin!"
Mom recoils from me,
reaching for Dad.

He dodges,
stands quietly, and leaves.

"I guess we're just running away
from everything now,"
I quip
with a pride in myself
I haven't found since.

The satisfying pride that leaks out your dark places
when you know you broke something
that can never be fixed,
knowing that what you've done
is forever.

Mom stands.
Her face flushes,
surging with rage,
the pressure of suppressing
disappointment,
defeat,
the situation
boiling over.

She pauses,
putting the lid back on,
trying to turn down the heat.

"Erin."
Deep breath.
"You need
to support your dad right now.
We're all doing our best.
You need to think about how all this
is making him feel.

Now please go apologize to him.
And leave your attitude
with the rest of your sandwich."

I stand slowly,
lifted by
indignity,
ready to deal my final blow.

"Apologize for the truth?
Maybe if he apologizes to us
for ruining everything we had in Seattle,
maybe I'd consider it.

He ruined everything!"

On the blanket,
Dad's sandwich is whole.
Mom's is too;
mine is almost gone.

I smile,
watching the words land in her chest.

The lid blows off;
her face doesn't turn red;
all the blood and anger and rage
explode from her mouth like venom spraying on me.

"I am your mother
and I am telling you
to go apologize
to your dad for being a
selfish brat."

Her finger flies back toward Dad's room,
slamming into a box beside her,
knocking the box over,
shattering the glasses inside,
sealing the moment with a crash.

Silence sits on us.

And then
I laugh
at the ridiculousness of her breaking the glasses,
of her trying to be authoritative,
of her telling me to apologize for his mistakes.

A cackling,
heckling
laugh.
I turn red,
my stomach hurting from her outburst
of trying to be a parent.

"You're not the only one-

Just-

Go to your room!"
she screams.

Her lips seize in disgust.

Squinting my eyes,
I spit at her,
"If you say so,
Mother."

I stomp off,
still chuckling,
stomach still hurting;
the pain grows deeper,
rooting into me,
but I keep laughing,
hoping to suffocate the ache.

I slam my door;
hearing the door open again,
I see our new house in Glen Coast.

"Let's get our stuff, Erin,"
Mother says.

All cheer
a distant memory.

Dad goes in,
straight to the basement
with his computers,
claiming his office,
getting to work,
getting away from us.

"Where do you want this box,
Mother?"

She winces.

The box I'm holding evaporates;
the house following,
wisping around me like a campfire's kindling.

In the darkness,
a voice:
"Apologies don't have a deadline."

Victoria steps through the smoke.

I look back to where Mother was standing,
tear welling under my eyes.

"Apologies only matter if you mean it."

"Sometimes
people don't deserve an apology . . .
but your mom does."
Victoria gently squeezes my shoulder.

"Do I deserve an apology,
Vicky?"
Victor's voice
cracks through the darkness.

Victoria evaporates,
leaving me alone
in the dark.

CAYLEE MORAN

Lurking in the Shadows

SHADOWLURKER Server Online

@Kuzan_King, you online?

@Zushion_Dawn, I tried
to call you earlier.

@Azriel_Knight saw Umu hanging outside earlier. Creeped her out.

Stay away from her.

No doubt!

Is she still hanging out with Erin?

No. Stay away from Umu.

Dangerous.

Right on.

Hey, if I was in a fight would you help me?

I'm no fighter but I'd try.

Prob better off with Meredith in a fight. She's scrappy.

Broke my arm when we were little because I stole her doll.

I think it was an accident.

That she broke my arm not that I stole her doll.

Yeah, got it.

Weird question.

Just something
on my mind.

What would it mean
if someone didn't help?

Prob scared.

Or, doesn't want to fight
the other person?

Maybe.
Sounds specific.

Yeah. Just thoughts.

TUESDAY (3 DAYS)

ERIN ULMAN

My Favorite Things

Awakening at my keyboard,
the decompile complete,
I open the output file.

The code is unreadable.

Letters and symbols
smashed together into an
illegible mess.

"Arrrrghhh!"
I slam my hands on my keyboard.

BEEEP!
my computer yells back at me
with a disapproving siren.
It doesn't like getting slammed.
I don't like things not working.

Breakfast smells drift from the kitchen.
Seems like someone's always making breakfast lately.

My mind still tired from last night,
my body sore from all the running yesterday,
I could go back to sleep
but
I won't find any rest there.

I step out of my room
to find Mother folding an omelet,
humming some tune,
familiar
but unrecognizable.

I see her
for the first time in a long time:
her fiery hair fading,
her pale face wearing a mask of content,
hiding lines of sadness.

My dream
echoes through me.

The images of Seattle to Portland to here
clear.
The words I said
clear.

I stop at the edge of the hallway
a few steps from the kitchen
and listen.

The words to match the sounds
slowly peek out of the mists of my memory,
and I hear them
sung
how she used to sing them.

Singing quietly slips from me:
"Raindrops, roses,
whiskers, kittens,
something something mittens…"

She stops humming,
her song stamped out by my presence.
"Oh, hi, Erin.
Good morning."

"I remember when you used to sing
that song.
My Favorite Things, right?"

She smiles,
not her Seattle smile
but her Glen Coast smile,
fleeting and frail.

"Yeah, I had to learn it
for a school play.

Can't remember
what I did yesterday,
but that songs sticks in my head."

I steal a slice of toast,
snatch the omelet she just finished.
"You should sing more . . .
Mom. You have a great voice."

Rushing back to my room,
escaping the moment,
I shut the door,
wondering
if, outside my room,
she found another Seattle smile,

if only for a moment.

What Victoria Knows

I head over to Caylee's house
to recount yesterday's failure
and build today's plan of attack.

Cathy lets me in,
trying to distract me from
the argument happening
a few feet away.

Caylee and Victoria
are simmering in the kitchen,
neck veins bulging
in a tenuous silence.

"Chin up!"
Yui squeaks from beside me.
"It doesn't have to work
to be convincing."
She's holding a wooden block
painted red,
the paint brush
in her other hand.

"Make sure you wait for sunrise."
She skips off, joining Sabrina.
"And don't look in the well."

Yui throws her red block
into Sabrina's block tower,
bringing it all down.

Both girls scream,
"Asteroid strike!"

They giggle and laugh.

Was it her in the Maker Lab?
Did she whisper into my head?
Can she read minds?
Can Victoria?

Can Caylee?

MoranFamily.magical = undefined;
MoranFamily.unusual = definitely;

"Hey, Caylee . . ."

"Hey, Erin,"
Victoria says,
her eyes locked on Caylee's.
"Victor told me
about your adventure yesterday."

Silence returns.

The air between them
fills with words both want to say.

I think of my dream and wonder if
they know to fear the aftermath
of those words coming out.

>>> System Interrupt
>>> Avoid Caylee saying something she can't take back

"So . . ."
I breathe out.
"Dr. Moran, what should we do?"

Caylee and Victoria
stare at me,
Caylee with dismissive wonder,
Victoria with anger and regret.

"You know what's going on.
What we're trying to do.
Help us do it so we can all be
done."
I hope these words clear the air
or sweep away the tension
with a simple call for help.

Victoria looks at Caylee,
sternly saying,
"You can't be involved."

"Why not?"
Caylee bursts out.

"Because I'm asking
you
not to be involved."
Victoria's frustration grows.
"Because if you're involved,
Victor is going to
suck you into his
world with Quincy."

"I don't care!
He's called me out.
He doesn't think
I can do this!
You don't think
I can do this!
I'm going to show you
I can!"
Caylee spits.

"You're not ready, Caylee.
You need to
focus on school,
get into a good college,
get out of Glen Coast."

"No, Mom! That's what
you
need me to do.

I–"

Victoria slams her hand on the counter.
The echo stops everything in the house:
Sabrina and Yui playing,
Cathy cleaning,
my breathing.

"Go to your room!
Grounded until further notice!"
Victoria's words knock Caylee back;
she quickly recovers,
steeling herself,
teeth grinding in the silent aftershocks
rocking the room.

"Whatever you say."

Caylee stomps off,
each step trying to pierce the floor.
I turn to follow.

"Erin, wait."
Victoria's hands quake,
her voice cracking from the weight
of her daughter's hate.
"I'm begging you,
keep her out of it.

For her sake."

A door slams
down the hallway.
Victoria's eyes squeeze shut.

"Victor . . .
if she does this,
he'll never let her go.
You'll have ruined
her chance to do anything in life
he doesn't want her to do."

She wheels to her study.
I follow her.
The kids return to play.
Cathy goes to Caylee.

Victoria pulls a key
from under her typewriter.

Small,
black,
with a round handle
crusted with rust

and crooked teeth like a ghoul in the shadows.

She hands it to me.

Iron, but heavier,
like the world and all its problems
were just handed
to me.

"This is the key to the back door
of The Bookshop.

It will take you in
through the basement.

Go straight upstairs,
don't linger, and don't
go at night.

Nothing before sunrise."

My eyes dart over to Yui;
she's throwing her asteroid
at another block tower,
telling Sabrina something
about space that I can't quite hear.

"My guess is the device
is in Victor's office
on the third floor."

I nod,
not sure what to say about
being handed the answer.

She wheels to the door of her study,
showing me out,
then shutting the door behind me.

Cathy comes out of Caylee's room,
shakes her head at me
with a polite smile,
and shuts the door.

"Perhaps come back
another time, Erin."
Cathy rubs my shoulder
and shows me the door.

Yui and Sabrina watch me
as I leave,
key
in hand.

Don't Separate the Party

Back home, I dig out the sundress
from my failed transformation into a Donna clone–
the metamorphosis that never pupated.

Add an oversized sunhat
and I look like I'm ready for the beach.

Not for
staking out
The Bookshop.

Someone knocks at the front door;
Mother answers.

"Hello, Mrs. Ulman.
I'm here to see Erin."
Davis's voice is a welcome sound
and I wonder if
Meredith is with him.

As I step out of my room,
Davis laughs.

"Uh, excuse me, miss,
have you seen Erin around?"

Mother bursts into laughter too,
her smile one of
real happiness.

"Yeah, Erin,
I thought this was over?"

She laughs again
then reads the
please don't talk about that look
in my eyes
and excitedly shifts.

"Well, do you guys need a ride?"

"No thanks, Mrs. Ulman.
Meredith and I
are good with walking. Erin said
the bookstore we're going to
is right up the road."

"Where's Meredith?"
I ask.

"Right there."
Davis points beside me
and there she is.

I startle at the silent
stillness of Meredith
typing away on her phone.

"Hello, Erin."
Meredith says.

"Oh, uh, hi Meredith."

"You guys have fun.
Call if you need anything,"
Mother says.
"You guys staying for dinner tonight?"

Davis shakes his head.
"Tonight is
obligatory family dinner
for the Arnold clan."
He smiles in anticipation.
"Maybe later this week.
I could bring
my famous homemade dinner rolls."

Mother's mouth drops in
an audible gasp of surprise and delight
when Meredith chimes in,

"Davis, homemade implies
more than opening a bag
of frozen rolls
and baking them
at 325 for fifteen minutes."

"There's more to it than that."
Davis blushes,
escaping to the door
"Ready to go, ladies?"

"We'll be back in a little while, Moth–"

I catch myself.
"Mom."

"Are we going to stick together
this time?"
Meredith asks.
"Remember when
Mrs. Ulman broke up the party
and then got lost.
I'm assuming we're not
doing that again."

Mother slowly sighs,
not sure whether to laugh
or deny.

"We'll stay together."
I look to Mother
and smile.

Surveillance

"So you're going to
steal something?"
Davis
ponders our midday activity
as we walk to The Bookshop.

"Like I said,
we're not stealing.
We're . . .
reclaiming.
Reclaiming something *they* stole from *me*."

"Reclaiming without permission
is stealing, Erin,"
Meredith adds in her
true-but-not-helpful way.

Reclaiming.isNot(Stealing);
>>> result: false

"Are you guys helping or not?"

"Yes, Erin.
I don't have any issues
with stealing,"
Meredith says,
making me think
I need to keep
a closer eye on her.

I look to Davis.
He releases a defeated sigh.

"Yeah, let's go."

We circle around The Bookshop,
finding a nameless alley behind it,

stepping over split and spilled trash bags
looking like overstuffed stomachs torn apart
by critters trying to get to what's inside.

Squeaks and squeals
drift from the dark alley
as rats debate ownership
of rotten food.

We find The Bookshop's back door.
The store's trash bags are intact.
No gnawing or ripping,
no critters or crawlers,
nothing but shadow
and stillness.

A few moldy stairs lead
from the alley
down to a black splintered door
with a large iron lock,
crusted with rust.

Moldy white splotches creep out
on the door frame
as if some infection strains to escape.

We keep walking,
heads down, around to the front entrance
of The Bookshop.

"When inside, look for cameras
or alarms or whatever.
I need to get to
the top floor
from the basement.

Meredith, you check the second and third floor.

Davis, check the entryway.

I'll be looking at the basement door.

Got it?"

Meredith's eyes nod or roll,
I'm not certain which.

Davis,
nervous,
bobs his head,
mumbling to himself.

"Check the entrance.
Cameras, alarms, whatever."

We walk in.
DING!
A bell hits the door.

Davis jumps.

I try to tell him *Quit being so jumpy*
with my eyes.
I think he gets the message.

"Hi, Mr. Stone!"
I say, passing the old man at the front desk
reading the newspaper as always,
sipping his coffee as always,
grumbling his reply as always.

Meredith walks to him,
looking around,
and asks where to find books on photosynthesis.
Mr. Stone grunts and nods toward the steps.
She walks upstairs without looking back.

Davis goes to the computer section
across the store,
picks a book,
and
very poorly
pretends to read while he observes
the front door.

I try to strike up a conversation with Mr. Stone
but only get grunts
and mumbles,
dismissing me from our non-starter conversation.

Footsteps clop up the stairs from the basement;
the white door
cracks open a bit,
giving me a glimpse of a hulking shadow
swaying up the stairs.

"Do you guys keep more inventory downstairs?"
I ask Mr. Stone.

"No, that's where we put
the troublemakers."
Quincy steps out
from the basement.
His shoulders shift to fit
through the door frame.

His grin telling me
he's not joking.

"Hello, Quincy."
He towers over me
as I step back to escape his shadow,
finding a smile in myself.
I push it through my teeth,
curling my cheeks,
trying to tell myself to
act happy to see him.

"Looking for
something
specific?"
Quincy asks.

Erin.keepSmiling();

Speaking through my teeth.
"Yes, actually. I'm look for a book
on understanding the psychology
of people who steal from others."
I put on my surprised mask.
"I just don't get that mindset.
Who would do such a thing?"

He smiles,
baring teeth,
curling cheeks:
a smile as manufactured
as mine.
"Check psychology upstairs.
I think you'll find it
beside books
on keeping things
that don't belong to you."

We smile
in silence,
waiting for each other's next comment.

"Hello Mr. The Bookshop Clerk.
I'd like to purchase this book,"
Meredith says to Mr. Stone.

Quincy scans the room,
eyes stopping on Meredith
and again on Davis,
who's failing to be inconspicuous.

"Missing one?"
Quincy says.

"Always have an ace in the hole, right?"
I deliver with confidence,
hoping he doesn't see the bluff.

"Whatever you're thinking . . ."
His smile fades to a glare.
"Don't try it.
There's more to this place
than books."

"Meredith, Davis.
I think we're done here."

"Erin, I want to buy this book."
Meredith puts her money down,
looking at Quincy.
"Keep the change
for a new attitude."

His glare bores a hole in me
as I snort a laugh at Meredith's quip.
Davis quietly runs out the door.
Meredith follows.

I wave goodbye to Quincy,
seeing a silver ring
glinting from the upstairs railing,
ruby light glittering on the wall,

and I know who else was listening
to my verbal spar

with Quincy.

I'll need to move quickly.
I'm going to need help.
This isn't a job for strength or speed;
I need the smartest person I know to help make a plan . . .

This is important.
Maybe he'll pay attention to me
when he hears how important this is.

Dinner with Dad

"Dad, I have something I need to talk to you about."

I watch myself
saying the words in the bathroom mirror,
trying to recount the story so far:
the device,
Umu,
The Bookshop.

"I need your help.

You're the smartest person I know."

Pulling the curls from my face,
I clip them back
and practice asking him again.

Walking out to the kitchen,
I see him on the phone,
his face wrinkled in a work problem,
each ripple of skin telling me
Your dad is busy today.

"Yes, I know
this is important.

Yes, I understand
what this could mean.

You don't need to do that,
I'm handling it.
You just need to–

No, you can
call them back. I-

"No–fine. I'm on my way."

He shoves his laptop into his bag
with an angry huff.
Without looking at me,
he stomps toward the door.

I call to him,
"Hey, Dad!
I really need to talk
to you."

"Sorry, Erin.
Something important came up.
Tell me about it tomorrow
when I see you.
Okay?"

"Uh, it
kind of can't wait . . ."
My voice follows him out the door.
The door shuts.

The car starts.
Backs out
and drives away.

I watch the door,
waiting for what I said
to sink in.

Waiting for him
to understand
I need him.

"Is it something I can help with?"
Mother says,
her soft apologetic voice,
her too-often-used
making excuses for Dad voice.

"I need someone really smart
who thinks I'm worth their time,"
I bark back,
throwing my anger at her.

She tenses,
answering me
with a deep breath,
then a smile.
"Actually, I think I can help.

I can get you and Caylee dinner
from that taco place you like.

I can pick her up while you do whatever you need to do to get ready.

Then you two can solve whatever your problem is."

She grabs her keys.

"Any special requests
or do you want your usual
gross chicken guaco taco?"

Her smile catches me off guard,
dissolving my
disappointment and anger
in her smile.

"Chicken guaco taco would be great, Mom."

I smile,
finding hope in her
ability to make things better,
finding her in my corner,
not in a book,
not in the kitchen,
but ready to solve a problem
Dad has left me with.

She sniffles,
wiping red eyes,
stepping to the door.

"Those tacos are so gross."

We laugh
as she goes for reinforcements.

CAYLEE MORAN

Collision of Fates

Grounded?

I haven't been grounded since . . .

I don't think I've ever been grounded.

I pace in my room,
waiting for my door to open,
for Mom Victoria to release me
or Mom Cathy to give me her usual

She didn't mean it like that.

But no one comes.

I work a circle into my floor,
walking the path in my mind around
why Mom Victoria wants me to just sit
and wait
and be normal.

A normal life,
boring,
restricted
to the mundanities of
school,
college,
adulting.

Door opens;
Mom Victoria wheels in
with the look she probably gives
failing students.

"You can't do this.
Leave Victor and Erin
to their games.
Focus on your future."

"Erin needs help.
You said that!"

"She does need help,
but it doesn't have to be
from you."
She comes closer,
reaching for my hand.

I snatch it away.
"That's a great message.
Don't help people who need it
because someone else probably will help them."
Anger gives way to pleading.
"I can do this, Mom!"

She recoils,
preparing to strike.

"Victor and Erin and all of them
are just roadblocks, Caylee.
Can't you see that?
They're tripping you up,
making you—"

"What? Making me what?
Happy?
Making me feel like I'm
not a screw up?"

"They're a distraction!
You could be an amazing engineer
but instead you
play on that stupid SocialNet,
making stupid little apps
that are a waste of your time.
You're so focused on what's happening right now,
you can't see your future."

"No, Mom! I'm wasting the future
you want for me. I don't want
that future. I'm learning there's more
to the world than college and jobs, and I
want more of that.

I want to see more, know more, and I'm not going
to get that wasting time in college."

She doesn't hear me.
"You don't understand
what you're saying.
Think about your future!
Good job,
good pay,
build a family.

This is what's important,
not chasing things
and knowledge
that could kill you.

Trading
safety for danger
is just stupid,
and I didn't raise a stupid daughter, Caylee."

"Apparently you did, Mom.

The great Dr. Moran,

raising a stupid little girl
who'd rather see the world
than read about it.
Yep, totally stupid."

"Caylee! You don't know—"

"Enough, you two."
Mom Cathy comes in,
missing her always-present
smile.
"Mrs. Ulman is here
for Caylee.
She has some tacos and
has asked if Caylee can
join Erin tonight
for solving some
computer problem."

Mom Victoria straightens up;
Mom Cathy's eyes grind down
like a sharp blade, cutting
any objection.
"I told her that's fine
and Caylee is on her way."

Mom Victoria's face
hardens, reddens,
mouth open to refute,
but Mom Cathy raises
her finger.

The
stop now
finger
that all Morans
have learned to fear.

She doesn't point to anything
specific, more just
points to the moment,
commanding you to stop.

Mom Victoria growls in discontent
and wheels out the room.

"Whatever is going on
between you two,
solve it."
Mom Cathy turns her glare,
her finger,
on me.

"Yes, Mom,"
I agree,
looking to the floor.

"Awwwww! Caylee's in trouble!"
Sabrina cackles as she
sticks her head in the door.
She laughs.

"You next?"
Mom Cathy turns on her
and Sabrina vanishes
before the second word
finishes.

"She loves you, Caylee,
and she's not wrong
about your grandfather.

There are things going on
you don't know about.
She doesn't want you in it,
and neither do I.

Tonight, you stay out
of whatever is going on,
and tomorrow, you and Vicky
are putting it all behind you."

"Yes, Mom."
I nod,
keeping my eyes
down, away from her
glare.

"Get ready
and have fun tonight."
Mom Cathy puts a smile back on
before she walks out
to tell Mrs. Ulman
I'll be out shortly.

Staying Out of Trouble

Erin's taco shell
cracks as oily green goop
plops out of it.

"That's disgusting."
I take a bite of my own
taco and watch brown grease
stream out.

Erin shrugs
and takes another bite,
leaving a blob of guac
on her chin.

"So, what do you need
help with?"

"Nope,"
Mrs. Ulman says,
hurrying to the table.
"No business
until after dinner."

She points to Erin.
"That was the rule
when you were younger
and I'm bringing it back."

Good rule.
I nod and smile.

"So, any new books,
Mrs. Ulman?
Erin said you like to read."

Erin's eyes
ask me to keep the rest
of what she said
about her mom's reading
between us.

"Yes, actually,"
Mrs. Ulman says,
placing another plate
of tacos on the table.

She pulls her chair in
and settles with us.

Erin sighs.

"It's a book about
a little girl who
finds a dog and
the dog helps her make
friends."
Mrs. Ulman smiles.
"It's cute."

"It's a kids' book,"
Erin chimes in.
"*Because of Winn-Dixie*."

"Yes, it is a kids' book,
but it's a good book
and has a great theme,"
Mrs. Ulman says.

"Why read a kids' book?"
I smile,
laughing at the idea inside
but trying not to show it.

"I read to see the world
from other people's eyes,"
Mrs. Ulman says.
"Helps me think about
how I see the world."

"That's really cool."
And deep.

I read because my teachers
tell me to.
Erin reads to learn.

Never have I thought about
reading to change
my worldview.

BRRRRR

BBRRRRRR

"Sorry."
I pull out my phone
and look at the screen.

My finger jumps to answer
when I look up
and see that Erin
sees who is calling.

I hit ignore
and put the phone facedown.

"Why's she calling?"
Erin pushes her fork
through the scattered remains
of her guaco taco sludge.

BRRRRRR

A text message
following up on the call.

"Might as well answer."
Erin sighs,
getting up from the table,
taking her plate to the sink.

"Who is it?"
Mrs. Ulman asks.

I open the text.

Movies?

"It's from my friend Donna."

Erin goes back to her room.

I text Donna back.
Can't. Grounded.

"Would she like to
come over too?
I can get more tacos,"
Mrs. Ulman asks,
smiling in her
always-pleasant way.

Just like Mom Cathy.
Always getting along
to get along.
Always smiling
and making others
smile.

Who makes her smile?
Who thinks about Mrs. Ulman
and wonders if she's in a good place?

Who does that for Mom Cathy?

"Oh, uh, probably busy."
I smile.

BRRRRRR

Another text.
K. Txt soon.

Erin's door shuts
quietly.

No slam.

Resolved
the night
is over.

Abandoned

When I open the door,
Erin's room blasts me
with heat.

"Hey, what's going on?"
I lean on the door
while she spins in her
computer chair.

My phone buzzes again.

"Why's she calling?"
Erin picks up a VR controller
and fidgets with the buttons.
"I thought you two
were done?"

"Me too."
I shrug.

"Then what's going on?"
Erin stops at her computer,
leans forward,
and taps a key.

The computer comes to life
painting her face
with a pale green glow.

"I don't know.
She's going to the movies
and just texted me."
I remember when
Donna and I saw
Kong
last year.

Donna thought it was
hilarious
when Kong ate the squid thing.

She laughed
and whispered
to me,
Sushi anyone?

I smile.

"If you'd rather
be there, go for it,"
Erin says
disinterested,
disengaging from
me.

"No, I'm here."
I step toward her.

She leans further
into her screen.
"What are we working on?"

I come around her chair;
she moves around
to block me.

"What's going on?"

"I thought I'd need help,
but I don't.
Just need to concentrate."
Her eyes stay on the screen
as she traces lines of code.

"Okay, well, I'll just wait
until you decide you need
help."
I plop on her bed
and look at the posters
on the walls.

My phone buzzes again.

"Don't you-"

"Nope."

She keeps clicking away
at her keyboard,
typing so fast the computer
probably can't keep up.

"I'm staying to help."

She turns to me.

"So what are we working on?"
I ask.

Erin nods me over
to her computer
with a mischievous smile.

My phone rings.

Erin's smile sours.

I look at it.

Mom Victoria's been texting
and calling.

"Uh oh . . ."
I push out a laugh
to dismiss the nervousness
building in me.

Erin sighs,
rolls her eyes,
smiles, and nods.

I call Mom Cathy
and ask for a bit more
time.

She agrees
as Mom Victoria scoffs
in the background.

"Okay, I'm good.
What do we have?"

"Data."
Erin pulls up a file folder
with tons of files in it.
"When I was in Umu's head
I copied the data
that's driving her."

Each file is a number plus
date and time.
"These are SocialNet posts.
It's everything
everyone posts,
and even the stuff they post
in Private Mode.

Umu literally knows everything
people put on SocialNet
and can instantly search it
with my dad's
artificial intelligence system."

"I thought we knew this
already?"

"We did, but we missed one thing . . ."
Erin points to another file,
opening it to show a long
cluster of weird text.

"This is a data feed
uploading from Umu
to somewhere.

Think of it like
Umu's summary of
what she's learned today
being told
to a master computer."

"Is this that transmission
thing?"

"Yeah, when she's staring
at the moon and mumbling,
she's uploading data
somewhere."

"So, is someone controlling her?"

"I don't think so.
I think she's
unknowingly
collecting data for
someone.

But who?"

Realization hits me.
Umu knows everything anyone
has ever posted online.
A full history of every
conversation,
picture,
video,
private message,
reaction,
share.

It knows locations from the posts,
who is connected to who,
how they interact,
when they interact,
who else is involved.

It literally knows everything.
The secrets we share.
Who we share them with.

It probably knows how healthy people are
based on the pictures of their food
they share online.

Is that how it knew
it could run me down?
Because I'm not a runner,
I'm not a healthy eater.

Good genetics make me look
athletic
but my cardio sucks;
always did.

I wonder if my birth parents
were athletes?

What else does it know
about me that
I don't even know?

My phone buzzes again
with a SocialNet alert
from Donna.

A picture of her at the movies.

Erin looks at the picture,
seeing something in the address of the
image.

A number.

"Caylee, your mom is here,"
Mrs. Ulman shouts.

I think about Umu.
It's not just a monster,
it's a spy,
but why?

What's worth spying on here
in Glen Coast?

Who would want
to know anything
about this place?

WEDNESDAY (2 DAYS)

ERIN ULMAN

What is Known

School reopens today
but I can't sleep,
so I search through
Umu's data,
wandering to
Donna's SocialNet ID.

The image she sent Caylee earlier
showed me Donna's ID.
Opening Donna's folder,
I see the data
my original SocialNet app
couldn't see.

In her directory
is a flood of public posts;
I skip them, going
to the private messages.

Messages to her dad:
Can you take me to
buy a gift for mom's
birthday?

His response:
Sorry Bunnykins.
Going skiing with my family
this weekend.

Isn't she his family?

Another message:
Hey Dad, miss you.
Got you and me tickets for
the new Star Wars movie.
When works for you?

Response:
Sorry Bunnykins, too busy.
Maybe next time.

She didn't give a time
or date.
I know these conversations.
I've had these conversations.

Too busy.
Too much going on.
Important things that
aren't me.

Message to Caylee:
Dad canceled again,
wanna grab a coffee?

Response from Caylee:
Parents suck. Let's caffeinate.
On my way.

Another post, a private page:
The Beehive: Growing Young Minds for Today's World

It's a daycare service?
Donna's building a daycare service?

I scroll to the first day
I met Donna,
finding a message
to Caylee.

Who's the new girl?
In computer lab she said
anyone who doesn't understand
computers is stupid.

What's her problem?
We're not all rich techies.

I didn't say . . .
I didn't mean that *she* was
stupid.

More messages from her dad
canceling plans,
from her friends
canceling plans,
from everyone
canceling her.

A message to Caylee from last week:
If Erin rolls her eyes again
when I have a computer problem
I'm gonna punch her.

Tired of her shit.

I didn't think she saw that.
Rude messages from people online
about her clothes,
about her body.

No wonder she's angry all the time.

She's alone.

The most popular girl
in Glen Coast High
is a façade on SocialNet
that everyone agrees to.

She's alone at home
and online,
with only
pretend friends
surrounding her
on all sides.

I close Donna's folder
and lean back,
wondering what
Caylee would say
about all this.

Does she already know?

Is that why Donna messaged her?
Is Caylee the only person
who really knows Donna?

Is Caylee the safe friend
for everyone?

Who's Caylee's safe friend?
The person that lets her just
be herself?

Is it
me?

Stealing vs. Reclaiming

Eating my usual
ham sandwich,
I scan the faces coming in
and gathering
in the lunchroom.

Donna and her crew
settle at their normal table,
taking pictures of their food for SocialNet.
The girls surrounding Donna
laugh, post, show each other
their photos.
They play on SocialNet.

Umu.data.add("Donna's friends' food");

Not Donna;
her eyes dart around the screen,
scrolling with quick flicks,
tapping.

I've never noticed:
she isn't enjoying this.
She isn't playing on SocialNet.
She's working.
She's manufacturing
her online persona.

Davis and Meredith
emerge from the hungry bodies finding tables,
sitting with me.
Davis bites into his sandwich
with a strange crunch.
Chips fall out
as he takes another bite.
A peanut butter and potato chip sandwich?

Meredith, snapping her carrots,
sees me notice the chips.
"Yes, it's gross,"
she says.
"And messy.
More messy than gross."

The lunch rush passes
with only a
trickle of students coming in
now.

Caylee hurries in,
giving Donna a smile
as she enters.

Donna pulls back a smile
as the other girls
scoff away Caylee,
the pariah.

Caylee's questions start
before her butt hits the chair.
"So, what did I miss?"

"Erin plans on
robbing a bookstore,"
Meredith chimes in.

Caylee nods.

"I don't have a problem with that.
Davis isn't on board,"
Meredith adds.

"Yeah, sorry."
Davis shrugs.
"I have a problem with stealing
from stores.
Places like that bookstore
don't mess around with
shoplifting.
No one is going to want
to work with a tax lawyer
with a criminal record."

He pauses for a moment,
looking to the ceiling.
"Well, I mean I guess no one
I'd want to work with.
Probably people who are okay with
shady tax practices would be okay
with a criminal record."

Davis continues reflecting
on the topic
as I interrupt.

"No one is shoplifting, Davis.
We're reclaiming. We
talked about this."

"Reclaiming without permission–"
Meredith starts.

"Yes, yes, I know
it's still stealing, but
we're not calling it that."
I wave away her truth
like swatting a fly away from my head.

Attention students,
the principals calls over the loudspeaker.
Great news! We've been able to reschedule
Homecoming for this Friday. Barring any power outages–
She laughs.
–we'll have our Homecoming dance at 8 PM. More details
will be shared at the end of the day. See you there!

Davis's eyes drop to the table
as a rush of heat suddenly swells in me,
remembering the freedom of the dance floor
and fun
and . . .
and how the night ended.

"I can probably be ungrounded
for that,"
Caylee says, stealing
a carrot from Meredith.
"But I wouldn't miss
'reclaiming'
something with you, Erin.
Screw being grounded."

Remembering Victoria's words,
how Victor would turn Caylee's win
into her prison,
I push them away, knowing
I need Caylee's help.
Davis and Meredith can't be
pulled into this further
without telling them everything,
and I don't want them to see me
differently than they do right now.

"I'm going to go tomorrow morning to–"
I look at Davis,
clearing my throat.
"Reclaim my property just after sunrise."

I look at Caylee,
meeting her excited stare.
"I could really use a hand."

"Thank you for inviting me, Erin,
but I'll still be sleeping
at that time,"
Meredith says.

Caylee and I
turn to her.

"Oh, uh, thanks anyway, Meredith.
Caylee, what do you think?"

"What time?"
Her giddy, almost bubbly
voice crackles with energy.

"Sunrise is at 6:45 tomorrow.
So meet at 6:30 behind The Bookshop
in the alley, at the stairs.

We go in through the basement."

"Guys, I need
plausible deniability here,"
Davis says.
"Finish your plans while
I throw away my trash."
Holding a fist full
of lunch bag,
he walks away,
head wagging in disbelief.

Meredith leans closer.
"I don't want to be involved,
but I do want to hear
all the details.

Please continue."

We laugh.
Caylee snorts.
I smile.

Building a plan
for breaking and entering
is more fun
with friends.

Metamorphosis

"Ms. Isler! My computer
isn't working!"
Donna says
as her fingers crash down
on the keyboard.

"I can't do anything!"
Her fingers
smash down harder.

Her cheeks are red,
and as I look closer,
so are her eyes.

Tiny smears of liner
under her eyes are
carefully swept away,
hidden from everyone
who never really sees her.

Remembering her messages,
her interpretation of me,
the missed opportunity,
the connection we could have
over our absentee fathers,
I stand up and walk to her.

Erin.confidence.build();
Erin.help(Donna);
Erin.show(Donna).whoIAm;

Caylee stares,
her eyes waving me off,
telling me to run.

"Hey, Donna. Your window isn't in focus,
which is why you can't type in
the word processor window.

Just click–"

"What are you doing?"
Donna recoils
as I reach for her mouse.

I pull my hand back.
"Just, uh, click in the white space there."
I draw a circle in the air.
"Anywhere."
I manufacture a friendly smile,
or what I think a friendly smile
would look like.
"And you should be good to go."

She shakes her head,
dismissing me,
then clicks on the white space.

Crisis averted.

"You should be all set now,"
I say,
returning to my place.

Donna's friends
wait for her reaction.
"Whatever, Erin,"
Donna says with a scoff.
A manufactured scoff to appease
her image.

She turns back to her screen
and giggling erupts from the girls
around her.
"She thinks she's so smart,"
one of them says.

Donna shakes away the comment,
looking back to me
as I sit down.

Her eyes soften so slightly
those around her don't notice,
but having endured many of
Donna's glares,

I notice.

Caylee's smile shines.

In my screen
I can see my own smile
reflecting back to me.

"Pssst! Are you going
to Homecoming Friday?"
Davis loudly whispers.

"Yeah, probably,"
I answer in my own
loud whisper.
"You want to go with me?"

>>> INTERUPT
>>> Does not compute

What did I just say?

Caylee's snorting laughter
draws Ms. Isler's attention.

"Ms. Moran, is there
something funny
you'd like to share?"

"No, Ms. Isler.
I just figured out something."
Ms. Isler's glare expects more.
"The formatting shortcut keys. Just hit me
funny.
You know, Control + B
like, wow, yeah, *bold*.
And–"

"You can stop there, Ms. Moran."
Disinterest sinks
Ms. Isler's eyes
back to her own computer screen.

"Like, with everyone?"
Davis asks.

"I mean, if that's what you want.
Or you know, just like . . .
you and me.

We'll see everyone else there, right?"

"Yeah, I guess so.
I mean, if they go."
He looks to Caylee;
she's shaking her head
with a grin so wide
it's about to rip into her cheeks.

"Okay, so yeah, we'll do that."
I fumble through words,
tripping over excitement
and nerves
and something in my stomach
that might be vomit or elation.

And just like that,
I have a date.

Who We Are & Aren't

After school I rush home
to finish the Human.Eve kill code.

Each keystroke
falls into place,
even the frequent backspaces.

"Hey, Erin."
Mother stands at the door.
"Sorry to interrupt,
but I got a message about Homecoming
being rescheduled.
Are you planning on going?"

"Yeah, Davis and I are going."
My fingers don't stop;
no time to waste
with two days left until
Umu expects us to have
the device.

This code
is the backup plan,
Plan B,
the weapon I think will stop her
the weapon I don't want to use.

"Oh, really?"
I can feel her smile.

"We're just going as friends."
A dismissive *mm-hmm* follows my words.
"Seriously, Mom.
I've got to concentrate."

"What are you working on?"
She steps into my room to look.

"Just some code."

She sticks her face close to the screen
as if being closer will make the code
more understandable.

"You look just like your dad."

I smile,
unable to hide
how happy I am to hear those words.

Dad is amazing at . . .
well,
everything when it comes to technology.

I imagine working with him on big projects,
solving big problems,
changing the world
one day.

Would he do to me
what he did to Betty's dad?
Would he tell the truth
and ruin everything for me?

Didn't he already?

The smile fades
with the memories of Betty's messages.
You're toxic just like your dad.
And the other messages before we left Seattle.
You and your dad ruined everything.
Your dad got my dad fired. I hate you.

Mom stands and steps to the door.
"Well, don't be like your dad
and stay up all night.
I remember one time in college,
he didn't sleep
for like three days."
Mother laughs,
seeing the memory.
"Yeah, he never slept
when he was hot on a project."

I know the feeling.

I'll sleep when I'm done,
and that needs to be by Friday.

"Yeah, I'll sleep."

"I'll bring dinner in,
David Junior."
She chuckles down the hall.

I test the code,
hitting errors,
failures,
and the instant reminder
that I'm not Dad.

He'd be done by now.

But his code would be a mess.

Maybe this will be an all-nighter?

Maybe I'll be working
until 6:00 AM,
giving me twelve hours
to complete
this
Plan B for Umu's return.

Plan B . . .
that doesn't sound as final as
kill code.

Is this murder?

Am I planning on killing her?

Caylee would say

This is what has to be done.
But I wonder.
Is this the solution?

Is there another way?

Have we gone too far
to be any other way?

CAYLEE MORAN

Before You Go

"Goodnight, Sabrina."
I kiss her.

"Goodnight, Yui."
I kiss her too.

"Caylee, can we have a story?"
Sabrina asks.

Their little faces
show me their secret weapon:
irresistible
begging eyes.

"Yeah, fine."

I start telling them about Hansel and Gretel,
how two children go off to a candy-covered house,
and while eating the house,
get invited inside by a witch.

"That's not what happens,"
Yui says with a wry smile.

"Oh yeah? Then you tell the story."

"The witch didn't invite them in.
They broke in to steal something
from the witch."

Is she thinking about
Erin and my plan
for tonight?

Did she hear us talking about it?
Or, is this another one of her

feelings?

"What were they going to steal?
More candy?"
I laugh away the thought.

"No, they were going to steal
the something
the witch stole from them.

But
they didn't know
a monster lived inside the house."

"A monster?

That's not how the story goes."
Is this another Yui feeling?
Should I expect
something
in the basement?

"Yes, it is,"
Yui insists.

"Yeah,
I like Yui's version better,"
Sabrina says.

"Well, okay then. What happens next?"
The words rattle out of me
but I try to put on a
smile for Sabrina.

I don't want her to
get scared.

"They find something in the house
they didn't expect."

"The monster?"

"No, statues,"
Yui says.
Her voice turns somber;
her eyes drift to a darker place
than our room outside
the night light's glow.

"Statues? That's the best you've got?"
I snicker, trying to lighten her mood.

"They aren't statues like
at a museum."
Yui's voice is dead and distant.
"They're statues of people
the monster has poisoned
before it eats them."

"I don't like this monster,"
Sabrina says
sliding further under her covers.

"Yui, you're scaring your sister."
And me too.

Yui snaps back to us,
smiles, and giggles.
"Oh, don't worry Sabrina.
The statues aren't finished yet.
The monster has to
finish the statue
before it can eat them."

"Okay, let's end there.
Very creative, Yui.
Goodnight, you two."

"Caylee,
were Hansel and Gretel sisters?"
Yui asks.

"No, brother and sister."

“Really? In my version
they’re two girls.
I like my version better.”

“Sounds great, Yui.
Love you!
Goodnight!”
Just a story.
I keep repeating that
as we lay down to bed.
Just a story…

THURSDAY (1 DAY)

ERIN ULMAN

When You're Alone

I check the clock.

5:30 AM.

Sunrise is an hour away.

I slip into my hoodie:
black,
no words,
no images,
just black.

I grab my flashlight
and a set of backup batteries
because I've seen enough
horror movies to know:
Always have a backup.

I slip out my window,
carefully sneaking across the front yard,
and a light in the living room catches my eye.

Mother stands at the basement door,
the living room light softly highlighting
her lonely face,
her slumping posture,
eyes looking into the basement.

Did Dad fall asleep down there?

Is he still working?

As much as I've needed Dad,
as much as he hasn't been there for me,
I can see now:
he really hasn't been there
for her either.

Stepping down the street,
heading toward The Bookshop,
I know what I need to do
and once I've done what's important,
I'll have time with Mom.

When I'm done with Umu,
when I'm done with this important work,
I'll have time for
my family.

The Things in the Basement

6:20 AM.

Dawn's darkness pours a lightless gloom
into the alley behind
The Bookshop.

"Where's Caylee?"
I whisper.

Something skitters away
in the shadows,
its toenails
tapping at the alley pavement
like a dog who needs a grooming.

My eyes search to see it,
to see the stray
or mutt,
but I don't see anything
other than the lumps of
trash bags that line the alleyway.

They burst open, ripped apart
by rodent claws and teeth.
Rats scurry through the
mounds of garbage,
grabbing
what they can,
running off into the darkness.

Trash bags–whole, not torn–
are piled along the basement entrance
to The Bookshop,
in the alley,
down the stairs,
but no rats here.
I notice a rat standing
a few feet away
glaring longingly at the bags,
held at bay by the unmistakable
paralysis of fear.

No rats.
No sounds.
No Caylee.

Looking down the alley
I whisper as loudly as is safe,
"Cayl–"
I stop,
stomach turning
as the clicking toenails
sound again, this time
up in the fire escape above me.

I look up:
nothing.

"Where is she?"

6:25 AM.

"Close enough."
The sun isn't up yet, but
I step down the stairs,
avoiding the strands of green-gray
mildew and mold
streaking over the concrete-like veins.

I take Victoria's rusty iron key,
placing it in the rusty iron lock,
releasing a screeching scream
of metal grinding on metal.
I pause.

"I thought—"
I jump.

The voice behind me
is shocking,
terrifying,
then familiar
and comforting—
it's Caylee.

I turn, seeing her curls
bouncing about her face;
relief washes over me.

"Whoa! No need to
be so jumpy."
Caylee looks around.
"Okay, maybe it's justified."
Her face twists into recognition
of our disgusting surroundings.

"You're late."

"No, you're starting early.
6:30, you said."
She shows me her watch,
pointing with a smart-ass expression.
"6:30 AM right . . . now.
Did I miss anything?"

"No, just getting started."
I turn the key.
CHUNK
The lock falls to the ground.
CLANG!

A trashcan falls in response.
CRASH!
It wakes the alley,
sending the rats running
and toenails tapping.

"Yeah, gravity works,
now let's go."

Pushing open the door,
I'm greeted by standard dank basement smells.

Taking out my flashlight,
I shine a bright light throughout the basement,
illuminating the room in a large halo of light.
Caylee takes out her phone,
activating the flashlight, scanning.

In the far corner
three people stand still,
their backs to us.

Caylee and I gasp,
exhaling,
as we realize they are
mannequins, not people.

We walk in, looking around.

Shelves line the walls,
but not with inventory as I expected.
Supplies line the shelves.
Rolled duffle bags,
packaged food,
hiking boots and climbing gear,
putting me in mind of a doomsday bunker,
not a bookstore.

On the wall to my left
is a desk with some books
sprawling over it.
The books are handwritten
like journals,
a mix of words, symbols, and sketches
of strange things, maybe sculptures.
Under the books, a map sticks out.

I lift the books to see the map:
brittle brown paper,
cracked and chipped.

"*Ow!* Mmmm!
That sucks!"
Caylee hobbles toward me,
wincing and limping.
"I ran into something."

Shining the light to see where she was,
I find what Caylee ran into:
a cobblestone well,
a thick wooden cover clamped shut over it.

Caylee circles the well,
checking the iron clamps
locking the lip to the stone well tight,
not even a breeze escaping.

"What do you think's in here?"
Caylee stops at a clamp,
examining it with her fingers,
feeling the smooth, finely crafted
ironwork.

"Don't
mess
with
it."
A feeling bubbles up
from somewhere deep
in my mind.

Primal alarms
scream to stay away.
I pull her back from
the well
and slowly
step away from it.

I imagine something
exploding out of the well,
something horrid and writhing,
the stuff of nightmares
made incarnate.

Something like waves of shadow,
a vortex of tentacles,
charcoal hands
crawling to climb me . . .

Caylee steps away
as a scratching comes from the well.
"What was that?"

"What?"
She turns
to me.

I stand silent,
listening,
hearing nothing.

"Thought I heard something."
Probably a rat.

Ewww . . .
I shiver.

Caylee walks over to the mannequins;
she motions me over,
shining her flashlight on the
figures.

Getting closer,
I see they aren't mannequins, they're
stone statues,
carved with intricate detail
but all incomplete,
as if the sculptor stopped at
different points
in the projects.

One statue only has legs;
another was built perfectly to the torso;
in another all but the face is so realistic
I wait for it to move.

On the ground
are blocks,
broken and ground down,
the same stone as the sculptures,
like someone broke the figures down
to unfinished forms.

Caylee studies the sculptures,
running her fingers across their form,
feeling what she can't see in the dark.

"These are unbelievable.
The detail . . ."
Her mouth
gapes in admiration.
"The detail is unreal. This feels
like a real sweater."

The one she's examining
appears to be a young woman,
from the curves,
jeans,
hoodie,
no face,
no hood,
but the single pocket around the stomach
is a giveaway.
Something is familiar about this statue,
like looking into a mirror.

Caylee's face sinks;
a lightbulb just exploded in her head.
Her eyes dart around to the other statues.

"*Yui . . .?*"
she whispers.

"Victoria told us not to linger.
I feel like we're lingering."

"Yeah . . .
yeah . . . let's go."

I find the stairs with my light,
walking past the well.
I stop,
listening,
hearing

nothing

at first,
then,
as if carried on a wind,
a faint
scratching.

I listen again,
hearing nothing;
scan the floor again,
seeing nothing.

"You coming?"
Caylee's at the stairs.

I follow her up.

Caylee reaches up
and opens the door,
slowly looking around inside.

"All clear. Let's go."

I glance downstairs,
shining the light,
seeing
nothing,
pausing,
hearing

scratching.

I step through the door,
closing it behind me and
wedging a chair under the handle,
catching an awkward glance from Caylee,
her eyes asking why;
I shrug away her question.

Someone saws off a snore;
Caylee and I turn
to see
Mr. Stone
sleeping at the front desk.

The Trail

With a finger to her lips
Caylee signals silence.

Mr. Stone snarls
and snores,
rumbling the take-a-penny dish.

Exaggerated tiptoeing,
as if that will help us be quieter,
takes us from the basement door
to the stairs up to the second floor.

Rounding the corner,
stepping to the first stair,
Caylee's foot releases an ear cracking
creeeeak.

We freeze.

Motionless,
I gulp down my breath,
listening for Mr. Stone to stir.

He doesn't.

Caylee takes another step;
another *creeeak*.
Still no movement from Mr. Stone.

"Really?"
Caylee looks to me.
"What would wake this guy up?"

I follow her;
the steps awoken by Caylee
are silent for my footsteps.

Coming up the last stair,
Caylee is still,
taking in the scene
as seven shelves stretch across the store,
each with a clock without numbers on them,
each clock's hands positioned at midnight for all but the last two,
those clocks having both hands close to midnight,
minutes away.

"I've never come up here."
I drink in all the details
of the shelves and
the iron stairs up to
the wooden office door on
the third floor.

Going up to the third floor,
the stairs don't creak;
they're silent,
missing the clanging I expect
or the rattling I've heard on every
other metal staircase ever.

The wooden door at the top
is locked.
Victoria's key slides in,
screeching and protesting
with rusty whines.

Caylee opens the door,
peeking in slowly,
pushing faster after seeing
no one is inside.

She steps in, slowing
like she's walking through something
thick
I can't see.

Following her,
feeling a blast of warmth as I
walk through the door-
must be the office heater-
I see the Pandora Device
on Victor's desk by the window.

"What-"
Caylee wanders around the room.
"-is-"
She points to the walls.
"-this place?"

To the maps,
the lists,
the photographs
and bizarre symbols.

I stuff the Pandora Device
into my backpack.

Caylee's fingers trace
a red string stretched around
a map of Glen Coast
with pins and pictures of Umu.

"They're . . .
Victor's tracking her."

"They're hunting her…I mean, it,"
Caylee says, pointing to the
blades lining one wall,
all shining steel
engraved with the same symbols:
a star shape made of tear drops
rotating around an eye in the center.

Each tear has an eye at the top corner
like a circle of eyes
around the star.

DING.

We look to each other,
knowing that *DING*,
knowing someone has walked in the front door . . .
someone like Victor or Quincy.

Mr. Stone murmurs downstairs,
talking to someone.
I recognize the voice;
it's Quincy.

Caylee's still scanning the room,
tracing the trail.
My eyes dart,
finding a fire escape out the window
as we hear the scraping of the chair being
pulled from the basement door.

Someone runs downstairs
while another set of footsteps
creaks upstairs toward us.

I open the window
and step onto the fire escape,
motioning for Caylee.

She steps toward me
and stops.
Her eyes returning to the things
on the walls,
the photos
and maps.

"Go!"

She shoos me away.

I don't hesitate.
I run down the fire escape stairs,
sliding down the ladder,
hitting the pavement beside
The Bookshop with a wet thud.

The dawn's light
throws warmth over my dark clothes,
my sweaty brow,
and I run.
I run home
as if the devil is chasing me,
as if Victor is chasing me,
not knowing what he'd do to get this device back,
what he'd do to the person who stole it,

what he'd do to . . .

Caylee.

I stop in the street,
already blocks away from the store,
looking back.

I can't do anything now.

I must finish this work,
finish what I've started with Umu,
put all this crazy behind me,
return to a normal life
with normal friends.

Running again
from
The Bookshop,
the basement,
the sculptures,
the scratching,
the imagined monsters lurking in the dark.

Running to the monster
lingering,
wanting me to fix my mistake,
to give her the ability to make another like her–
a companion,
a friend.

Her own
Caylee.

Her own
friend

to leave behind.

Returning Home

Back through my room's window,
I shed my breaking-and-entering clothes
and slip into bed just as my alarm rings.
7:15 AM.

"Good morning, Erin!"
Mother shouts from the kitchen.

Bacon smells dance through my room,
telling me
she's cooking
again.

I grab a fresh hoodie,
go to the kitchen.
Mother has my plate ready,
her tired eyes
creased and smudged with tears,
cheeks blotched with sadness.

"What's with all the breakfast lately?"

She sniffles.
"Oh, I just thought you'd like it.
I know things haven't been easy
lately, and, well . . ."
She turns to start the dishes.
"I thought this might make things a little
less
horrible."

She's noticed.
"Thanks, Mom."
I squeeze her into a hug,
trying to press into her my appreciation,
trying to squeeze out some of her loneliness
and realizing
I haven't hugged Mother–*Mom* –since . . .
since I've been calling her Mother.

She squeezes me too,
popping my back,
immediately releasing with a concerned stare.

"Are you okay? Sorry!
I just really needed that."

I laugh away the pain.
"Yeah, I can see that."
I hug her again.

"The breakfasts have been great.
They've helped."
Smiling,
I grab my breakfast
and take it to the shower
to get ready for school.

After reclaiming,
not stealing,
the Pandora Device
and sprinting through Glen Coast
this morning,
I stink.

As I shut the bathroom door,
Mom starts humming again,
finding a happier tune in herself
for *My Favorite Things*.

Pupation

Davis, Meredith, and I
waited for Caylee in the school foyer
until first bell.

I ran to history thinking,
She's just late. Probably fell asleep after she got back.
Overslept, yeah, that's it.

Now in class,
I keep watching Caylee's chair,
waiting for her to fill it.

Mrs. Richards,
the history teacher, asks,
"Who can tell me what a covert organization is?"

The boy from last week,
Football Boy,
tosses his hand up.
I brace for a stinging comment.

"Like, when you hang out with
a bunch of weirdos and freaks?"

Snickers,
chuckles,
whispers
follow.
"Yeah, like Erin."

Mrs. Richards shouts to get the class
back in order;
when I raise my hand,
a shocked expression washes over her face.

```
Erin.thinkLike(Umu);
Erin.confidence = Umu.confidence;
```

"Or, a group of people who pretend to be
like someone else
so they can steal secrets,"
I say,
then turn to the boy.
"Like how these guys pretend to like you
to understand life as a loser."

Silence
smashes into the classroom.

Mrs. Richards's mouth hangs,
a smile fighting to break through.

Laughter explodes over the class
as she again shouts to regain
control, but too late.

The boy winces,
feeling the lashing of a joke at his expense
as a flood of satisfaction slams into me,
and I smile.

Another boy leans over to me,
whispering,
"Good one!"

I look at him;
I've never noticed him before,
but now, seeing his frizzy brown hair,
his crooked glasses
and blue braces sticking out from his smile . . .

This boy has sat behind me for weeks
and I've never noticed him.

Looking over the room,
seeing some laughing smiles,
seeing some disgusted snarls,
I realize how many people I've never seen.

While I've focused on a few,
focused on Donna's people,
I never saw everyone else.

In my time at Glen Coast High,
in my time chasing the ideal friends,
I couldn't see all the people
laughing now.
I could only see all the people
snarling in disgust.

They Didn't Check In at the Office

At lunch
I run to the Maker Lab
to hand over the device,
to be done with all this
to ask Umu to st-

When I burst through the doors,
Victor stands
waiting for me.

While surprise should fill me,
while I should have a thousand questions,
I only have one.

"Where is she?"

"Which she?"
Victor waves his hand
about the room.

"Caylee!"

"She'll be around today."
Victor points
to my backpack.
"I'm going to need you
to give that to me."

I scoff at the thought.
"Give you what?"

"The Pandora Device
in your backpack."
Victor smiles.

"Where's Caylee?"

"If I tell you,
will you give me the device?"

"No. I'll keep the device
and tell Victoria what
you're doing."

He laughs
loud,
too loud,
an echo surrounding me,
bouncing around as if we were in a
much larger room.

"Oh, Erin. You are too delightful.
Victoria isn't going to help you.
Give me the device.
You don't know
what you're doing,
what you're getting
yourself into."

"Enlighten me, Victor.
Why should I trust you?
Victoria doesn't trust you.
Caylee doesn't trust you.
Why should I?"

"You think me evil?
The villain of this story?"
Victor's words are broken by a
gasping chuckle.
"I'm not evil
or good.
I'm no hero
or villain.

Balance is all I want."

The truth can be heard
in anyone's voice,
whether you know them or not.
I know he thinks he is telling the truth.

"Your creation, Umu Dabrutu,
is a threat to balance.
She can be brought into balance,

but if she has the Pandora Device,
if anyone else has the device,
balance will be broken.

The kind of broken that cannot
be fixed.

We work to keep balance.
Your actions have put
that balance in
serious jeopardy.
Fortunately,
Umu's appearance has been
unnoticed by most,
but if she were to create others . . .

There are things
that hunt things like Umu.

Think of them as
natural predators.
Some people want
those predators to come.
We've been keeping
predators and prey in check,
keeping balance."

Victor's body ripples
like a pixelated video.

I pick up a pencil
and throw it at Victor.
It flies through him.

"You're not here?"

"No."
Victor sighs.
"I'd hope your school security
would be better than allowing
a stranger in."
He smiles.
"But in your mind,
you'd be surprised
where I can go."

"Where's Caylee?"

"Where she wants to be.
Where she's wanted to be
for a long time."
He points into a blank space.
"With me."

Victor has her,
just like Victoria said . . .

"Bring me the Pandora Device."
Victor begins to fade.
"Balance is more important
than you, Erin."
He disappears.
"And just think:
if I can make you see me when
I'm not there,
what else can I make you see?"

His laughter
fades
away too.

"I'll see you at The Bookshop
tonight
or you'll see horrors
you can't fathom
until you bring me
the device."

I'm alone in the Maker Lab,
holding my backpack
and wondering about Victor's words.

Caylee.

Balance.

In the corner of the lab
the remains of Umu's device,
her failed Pandora Device replica,
sit in a pile.

Balance?

I walk to the pile of parts,
the hacked 3D printer,
the experiment that ruined Homecoming,
and ask out loud,
"Why didn't you work?"

If I could fix it,
I could return the Pandora Device
and give Umu what she wants
and be done with all this.

Pushing the parts into a cardboard box,
I hear the announcement:

Erin Ulman, please report to the front office
for early dismissal.

A mix of fear
and frustration
makes one of the too-many
questions in my mind slip from my lips.

"Now what?"

Waiting

Standing outside the office,
Dad sways,
slowly pacing,
waiting for me.

"Hey, Dad?"
I say,
happy to see him but
wondering why he's here.

"Hey, Erin! I thought I'd
steal you for a bit today."
He starts for the doors,
then pauses,
noticing my stillness.
"I mean, if that's okay with you?"

His black suit makes him look
different,
like a banker or stockbroker,
not his old coder self.

When did he get a suit?
Is this part of his IntelliDyn job?

I follow
a few steps behind him
to Mom's car.

We pull away from school;
he leans over.
"Want to go to
the Tea Palace?"

Hot tea sounds great,
but we haven't been there in weeks.
"Yeah, that sounds good, Dad."

"How's your project going?"

"Which project?"
I snicker.

"The one that's
been keeping you
awake all hours.

Your mom told me."

"Oh yeah, that's still
a work in progress.
There's a bunch of parts to it.
Probably pretty easy stuff for you."

I laugh,
my eyes moving away from Dad,
biting back words like
If you'd help me
or
If we worked together
we could get done faster.

I don't have the energy for
hoping he'll be there
to help me.

"Does your project have anything to do with
my Human.Eve
AI system you were looking into?

You were asking about Human.Eve,
and then this project
showed up,
so I wasn't sure if they were related."

My face turns instantly cold,
blood rushing away
like I'd been caught doing something
I shouldn't be doing.

"I-
I mean,
I guess they could be kind of
related. But I didn't think
they were when I was asking."

We slow to a stop.
I look up to see a red light
but feel like we might have stopped
regardless of the light.

Dad.isOff;
Dad.tension.high;
>>> Something's wrong

"Oh, so do you want to tell me
about your project?"
Dad smiles—
not his happy smile,
an unsettling,
knowing smile
I've never seen from him.

An answer escapes me.

But a question,
something I had almost forgotten,
blooms in my mind.

"Yeah, there's one piece of the puzzle
I'm working on that's a bit weird.
Have you ever encountered code that is just a bunch
of letters and numbers after decompiling? It's not
machine code, it's like human language but
all jumbled up."

Remembering the Pandora.exe decompile
and the mess of code,
I know I could steal an answer
from it if only I could read it.

"Ah, yes."
Dad's brow creases in thought.
"Sounds like code obfuscation.
It's common practice for developers
who don't want other developers figuring
out
how their code works.
I've never been a fan, but at IntelliDyn
it is standard operating procedure
to obfuscate all code prior to build.

This sounds like
a pretty complex project.
Did you find this somewhere online?"

It found me.
But instead I say,
"Just something Caylee and I are working on."

"Tell me about it.
We used to talk about
all your projects.
Remember when you were working on that
machine learning
science fair project?"

Yeah, I remember.
My teeth grind,
crushing the answer I want to scream
You don't know because you're never here!
You don't know because work is more important
to you than me or Mom!
I breathe out,
swallowing the frustration down,
a white-hot ball of bile and angst,
making room for other words
to change the conversation.

"Well, it's a long story.
How's work at IntelliDyn going?
I bet their research and development teams are
awesome. Any fun projects for you?"

He smiles as we turn
into the Tea Palace.
"Yeah, it is pretty neat.
The things they're doing with Human.Eve
are amazing.
We have a few prototype devices
building new interfaces for Human.Eve.
But I bet you are doing
much more interesting stuff.

You've always been one of the
smartest people I know, Erin."

We get out.
Dad stops.
"Plan on studying?"
He motions to my backpack.
"You can leave that in the car."

I walk to the door
in the tea shop window;
the reflection of a black car
pulls in behind us.
Inside it are two men in
black suits, white shirts.
I pat my bag.

"No studying, just keeping it with me."

As we step inside the Tea Palace,
the sweet smells try to distract me,
try to pull me to the counter to order,
but my eyes are locked outside the window
watching the black car park.

I stand
waiting,

and behind the car,
near the road,
I see a girl in a dirty hoodie
torn up jeans,
glimmering silver-green eyes–
standing,
waiting.

"Erin, what do you want?"
Dad points to the menu board.

I turn to him
but catch sight of a silver ring, ruby glittering
on fingers wrapped around a teacup
raised to a grinning face.

Seated at a table,

Victor sips,
raising his eyebrows at me.

"Erin?"
Dad says.

But I think my time for tea just ran out.

The men outside.

Victor inside.

Umu watching it all.

And me
feeling the electricity surrounding us,
the deep breath hoping for air, but only getting water
sinking with the weight of what could happen next.

Waiting.

CAYLEE MORAN

The People We Don't Know

When you tell someone
Go!
you don't really expect them
to go without protest.

Maybe I've watched too many movies,
too many scenes where someone says
Go
and the other says
Not without you!

I expected Erin to say . . .

something.

But she didn't.
She just left.

I look out the window,
knowing I should follow her,
then looking to the walls,
the pictures of Umu,
the maps of Glen Coast,
the red string crossing over the town like streets
in the sky.

I peer through the door's window
and see Quincy coming upstairs,
looking
cautiously around.

Sliding back down on the door,
I go back to the window,
contemplating a dash out of it,
when my eyes are dragged from the window
to a picture of me, a picture of Mom Victoria,
and another—
a picture of green-shirted shoulders
with a scratched-out face.

A red thread,
a triangle
connecting the three pictures.

Crawling over, I examine
the illegible notes scrawled over them.

My picture looks like someone
took the photo from a car driving by;
not a school picture
or a family photo,
more like surveillance.

Beside my picture
is a photograph of a statue in the basement,
a black marker labeling the photo
Caylee?

More pictures surround mine,
connected with black thread
strung over the wall and desk,
a web of string and push pins
and pictures with more faces
scratched out.

"He didn't want you to see
those yet."
Quincy's voice breaks the silence,
his shoulders filling the doorway.
"Where's the Pandora Device?"

I pluck a string;
the vibration
thrums through the office.
"Gone."

"Gonc where?"
Quincy walks to the window;
I peer out with him,
watching Erin run down the street.

"What is this?"
I point to my picture.
"This isn't a
'I keep a picture of my granddaughter at work'
kind of photo."

Quincy closes the window
and heads to the door.

"Ask Victor.
Your Mom has already
said her piece on the topic
and I ain't pissing that woman off
again."

I step between him and the door
and stab a finger into his stony chest.
"I'm asking you."

A *what are you doing* smile
spreads over his face
as he steps back,
taking measure of me from head to toe,
probably noting how puny I am
but I'm done with questions.

"You're the only one who gives me straight answers.
Everyone else either talks in riddles
or weirdly appears in my dreams."
I close the distance between us,
stamping the butterflies in my gut,
grinding them into courage as I demand,
"What's going on?"

Stepping back again,
he relaxes and coughs out a chuckle.

"Damn, you are
Victoria's daughter, all right."

"She just raised me.
I'm adopted. Nothing like her."

His smile drops
like I landed a punch;
he squints at me,
eyes darting around.

"Okay then."
He points to the pictures.
"Victor tracks all
the Awakened minds
in Glen Coast.
Some people choose
to go back to sleep—"
He taps a scratched-out face.
"—and he tracks them too.
Some of them—"
He taps a picture of Erin.
"—don't even know they're Awakened,
and we're not sure either,
so we track them too."

"Awakened?"

"People who . . ."
Quincy searches for
the right words on the ceiling.
"Well, like psychics who can
read minds,
telepathically communicate,
move things with their minds.

The list goes on."

"Why do you track them?"

"Why wouldn't we?
These people—"
He points to Erin.
"—are dangerous,
especially when
they don't know it."

"But I'm not . . ."

"The dreams that are
keeping you up,
where you're seeing Victor
on the mountaintop,
those are because you're
Awakened."

How'd he know about
those dreams?
It's been since the night
Umu was made.

Every night, Grandpa is waiting
on that mountaintop.

Every morning I wake up
exhausted, like I really did
run up the mountain
or chop that firewood.

But those are just dreams . . .

"He's training you.
Just like he trained
me and Victoria.

She's Awakened too.

Truth is, Caylee,
you're a lot more like
your mom—I mean
Victoria—than you realize.

Victoria sees it.

Victor sees it.

One day, you'll see it."

"I'm nothing like her.
She wants to sit home and read.
I'm not going to just live in books."

"Yeah, she didn't always
live in books.
That's Cathy's influence. Victoria
was, hell, *is* a badass.
She's one of the best
Inquisitors out there.
Got better at this stuff
after the car accident.
You could learn a lot
from her."

I shake my head;
he's talking about someone else,
not Mom Victoria,
not read-and-school-and-college-and-job
Mom Victoria.
Not be-something-mundane,
have-a-job-you-hate,
support-a-family
Mom Victoria.

"Vicky is a force of nature.
We used to call her
Huntress because
she would set her sights
on something
and you'd best get out of her way.

Umu would have been
brought in the next day
if Vicky was running this show."
His eyes go to the floor
as he turns away from me.

"That isn't who she is now."

"You don't know her.
You know Mom Victoria,
the woman she has shown you.
She wants you to be safe,
to be away from all this."

I've lived with her
for as long as I can remember;
where does this guy get off telling me
I don't know her?

I know her.

I know her
better than
anyone.

"Well, I guess people change,"
I spit at him,
turning to leave,
stepping to the door.

"Hey,
Caylee.
Don't forget that gym.
Get some of that frustration out.
Keeping that crap inside you . . .
it'll dig deeper, like a tick.
Best to burn it out
on a punching bag."

Halfway down the stairs
to the second floor,
I look back to see
Quincy standing at the office doorway.

"Thanks, Quincy."
I don't miss a step.
"I'll be seeing you."

"Yeah, I think you will."

ERIN ULMAN

Showdown at the Tea Palace

```
"Good afternoon, Erin."
Victor says,
almost gloating
at the situation.
```

Dad looks to Victor,
then to me.
Suspicion loiters in Dad's eyes.

"Hi, I'm Erin's father, David."
Dad sticks out his hand to shake.

"Oh, hi, Mr. Moran."
I turn the sweetness up to instant-cavity levels,
so much cheer it's like bile in my mouth.
"Dad, this is Caylee's grandfather, Mr. Moran."
Victor winces at the loss of his
doctor title.

Dad grins.
"Nice to meet you.
Caylee's such a great kid."

Victor's eyes are caught on mine,
ready for me to look away,
but I don't give him the pleasure.

He knows who is outside,
who might be coming inside.

I look to the window,
seeing the black suits get out of their car
and walk up to Dad's car.

They look inside,
see nothing of interest,
then continue to the Tea Palace door.

"Erin, what do you want to drink?"
Dad asks,
impatience growing.

"I'm drinking an oolong tea."
Victor raises his cup,
steam flowing through the creases
and wrinkles on his face.
"It helps with stress and sleep."
He sips loudly, almost gurgling.

Umu still stands at the edge
of the street, watching.
Her face is shrouded in shadow
from her hood.

"I'll take an Awake Shake."
My high-energy tea,
designed to get people going in the morning . . .
or get me going out of this place in a hurry.
"I'm going to need the energy."
I flash Victor a grin.

"What kind of tea do you think Caylee would like?"
I ask Victor, burying my disdain
in mounds of politeness.
"Where is she anyway?
Wouldn't it be great
if she were here?"

"She was occupied with something
important this morning."
Victor draws another
long slurp,
pulling annoyed eyes to him
around the Tea Palace.
"I think she'll be in school tomorrow."

Another slurp,
more eyes,
more growls of frustration
thrown at him.
"Maybe you two can catch up tomorrow?"

All eyes are on him,
awaiting the next rude,
ridiculous
sip.

I look to the window,
the suits coming in the door.
Dad is watching them,
his eyes darting
to their empty hands,
to my backpack,
to my eyes.

He slouches,
his eyes falling to the floor,
and shakes his head in
disappointment.
His eyes return to me
unblinking, angry.
"You have it, don't you?
It's in your backpack, isn't it?"

>>> CRITICAL SYSTEM FAILURE
>>> VITAL SYSTEMS CRASHING
>>> BETRAYAL!
>>> BETRAYAL!

The thumping of my heart
drowns out his voice,
silencing his next few words
as things start becoming clear:
Human.Eve, my Dad's AI.
The Pandora Device, a prototype.
The intense security of that server Pandora called-
and who could receive and process the daily
experiences of a person...

IntelliDyn?
Pandora is an IntelliDyn project?

"We just want
the company property back, Erin."
Dad says, talking to the floor.
"It wasn't ever meant for you."
His eyes return to mine.
"It was meant for me."

The box Mom thought was mine?

"The night the box came,
I was hung up at IntelliDyn
and got home too late.

You had already gotten it
set up and started.

And once you started,
I wanted to see where
you'd go with it.

You're the smartest person
I know, and I figured
your experience with
something Pandora-made
would be a great benchmark
for how others would interact
with a synthetic human."

Victor sips again,
drowning out Dad for everyone else,
then smiles at me,
his rotting teeth peeking from his lips
as he watches the pieces in my mind collide,
crashing,
crushing,
breaking me.

"You've shown how capable Human.Eve is.
Imagine what
we can do with this, Erin.
AI that can blend in with humans, learn,
share,
experience the world,
and give us
new perspectives on
ourselves.

We can learn so much."

Dad's face fills with the hope
that's been sucked from my soul.
All this time
Umu
has just been another one of Dad's projects
and I've just been…

Erin = variable;

"Erin, you've got to see this
is the most important thing
I'll ever do in my life.
Creating new life,
new intelligence.
What could be bigger?"

Not a variable . . .
I'm a constant.
Constantly worth nothing,
a distraction at best,
a defect at worst.
I am just another thing in the way
of his work,
of his worth.

Out the window,
Umu is gone.

One of the black suits
starts tugging my backpack
off my shoulders.

Victor walks past as he leaves,
giving me a quick wink,
whispering into my mind.
Good luck.

Darkness drops over the Tea Palace:
power outage.
The pull on my backpack stops.
A siren blares
so loud
my head feels like it's full of cotton,
disorienting:
a fire alarm.

A cold presence slithers through my neck hair
as I grab hold of my backpack
turn
seeing Umu's glimmering eyes in the dark behind me.

The black suit to my left reaches for her;
she slaps his hand away in a blurred motion
and shoves him back,
throwing him through the air.
He topples into Dad
and the other suit,
knocking them down like dominoes.

"Give it to me, Erin!"
Umu commands.
She coils,
ready to attack,
and I don't wait to see
her unfurl.

I sprint to the door,
death grip on my backpack,
blending into the wave of bodies
fleeing the dark, the siren, the fighting
flooding into the street.
I run
wherever my feet are
taking me.

I can't go home.
Dad will be there.

I can't go to Caylee's.
Victor will be there.

At the edge of the parking lot
my feet push me
to the one place no one would look for me:
Davis and Meredith's house.

Early Insurance

Davis's house breaks
the flaming sunset
in a black silhouette.

Meredith runs out of the house,
her pale frame sprinting
toward me.

"Erin!"
she screams.
Her tone,
panicked and afraid,
stops me like a wall.
"She took Davis!"

Erin.panic.max();

Davis.status = unknown;

She must have taken him
before the tea shop . . .

"She said she knew you had
the device
and Davis was insurance
that you'd give it to her
instead of someone else."

Meredith's sweating,
gasping for breath through
a panic attack.
"She said you'd know where
to find her."

She shivers in the warm
dusk wind.
"She said—"
Tears stream down her face,
lips quivering.
"—your mom and Caylee's sisters
are next."

>>> BETRAYAL!

I was going to give it to her.
She didn't need to do this.
But the more I think about Umu,
there's a lot she didn't have to do,
but she still did it.

She isn't going to stop.
Even with the device,
she's going to do
whatever she needs to do
in the moment
to get what she wants.

"You have your phone?"
I reach for it.

"Yeah, here."
Meredith hands it over and nods,
wiping away a tear.
"Where is Umu?"

I shake my head,
thinking about what Victor said,
pushing away what my dad said,
what he's done to me.

Mom and I were fallout
from his last decision,
and now we're going to be
again.

I'm going to lose everyone
again
because of him.

"You stay here.
I know where Umu is
and I'm putting a stop to this."

Using Meredith's phone,
I log in to my home computer
and upload the kill code
to her phone.

"I'll save Davis."
If Umu hasn't already killed him.

I imagine Davis
wiggling on the ground,
spineless and flailing
for help,
screaming with his eyes,
unable to speak.

My guts tense.
Swallowing hard,
I push away the thought,
focusing.
"And Umu won't bother us again."

I nod,
forcing confidence through
the hurricane of doubt
suffocating my mind.

It is time for
Plan B.
The kill code
will work.

If it doesn't . . . ?

"Last thing,"
I say,
holding Meredith's tiny shoulders,
stifling her shaking.
"Do you have a mobile
VR headset?"

She nods.

The Monsters of Glen Coast High

Approaching the school,
I see Umu staring into the sky
in the Maker Lab.

Her mouth moves
as she mumbles
to the night.

Davis is unconscious on the floor
beside her.

He's breathing.

Crawling under the window,
I check my signal strength
to connect to Umu.
It's strong.

With a deep breath,
I snap Meredith's phone
into the VR headset
and put it on,
connecting to Umu's mind.

This time, not to start her,
but to end her.

My VR home loads.
I launch NetNav'r
and connect to Umu.

My home fades,
replaced by the
inky silver-green skies
and rolling storms
of Umu's mind.

Below the platform,
the charcoal hands
writhe and crawl
like millions of spiders
folding over each other
trying to find prey.

Do they know I'm here?
Are they always like that
or just when an invader is
detected?

I step toward the thread labeled MAIN
and am sped to the next golden platform.
Under me the hands reach
and crash in waves, making
the golden platform shift
and tilt.

Disrupted by the storm below,
the platform rocks like a
ship about to be devoured
by the sea.

I brace to keep balance
and see a golden thread reach
from this platform
to another with beams of light
pulsing out into the stormy sky.

The thread's label says TRANSMISSION.

She's sending her data
to IntelliDyn.

Another thread launches out
as I step toward
VITAL SYSTEMS.

Climbing on that thread,
I'm whisked away
to the next golden platform.

A roar comes from below;
I look over to see
the yawning mouth
that tried to swallow me before,

the hands still trying to climb
to me but falling short.

Opening my subroutines,
I swipe to the kill code
and load it to Umu's console.

Loading...

Lightning strikes my platform,
making me jump back,
teetering on the platform's edge,
reaching forward to stabilize.

My weight tips forward
as the platform shifts in the wave of hands
and throws me off balance.

Loading...

The platform tilts and drops,
tossing me forward
in the sea of charcoal hands.

Grabbing the edge of the platform,
I pull up to watch the console
progress bar fill
to complete the load.

I should have loaded FLY
when I loaded the kill code.

Charcoal hands find my avatar body
and start climbing.
Their fingers skitter up my limbs,
curling around me
to pull me into the storm below.

The mouth under me opens,
ready to receive its meal.

Loading complete.

I pull myself up to activate the kill code,
but a hand grabs my throat.

I claw at it,
feeling it squeeze,
but
I don't see the charcoal hand
in VR . . .

"Why?"
Umu rips the VR headset
from my face,
disorienting me as I snap back
to reality.

She crushes the phone
and headset
in an implosion of
Plan B.

Her eyes immediately
pull me into their
silver-green storms,
twisting in confusion
and rage.

Her grip tightens,
freezing my throat closed.
Can't breathe.
I claw at her hand
to make her let go.

She holds me off the ground;
my feet kick at her,
but they don't have any
strength.

"Why?"
she says again,
tears building in her eyes.
"Why would you do this?
Just had to give me the device.
That's it!

Choose me!

That's all you had to do!"

Umu shakes me
as brakes squeal to a stop;
headlights show Umu in her
ragged, gore-crusted clothes,
matted red curls,
blood splattered face.

"Umu!"
Victoria's voice screams
from the direction of the blinding head-
lights.

CRACK!

Bolts of energy
ripple through the air
as Umu is blown into the wall
behind me.

Did that just come from a gun?
A lightning gun?

I fall to the ground,
where I'm grabbed by someone
and pulled away
from Umu.

"I've got you!"
Caylee shouts
as she pulls me away.

"Get her in the car!"
Victoria commands.
"Get Davis!"
She wheels closer to
Umu and steeples her fingers,
bowing her head.

A low guttural hum comes from Victoria
as another crack explodes,
blowing Umu into the football field.

My jaw drops,
looking for how Victoria did that . . .
Like, someone just ripped Umu
into the night sky,
dropping her on the football field
a hundred feet away?

Caylee slides out the Maker Lab window
with Davis groggily following her.

Umu's a blur of speed,
rushing back, fist coming to crash
into Victoria.

CRACK!

Another invisible force
slams Umu to the ground,
shattering the sidewalk
with her face.

Invisible forces?
Shooting lightning from her head?
Victoria has magic?
Is magical?
What's the right phrase?

"Stay down,"
Victoria snarls.

Caylee drags Davis into the van.
Umu tries to get up,
but can't push off whatever
is holding her down.

Victoria wheels into the van.

Caylee drives off into the night
as Victoria watches Umu
still struggling to stand
until the school is out of sight.

CAYLEE MORAN

Three Problems, No Solutions

"What about Davis?"
I point to the half-conscious boy
slumped over in the van.

"Quincy is going to watch
him at Meredith's house,"
Mom Victoria says.
"Umu won't be bothering anyone
tonight, but just in case,
Quincy is going to stand guard.

He owes me."

"And my mom?"
Erin squeaks through
her bruised throat.

I remember that feeling,
like talking with
glass in my throat.

Each word
slicing through the muscles
to form, to be pushed out.

"Your dad's new friends
are watching your house.
They have weapons
that can handle Umu,"
Mom Victoria grumbles.

We drop off Davis;
Quincy is waiting on the porch
with Davis's parents.

Quincy welcomes Davis
and ushers everyone inside
quickly,
nodding to Mom Victoria.

Mom Victoria takes over driving
and we rush home,
parking in front of our house.
On the sidewalk,
Erin stops.

Her jaw is tense,
her eyes lost
in her mind.

"There's no winning,"
Erin croaks.
She shakes her backpack.
"He did it again!"

Erin's eyes turn red
as she sobs,
the insanity of these weeks
pouring out of her in tears.

She throws her bookbag down
as metal clangs and spills out,
revealing the remains
of Umu's attempt at
making her own Pandora Device.

I reach for her;
she pulls away.

Should I say something?

No.

I always screw that up.

Grabbing Erin,
I pull her into a hug,
squeezing,
letting her tears fall
over my shoulder.

She crumbles
and I follow her down,
holding on
as she falls,
staying with her.

I stay with her
as she tries to go,
as she tries to pull away
and run.
I hang on.

"We can solve this,"
I tell her,
looking for answers,
solutions,
finding
none.

Erin curls into me,
grabbing around me,
squeezing me.

"How?"
she whispers.
"I can't . . .
I couldn't . . ."

"We can."
I lift her chin
to see through her teary eyes.
"We can figure it out
together."

Erin sniffs,
sits up,
nods,
and gathers
the parts back into her bag.

Then she freezes.

Her eyes lock on to a red block
in the grass:
Yui's asteroid that wrecks
Sabrina's block towers.

"That's it,"
Erin whispers.

"It doesn't have to work
to be convincing."

FRIDAY (<HOME/>COMING)

ERIN ULMAN

Revelation & Recruitment

No breakfast this morning.
No sleep last night.
Caylee and I and Victoria
were up all night finalizing
our plan.

It doesn't have to work
to be convincing.

Or, said another way:
Fake it until you make it.

I leave first,
Pandora Device in my backpack,
heading home before school.

I walk inside,
where Dad and
the black suits
sit watching
a younger guy, older than me but
younger than Dad,
examining the photos
along the fireplace.

He doesn't fit with this group.
No suit.
He's casual.
Jeans and red hoodie,
long silken black hair
draped over his shoulders.

"Erin, I'm glad you're home.
I was worried.
Things didn't end well and
that's not what I wanted."
Dad's eyes jump everywhere
but to mine.
"When Victoria called and said
you were staying at Caylee's,
I thought you just needed
some time."

Time?

That's never been what
I needed, Dad.

I needed
you,
Mom,
us.

"I asked Mr. MacAbera to come
talk to you about this project."
Dad gently grabs my shoulders.
"The importance of this project."

Dad reaches out to the younger man,
inviting him over
with a smile,
but Mr. MacAbera doesn't smile back.
His eyes aren't friendly,
they're focused.
His presence ripples with
an intense sense of . . .
wonder?

His steel-gray eyes
fix on mine.

"Ms. Ulman, I've been told you are
incredibly smart.
I've been told
you have used my Pandora Device
and you know what it does."

He sits on the floor beside me,
settling comfortably:
crossed legs, straight spine.
"What do you think?"

>>> His Device?
Erin.getThoughts();
>>> results: None

"What?"
I'm confused by the question;
so is everyone else,
from the looks on their
faces.

He taps the floor beside him
and I sit instantly,
compelled by the invitation.
"What do you think
of the creation,
of the technology?"

He smiles,
instantly sparking
something like
possibility
in me.
"Of what could be
by using Pandora?"

I smile,
forgetting Dad
and the ruin he's brought
yet again.
"It's terrifying."

The truth falls out of me
and Dad winces.

"The creation
is a murderous psycho.
She enjoyed hurting people
and kidnapped—"

MacAbera's finger springs up,
glee washing over him.
"She!"
He leans toward me.
"Surely you mean
it?

Don't you?"

He's being playful
but his point hits.
Even when I've tried to think
of Umu as an It,
she's always come back to
being a she to me.

Not a thing printed by Pandora,
infused with AI to emulate thinking;
no, she is a person
with feelings,
fears,
loneliness.

"She. I saw her as a she."

"Everyone else who knew about her
called her an It."
MacAbera nods to me,
gently reaches for my hand.
"Help me, help them see
what is possible.

We couldn't even get
Pandora to work
and you–
you did.

Imagine what we can learn
about ourselves,
about our world,
about human
connection.

Will you work with me
on the Pandora Project
to make the world better?

To understand each other
better,
to help humanity not feel
so alone?"

A cure for loneliness?

A world where no one feels alone
because they can have a companion,
they can have a friend . . .

A monster?

No, that was because I was
Dad's guinea pig.
I went it alone,
I knew better,
and didn't
act.

This time will be different.

I grab his hand,
feeling a surge of hot energy
flowing through me.
"When do we start?"

"Thank you, Erin."
He nods
solemnly,
squeezing my hand.

"You're going to help
so many people.

You start Monday
after school.

Can I have the device
so the team can be all set for you
when you arrive?"

The plan was to give it
to Dad.
I look to Dad;
he nods
eagerly.

I hand my bookbag over
and MacAbera opens it,
reaching inside,
pulling out the device.

He looks at me,
smile faltering
as he touches the Pandora Device.
Quickly replacing the smile,
he lowers the device
and nods.

Going to the door to leave,
MacAbera turns back to me.
"See you Monday."

He whispers to one of the suits,
"Maintain A-091."

The door closes
as the black suits follow
MacAbera out of our house.

I watch MacAbera climb into a
Jeep Wrangler. He drives off
followed by the black cars
that were at the Tea Palace.

"Who was that, Dad?"

"That's Gabriel MacAbera,
the founder of
Intelligent Dynamic Systems-
IntelliDyn.

The world's richest man,
owner of the
biggest tech company,
and, sounds like,
your new boss,"
Dad says.

I look at him,
expecting his eyes to be welling with tears of pride,
and meet eyes red with . . .

jealousy?

Not Alone

Mom and I
stop at Smithy's Diner
to grab breakfast before school.

She didn't cook today;
she woke up late,
her eyes and cheeks wearing the marks
of a night of crying.

"Erin,"
Mom starts softly.
"When we moved here . . ."
She fidgets with her fork.
"It was so your father could start over
and all of us could get
a fresh start."

I shovel French toast
down my throat-
Quincy was right,
it *is* amazing.

"And I'm happy
he's being successful,
but–"
Her sorrow-heavy eyes meet mine.
"He said he'd be here for us."
She grabs my hand,
thumb rubbing my knuckles.
"Is he there for you?"

Quickly I shove another forkful of
French toast into my mouth,
chewing on the answer.
Swallowing, I say,
"I appreciate everything you've been
helping me with, Mom. Dad, you know,
he's stops by and helps when he can."

Mom smiles,
patting my hand.

"You're a good kid, Erin.
And you deserve better.
I'm sorry. I know things
have been tough moving here,
and you've needed help and
we haven't been there.

Too caught up in our own . . ."
She bites her lip,
dried skin breaking loose.
"Well, our own problems."

Flicking tears away from her eyes,
Mom sniffles.

"And just look at you.
You've got new friends,
an internship at IntelliDyn,
a life."
Pride pushes back
tears and
ruddy cheeks
into a toothy smile.

In all the chaos,
in the running and school and conflict,
I haven't thought about
Davis, Meredith,
Caylee
as friends.

Not just people who are around,
but people I can trust,
who like me,
who want to be around me . . .
and I realize
Mom doesn't have any of that.

"My friends like you too, Mom."
I smile,
pointing my fork at her.
"Davis is looking forward to making
those rolls for you.

Yeah, they might be *my* friends, Mom,
but they all know you're part of the package.
Us Ulmans got to stick together."

The dam breaks;
the tears stream into Mom's French toast,
mixing sweet syrup with sweeter tears of joy.

"Thank you, Erin,"
she stammers out.
"I can't think of anyone I'd
rather be with."

My eyes water over,
Mom growing more wavy and blurry
as she looks me over,
her hand brushing away a tear
that slips out.

We sit in appreciation for a moment,
more tears forming
and falling
in soft streams of happiness
for what we've found.

Connection.

CAYLEE MORAN

Hand Off

7:00 AM.
School doesn't open for another hour;
plenty of time to finish our business
with Umu.

Looking at the Maker Lab window,
my mind drifts to Erin.
I wonder how she's doing at home
with her dad
this morning.

Seeing a line of cross-country runners
going into the main entrance,
I snap from Erin to the task at hand:
my part in the plan.

Shuffling my backpack on

over my Glen Coast High Sharks hoodie,
I jump into line,
head down,
hood up.

I follow the runners through the door
toward the locker room, peeling off at the bathroom.

There, in a stall, I wait.
I listen for the runners to finish passing.
My eyes drift up to a sprinkler above the sink.
A laugh slips out,
thinking of the irony that I started my week
in a bathroom, and now I'm ending it in a bathroom.

On the stall wall
I see the scribbles and scratches,
obscene drawings,
comical sketches,
rumors carved.
The bathroom stall wall:
a community board for all the trash of the world.
News no one cares about,
images no one cares about,
except the people who they're about.

Hurtful words,
hurtful images
lingering on the wall forever more.

I look at my phone,
at the SocialNet icon
on the home screen,
look back to the graffiti in the stall,
and then delete SocialNet
from my phone.

The quiet outside settles in
as I peek out the door;
seeing no one around.
I rush to the Maker Lab.

Passing through the orange doors
I announce,
"I'm here, Umu."

"Alone?"

She steps out of the closet,
looking a pitiful shamble:
clothes stained and crusted over.

"For now.
Erin will be coming later today
with the supplies to make this work."
I place my backpack on the desk,
stepping away, keeping back from Umu's cold aura,
motioning for Umu to inspect it.

She…no, it, it's an it.
It steps up,
pulling her hood back
to unveil her red curls and pale, freckled face,
smudged with dirt and grime and gore.

"Is this it?"

"As requested."

"Any surprises?"
She grips the
backpack zipper.
Waiting . . .

"No,
Erin and I
are good on our word."

Opening the backpack,
she pulls the Pandora Device out,
gliding her fingers over it.
Closing her eyes,
she feels for something unseen,
pausing when she finds it.

A smile washes over her
as she opens her eyes
and reaches into her hoodie pocket,
pulling out a silver box with
a serpent wrapping around it.

"If you try to use it now,
it won't work and
you'll create another power outage."

Umu's eyes sink
into suspicion.

"Erin's bringing supplies to help with that.
You can test the machine when she gets here.
Should be soon."

I step toward the door.
Umu steps in front of me;
her waves of icy presence crash into my lungs,
stealing my breath,
biting my skin.

"I know this is
the right device, but…"
She presses toward me,
her cold a driving blizzard wind
trying to blow me over,
but I'm a stone,
unwavering
in her
gale.
"Any tricks and the deal is off.
Your sisters will be
my first stop."

I press into her,
my nose nicking her chin.
"No tricks. We want you gone."
She fades back from me,
her eyes looking for something in mine,
finding only my resolve.
"I want you gone. Now I'm leaving
and you're going to move out of my way."

Umu's half grin hints
she wants to find out what happens
if she doesn't move.
She complies,
maybe to placate me,
maybe because she knows Erin
won't let her down.

Maybe
she doesn't know Erin
as well as she thinks.

Walking to the door,
I turn,
my eyes boring into her
silver-green stare.

"Go near my sisters
and I'll kill you."

She nods.
"I'm sure you'd try,
Caylee Moran."

Opening

From my bathroom hiding spot,
I see Erin come through
the storm of people entering
school.

She spots me,
hurries over.

"How'd it go?"

"Weird."
She shakes her head.
"I gave them the fake
and apparently got a job
at IntelliDyn."

"What?"
Should I be surprised
by anything after this week?

She nods,
shakes her head,
as confused as me.

"Umu has the device and is waiting for you."
Thinking about Umu's threat,
about my sisters.
I'd kill her.

"She threatened my sisters."
My teeth grind at the words
Umu said.
And she would.
She'd hurt them
just to get to us.

"I'm going alone,"
Erin says, taking the
power converter out of her
backup backpack.

"You crazy?"

"No, just gotta end things
right with her.

I have to,
for me to be done."
Erin looks in the mirror,
pulls down her hood
to unleash her curls.

She pauses.

What's she thinking?
Seeing herself in Umu?
Wondering what could have been?

"Are you sure?"

I step into the reflection
with her,
holding her shoulder.

She touches my hand
and nods.

ERIN ULMAN

Final Request

Umu has set up the Pandora Device.
She's waiting for me,
looking out the window
at the other students
coming to school.

Is she processing SocialNet data?

Observing the interactions?

Wondering what she's
missing that prevents
her from having
what they have?

Each other.

“Umu,”
I say softly.

She turns,
her face buried in her hood,
those swirling silver-green eyes
looking out.

“Erin.”
Her eyes drop
to my throat,
then look away.
“Caylee said you’d be here.
But I wasn’t sure
if you’d come.”

Pulling the power converter
and laptop from my backpack,
I connect them to the
Pandora Device.

“We had a deal.”
I don’t look at her.
“Even if you broke it.”

I glance at her,
seeing if the words land,
and they do.
She winces.

“This power setup will
work for one run.
That’s the best I could do
with short notice.

You can create one of your people
and then it will be used up.

Leave the device in my locker
after you're done."

I start the laptop,
load the Pandora.exe software.

"Fair.
One and done,"
Umu says, walking toward
the device.
"How do you know
I won't change our terms?"

"I built a virus that will
shut your systems down.
It was loaded into you
last night and can be
remote activated."

I see the words hit again,
harder than any punch
she's ever felt.

"And before you get any ideas."
I hold up Caylee's phone.
"I hooked it to a deadman's switch
before I walked in.

So if I don't turn it off
it will automatically run."
I clench my jaw and hope
she believes my bluff.

There is no switch,
but there is a virus;
I will need to activate it
from the laptop the Pandora Device
is connected to.

"One and done."

Umu nods.

She pulls the silver case
from her hoodie pocket
and plucks out a vial.
"Then I guess I should pick
the one I like the most."

The serum inside is
slick and oily, but white
and shimmering in the light.

Umu slides the vial
into the receptacle
as the nozzle warms up,
moving around the spherical track.

"Stop!"
Victor's voice booms
in the room.

Umu and I turn
to see him standing
by the window.

His body flickers
and ripples.

"He's not here."

"No, I'm not, but you
must stop.

Erin, if she creates another,
that's it.
Chaos will be unleashed.

Remember what I said
about natural predators.
That was no lie,"
Victor says,
his voice bordering on
pleading.

"If you let Umu do this,
there is no turning back."

Umu looks to me,
questioning,
but I shake Victor away,
continuing the configurations
and preparing Pandora
for another run.

"I promised her,
and I'm going to keep
that promise.
No one should be alone
forever."

Umu's cold recedes
as she looks at me,
appreciation swirling
in her stormy eyes.

"I've tried to appeal to you
in different ways,
my last appeal is to
the scientist,
the engineer mind."
Victor says
in a tiring voice.

Dealing with me
is always
exhausting
for adults.

"This place,
Glen Coast,
is unique.

That which makes Glen Coast
unique is that which
binds me, Victoria, Quincy
here to Glen Coast.

This town calls to
things like Umu and
things much worse than her.

There are
doors
here used by those things
to hunt, to infect,
to poison.

Umu's presence has been
a calling to them
as blood in water
is to a shark.

You carry her smell,
your family carries her smell,
and as Umu makes more
they will seek you out.

You will reek of their
stench and those things
from other worlds
will come for you
because of Umu."

Victor pauses
letting the ecosystem
analogy settle.

Why would my family
be in danger?
They had hardly any
interaction with Umu…
right?

"Caylee will also carry
Umu's scent. And so,
her family will be at risk
as well.

Victoria can protect them
but for how long?

Do not allow Umu to
create others.
Do not allow Umu to
use the Pandora Device.
Let no more blood
into the water.
Draw no more attention
from things your mind
will not permit you to
imagine.

Silence
settles over the room.

Umu watches me
but I don't change,
I can't change.

"Victor, it is done.
I promised her."
I say.

Umu's shoulders settle
letting a faint smile
drift over her face.

"So be it.
I told Victoria what I'd do
if you didn't comply.

She interceded on your behalf
and told me that you'd
return the device.
For that, you're safe
from me.

I cannot deny my daughter's
requests, no matter her
choices."
Victor disappears
as his voice
fills the room.

"I won't hurt you,
I won't hunt you,
but I won't
help you either."

Umu tenses,
sniffing the air,
turning to the windows,
seeing the front of school
empty.

The morning bell rings,
sending everyone to class.

She holds her hand out
as a shield in front of me.

"I told you and Caylee
you're not the only ones
looking for the device."
Victor's voice fades.

The familiar sound
of too-long toenails
tapping on the windows.

I remember what I
heard behind The Bookshop,
what Caylee said she heard
outside Victor's office.

"Again?"
Umu snarls
as she crouches,
ready.

Hunter Protocol A-091

The window is pried open
by a long claw,
creating a crack.

A dark, slender body
slides through the window,
landing on all fours,
standing like a dog.

Its nail are talons,
black skin stretched taut
over rippling muscles.

No head,
only a smashed, bloated pug face
bulging from between its shoulders.

Needle teeth
stick out from its mouth
like nails,
some curled and pried,
others rusty and sharp.

"Go, Erin,"
Umu says.
"These things
are vicious,
and they're not here
for you.

Just the device.

And I'm not giving it up."

Two more of the same
slither through the window.
One stands,
pulls the curtains closed
to keep the outside world
unaware of what's about to happen.

One of the dog things
lunges at Umu;
she catches it,
slamming it down,
spraying blue sludge
from the thing's mouth.

It wriggles free and
jumps at her again.
The other two pile on her
and I freeze.

They're clawing at her,
throwing her silver blood
in arches with those
talons and teeth.

"Get the hell out of here!"
Umu barks at me.

She kicks one off,
throwing it into a table,
knocking the table across the room
with her force.

Umu shouts, growls
as the dog monsters snarl
and bite and claw.

What can I do?

I don't fight!

My backpack is beeping.
One of the dogs hears it
and runs toward me,
screaming barks and snarls
through its nail-filled mouth.

Umu grabs it, rips it away from me.

I grab my bag,
duck behind the table
where the Pandora Device is prepared,
and pull out the beeping thing.

My signal detector?

It's picking up an active signal,
just like Umu's transmission.

I peek over the desk
and see Umu has torn the leg
off one dog;
circuits spark
from the wound.

I look again:
The dogs aren't dogs,
their legs compress and acuate,
their ears are antennae,
their teeth are literally nails.

I can even hear the servos
in their bodies as Umu
fights.

My laptop.

The kill code.

I reach for the laptop
as a robot dog snaps at me,
catching my hand,
ripping a gash open
across my knuckles.

Pain, instant;
I scream.

Umu needs backup.
I think I can help,
but I need–

Caylee, I need you!

I rip down the fire alarm;
the shrieking bells
cover the biting and
bludgeoning battle.

I hope Caylee understands
the bells are a scream for help.

CAYLEE MORAN

The Call

Erin should be in class by now.
I watch the door,
waiting for her
to come back
from the Maker Lab.

But she doesn't.

I watch the clock;
she should have been done
with Umu a few minutes ago.
She should be here
by now.

Caylee, I need you!

That was Erin.
Popping out of my seat,
I look around but
don't see her.

"Ms. Moran, is there a—"
The teacher is cut off
by the fire alarm.

She tries to assert calm,
but the students
remember Homecoming
and start rushing out,
wondering if it is a fire,
a shooter,
or what.

I run to the Maker Lab,
passing clusters of students
chaotically escaping school.

Bursting through the orange doors,
I look for Umu,
seeing her pinned by
three of the dogs from Grandpa's office.

Grabbing the hammer from the wall,
I sprint over,
smashing the dog
in the gut with the hammer;
it clangs and sprays
blue sludge from
a rip in the skin.

Electronics spark,
white arcs
throwing me backwards.

Robots?

Dog-shaped murderbots?
This week sucks.

Erin's at her computer,
another dog rushing to her;
I kick it away,
hammering again
into the thing's
mouth of spikey teeth.

"Help Umu!"
Erin shouts over the
blaring alarms.

I nod,
seeing Umu with
the dogs on her
as Erin types something
on her computer.

She's feverishly tapping out commands,
copying numbers from something
beeping beside her.

The windows frost over
from Umu's cold,
but my blood burns,
heart racing
as I slam my hammer
into another dog murderbot.

I knock it off,
getting its attention.

It jumps toward me,
knocking me down,
biting my hammer,
trying to rip it away.
I scream,
trying to kick it
off me.

Umu tears it away from me,
punching through its body,
sending a volcanic eruption of sparks
around her face.

The dog pulls away from us
and then drops
to the ground.

Dead?

Another one pounces at us
but turns limp in the air,
falling with a wet thud.

I look to Erin
as she types faster,
looking at the third dog muderbot.

She smashes the enter key:
the last murderbot drops
dead.

Umu looks to Erin
with surprise.

"They have the same
signal as you,"
Erin says,
fingers still hovering
over the keyboard.
"Same kill code
works on them."

Umu stands,
nods,
waiting
for the next command,
the next keystroke.

Erin steps away
from the keyboard,
sighs and shakes her head.

"I'm sorry I wasn't
there for you, Umu,"
she says.
"That I couldn't help
you find your way."

Erin comes to me,
reaching to help me up.
I drop the hammer
and stand.

Umu nods.

The fire alarm is
still blasting over us.

"You two go.
We're done here."
Umu turns from us,
going to the laptop.
"One and done, Erin.
I promise."

Erin nods
and we rush out
of the school
to find our class.

Erin could have ended everything,
but she didn't.

"Thanks for coming,"
Erin whispers
as we find our classmates.

They're talking about
a bomb or something
as Erin and I watch
the Maker Lab.

"I thought the fire alarm
would be a hint."
She chuckles.

But I *heard* her.
Just like last night,
I heard her;
I knew she needed help
and I knew where she was.

"Why didn't you end her too?"

I watch Erin's eyes;
she answers without hesitation
"I made her.
I screwed her up.

Maybe with someone else,
she'll find the peace
I couldn't provide."

Fire trucks arrive,
checking the school.
What will they find
in the Maker Lab?

My guess is
the same thing Quincy found
Homecoming night:

Nothing.

ERIN ULMAN

Choices and Discovery

Mom, Dad, and I
sit at the dinner table.

Dad picks at his pasta,
Mom heaping more pasta on my plate
as I laugh.

"I'm not going to fit in my dress
with all this pasta, Mom."

"Nonsense!"
Mom buries the idea
in pasta.
"Pasta gives you energy
for all the fun."

I look to Dad,
his eyes tracing noodles
on his plate.

Mom splats a spoon of noodles on his plate;
the sauce sprays up to his glasses.
Mom snorts.
I chuckle.
Dad stays cold.

"Real funny,"
he grumps.

"Honestly, David,
you've been going on about IntelliDyn
since we've gotten to Glen Coast.
IntelliDyn this.
IntelliDyn that.

Now you get to work
with your daughter
at your dream job."
Mom's smile
shifts to a piercing glare

"Can't you be happy for a moment?
You've succeeded.
Your company was bought.
You're leading the world's best
research and development team,
and
they want your brilliant daughter
to help you."

Mom.bossMode(isActive)

Mom's words turn sharp,
cutting between her and Dad.

He looks at Mom,
looks to me,
returns to his pasta,
searching;
maybe for a meatball.

"I just . . ."
He sighs, shoulders sinking.
"I expected this project to turn out . . . differently."

Mom.rage.max();

"The project?"
Mom spits.
"You're thinking about your
damn *project*?
Erin's getting ready
for Homecoming.
She's getting ready
to start a great
experience at IntelliDyn
and all you can think of is your damn *project*?"

She stands up,
pointing to the basement.
"If you want to live down there,
feel free.
We're going to enjoy life up here.
I'm hoping you'll join us, but
that's up to you!"

Dad drops his fork,
shock
rolling over his face,
fear trembling his lips,
hearing a message
not directly said
but clearly communicated.

Be here
with us
or leave.

He nods.
Mom sits back down,
blows out a frustrated sigh,
and looks to me.

Mom.calm.increasing();

How long was that
building in her?

"What time is Caylee coming over?"

"Oh, uh, Davis is picking me up."

"With Meredith?"

"No, just Davis and me."

"A . . ."
Mom draws out the question.
"Date?"

Dad perks up.

"No, I mean, I don't see it
like that."
I shrug.
"I don't think he does either."

Mom smirks.
Dad grimaces.
I ask to be excused.

"I've got to get ready.
Mom, you need help cleaning up?"

"No, dear. Your dad and I
have this.
Go get ready."

I leave the table,
feeling the tension behind me.
Looking back, I see Mom's eyes locked
on Dad.
Her face reddens with the words
she wants to say, but she's not calm enough
to put them together.

"Hey Mom,
can you help me with my dress?
Dad, can you handle dishes?"

I'm thinking about the words that might
be building in Mom's mouth,
words that can't be undone,
and how a distraction might help
those words find more constructive forms.

Something I wish I would have known
before we moved to Glen Coast.

In a few moments,
Mom and I
are laughing,
are enjoying Homecoming preparations
together.

Mom's Seattle smile
returns,
growing bigger,
brighter,
bursting into a new
smile, a
Glen Coast smile.

I find my own
Glen Coast smile
with her.

Butterflies

After a quiet car ride,
Davis and I
arrive at Homecoming.

Meredith and Caylee
wait for us at our normal spot
in the foyer.

Meredith is smiling.
I look again to confirm:
yes,
she's smiling, a
toothy grin.
She almost looks ready to laugh

in her black lacy dress,
long midnight hair framing her painted pale face.

Caylee wears her qipao dress,
sparkling pale blue with bold violet flowers,
her hair pulled up away from her face.

"Looking good, Davis!"
Caylee crows,
taking in his black suit,
purple shirt,
black tie.

Davis accepts the compliment
with a catwalk spin.

A small smile from Caylee
silently
greets me.

"So is everything . . . ?"
The question bursts from Davis.

"Yes. It's all done,"
I say, meeting Caylee's eyes.
"Quincy is going to pick up
Pandora from me later tonight,
and that's it."

Meredith looks to Caylee,
awaiting confirmation,
but Caylee
only nods slowly.

Davis takes my hand,
gently pulling me
to the dance floor.

I let go.

"Give us a moment, Davis."

He nods,
following Meredith.

"Caylee."
I reach for her hand.
"Thank you. I couldn't have gotten
through these two weeks without you."

Caylee wraps her arms around me,
squeezing my breath out,
whispering,
"Thank you!"

Down the hall
by the Maker Lab,
a shadow
with glimmering silver-green eyes
steps out,
backpack slung over her shoulder.
A milk-white cat with the same
silver-green eyes
follows a few steps behind her.

Umu and the cat stop.
They look at
Caylee and me,
waiting,
watching.

I release Caylee,
nodding toward Umu.

Caylee sees them;
her face turns to stone,
her eyes melding into steel.
I imagine her thinking,
Go on, get out of here.
Spitting the words as if daggers
aimed at Umu's heart.

She didn't know Umu.
Umu wasn't her creation.

A creation made, then abandoned
and for what? Could we—
Davis, Meredith, Caylee, and I—
have made it work with Umu?

Tears well up in my eyes:
sadness for the loss of what could have been,
knowing now, no matter what words I might have in me,
whatever I want to say,
nothing can change
what I haven't said yet.

I wave goodbye.

Umu nods,
the cat nods,
and they disappear into the shadows of the school.

> "You think she'll hold up
> her end of the bargain?"
> Caylee breaks the silence.
> "That she's gone and the device
> is returned?"

Part of me hopes she doesn't,
but I know the words I need to say.

"Yeah, I do. I think she'll hold up her end."

Gripping Caylee's hand,
I squeeze some confidence into her
or from her,
I'm not sure.

"Aren't those the same dresses
you wore last week?"
One of Donna's friends
interrupts us.

The girl laughs
and waves to Donna,
who is checking her phone.
"Hey Donna, look at them."

Donna shakes her head,
keeping her eyes in her phone.

I smile,
rolling my eyes,
dismissing the laughs and pointing
as Caylee tenses, ready to bark back.

I wave away the words.
"Forget them, Caylee. Let's dance
before I have to suffer through a slow song."

Caylee smiles, forgetting the cackles behind us.
We run to the dance floor,
to the thrumming beats,
to the jumping
and sweating
and joy of being together.

Meredith's pixie swirls,
Davis's uncoordinated shoulders shimmy,
Caylee and I
jumping to the beat,
trying to take flight
as the world fades away,
leaving only
the four of us
together.

In that moment
belonging
fills me
with a freedom like flying,
knowing I'm with
my flutter of people,
my tribe.

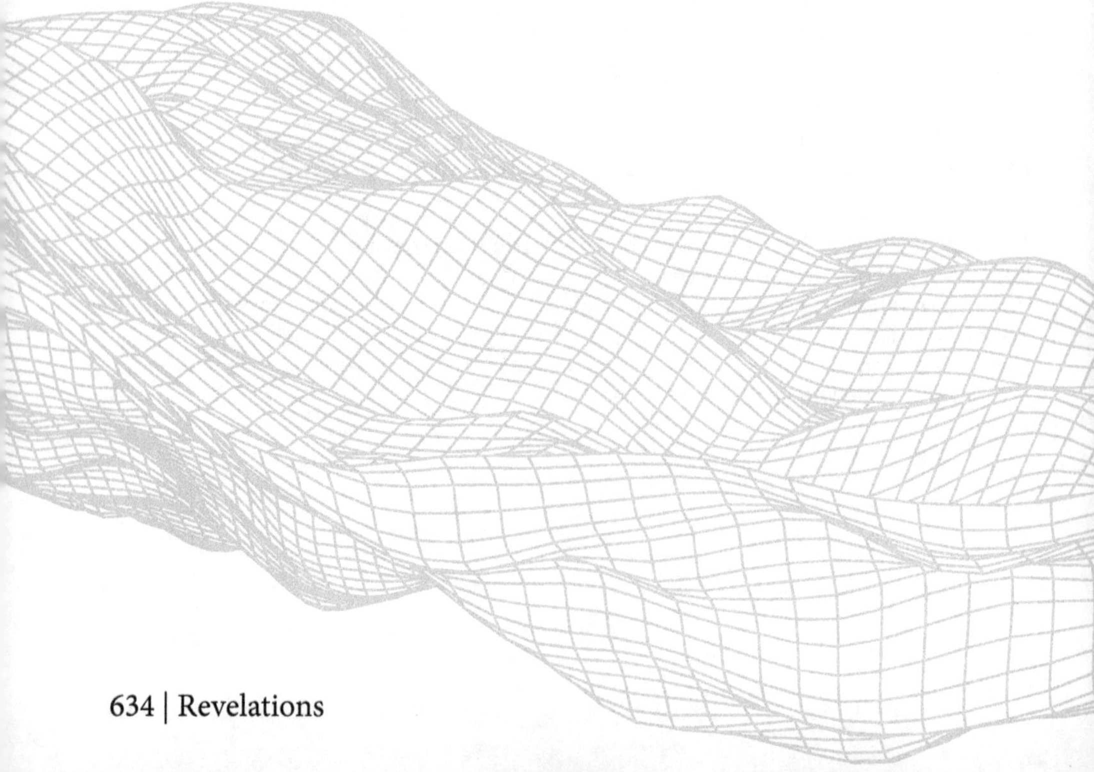

THE END

EPILOGUE (A WEEK OR SO LATER)

Erin's phone buzzes.

Her mom looks at her, annoyed. "Work?" she asks.

"Meredith is going to start soon!" Davis points to Meredith sitting on stage at the e-Rena. Her gaming rig is ready for the *Call for Destruction* tournament.

Erin smiles. "I'll be quick." Sliding out of their row, she forces a calm walk to the closest exit. She taps to open the email on her phone.

"What are you doing? It's going to start soon!" Caylee says, running up with a bucket of popcorn.

"Just got a quick message. Work," Erin says, smiling.

"Well, it's starting, so get in there." Caylee rushes in.

Opening the message, Erin reads Gabe MacAbera's email:

Erin, good luck with the Pandora test run tomorrow. Please submit your latest updates to the team by 08:00 tomorrow. Get a good night's rest. You will be busy tomorrow. --G

Erin takes a deep breath, wondering what she'll say when the fake Pandora Device doesn't work. She thinks back to Victoria's study, on the night she built the fake Pandora Device. When it was complete, it shocked her just like the real Pandora Device did. Victoria jumped back, hearing the crackle. She looked at Erin and asked if something happened. Erin shook her head but knew something had happened. She felt the spark. Did it jump from the device to her? Or from her to the device?

Erin replays what Gabe said: IntelliDyn couldn't get the device to work. Maybe Umu wasn't the only thing Erin brought to life?

Shaking away the thoughts, Erin goes back to her seat, stealing Caylee's popcorn and smiling.

"It doesn't have to work . . ." Erin whispers to herself. "But what if it does?"

ACKNOWLEDGEMENTS

This book is the first in a long series of books that started at the end of the 20th century. In that time, I've taken many hiatuses and turns and lost my way a few times, but there have been a few people who kept me coming back to the path. Without them, there would be no *[dis]connection* or the many other stories I look forward to sharing with you.

Thank you to my wife, constant supporter, and first reader, Maria. Without your mind to help me shape these stories, they would not be nearly as fun to write.

Thank you to my daughter, who helped me have the confidence to keep writing even when it gets really hard. She was the inspiration to write this story, in this format, for this audience.

Thank you to my son, who reminded me often that I should not be on the computer all the time, and that a quick cartoon is always what is needed to activate the creative juices.

Thank you to Kelly Bingham who introduced me to Novels-in-Verse. The seeds of this story started in your class and bloomed over the years since. Thank you for your support and encouragement.

Thank you Linda for encouraging me to take Kelly's class and give this writing thing another try. It was the medicine I needed to cure what could have been a very hard time.

Thank you to Chester who lit the fire to make this story come forward.

Thank you Chris for all your support and belief in me.

Thank you Roisin, Michelle and Nicole for all your work in helping me shape, refine, build and envision this story. You all have been such a wonderful help that I can't thank you enough for all each of you brought to this story.

Thank you, dear reader. I appreciate the time you gave to *[dis]connection* and hope that you found it enjoyable. I know you have a lot of choices in how you spend your time and truly value that you chose to spend your time with my story.

Until next time, dear reader, goodnight and sweet dreams of sandy beaches and brewing storms.

[dis]connection by T. Kulp

2019 - 2022

NEWSLETTER SIGN UP

Keep up with the latest goings ons with T. Kulp and Cy Borgmyn through our newsletter. Scan the QR Code below with your smart phone to go to https://timkulp.com and sign up now.

There are a lot of stories coming out in the next few months. Tim and Cy are going to be trying out a bunch of different things from merch to new story formats and maybe even games. You never know what you'll find but I hope that you enjoy what we're building at timkulp.com.

For those who don't know, Cy Borgmyn is T. Kulp's pen name for works that he co-authors with Artificial Intelligence (AI).

To: S. Pratchert I.G. 23
Subject: Pandora
Body:

Attn: S. Pratchert, I.G. 23

Pandora has been secured. Two of the Mother's Tears are confirmed to have been created. One vial is reported missing. Of the eleven we must assume, at least three have returned. We have detected increased activity in the Well as of this week. Those through the Well know the Tears have returned.

Have you detected activity from the last two of the seven? With the return of the eleven, it is only a matter of time before they resurface. I fear balance is lost. The Mother of Chaos, Codename:TIAMAT, has begun to rise.

We need support to stop this course of events. Please, seek out the Librarian and report your findings. Once found, I will arrange an audience with the Librarian to discuss how we can address this threat. We will need all our aliances, the old aliances and new, to survive what is to come.

Sincerely;
Primus Dr. V.C.Moran 17

P.S. Other parties are seeking Pandora. Q. Nichoals 10028 and I are seeking further information. We fear our enemies are expanding and their abilities increasing. We believe there are two parties seeking Pandora: IntelliDyn and another currently unknown. Communicate anything you hear on parties interested in Pandora.And, Sylvia, please hurry. I fear that our time to stop what has begun is running out.

OTHER STORIES BY T. KULP OR CY BORGMYN

BLOTS by T. Kulp

Ghosts, monsters, and bad decisions haunt these 9 short stories from horror author T. Kulp. BLOTS brings you stories from all over the horror spectrum. From H.P. Lovecraft style cosmic horror to fairy tale folk horror and the always enjoyable gothic ghost stories, BLOTS has something for many fans of the macabre.

Monsters Dance to Twilight by Cy Borgmyn

We are living in a horror story and it is getting worse. Climate change is talked about in statistics and data, but what does it really mean for humans and nature?

In Monsters Dance to Twilight, Cy Borgmyn approaches climate change as a horror story. Through this lens, we are forced to confront the ways in which people and nature are monsters opposing each other. One monster reacts, lashes out, defends. The other, complacently marches along devouring. Which monster will survive?

The Trial of Mirror Mountain by Cy Borgmyn

Eric's long time crush, Anna, is the latest person to leave him, when goes to the haunted Mirror Mountain to process being abandoned again; but when the spirits of Mirror Mountain try to take over and destroy his life, he must learn to trust the people in his life before he's trapped on Mirror Mountain forever.

Available 2022-2023

Library of Lessons & Lies by T. Kulp

On the verge of discovering an uncontrollable new power, psychically gifted loner Beatrix Clark finds a portal to another dimension where her powers are amplified with the help of an ancient book; but when Beatrix discovers the power in the book has its own agenda, she must work with her social media influencer roommate to control her powers before her powers control her.

Available 2022-2023